DEATH BY ESPIONAG

DEATH BY ESPIONAGE

INTRIGUING STORIES OF DECEPTION AND BETRAYAL

Edited by MARTIN CRUZ SMITH

CUMBERLAND HOUSE
NASHVILLE, TENNESSEE

Published by Cumberland House Publishing, Inc.
431 Harding Industrial Drive, Nashville, TN 37211.

Jacket/cover design by Gore Studio, Inc.
Text design by Mike Towle

Library of Congress Cataloging-in-Publication Data

Death by espionage : intriguing stories of betrayal and deception / edited by Martin Cruz Smith.
     p. cm.
   ISBN 1-58182-040-2
   1. Spy stories. I. Smith, Martin Cruz, 1942–.
  PN6071.S64D43   1999
  808.83'872—dc21   99-26711
                                               CIP

Printed in the United States of America
1 2 3 4 5 6 7 8—03 02 01 00 99

THE INTERNATIONAL ASSOCIATION OF CRIME WRITERS PRESENTS:

Introduction

S PIES HAVE ALWAYS BEEN with us. My favorite is the very first—the serpent in the Garden of Eden. The most subtle of God's creatures, he talked poor, innocent Eve into plucking the fruit from the Tree of Knowledge of Good and Evil. Truth be told it didn't take a lot of prodding—such is the attraction of classified information. So, Adam and Eve got booted out of Eden and the serpent was condemned to travel on his belly for the rest of his days, a cashiered agent if ever there was one.

If spies have always been with us, so have spy stories. I am more of a mystery writer myself. What I like about the mystery story is the excuse a dead body gives for the investigation of the living. Whether it's in a Victorian parlor or the corridors of the Kremlin, the rules of etiquette and ideology are, by necessity, temporarily suspended. A cross section of society is exposed, corset strings snap, and the next blunt instrument might be a bust of Marx. But there's always a motive.

Espionage is more intellectual. There may be no weapon, no gore, no corpse at all when the main goal is information. Secret agents tend to be better educated, speak a number of languages, know a demitasse from a derringer. The information they seek can be as specific as the disposition of Assyrian hosts or Russian missiles, or as vague as Alfred Hitchcock's legendary McGuffin. John D. MacDonald has a piece in here about an antimissile system eerily like Ronald Reagan's Star Wars, the most costly McGuffin of them all.

The point is that the quest for information, finding it and trading it, makes for particularly complex and interesting characters, which is why so many writers, from the best to the worst, have experimented in this genre. There is the matter of sympathy. After all, a successful spy must possess the skills of a successful writer, knowing how to pique a buyer's interest, string him along, and leave him wanting more. (No wonder so many agents are double agents; how many writers can say they never sold the same story twice?)

There is the matter of masquerade: Who is an agent and who is not? See Guy de Maupassant's sly tale of two French fishermen and Mark Twain's account of spy fever during the Civil War. Then there is the exquisite seediness of spies. Howard Engel's "The Ant Trap" features a secret agent whose station is the café at the Hotel Sacher in Vienna. Shabby, next to penniless, and no longer able to distinguish between rumor and deadly threat, he nurses his drink and awaits one more assignment. You can almost hear a zither in the background.

With the end of the Cold War the old simplifications have come to an end. It's not just a matter of black hats and white hats being replaced by gray hats. There are so many hats now. Since an age of diversity demands spies from the Irish Republican Army, MI5, Hamas, Mossad, it's only appropriate that fiction follow suit. Hence, *Death by Espionage* introduces foreign writers with points of view we wouldn't have seen even a few years ago. I'm thinking in particular of two stories from Cuba, both of them original and sophisticated. In "Golam,"

José Latour takes us to an Israeli spymaster who has, disastrously, decided to tell all. In "Spy's Fate," Arnaldo Correa reconsiders two old adversaries from both sides of the Cuban-American divide.

This is a great time for espionage fiction. The old subtle serpent speaks many languages now, each tale more intriguing than the last.

Martin Cruz Smith

DEATH BY ESPIONAGE

The Adventure of the Bruce-Partington Plans

SIR ARTHUR CONAN DOYLE

I N THE THIRD WEEK of November, in the year 1895, a dense yellow fog settled down upon London. From the Monday to the Thursday I doubt whether it was ever possible from our windows in Baker Street to see the loom of the opposite houses. The first day Holmes had spent in cross-indexing his huge book of references. The second and third had been patiently occupied upon a subject which he had recently made his hobby—the music of the Middle Ages. But when, for the fourth time, after pushing back our chairs from breakfast we saw the greasy, heavy brown swirl still drifting past us and condensing in oily drops upon the window panes, my comrade's impatient and active nature could endure this drab existence no longer. He paced restlessly about our sitting room in a fever of suppressed energy, biting his nails, tapping the furniture, and chafing against inaction.

"Nothing of interest in the paper, Watson?"

I was aware that by anything of interest, Holmes meant anything of criminal interest. There was the news of a revolution, of a possible war, and of an impending change of government; but these did not come within the horizon of my companion. I could see nothing recorded in the shape of crime which was not commonplace and futile. Holmes groaned and resumed his restless meanderings.

"The London criminal is certainly a dull fellow," said he in the querulous voice of the sportsman whose game has failed him. "Look out of this window, Watson. See how the figures loom up, are dimly seen, and then blend once more into the cloud bank. The thief or the murderer could roam London on such a day as the tiger does the jungle, unseen until he pounces, and then evident only to his victim."

"There have," said I, "been numerous petty thefts."

Holmes snorted his contempt.

"This great and somber stage is set for something more worthy than that," said he. "It is fortunate for this community that I am not a criminal."

"It is, indeed!" said I heartily.

"Suppose that I were Brooks or Woodhouse, or any of the fifty men who have good reason for taking my life, how long could I survive against my own pursuit? A summons, a bogus appointment, and all would be over. It is well they don't have days of fog in the Latin countries—the countries of assassination. By Jove! here comes something at last to break our dead monotony."

It was the maid with a telegram. Holmes tore it open and burst out laughing.

"Well, well! What next?" said he. "Brother Mycroft is coming round."

"Why not?" I asked.

"Why not? It is as if you met a tram car coming down a country lane. Mycroft has his rails and he runs on them. His Pall Mall lodgings, the Diogenes Club, Whitehall—that is his cycle. Once, and only once, he has been here. What upheaval can possibly have derailed him?"

"Does he not explain?"

Holmes handed me his brother's telegram.

MUST SEE YOU OVER CADOGAN WEST. COMING AT ONCE.

Mycroft

"Cadogan West? I have heard the name."

"It recalls nothing to my mind. But that Mycroft should break out in this erratic fashion! A planet might as well leave its orbit. By the way, do you know what Mycroft is?"

I had some vague recollection of an explanation at the time of the Adventure of the Greek Interpreter.

"You told me that he had some small office under the British government."

Holmes chuckled.

"I did not know you quite so well in those days. One has to be discreet when one talks of high matters of state. You are right in thinking that he is under the British government. You would also be right in a sense if you said that occasionally he *is* the British government."

"My dear Holmes!"

"I thought I might surprise you. Mycroft draws four hundred and fifty pounds a year, remains a subordinate, has no ambitions of any kind, will receive neither honor nor title, but remains the most indispensable man in the country."

"But how?"

"Well, his position is unique. He has made it for himself. There has never been anything like it before, nor will be again. He has the tidiest and most orderly brain, with the greatest capacity for storing facts, of any man living. The same great powers which I have turned to the detection of crime he has used for this particular business. The conclusions of every department are passed to him, and he is the central exchange, the clearing house, which makes out the balance. All other men are specialists, but his specialism is omniscience. We will suppose that a minister needs information as to a point which involves the Navy, India, Canada, and the bimetallic question; he could get his separate advices from various departments upon each, but only Mycroft can focus them all, and say offhand how each factor would affect the other. They began by using him as a short-cut, a convenience; now he has made himself an essential. In that great brain of his everything is pigeon-holed and can be handed out in an instant. Again and again his word has decided the national policy. He lives in it. He thinks of nothing else save when, as an intellectual exercise, he unbends if I call upon him and ask him to advise me on one of my little problems. But Jupiter is descending today. What on earth can it mean? Who is Cadogan West, and what is he to Mycroft?"

"I have it," I cried, and plunged among the litter of papers upon the sofa. "Yes, yes, here he is, sure enough! Cadogan West was the young man who was found dead on the Underground on Tuesday morning."

Holmes sat up at attention, his pipe halfway to his lips.

"This must be serious, Watson. A death which has caused my brother to alter his habits can be no ordinary one. What in the world can he have to do with it? The case was featureless as I remember it. The young man had apparently fallen out of the train and killed himself. He had not been robbed, and there was no particular reason to suspect violence. Is that not so?"

"There has been an inquest," said I, "and a good many fresh facts have come out. Looked at more closely, I should certainly say that it was a curious case."

"Judging by its effect upon my brother, I should think it must be a most extraordinary one." He snuggled down in his armchair. "Now, Watson, let's have the facts."

"The man's name was Arthur Cadogan West. He was twenty-seven years of age, unmarried, and a clerk at Woolwich Arsenal."

"Government employ. Behold the link with brother Mycroft!"

"He left Woolwich suddenly on Monday night. Was last seen by his fiancée, Miss Violet Westbury, whom he left abruptly in the fog about 7:30 that evening. There was no quarrel between them and she can give no motive for his action. The next thing heard of him was when his dead body was discovered by a plate-layer named Mason, just outside Aldgate Station on the Underground system in London."

"When?"

"The body was found at six on the Tuesday morning. It was lying wide of the metals upon the left hand of the track as one goes eastward, at a point close to the station, where the line emerges from the tunnel in which it runs. The head was badly crushed—an injury which might well have been caused by a fall from the train. The body could only have come on the line in that way. Had it been carried down from any neighboring street, it must have passed the station barriers, where a collector is always standing. This point seems absolutely certain."

"Very good. The case is definite enough. The man, dead or alive, either fell or was precipitated from a train. So much is clear to me. Continue."

"The trains which traverse the lines of rail beside which the body was found are those which run from west to east, some being purely Metropolitan, and some from Willesden and outlying junctions. It can be stated for certain that this young man, when he met his death, was traveling in this direction at some late hour of the night, but at what point he entered the train it is impossible to state."

"His ticket, of course, would show that."

"There was no ticket in his pockets."

"No ticket! Dear me, Watson, this is really very singular. According to my experience it is not possible to reach the platform of a Metropolitan train without exhibiting one's ticket. Presumably, then, the young man had one. Was it taken from him in order to conceal the station from which he came? It is possible. Or did he drop it in the carriage? That also is possible. But the point is of curious interest. I understand that there was no sign of robbery?"

"Apparently not. There is a list here of his possessions. His purse contained two pounds fifteen. He had also a checkbook on the Woolwich branch of the Capital and Counties Bank. Through this his identity was established. There were also two dress circle tickets for the Woolwich Theatre, dated for that very evening. Also a small packet of technical papers."

Holmes gave an exclamation of satisfaction.

"There we have it at last, Watson! British government—Woolwich Arsenal—technical papers—Brother Mycroft, the chain is complete. But here he comes, if I am not mistaken, to speak for himself."

A moment later the tall and portly form of Mycroft Holmes was ushered into the room. Heavily built and massive, there was a suggestion of uncouth physical inertia in the figure, but above this unwieldy frame there was perched a head so masterful in its brow, so alert in its steel-gray, deep-set eyes, so firm in its lips, and so subtle in its play of expression, that after the first glance one forgot the gross body and remembered only the dominant mind.

At his heels came our old friend Lestrade, of Scotland Yard—thin and austere. The gravity of both their faces foretold some weighty quest. The detective shook hands without a word. Mycroft Holmes struggled out of his overcoat and subsided into an armchair.

"A most annoying business, Sherlock," said he. "I extremely dislike altering my habits, but the powers that be would take no denial. In the present state of Siam it is most awkward that I should be away from the office. But it is a real crisis. I have never seen the Prime Minister so upset. As to the Admiralty—it is buzzing like an overturned beehive. Have you read up the case?"

"We have just done so. What were the technical papers?"

"Ah, there's the point! Fortunately, it has not come out. The press would be furious if it did. The papers which this wretched youth had in his pocket were the plans of the Bruce-Partington submarine."

Mycroft Holmes spoke with a solemnity which showed his sense of the importance of the subject. His brother and I sat expectant.

"Surely you have heard of it? I thought everyone had heard of it."

"Only as a name."

"Its importance can hardly be exaggerated. It has been the most jealously guarded of all government secrets. You may take it from me that naval warfare becomes impossible within the radius of a Bruce-Partington's operation. Two years ago a very large sum was smuggled through Estimates and was expended in acquiring a monopoly of the invention. Every effort has been made to keep the secret. The plans, which are exceedingly intricate, comprising some thirty separate patents, each essential to the working of the whole, are kept in an elaborate safe in a confidential office adjoining the arsenal, with burglarproof doors and windows. Under no conceivable circumstances were the plans to be taken from the office. If the chief constructor of the Navy desired to consult them, even he was forced to go to the Woolwich office for the purpose. And yet here we find them in the pockets of a dead junior clerk in the heart of London. From an official point of view it's simply awful."

"But you have recovered them?"

"No, Sherlock, no! That's the pinch. We have not. Ten papers were taken from Woolwich. There were seven in the pockets of Cadogan West. The three most essential are gone—stolen, vanished. You must drop everything, Sherlock. Never mind your usual petty puzzles of the police court. It's a vital international problem that you have to solve. Why did Cadogan West take the papers, where are the missing ones, how did he die, how came his body where it was found, how can the evil be set right? Find an answer to all these questions, and you will have done good service for your country."

"Why do you not solve it yourself, Mycroft? You can see as far as I."

"Possibly, Sherlock. But it is a question of getting details. Give me your details, and from an armchair I will return you an excellent expert opinion. But to run here and run there, to cross-question railway guards, and lie on my face with a lens to my eye—it is not my *métier*. No, you are the one man who can clear the matter up. If you have a fancy to see your name in the next honors list—"

My friend smiled and shook his head.

"I play the game for the game's own sake," said he. "But the problem certainly presents some points of interest, and I shall be very pleased to look into it. Some more facts, please."

"I have jotted down the more essential ones upon this sheet of paper, together with a few addresses which you will find of service. The actual official guardian of the papers is the famous government expert, Sir James Walter, whose decorations and subtitles fill two lines of a book of reference. He has grown gray in the service, is a gentleman, a favored guest in the most exalted houses, and, above all, a man whose patriotism is beyond suspicion. He is one of two who have a key of the safe. I may add that the papers were undoubtedly in the office during working hours on Monday, and that Sir James left for London about three o'clock taking his key with him. He was at the house of Admiral Sinclair at Barclay Square during the whole of the evening when this incident occurred."

"Has the fact been verified?'"

"Yes; his brother, Colonel Valentine Walter, has testified to his departure from Woolwich, and Admiral Sinclair to his arrival in London; so Sir James is no longer a direct factor in the problem."

"Who was the other man with a key?"

"The senior clerk and draughtsman, Mr. Sidney Johnson. He is a man of forty, married, with five children. He is a silent, morose man, but he has, on the whole, an excellent record in the public service. He is unpopular with his colleagues, but a hard worker. According to his own account, corroborated only by the word of his wife, he was at home the whole of Monday evening after office hours, and his key has never left the watchchain upon which it hangs

"Tell us about Cadogan West."

"He has been ten years in the service and has done good work. He has the reputation of being hot-headed and impetuous, but a straight, honest man. We have nothing against him. He was next to Sidney Johnson in the office. His duties brought him into daily, personal contact with the plans. No one else had the handling of them."

"Who locked the plans up that night?"

"Mr. Sidney Johnson, the senior clerk."

"Well, it is surely perfectly clear who took them away. They are actually found upon the person of this junior clerk, Cadogan West. That seems final, does it not?"

"It does, Sherlock, and yet it leaves so much unexplained. In the first place, why did he take them?"

"I presume they were of value?"

"He could have got several thousands for them very easily."

"Can you suggest any possible motive for taking the papers to London except to sell them?"

"No, I cannot."

"Then we must take that as our working hypothesis. Young West took the papers. Now this could only be done by having a false key—"

"Several false keys. He had to open the building and the room."

"He had, then, several false keys. He took the papers to London to sell the secret, intending, no doubt, to have the plans themselves back in the safe next morning before they were missed. While in London on this treasonable mission he met his end."

"We will suppose that he was traveling back to Woolwich when he was killed and thrown out of the compartment."

"Aldgate, where the body was found, is considerably past the station for London Bridge, which would be his route to Woolwich."

"Many circumstances could be imagined under which he would pass London Bridge. There was someone in the carriage, for example, with whom he was having an absorbing interview. This interview led to a violent scene in which he lost his life. Possibly he tried to leave the carriage, fell out on the line, and so met his end. The other closed the door. There was a thick fog, and nothing could be seen."

"No better explanation can be given with our present knowledge; and yet consider, Sherlock, how much you leave untouched. We will suppose, for argument's sake, that young Cadogan West *had* determined to convey these papers to London. He would naturally have made an appointment with the foreign agent and kept his evening clear. Instead of that he took two tickets to the theater, escorted his fiancée halfway there, and then suddenly disappeared."

"A blind," said Lestrade, who had sat listening with some impatience to the conversation.

"A very singular one. That is objection No. 1. Objection No. 2: We will suppose that he reaches London and sees the foreign agent. He must bring back the papers before morning or the loss will be discovered. He took away ten. Only seven were in his pocket. What had become of the other three? He certainly would not leave them of his own free will. Then, again, where is the price of his treason? One would have expected to find a large sum of money in his pocket."

"It seems to me perfectly clear," said Lestrade. "I have no doubt at all as to what occurred. He took the papers to sell them. He saw the agent. They could not agree as to price. He started home again, but the agent went with him. In the train the agent murdered him, took the more essential papers, and threw his body from the carriage. That would account for everything, would it not?

"Why had he no ticket?"

"The ticket would have shown which station was nearest the agent's house. Therefore he took it from the murdered man's pocket."

"Good, Lestrade, very good," said Holmes. "Your theory holds together. But if this is true, then the case is at an end. On the one hand, the traitor is dead. On the other, the plans of the Bruce-Partington submarine are presumably already on the Continent. What is there for us to do?"

"To act, Sherlock—to act!" cried Mycroft, springing to his feet. "All my instincts are against this explanation. Use your powers! Go to the scene of the crime! See the people concerned! Leave no stone unturned! In all your career you have never had so great a chance of serving your country."

"Well, well!" said Holmes, shrugging his shoulders. "Come, Watson! And you, Lestrade, could you favor us with your company for an hour or two? We will begin our investigation by a visit to Aldgate Station. Good-bye, Mycroft. I shall let you have a report before evening, but I warn you in advance that you have little to expect."

An hour later Holmes, Lestrade, and I stood upon the Underground railroad at the point where it emerges from the tunnel immediately before Aldgate Station. A courteous red-faced old gentleman represented the railway company.

"This is where the young man's body lay," said he, indicating a spot about three feet from the metals. "It could not have fallen from above, for these, as you see, are all blank walls. Therefore, it could only have come from a train, and that train, so far as we can trace it, must have passed about midnight on Monday."

"Have the carriages been examined for any sign of violence?"

"There are no such signs, and no ticket has been found."

"No record of a door being found open?"

"None."

"We have had some fresh evidence this morning," said Lestrade. "A passenger who passed Aldgate in an ordinary Metropolitan train about 11:40 on Monday night declares that he heard a heavy thud, as of a body striking the line, just before the train reached the station. There was dense fog, however, and nothing could be seen. He made no report of it at the time. Why, whatever is the matter with Mr. Holmes?"

My friend was standing with an expression of strained intensity upon his face, staring at the railway metals where they curved out of the tunnel. Aldgate is a junction, and there was a network of points. On these his eager, questioning eyes were fixed, and I saw on his keen, alert face that tightening of the lips, that quiver of the nostrils, and concentration of the heavy, tufted brows which I knew so well.

"Points," he muttered; "the points."

"What of it? What do you mean?"

"I suppose there are no great number of points on a system such as this?"

"No; there are very few."

"And a curve, too. Points and a curve. By Jove! if it were only so."

"What is it, Mr. Holmes? Have you a clue?"

"An idea—an indication, no more. But the case certainly grows in interest. Unique, perfectly unique, and yet why not? I do not see any indications of bleeding on the line."

"There were hardly any."

"But I understand that there was a considerable wound."

"The bone was crushed, but there was no great external injury."

"And yet one would have expected some bleeding. Would it be possible for me to inspect the train which contained the passenger who heard the thud of a fall in the fog?"

"I fear not, Mr. Holmes. The train has been broken up before now, and the carriages redistributed."

"I can assure you, Mr. Holmes," said Lestrade, "that every carriage has been carefully examined. I saw to it myself."

It was one of my friend's most obvious weaknesses that he was impatient with less alert intelligences than his own.

"Very likely," said he, turning away. "As it happens, it was not the carriages which I desired to examine. Watson, we have done all we can here. We need not trouble you any further, Mr. Lestrade. I think our investigations must now carry us to Woolwich."

At London Bridge, Holmes wrote a telegram to his brother, which he handed to me before dispatching it. It ran thus:

SEE SOME LIGHT IN THE DARKNESS, BUT IT MAY POSSIBLY FLICKER OUT. MEANWHILE, PLEASE SEND BY MESSENGER, TO AWAIT RETURN AT BAKER STREET, A COMPLETE LIST OF ALL FOREIGN SPIES OR INTERNATIONAL AGENTS KNOWN TO BE IN ENGLAND, WITH FULL ADDRESS.

Sherlock

"That should be helpful, Watson," he remarked as we took our seats in the Woolwich train. "We certainly owe brother Mycroft a debt for having introduced us to what promises to be a really very remarkable case."

His eager face still wore that expression of intense and high-strung energy, which showed me that some novel and suggestive circumstance had opened up a stimulating line of thought. See the foxhound with hanging ears and drooping tail as it lolls about the kennels, and compare it with the same hound as, with gleaming eyes and straining muscles, it runs upon a breast-high scent—such was the change in Holmes since the morning. He was a different man from the limp and lounging figure in the mouse-colored dressing gown who had prowled so restlessly only a few hours before round the fog-girt room.

"There is material here. There is scope," said he. "I am dull indeed not to have understood its possibilities."

"Even now they are dark to me."

"The end is dark to me also, but I have hold of one idea which may lead us far. The man met his death elsewhere, and his body was on the roof of a carriage."

"On the roof!"

"Remarkable, is it not? But consider the facts. Is it a coincidence that it is found at the very point where the train pitches and sways as it comes round on the points? Is not that the place where an object upon the roof might be expected to fall off? The points would affect no object inside the train. Either the body fell from the roof, or a very curious coincidence has occurred. But now consider the question of the blood. Of course, there was no bleeding on the line if the body had bled elsewhere. Each fact is suggestive in itself. Together they have a cumulative force."

"And the ticket, too!" I cried.

"Exactly. We could not explain the absence of a ticket. This would explain it. Everything fits together."

"But suppose it were so, we are still as far as ever from unraveling the mystery of his death. Indeed, it becomes not simpler but stranger."

"Perhaps," said Holmes thoughtfully, "perhaps." He relapsed into a silent reverie, which lasted until the slow train drew up at last in Woolwich Station. There he called a cab and drew Mycroft's paper from his pocket.

"We have quite a little round of afternoon calls to make," said he. "I think that Sir James Walter claims our first attention."

The house of the famous official was a fine villa with green lawns stretching down to the Thames. As we reached it the fog was lifting, and a thin, watery sunshine was breaking through. A butler answered our ring.

"Sir James, sir?" said he with a solemn face. "Sir James died this morning."

"Good heavens!" cried Holmes in amazement. "How did he die?"

"Perhaps you would care to step in, sir, and see his brother, Colonel Valentine?"

"Yes, we had best do so."

We were ushered into a dim-lit drawing room, where an instant later we were joined by a very tall, handsome, light-bearded man of fifty, the younger brother of the dead scientist. His wild eyes, stained cheeks, and unkempt hair all spoke of the sudden blow which had fallen upon the household. He was hardly articulate as he spoke of it.

"It was this horrible scandal," said he. "My brother, Sir James, was a man of very sensitive honor, and he could not survive such an affair. It broke his heart. He was always so proud of the efficiency of his department, and this was a crushing blow."

"We had hoped that he might have given us some indications which would have helped us to clear the matter up."

"I assure you that it was all a mystery to him as it is to you and to all of us. He had already put all his knowledge at the disposal of the police. Naturally he had no doubt that Cadogan West was guilty. But all the rest was inconceivable."

"You cannot throw any new light upon the affair?"

"I know nothing myself save what I have read or heard. I have no desire to be discourteous, but you can understand, Mr. Holmes that we are much disturbed at present, and I must ask you to hasten this interview to an end."

"This is indeed an unexpected development," said my friend when we had regained the cab. "I wonder if the death was natural, or whether the poor old fellow killed himself! If the latter, may it be taken as some sign of self-reproach for duty neglected? We must leave that question to the future. Now we shall turn to the Cadogan Wests."

A small but well-kept house in the outskirts of the town sheltered the bereaved mother. The old lady was too dazed with grief to be of any use to us, but at her side was a white-faced young lady, who introduced herself as Miss Violet Westbury, the fiancée of the dead man, and the last to see him upon that fatal night.

"I cannot explain it, Mr. Holmes," she said. "I have not shut an eye since the tragedy, thinking, thinking, thinking, night and day, what the true meaning of it can be. Arthur was the most single-minded, chivalrous, patriotic man upon earth. He would have cut his right hand off before he would sell a State secret confided to his keeping. It is absurd, impossible, preposterous to anyone who knew him."

"But the facts, Miss Westbury?"

"Yes, yes; I admit I cannot explain them."

"Was he in any want of money?"

"No; his needs were very simple and his salary ample. He had saved a few hundreds, and we were to marry at the New Year."

"No signs of any mental excitement? Come, Miss Westbury, be absolutely frank with us."

The quick eye of my companion had noted some change in her manner. She colored and hesitated.

"Yes," she said at last. "I had a feeling that there was something on his mind."

"For long?"

"Only for the last week or so. He was thoughtful and worried. Once I pressed him about it. He admitted that there was something, and that it was concerned with his official life. 'It is too serious for me to speak about, even to you,' said he. I could get nothing more."

Holmes looked grave.

"Go on, Miss Westbury. Even if it seems to tell against him, go on. We cannot say what it may lead to."

"Indeed, I have nothing more to tell. Once or twice it seemed to me that he was on the point of telling me something. He spoke one evening of the importance of the secret, and I have some recollection that he said that no doubt foreign spies would pay a great deal to have it."

My friend's face grew graver still.

"Anything else?"

"He said that we were slack about such matters—that it would be easy for a traitor to get the plans."

"Was it only recently that he made such remarks?"

"Yes, quite recently."

"Now tell us of that last evening."

"We were to go to the theater. The fog was so thick that a cab was useless. We walked, and our way took us close to the office. Suddenly he darted away into the fog."

"Without a word?"

"He gave an exclamation; that was all. I waited but he never returned. Then I walked home. Next morning, after the office opened, they came to inquire. About twelve o'clock we heard the terrible news. Oh, Mr. Holmes, if you could only, only save his honor! It was so much to him."

Holmes shook his head sadly.

"Come, Watson," said he, "our ways lie elsewhere. Our next station must be the office from which the papers were taken.

"It was black enough before against this young man, but our inquiries make it blacker," he remarked as the cab lumbered off. "His coming marriage gives a motive for the crime. He naturally wanted money. The idea was in his head, since he spoke about it. He nearly made the girl an accomplice in the treason by telling her his plans. It is all very bad."

"But surely, Holmes, character goes for something? Then, again, why should he leave the girl in the street and dart away to commit a felony?"

"Exactly! There are certainly objections. But it is a formidable case which they have to meet."

Mr. Sidney Johnson, the senior clerk, met us at the office and received us with that respect which my companion's card always commanded. He was a thin, gruff, bespectacled man of middle age, his checks haggard, and his hands twitching from the nervous strain to which he had been subjected.

"It is bad, Mr. Holmes, very bad! Have you heard of the death of the chief?"

"We have just come from his house."

"The place is disorganized. The chief dead, Cadogan West dead, our papers stolen. And yet, when we closed our door on Monday evening, we were as efficient an office as any in the government service. Good God, it's dreadful to think of! That West, of all men, should have done such a thing!"

"You are sure of his guilt, then?"

"I can see no other way out of it. And yet I would have trusted him as I trust myself."

"At what hour was the office closed on Monday?"

"At five."

"Did you close it?"

"I am always the last man out."

"Where were the plans?"

"In that safe. I put them there myself."

"Is there no watchman to the building?"

"There is, but he has other departments to look after as well. He is an old soldier and a most trustworthy man. He saw nothing that evening. Of course the fog was very thick."

"Suppose that Cadogan West wished to make his way into the building after hours; he would need three keys, would he not, before he could reach the papers?"

"Yes, he would. The key of the outer door, the key of the office, and the key of the safe."

"Only Sir James Walter and you had those keys?"

"I had no keys of the doors—only of the safe."

"Was Sir James a man who was orderly in his habits?"

"Yes, I think he was. I know that so far as those three keys are concerned he kept them on the same ring. I have often seen them there."

"And that ring went with him to London?"

"He said so."

"And your key never left your possession?"

"Never."

"Then West, if he is the culprit, must have had a duplicate. And yet none was found upon his body. One other point: if a clerk in this office desired to sell the plans, would it not be simpler to copy the plans for himself than to take the originals, as was actually done?"

"It would take considerable technical knowledge to copy the plans in an effective way."

"But I suppose either Sir James, or you, or West had that technical knowledge?"

"No doubt we had, but I beg you won't try to drag me into the matter, Mr. Holmes. What is the use of our speculating in this way when the original plans were actually found on West?"

"Well, it is certainly singular that he should run the risk of taking originals if he could safely have taken copies, which would have equally served his turn."

"Singular, no doubt—and yet he did so."

"Every inquiry in this case reveals something inexplicable. Now there are three papers still missing. They are, as I understand, the vital ones."

"Yes, that is so."

"Do you mean to say that anyone holding these three papers, and without the seven others, could construct a Bruce-Partington submarine?"

"I reported to that effect to the Admiralty. But today I have been over the drawings again, and I am not so sure of it. The double valves with the automatic self-adjusting slots are drawn in one of the papers which have been returned. Until the foreigners had invented that for themselves they could not make the boat. Of course they might soon get over the difficulty."

"But the three missing drawings are the most important?"

"Undoubtedly."

"I think, with your permission, I will now take a stroll round the premises. I do not recall any other question which I desired to ask."

He examined the lock of the safe, the door of the room, and finally the iron shutters of the window. It was only when we were on the lawn outside that his interest was strongly excited. There was a laurel bush outside the window, and several of the branches bore signs of having been twisted or snapped. He examined them carefully with his lens, and then some dim and vague marks upon the earth beneath. Finally he asked the chief clerk to close the iron shutters, and he pointed out to me that they hardly met in the center, and that it would be possible for anyone outside to see what was going on within the room.

"The indications are ruined by the three days' delay. They may mean something or nothing. Well, Watson, I do not think that Woolwich can help us further. It is a small crop which we have gathered. Let us see if we can do better in London."

Yet we added one more sheaf to our harvest before we left Woolwich Station. The clerk in the ticket office was able to say with confidence that he saw Cadogan West—whom he knew well by sight—upon the Monday night, and that he went to London by the 8:15 to London Bridge. He was alone and took a single third-class ticket. The clerk was struck at the time by his excited and nervous manner. So shaky was he that he could hardly pick up his change, and the clerk had helped him with it. A reference to the timetable showed that the 8:15 was the first train which it was possible for West to take after he had left the lady about 7:30.

"Let us reconstruct, Watson," said Holmes after half an hour of silence. "I am not aware that in all our joint researches we have ever had a case which was more difficult to get at. Every fresh advance which we make only reveals a fresh ridge beyond. And yet we have surely made some appreciable progress.

"The effect of our inquiries at Woolwich has in the main been against young Cadogan West; but the indications at the window would lend themselves to a more favorable hypothesis. Let us suppose, for example, that he had been approached by some foreign agent. It might have been done under such pledges as would have prevented him from speaking of it, and yet would have affected his thoughts in the direction indicated by his remarks to his fiancée. Very good. We will now suppose that as he went to the theater with the young lady he suddenly, in the fog, caught a glimpse of this same agent going in the direction of the office. He was an impetuous man, quick in his decisions. Everything gave way to his duty. He followed the man, reached the window, saw the abstraction of the documents, and pursued the thief. In this way we get over the objection that no one would take originals when he could make copies. This outsider had to take originals. So far it holds together."

"What is the next step?"

"Then we come into difficulties. One would imagine that under such circumstances the first act of young Cadogan West would be to seize the villain and raise the alarm. Why did he not do so? Could it have been an official superior who took the papers? That would explain West's conduct. Or could the chief have given West the slip in the fog, and West started at once to London to head him off from his own rooms, presuming that he knew where the rooms were? The call must have been very pressing, since he left his girl standing in the fog, and made no effort to communicate with her. Our scent runs cold here, and there is a vast gap between either hypothesis and the laying of West's body, with seven papers in his pocket, on the roof of a Metropolitan train. My instinct now is to work from the other end. If Mycroft has given us the list of addresses we may be able to pick our man and follow two tracks instead of one."

Surely enough, a note awaited us at Baker Street. A government messenger had brought it post-haste. Holmes glanced at it and threw it over to me.

> There are numerous small fry, but few who would handle so big an affair. The only men worth considering are Adolph Meyer, of 13 Great George Street, Westminster; Louis La Rothière, of Campden Mansions, Notting Hill; and Hugo Oberstein, 13 Caulfield Gardens, Kensington. The latter was known to be in town on Monday and is now reported as having left. Glad to hear you have seen some light. The Cabinet awaits your final report with the utmost anxiety. Urgent representations have arrived from the very highest quarter. The whole force of the State is at your back if you should need it.
>
> MYCROFT

"I'm afraid," said Holmes, smiling, "that all the queen's horses and all the queen's men cannot avail in this matter." He had spread out his big map of London and leaned eagerly over it. "Well, well," said he presently with an exclamation of satisfaction, "things are turning a little in our direction at last. Why, Watson, I do honestly believe that we are going to pull it off, after all." He slapped me on the shoulder with a sudden burst of hilarity. "I am going out now. It is only a reconnaissance. I will do nothing serious without my trusted comrade and biographer at my elbow. Do you stay here, and the odds are that you will see me again in an hour or two. If time hangs heavy get foolscap and a pen, and begin your narrative of how we saved the State."

I felt some reflection of his elation in my own mind, for I knew well that he would not depart so far from his usual austerity of demeanor unless there was good cause for exultation. All the long November evening I waited, filled with impatience for his return. At last, shortly after nine o'clock, there arrived a messenger with a note:

> Am dining at Goldini's Restaurant, Gloucester Road, Kensington. Please come at once and join me there. Bring with you a jemmy, a dark lantern, a chisel, and a revolver.
>
> S. H.

It was a nice equipment for a respectable citizen to carry through the dim, fog-draped streets. I stowed them all discreetly away in my overcoat and drove straight to the address given. There sat my friend at a little round table near the door of the garish Italian restaurant.

"Have you had something to eat? Then join me in a coffee and curaçao. Try one of the proprietor's cigars. They are less poisonous than one would expect. Have you the tools?"

"They are here, in my overcoat."

"Excellent. Let me give you a short sketch of what I have done, with some indication of what we are about to do. Now it must be evident to you, Watson, that this young man's body was *placed* on the roof of the train. That was clear from the instant that I determined the fact that it was from the roof, and not from a carriage, that he had fallen."

"Could it not have been dropped from a bridge?"

"I should say it was impossible. If you examine the roofs you will find that they are slightly rounded, and there is no railing round them. Therefore, we can say for certain that young Cadogan West was placed on it."

"How could he be placed there?"

"That was the question which we had to answer. There is only one possible way. You are aware that the Underground runs clear of tunnels at some points in the West End. I had a vague memory that as I have traveled by it I have occasionally seen windows just above my head. Now, suppose that a train halted under such a window, would there be any difficulty in laying a body upon the roof?"

"It seems most improbable."

"We must fall back upon the old axiom that when all other contingencies fail, whatever remains, however improbable, must be the truth. Here all other contingencies *have* failed. When I found that the leading international agent, who had just left London, lived in a row of houses which abutted upon the Underground, I was so pleased that you were a little astonished at my sudden frivolity."

"Oh, that was it, was it?"

"Yes, that was it. Mr. Hugo Oberstein, of 13 Caulfield Gardens, had become my objective. I began my operations at Gloucester Road Station, where a very helpful official walked with me along the track and allowed me to satisfy myself not only that the back-stair windows of Caulfield Gardens open on the line but the even more essential fact that, owing to the intersection of one of the larger railways, the Underground trains are frequently held motionless for some minutes at that very spot."

"Splendid, Holmes! You have got it!"

"So far—so far, Watson. We advance, but the goal is afar. Well, having seen the back of Caulfield Gardens, I visited the front and satisfied myself that the bird was indeed flown. It is a considerable house, unfurnished, so far as I could judge, in the upper rooms. Oberstein lived there with a single valet, who was probably a confederate entirely in his confidence. We must bear in mind that Oberstein has gone to the Continent to dispose of his booty, but not with any idea of flight; for he had no reason to fear a warrant, and the idea of an amateur domiciliary visit would certainly never occur to him. Yet that is precisely what we are about to make."

"Could we not get a warrant and legalize it?"

"Hardly on the evidence."

"What can we hope to do?"

"We cannot tell what correspondence may be there."

"I don't like it, Holmes."

"My dear fellow, you shall keep watch in the street. I'll do the criminal part. It's not a time to stick at trifles. Think of Mycroft's note, of the Admiralty, the Cabinet, the exalted person who waits for news. We are bound to go."

My answer was to rise from the table.

He sprang up and shook me by the hand.

"I knew you would not shrink at the last," said he, and for a moment I saw something in his eyes which was nearer to tenderness than I had ever seen. The next instant he was his masterful, practical self once more.

"It is nearly half a mile, but there is no hurry. Let us walk," said he. "Don't drop the instruments, I beg. Your arrest as a suspicious character would be a most unfortunate complication."

Caulfield Gardens was one of those lines of flat-faced, pillared, and porticoed houses which are so prominent a product of the middle Victorian epoch in the West End of London. Next door there appeared to be a children's party, for the merry buzz of young voices and the clatter of a piano resounded through the night. The fog still hung about and screened us with its friendly shade. Holmes had lit his lantern and flashed it upon the massive door.

"This is a serious proposition," said he. "It is certainly bolted as well as locked. We would do better in the area. There is an excellent archway down yonder in case a too zealous policeman should intrude. Give me a hand, Watson, and I'll do the same for you."

A minute later we were both in the area. Hardly had we reached the dark shadows before the step of the policeman was heard in the fog above. As its soft rhythm died away, Holmes set to work upon the lower door. I saw him stoop and strain until with a sharp crash it flew open. We sprang through into the dark passage, closing the area door behind us. Holmes led the way up the curving, uncarpeted stair. His little fan of yellow light shone upon a low window.

"Here we are, Watson—this must be the one." He threw it open, and as he did so there was a low, harsh murmur, growing steadily into a loud roar as a train dashed past us in the darkness. Holmes swept his light along the window sill. It was thickly coated with soot from the passing engines, but the black surface was blurred and rubbed in places.

"You can see where they rested the body. Halloa, Watson! What is this? There can be no doubt that it is a blood mark." He was pointing to faint discolorations along the woodwork of the window. "Here it is on the stone of the stair also. The demonstration is complete. Let us stay here until a train stops."

We had not long to wait. The very next train roared from the tunnel as before, but slowed in the open, and then, with a creaking of brakes, pulled up immediately beneath us. It was not four feet from the window ledge to the roof of the carriages. Holmes softly closed the window.

"So far we are justified," said he. "What do you think of it, Watson?"

"A masterpiece. You have never risen to a greater height."

"I cannot agree with you there. From the moment that I conceived the idea of the body being upon the roof, which surely was not a very abstruse one, all the rest was inevitable. If it were not for the grave interests involved, the affair up to this point would be insignificant. Our difficulties are still before us. But perhaps we may find something here which may help us."

We had ascended the kitchen stair and entered the suite of rooms upon the first floor. One was a dining room, severely furnished and containing nothing of interest. A second was a bedroom, which also drew blank. The remaining room appeared more promising, and my companion settled down to a systematic examination. It was littered with books and papers, and was evidently used as a study. Swiftly and methodically Holmes turned over the contents of drawer after drawer and cupboard after cupboard, but no gleam of success came to brighten his austere face. At the end of an hour he was no further than when he started.

"The cunning dog has covered his tracks," said he. "He has left nothing to incriminate him. His dangerous correspondence has been destroyed or removed. This is our last chance."

It was a small tin cash box which stood upon the writing desk. Holmes pried it open with his chisel. Several rolls of paper were within, covered with figures and calculations, without any note to show to what they referred. The recurring words, "water pressure" and "pressure to the square inch" suggested some possible relation to a submarine. Holmes tossed them all impatiently aside. There only remained an envelope with some small newspaper slips inside it. He shook them out on the table, and at once I saw by his eager face that his hopes had been raised.

"What's this, Watson? Eh? What's this? Record of a series of messages in the advertisements of a paper. *Daily Telegraph* agony column by the print and paper. Right-hand top corner of a page. No dates—but messages arrange themselves. This must be the first:

> "Hoped to hear sooner. Terms agreed to. Write fully to address given on card."
>
> "Peirrot

"Next comes:

> "Too complex for description. Must have full report. Stuff awaits you when goods delivered."
>
> "Peirrot

"Then comes:

> "Matter presses. Must withdraw offer unless contract completed. Make appointment by letter. Will confirm by advertisement."
>
> "PEIRROT

"Finally:

> "Monday night after nine. Two taps. Only ourselves. Do not be so suspicious, payment in hard cash when goods delivered."
>
> "PEIRROT

"A fairly complete record, Watson! If we could only get at the man at the other end!" He sat lost in thought, tapping his fingers on the table. Finally he sprang to his feet.

"Well, perhaps it won't be so difficult, after all. There is nothing more to be done here, Watson. I think we might drive round to the offices of the *Daily Telegraph*, and so bring a good day's work to a conclusion."

MYCROFT HOLMES AND LESTRADE had come round by appointment after breakfast next day and Sherlock Holmes had recounted to them our proceedings of the day before. The professional shook his head over our confessed burglary.

"We can't do these things in the force, Mr. Holmes," said he. "No wonder you get results that are beyond us. But some of these days you'll go too far, and you'll find yourself and your friend in trouble."

"For England, home and beauty—eh, Watson? Martyrs on the altar of our country. But what do you think of it, Mycroft?"

"Excellent, Sherlock! Admirable! But what use will you make of it?"

Holmes picked up the *Daily Telegraph* which lay upon the table.

"Have you seen Pierrot's advertisement today?"

"What? Another one?"

"Yes, here it is:

> "Tonight. Same hour. Same place. Two taps. Most vitally important. Your own safety at stake.
>
> "PEIRROT"

"By George!" cried Lestrade. "If he answers that we've got him!"

"That was my idea when I put it in. I think if you could both make it convenient to come with us about eight o'clock to Caulfield Gardens we might possibly get a little nearer to a solution."

ONE OF THE MOST remarkable characteristics of Sherlock Holmes was his power of throwing his brain out of action and switching all his thoughts on to lighter things whenever he had convinced himself that he could no longer work to advantage. I remember that during the whole of that memorable day he lost himself in a monograph which he had undertaken upon the Polyphonic Motets of Lassus. For my own part I had none of this power of detachment, and the day, in consequence, appeared to be interminable. The great national importance of the issue, the suspense in high quarters, the direct nature of the experiment which we were trying—all combined to work upon my nerve. It was a relief to me when at last, after a light dinner, we set out upon our expedition. Lestrade and Mycroft met us by appointment at the outside of Gloucester Road Station. The area door of Oberstein's house had been left open the night before, and it was necessary for me, as Mycroft Holmes absolutely and indignantly declined to climb the railings, to pass in and open the hall door. By nine o'clock we were all seated in the study, waiting patiently for our man.

An hour passed and yet another. When eleven struck, the measured beat of the great church clock seemed to sound the dirge of our hopes. Lestrade and Mycroft were fidgeting in their seats and looking twice a minute at their watches. Holmes sat silent and composed, his eyelids half shut, but every sense on the alert. He raised his head with a sudden jerk.

"He is coming," said he.

There had been a furtive step past the door. Now it returned. We heard a shuffling sound outside, and then two sharp taps with the knocker. Holmes rose, motioning us to remain seated. The gas in the hall was a mere point of light. He opened the outer door, and then as a dark figure slipped past him he closed and fastened it. "This way!" we heard him say, and a moment later our man stood before us. Holmes had followed him closely, and as the man turned with a cry of surprise and alarm he caught him by the collar and threw him back into the room. Before our prisoner had recovered his balance the door was shut and Holmes standing with his back against it. The man glared round him, staggered, and fell senseless to the floor. With the shock, his broad-brimmed hat flew from his head, his cravat slipped down from his lips, and there were the long light beard and the soft, handsome delicate features of Colonel Valentine Walter.

Holmes gave a whistle of surprise.

"You can write me down an ass this time, Watson," said he. "This was not the bird that I was looking for."

"Who is he?" asked Mycroft eagerly.

"The younger brother of the late Sir James Walter, the head of the Submarine Department. Yes, yes; I see the fall of the cards. He is coming to. I think that you had best leave his examination to me."

We had carried the prostrate body to the sofa. Now our prisoner sat up, looked round him with a horror-stricken face, and passed his hand over his forehead, like one who cannot believe his own senses.

"What is this?" he asked. "I came here to visit Mr. Oberstein."

"Everything is known, Colonel Walter," said Holmes. "How an English gentleman could behave in such a manner is beyond my comprehension. But your whole correspondence and relations with Oberstein are within our knowledge. So also are the circumstances connected with the death of young Cadogan West. Let me

advise you to gain at least the small credit for repentance and confession, since there are still some details which we can only learn
from your lips."

The man groaned and sank his face in his hands. We waited, but
he was silent.

"I can assure you," said Holmes, "that every essential is already
known. We know that you were pressed for money; that you took
an impress of the keys which your brother held; and that you
entered into a correspondence with Oberstein, who answered your
letters through the advertisement columns of the *Daily Telegraph*.
We are aware that you went down to the office in the fog on
Monday night, but that you were seen and followed by young Cadogan West, who had probably some previous reason to suspect you.
He saw your theft, but could not give the alarm, as it was just possible that you were taking the papers to your brother in London.
Leaving all his private concerns like the good citizen that he was, he
followed you closely in the fog and kept at your heels until you
reached this very house. There he intervened, and then it was,
Colonel Walter, that to treason you added the more terrible crime of
murder."

"I did not! I did not! Before God I swear that I did not!" cried
our wretched prisoner.

"Tell us, then, how Cadogan West met his end before you laid
him upon the roof of a railway carriage."

"I will. I swear to you that I will. I did the rest. I confess it. It was
just as you say. A Stock Exchange debt had to be paid. I needed the
money badly. Oberstein offered me five thousand. It was to save
myself from ruin. But as to murder, I am as innocent as you."

"What happened, then?"

"He had his suspicions before, and he followed me as you
describe. I never knew it until I was at the very door. It was
thick fog, and one could not see three yards. I had given two
taps and Oberstein had come to the door. The young man
rushed up and demanded to know what we were about to do
with the papers. Oberstein had a short life-preserver. He always

carried it with him. As West forced his way after us into the house Oberstein struck him on the head. The blow was a fatal one. He was dead within five minutes. There he lay in the hall, and we were at our wit's end what to do. Then Oberstein had this idea about the trains which halted under his back window. But first he examined the papers which I had brought. He said that three of them were essential, and that he must keep them. 'You cannot keep them,' said I. 'There will be a dreadful row at Woolwich if they are not returned. 'I must keep them,' said he, 'for they are so technical that it is impossible in the time to make copies.' 'Then they must all go back together tonight,' said I. He thought for a little, and then he cried out that he had it. 'Three I will keep,' said he. 'The others we will stuff into the pocket of this young man. When he is found the whole business will assuredly be put to his account.' I could see no other way out of it, so we did as he suggested. We waited half an hour at the window before a train stopped. It was so thick that nothing could be seen, and we had no difficulty in lowering West's body on to the train. That was the end of the matter so far as I was concerned."

"And your brother?"

"He said nothing, but he had caught me once with his keys, and I think that he suspected. I read in his eyes that he suspected. As you know, he never held up his head again."

There was silence in the room. It was broken by Mycroft Holmes.

"Can you not make reparation? It would ease your conscience, and possibly your punishment."

"What reparation can I make?"

"Where is Oberstein with the papers?"

"I do not know."

"Did he give you no address?"

"He said that letters to the Hôtel du Louvre, Paris, would eventually reach him."

THE ADVENTURE OF THE BRUCE-PARTINGTON PLANS 43

"Then reparation is still within your power," said Sherlock Holmes.

"I will do anything I can. I owe this fellow no particular goodwill. He has been my ruin and my downfall."

"Here are paper and pen. Sit at this desk and write to my dictation. Direct the envelope to the address given. That is right. Now the letter:

> "Dear Sir:
>
> "With regard to our transaction, you will no doubt have observed by now that one essential detail is missing. I have a tracing which will make it complete. This has involved me in extra trouble, however, and I must ask you for a further advance of five hundred pounds. I will not trust it to the post, nor will I take anything but gold or notes. I would come to you abroad, but it would excite remark if I left the country at present. Therefore I shall expect to meet you in the smoking room of the Charing Cross Hotel at noon on Saturday. Remember that only English notes, or gold, will be taken."

"That will do very well. I shall be very much surprised if it does not fetch our man."

And it did! It is a matter of history—that secret history of a nation which is often so much more intimate and interesting than its public chronicles—that Oberstein, eager to complete the coup of his lifetime, came to the lure and was safely engulfed for fifteen years in a British prison. In his trunk were found the invaluable Bruce-Partington plans, which he had put up for auction in all the naval centers of Europe.

Colonel Walter died in prison toward the end of the second year of his sentence. As to Holmes, he returned refreshed to his monograph upon the Polyphonic Motets of Lassus, which has since been printed for private circulation, and is said by experts to be the last word upon the subject. Some weeks afterward I learned incidentally that my friend spent a day at Windsor, whence he returned with a remarkably fine emerald tie pin. When I asked him if he had bought it, he answered that it was a present from a certain gracious lady in whose interests he had once been fortunate enough to carry out a small commission. He said no more; but I fancy that I could guess at that lady's name, and I have little doubt that the emerald pin will forever recall to my friend's memory the adventure of the Bruce-Partington plans.

Enemy Territory

EDWARD D. HOCH

REINHARDT REMEMBERED HIS first days at the Nazi spy school in the Netherlands quite clearly. He'd arrived at the renovated estate near The Hague in May of 1944, when rumors of an Allied invasion of Western Europe were at their peak. Immediately he'd been assigned to a group of five men and one woman for a month of intensive training. It was made clear at the beginning that they were being trained for a mission so secret even the director of the school had no knowledge of its nature. Of the six, it was likely only two would be chosen.

They especially liked Reinhardt because he was an American by birth and spoke perfect English. Like many Germans who came to America before the First World War, his parents found themselves the objects of suspicion and mistrust during the conflict and its aftermath. In the 1930s they had to hide their admiration for Hitler, though they conveyed it to their son every day of his young life. As soon as he was eighteen he left home and found a job as a seaman aboard a German merchant ship sailing out of Boston. Reinhardt

was in Bremen when war broke out in 1939. He immediately tried
to enlist in the German army. It was suggested instead that he might
be more valuable to the cause if he found a job on an American merchant ship and reported on ship movements and cargoes. His success at this type of spying finally led to the espionage school in the
German-occupied Netherlands.

He shared a room in one of the estate's outbuildings with Franz
Keller, an electrical engineer, though neither man knew the other's
real name or specialty at first. Everyone there, instructors and stu-
dents alike, used aliases to protect their true identities. Keller was a
blond German who spoke English with a slight accent. They became
friendly at once.

On the first day of classes the instructor, a slender gray-haired
man named Major Essen, told them they would learn to ride
motorcycles and be trained in gunnery, radiotelegraphy, codes,
secret ink, and the use of plastic explosives for booby traps. In his
class they spent a week learning to photograph documents using a
Leica with a special lens, then developing and printing the pictures.
Special training was given in microphotography, reducing the
Leica's negatives of documents to microdots that had to be read
under strong magnification. "Always," he said, "we stress backup—
redundancy in all matters. It is always better to have too much
knowledge, too much backup, than to fail in a mission because of
some deficiency."

The other three men were all in their twenties or early thirties,
the same ages as Reinhardt and Keller. The woman was about the
same age too, a dour but comely blonde German with large eyes
named Lola Brandt, who excelled at rigging booby traps with plastic explosives and a simple mousetrap detonator. Keller enjoyed
the training but did worse than Reinhardt with the automatic pistols and submachine guns they had to fire skillfully with either
hand. One of the other three men was a German Swede named
Erickson, a jovial fellow who told endless stories during their free
time together. The other two, Wapper and Seffel, kept pretty much
to themselves.

"What do you think they're training us for?" Reinhardt asked one night when they were back in their room after a full day of hand-to-hand combat and pistol training in the thick-walled basement of the main house.

Keller, his bleak eyes staring into space as if awaiting the appearance of the next pop-up target, said only, "We'll know soon enough. They're sending us somewhere."

"If we're chosen."

"You'll be chosen," Keller assured him. "They want someone who speaks perfect English." His own English was passable, and he was trying to lessen the accent with Reinhardt's help. They couldn't help noticing that the other four also spoke passable English, and some classes were conducted entirely in English.

Neither of them said what was uppermost in their minds. They were being trained for a mission somewhere behind American lines.

DURING THE FOLLOWING WEEK Reinhardt noticed that one of their number, the tall German using the alias Hans Seffel, had dropped out of the class. The others confirmed that he'd been transferred to another unit at the school. Now there were just five of them left.

The course ended as abruptly as it had begun. The woman, Lola, simply failed to appear for breakfast one morning. Then Reinhardt and Keller were spirited away without an opportunity to bid the others good-bye. They found themselves in a small plane with Major Essen, headed for Berlin more than six hundred miles away. The following morning they were taken in a car through the bomb-damaged city to the home of a high-ranking intelligence officer in the suburbs.

"You are about to receive your final briefing," Major Essen told them. Inside the house he introduced them to a white-haired man of military bearing who sat behind an ornate desk wearing a bathrobe. He rose as they entered and reached out his hand. "Congratulations, gentlemen. You have successfully completed the course and been chosen for a highly important mission. Please be seated."

"Thank you, sir," Reinhardt said.

"As you may have guessed from the training you received, you will be going to America. Although we already have agents in place there, they are tied down by specific duties, usually involving foreign embassies. What we especially need is technical data on shipbuilding, planes, rockets, and the like. Engineering data." He glanced at Franz Keller. "That would be your field, I believe. Even in wartime, American society has remained remarkably open. Some of the information we desire can no doubt be found in newspapers, magazines, and technical journals. The problem with obtaining this material through normal diplomatic channels is one of time. Something as simple as an issue of the *New York Times* takes four weeks to reach us here. A skilled technician like yourself, working full-time with publications that are generally available, could radio us information at once. Longer pieces could be reduced to microdots and mailed to us via addresses in neutral countries like Switzerland."

"What would be my part in all this?" Reinhardt asked the man, who had given no hint of his name or rank.

"As a native-born American you will serve as Keller's front man, helping to protect him in any possible way."

"I'm to be his bodyguard?"

The man in the bathrobe smiled. "Much more than that, I assure you. Further instructions will be communicated to you once we know your insertion has been successful."

"Where will we be stationed?" Keller asked.

"In America's information center, New York City. A submarine will deposit you on a remote stretch of the Maine coastline. You will make your way to New York and find an apartment there. Special instructions will be radioed to you as soon as we have established a shortwave link."

"Very well," Reinhardt said. He had little choice at this point. If he refused the mission they would hardly allow him to remain free and speak to others about it. "Tell me one thing. Why were the two of us chosen over the others?"

It was Major Essen who answered. "We feel a pair will work better than individuals because they can support and complement one another. As you know, we landed four agents on Long Island and another four in Florida back in 1942. Their mission was sabotage and it failed because two were captured and told everything to save themselves from the electric chair. The other six were caught and executed within two months of their landings. We do not want anything like that to happen again." He opened the briefcase he'd carried on the journey and removed two identical .32 caliber Colt automatic pistols along with clips holding seven bullets each. He handed a weapon to each of them before continuing. "Here also are special document-copying lenses for your Leica cameras, and microdots with detailed instructions for building a radio and transmitting messages to Berlin. Call signs, times of transmission, and radio cover names are also given. You will sail from Kiel in one week's time, when you will be given your false identity papers as well."

"How long will we be there?" Reinhardt asked.

The nameless man behind the desk answered. "We are planning on a two-year mission. If your extraction becomes necessary before that time, radio a properly coded message and a submarine will rendezvous with you at a predetermined location."

"You seem to have thought of everything," Keller said with a smile.

"No one ever thinks of everything."

REINHARDT AND KELLER WERE taken to the northern port of Kiel and put aboard a liner in dry dock for repairs. "It's not a military ship," Major Essen explained. "The probability of an American bombing is very slight."

In these days following the Normandy invasion, nothing seemed improbable for the Americans. When they were alone in the stateroom that would be home for the next few days, Keller ran a comb through his blond hair and said, "I don't suppose there'll be any shore leave before we sail off on that U-boat."

Reinhardt shook his head. "They have too much time and effort invested to risk losing us now."

"I only hope the war lasts two more years. What happens if it ends while we're over there?"

Reinhardt, who refused to speculate on the possibility of a German defeat, said simply, "We'll be the first of the occupying army."

They saw nothing of Major Essen for the next several days, and life was tedious aboard the dry-docked liner. Once the air raid sirens sounded and Reinhardt looked up at the bright night sky. "It's a bomber's moon," he said, but they saw no planes and presently the all clear sounded.

Essen returned on the evening before the submarine was due. He sat down in their stateroom and opened his briefcase. "Gentlemen, here we have all the papers you will need—birth certificates, Selective Service registration cards, driver's licenses, ration books. Some of the documents bear dates in 1945 and '46, for use in the later parts of your mission." Next he took out bundles of American currency and stacked them on the little table between their beds. "Count it! There should be sixty thousand dollars. It will cover all your expenses for two years."

Reinhardt moistened his lips. It was more money than he had ever seen in his life. "Ah—what if there is an unexpected emergency? What if the Americans change their currency as they did in Hawaii after Pearl Harbor?"

The major smiled and produced a necktie of a conservative pattern. "There is always a backup, as I told you early in your training. Sewn into the lining of this tie are a dozen chip diamonds that can be converted into cash without difficulty. I hope you will not need them."

The following morning at dawn they boarded a Type IXC submarine, the longest-ranged of Atlantic U-boats. The voyage to America was under way.

THERE WAS A STOP on the southern tip of Norway for fuel and supplies, and then they sailed submerged for the next several days, coming up only far enough for the snorkel to take in fresh air from the surface at night. It was a weaving, wandering route across the Atlantic as the submarine's commander sought to avoid detection. Reinhardt found the U-boat's cramped quarters to be unbearably dank and smelly, and when they finally surfaced for an hour one night he joined the rest of the crew on deck with a feeling of utter relief.

It was a night in early August when the submarine finally reached Frenchman Bay on the coast of Maine. The sun rose early at that time of year, and the rubber boat from the submarine had to start out before 4:00 A.M. in order to deposit Reinhardt and Keller on the beach and return safely to their ship before dawn. Alone for the first time, the men walked quickly with their suitcases, heading for the nearest highway.

By daylight they had reached a town and found a taxi willing to drive them the thirty miles into Bangor for six dollars. From there they caught a train to Portland and then to Boston, where they took a hotel room for the night. The following day they reached New York. The city was crowded with servicemen in uniform but they managed to find a small hotel room on East Twenty-third Street. It would do until they were settled in an apartment.

The following morning Reinhardt bought some newspapers and read of the latest Allied victories in Europe. A front-page map indicated that Paris was in danger of falling. "Can we believe that?" Keller wondered.

"Of course not! It's propaganda!" But he wondered about it himself.

The search for an apartment moved slowly because the short-wave radio would not operate properly inside a building with steel construction. They finally located one on Beekman Place, the top floor of a townhouse that was perfect for their needs. They sublet it for $150 a month. Reinhardt made the arrangements and paid two months' rent in advance. The first thing he did after they moved in was to find a hiding place for their money, diamonds, and pistols. The metal medicine cabinet in the tiled bathroom was a loose fit and when he pulled it out he found a small wall cavity of just the right size.

Within days Keller had purchased a radio and the equipment needed for converting it into a transmitter. They purchased magazines and technical journals, and scanned the papers for any hint of experiments with rockets, atomic energy, or radio-controlled missiles. Wartime censorship allowed very little. Keller's first cipher message to Berlin was a summary of an article giving new information about Pearl Harbor and stating that several of the older battleships and cruisers sunk there had been raised and refitted with massive antiaircraft batteries.

A few days later, on August 26, the *New York Times* proclaimed, "Nazi Rout Grows; German Commander Surrenders in Paris." Reinhardt read the stories with growing apprehension, then showed the paper to Keller. "We're losing the war," he said simply.

"You told me a few weeks ago it was all propaganda."

"Some of it is, but—"

"What would happen if the war ended while we were still here?" Keller wanted to know.

"We'd be safe. We have forged documents running through 1946, and enough cash and diamonds to last us longer than that."

"You can say that. You were born here. It's your home. I am a stranger here."

"We'll stick together," Reinhardt assured him.

"I hope so."

As his depression deepened, Keller started going out nights to nearby bars along First Avenue. During the day he did his job well, sending and receiving several shortwave transmissions to and from Berlin. But with the coming of dark his restlessness always grew. At first Reinhardt would accompany him, but it was not a life for him, especially when Keller began engaging in conversation with some of the women in the place.

The downstairs floors of their townhouse were occupied by an older man named Samuels, a widower whose wife had died the previous year. Keller thought he was probably Jewish, but Reinhardt assured him it made no difference. "You're in America now, not Germany."

It was Samuels who stopped him one day in early September as he was going upstairs to their apartment. "Your friend stays out pretty late some of these nights. I hear him going up the stairs way after midnight."

"He's restless," Reinhardt said.

"You fellas veterans?" he asked.

"I am. Franz is a refugee."

Samuels eyed him uncertainly. "How come they let you out?"

"I was wounded. Punctured eardrum from a bomb blast in North Africa."

"Sorry to hear that."

"I can live with it."

The man went back to his door. "Look after your friend. You don't want him getting into trouble."

The following evening when Keller went out for a drink, Reinhardt decided to join him. This time, because neither had eaten dinner, Keller suggested an Irish bar called the Shamrock that served sandwiches and light suppers. It was a noisy place with more than its share of American servicemen. They sat at a table and ordered beer and sandwiches. Once he noticed a dark-haired woman glancing at them from the bar, but she made no move to approach them and the next time he looked that way she was gone. Keller had two beers and then ordered a third with dinner. They seemed to cheer him up and after the meal he made no objection when Reinhardt suggested they call it a night. They were back in the apartment before ten o'clock.

"Here's a list of some journal articles I need from the New York Public Library. Maybe you can get them tomorrow."

Reinhardt glanced over the titles. "Most of these can't be taken out of the library. I'll have to try photographing them there. It'll take time. I don't want to be noticed."

"Do the best you can. I need them."

Reinhardt spent most of the following afternoon at the library on Fifth Avenue, trying to photograph articles in magazines like *Scientific American*. He took out a library card and actually managed to borrow a three-volume set titled *A First Course in Cryptanalysis*, published the previous year by the Brooklyn College Press. By the time he returned to the apartment at five o'clock, he felt it had been an afternoon well spent.

He climbed the stairs and let himself into their apartment, carrying the three books in a bag under one arm. Keller was seated in the room's single armchair, apparently asleep. It was a moment before Reinhardt noticed the blood trailing from the wound in his right temple and saw Keller's .32 caliber Colt automatic on the floor beneath his hand.

Reinhardt's partner had killed himself.

HIS FIRST EMOTION WAS a feeling of sheer terror. Keller had deserted him, left him alone in an enemy country. Why had he done such a thing? Certainly the war seemed to be going badly, but they had money and identification. It was a big country, and even if Hitler lost the war there were lots of places to hide.

Then Reinhardt remembered this was his country, not Keller's. The German might have felt emotions he could barely imagine.

He walked around the apartment, head in his hands, wondering what to do next. Should he send a message to Berlin? Was there even a code number for "partner a suicide"? Probably not. Such things were not allowed.

He could hardly call the police and have them snooping about, yet what was he to do with Keller's body?

Suddenly a firm knock on the door cut through his thoughts. He walked to it and called out, "Who's there?"

"Samuels, your downstairs neighbor. Are you alone?"

Reinhardt opened the door a crack. "Keller is out, but I'm doing some work. What do you want?"

The older man spoke quietly, as if afraid of being overheard. "You should know he had a woman up here this afternoon, while you were gone."

"A woman?" Reinhardt repeated, incredulous.

"Dark-haired lady. Couldn't see her face. Just saw her going up the stairs with him."

"Thank you, Mr. Samuels," he told the man. "I promise that won't happen again."

"I hope not." He might have had more to say but Reinhardt closed the door gently in his face. Then he turned and stared again at Keller's body. If it was true that a woman had been here with him, she might have been present at his suicide.

If it really was suicide.

A chill ran down his spine as he remembered the money and diamonds. He hurried to the bathroom hiding place, fearing the worst, but everything was still there behind the loose medicine cabinet—the money, the diamonds, the two Colt automatics.

Then, as if a sudden bolt of lightning had illuminated everything, he knew Franz Keller had been murdered. He knew who had done it, and he knew he would be the next victim.

REINHARDT SPENT THE EVENING trying to work out a plan. Time was important. He could see no way of getting Keller's body out of the apartment, not with old Samuels attuned to every sound and movement on the stairs. And with each passing hour he imagined the odor of death becoming more noticeable. He would have to leave this place by morning.

But first he had to face the killer. There was no other way. He picked up the pistol that had killed Keller and put it in his pocket.

As soon as it was fully dark he went quietly down the stairs to the wet street where a summer shower had just ended. He hurried along to the Shamrock, where he'd noticed the dark-haired woman the previous night. As he entered he scanned the tables but there was no sign of her. Unable to eat at the apartment with Keller's body slumped in the armchair, he ordered a sandwich and a beer from the Shamrock's waitress and lingered over his meal.

At ten o'clock, convinced that the woman would not return, he paid his check and left. He walked across Forty-second Street and turned north on First Avenue, heading back toward Beekman Place. The streets were still wet enough to reflect the glow of the overhead lights.

Then he saw her. She was wearing a dark raincoat, striding toward him down the nearly deserted street. As they passed, her face showed no recognition. Then her hand was coming out of the raincoat pocket and he caught the glint of reflected light on metal. Acting on instinct he grabbed her arms, pinning them to her sides. The gun clattered to the sidewalk by their feet.

"Lola Brandt, I believe," Reinhardt said. "Though it's been four months since The Hague, and your hair was a different color then."

HE POCKETED THE COLT AUTOMATIC and walked her back to the town-house on Beekman Place. "Let me explain—" she began once in her not-quite-perfect English, but he only gripped her arm harder.

"We'll talk back there, with Keller's body to keep us company. I know you killed him."

"Our war is lost. I came here to flee with him."

"Shut up!"

Outside the building he whispered in her ear, "Make one sound on our way up and I'll kill you."

Samuels's windows were already dark and he had probably retired for the night, but Reinhardt took no chances. He didn't speak again until they were safely up the stairs and into the apartment. Lola Brandt seemed startled to see Keller's body still in the chair and quickly averted her eyes. "How did you know?" she asked finally.

"Major Essen's stressing of backup and redundancy. The earlier effort in 1942 landed four men on Long Island and another four in Florida. They would hardly go through all this training and risk everything on a two-man landing. I suspected at least one other pair had been landed, but I was betting on Wapper and Erickson at first. They were clever, though. They put a woman on the other team, with Seffel, I imagine."

"With Seffel, yes," she admitted.

"Where were you? How did you find us here?"

"They landed us in Maine, near the same place as you, ten days earlier. No one spotted us, so they tried the same area again with you and Keller. We went to Boston because there are many universities in the area. I got word to Keller before I left, and when you two found an apartment here he sent me a coded message in care of general delivery in Boston."

"You and Keller—?"

She got up from the chair and roamed around the room, avoiding his body. "We had a brief affair. I foolishly thought he cared about me."

"Why did you come here?" Reinhardt asked. "To kill him?"

"No! The war is lost! Paris has fallen. I wanted him to run away with me but he wouldn't."

Reinhardt was shaking his head. "You knew we'd gotten sixty thousand dollars and diamonds, just like you and Seffel. You wanted to have it all for yourself, to help finance your new life here. When Keller wouldn't go along you shot him and tried to make it look like suicide."

"You knew that too?"

"Yes," he told her. "You didn't find our money or our weapons, so you had to kill him with your own identical Colt automatic. When I saw that our weapons were still in their hiding place I knew he was killed by someone who not only carried the same make, model, and caliber of pistol we did, but also had knowledge of that fact. Only a member of the other team could possibly have killed him under those circumstances. When the man downstairs said Keller had a woman up here this afternoon I knew it had to be you, even with the dark hair. And since you didn't find the money or diamonds I knew you'd be back."

She sat down again, her big eyes on his face. "Keller was a fool. But that's one less share to divide up now. Bring out your stash and we'll divide it three ways. Seffel is waiting for me back in Boston."

Reinhardt shook his head. "Seffel is dead. You killed him too."

"That's crazy!"

"Is it, Lola? Consider this. Four of us landed here and each of us was issued a .32 caliber Colt automatic. Keller's and mine are still in their hiding place. You used one to kill Keller and left it here with his body. I took the fourth one from you in the street just now. One of those last two had to be Seffel's weapon. He wouldn't have let you take them both to New York while he waited in Boston."

"All right," she sighed, knowing she was trapped but unwilling to quit. "You're right. There are only two shares now, yours and mine. I searched this apartment twice. Where is it hidden?"

He shook his head. "You first."

"Back in my hotel room. The Commodore at Grand Central Station." She tossed a key on the table with its numbered tag attached. "Room 1128. There's an overnight bag on the floor in the closet. It's in there, under some dirty laundry."

"All right. We'll go back there together."

"What about yours?"

He motioned toward the bathroom. "In there."

"I searched the bathroom, toilet tank and everything."

"The medicine cabinet is a loose fit. It's behind there."

She strode quickly across the floor to the bathroom door. Reinhardt picked up a pillow from the sofa and followed her in. "What's that for?" she asked.

"To muffle the sound. I don't want old Samuels downstairs hearing any clanking."

He edged the cabinet free, holding the pillow under it, and set it carefully on the floor. Lola saw the envelopes of money and diamonds, along with the two pistols, and reached into the wall cavity for them.

He slid the Colt automatic out of his pocket, placed the pillow over the muzzle, and shot her in the back of the head.

LOOKING OVER THE SCENE before he left the apartment for the last time, Reinhardt decided it seemed convincing enough at first glance. Keller had killed her and then shot himself with the same pistol. There was a war on, and if he was lucky they might be too busy to ever discover that Keller had died several hours earlier than Lola. And if they did discover it, he'd be far away beyond their reach.

He walked down First Avenue to Forty-second Street, then west to Grand Central Station and Lola's hotel. His and Keller's money and diamonds were in his pockets along with the other three guns. He'd dispose of two of them later, but first he wanted to collect the sixty thousand dollars and diamonds that had been given to Lola and Seffel. Neither of them would need it now. Taking the elevator to the eleventh floor of the Commodore Hotel, he slid the key effortlessly into the lock of room 1128.

He turned on the overhead light and crossed quickly to the closet. The bag was there, just as she'd promised. He pulled out the dirty clothes to reach the bottom, and it was only in the split second when he saw the battery and wires and mousetrap that he remembered she'd been an expert at rigging booby traps with plastic explosives.

A Part of History

MICHAEL COLLINS

L IFE BECOMES CROWDED: DAYS are busy and weeks short; months fly by and then years. One day you suddenly feel you haven't done much with your life, not really. Yes, you have the wife you married forty years ago and love very much, the family all grown and successful, the good job as a solicitor in Birmingham you're phasing out, the house in the suburbs beyond Kingstanding. All wonderful and a good life. But something is missing, and all the more so if once in your life you had a role in a larger world. You were a part of history.

All that was going through George Russell's mind as the British Airways jet dropped lower and lower over the countryside of well-tended fields and meadows, of green forests and small farmhouses from earlier centuries. When he'd finally decided to take the trip at last, he realized it must have been on his mind ever since the war ended all those years ago. To go and see the small nation the exiles had spoken of in such loving tones over the droning engines of the darkened Halifax bomber flying low over hostile territory, to try to feel a little of what had made them risk so much for their enslaved countrymen, to pay tribute to their memory if not to their graves. Honor the great triumph that had made their deaths have meaning far beyond the lives of three small men or a single country.

Now, as the jet dropped lower in its glide path to the capital city's international airport, George had his first view of the ancient city with its church spires and great castle, narrow streets and famed square, and sensed all the centuries it had been in the center of the history and culture of Europe. He felt himself smile as he glimpsed the silver ribbon of river through the core of the city. The river those doomed heroes had seemed to consider the symbol and very embodiment of the heart, soul, and history of their people, and for a moment he wasn't in the descending jet but in that other, noisier plane peering down through the dark night at the unknown land below.

It was December 1941, and he was eighteen. Officially. Actually, he'd lied about his age to get into the action and had been only a bare seventeen. It wasn't a time when Britain asked too many questions of a boy who wanted to serve. So when he was assigned to the crew of the *Halifax* that night because one of the regulars was drunk, he was the most junior airman on the flight, and he'd been excited to be even a small part of such a daring operation. It would be the first, and, as it turned out, only time he flew a single-bomber clandestine mission deep into enemy territory for Special Operations Executive and Section D of SIS (MI6), and every second of it was still burned into his memory after fifty-five years.

The solitary bomber flew low to avoid early detection. Observers on the ground would hear it, of course, and pass the information along, but in those days a single plane wasn't going to cause much damage even if it carried bombs. It would be most likely considered a friendly aircraft, a damaged plane from a larger bombing run trying, perhaps, for neutral Sweden. Possibly a reconnaissance run, or what it actually was: a parachute drop. The Germans were unlikely to scramble fighters at night for such a minor target, or waste antiaircraft ammunition, even if they spotted it in time.

Inside, the body of the plane was dark and the flight long. The gunners were at their guns. Captain Montagu, the SOE handler of Mission Purple, was up front with the pilots and navigator. Assigned to aid the three parachutists with their equipment when the time came for the drop, and man a gun if necessary, there was little for George to do as the bomber and the hours droned on. He sat in the faint moonlight with the exiles and tried to imagine being them. About to jump from a low-flying plane at night into enemy-held territory where they could never be sure what they would jump into and who might be waiting for them.

They were all soldiers in the British-equipped and trained exile brigade and had all volunteered for the deadly work. The chance of recognition for their bravery and heroism was low, and of surviving the mission even lower. Yet here they sat, quietly waiting to jump out of the plane into total uncertainty. In the hope of striking a blow that would help defeat the Germans and free their country.

"You are wondering why we do this, airman George?" He was the oldest of the three, a dark-haired man with a limp and a long scar on his face that could have been made by a saber. His code name was Kaspar. They all had code names: Kaspar, Old Nick, and Lucifer. The team was Mission Purple, and Kaspar appeared to be the leader. Where he sat quietly against the curved interior of the bomber, he studied George as if George held the answer to some larger question. "I often wonder about that myself. Especially this mission."

Old Nick, a younger man dressed like a farmer, said, "Don't start again with such talk, Sergeant. You know we must do this."

"The butcher deserves to die," Lucifer said to no one in particular except himself. "A hundred times over."

The youngest, Lucifer, was blond and handsome and his left hand twitched in spasms he couldn't seem to control.

George asked Kaspar, "Why do you wonder especially about this mission?"

"Because I think if we are successful, the result will perhaps not be good for our nation or our countrymen."

"It will be worse for our country if the butcher continues his butchery," Old Nick growled. "Our people are murdered by the thousands, are forced to collaborate with the bastard Germans. We will show the world the Nazis are not supermen, that they are safe nowhere. Our little country will kill the first Nazi ruler. This has all been discussed at higher levels than you, Sergeant, and we have our orders. Do not be defeatist."

"Defeatist, no. But not blind either," Kaspar snapped back.

Old Nick stood and held to the bulkhead for balance as he stalked forward to the cockpit.

"The butcher deserves to die," Lucifer said again, his blond hair hanging over his forehead and one eye as he stared ahead at the opposite bulkhead. "A hundred times over."

Kaspar watched the handsome young man as Lucifer said it again. "The butcher deserves to die. A hundred times over."

Like a mantra.

"Is he okay?" George wondered.

"He'll be fine," Kaspar said, and smiled. "Have you ever been to our country, young airman George?"

"No."

"It is a very beautiful country, very old. The mountains and forests are so green, the meadows so soft, the rivers so clear and clean. Our people laugh and dance. I have not seen it now for three years. I have not seen my family, my wife and my children. We knew the Germans would come, and so I had to leave. The Germans always come. One kind of German or another. For centuries. We are a small nation in the wrong place."

Lucifer's voice suddenly changed, had a smile inside it. "We're going home, Sergeant. I'll see my mother, my father. They live in the capital city. I will see the city again, and my little sister." His voice clouded. "But not my brother. The butcher killed my brother."

"Yes," Kaspar said to the young man, "we're going home. Perhaps that is worth it all. Soon you'll be in your city, we'll be walking along the river, and everything will be fine. Then, when it is over, I will go to my village. You must visit my village after the war, airman George. It is called Blanik. It is very small, and you will like it there."

Lucifer said, "We're going to die, aren't we, Sergeant? We're all going to die."

"No," Kaspar told him, "we are not going to die. The butcher is going to die, and that will be worth all the training and danger. The Germans don't know it, but they have a tiger by the tail, Lucifer, a national tiger."

Old Nick and Captain Montagu came back from the cockpit.

"Drop point in ten minutes," the SOE handler announced. "Let's get you all loaded, shall we? I'm afraid there's heavy cloud cover down low, but the pilot's sure he can drop you fairly close to the target."

"How close, Captain?" Kaspar asked. "And how sure?"

"Perhaps a twenty-odd-mile radius," Captain Montagu told him. "And relatively sure."

"Meaning we could come down somewhere in the target district, or in the courtyard of the castle in the city where the butcher has his headquarters."

"Not quite that bad, old man," the captain assured him, "but a bit dicey. Do you want to scrub it?"

"We are here," Old Nick said. "There is danger whenever we go and wherever we land."

Lucifer said, "I jump. I want to go home."

"Then," Kaspar said, firm and even cheerful, "we go."

"Good." Captain Montagu nodded. "Airman Russell, get them loaded."

George immediately went to work helping the parachutists to hook on their weapons—the Sten submachine guns developed to be dropped to resistance groups in all German-occupied countries, and the special handheld bombs designed and assembled by SOE for assassinations behind enemy lines where there would be little time for accuracy and no second chances. They would penetrate anything but armor plate. Those, with their pistols and emergency rations, made a considerable load to carry on a low-level drop, but necessary. Their transmitter would drop on its own parachute, with the extra crystals for the transmitters of previous teams on the ground, and codes for the resistance groups.

Their parachutes hooked to the harnesses, the three exiles stood near the open door of the *Halifax*, looking down at the heavy cloud cover over their country, the wind drowning out any last words they might have wanted to say to Captain Montagu or George, or even to one another.

At a nod from Montagu, Kaspar moved to the doorway, holding the frame with both hands. The word came through Montagu's headphones, and he tapped Kaspar on the shoulder. With a grin and a thumbs-up sign, the team leader leaped out into the dark night. Lucifer followed, and Old Nick, and the transmitter.

The last George saw of them were four faint flashes of white disappearing into the clouds below.

THERE ARE NO MONUMENTS to Kaspar, Old Nick, and Lucifer in their small nation. No graves to visit. No words of honor. The real names of the heroes and martyrs are as unknown to most of their countrymen, then and today, as they were to George all those years ago. There is no national celebration on this special day, the fifty-fifth anniversary of the Nazi butcher's assassination.

George had, of course, been in England, doing his own job in other bombers, when the arrogant butcher with one of those obscene SS ranks, *Obergruppenführer,* had been killed. No matter how much he read the newspapers back then, or over the years, he'd never found out exactly how they managed to kill the monster, or how Kaspar, Old Nick, and young Lucifer, not much older than he'd been that night in the darkened Halifax, had died themselves.

He only knew they had all died, and, along with the nation and the whole world back then in the war, what had happened to Kaspar's doomed village, Blanik.

A few weeks after the successful assassination of the Nazi ruler the village had been wiped off the face of the earth. All its men were shot, all its women sent to the death camps, all its children adopted by German SS families if deemed worthy of that honor, or sent to die with their mothers if not. All its buildings were blown up, burned, bulldozed, and obliterated. It would become, the Germans announced, a corn field, to teach the tiny nation the folly of opposing the great Third Reich.

After the war the village was rebuilt as a monument to itself and the victory of the nation—without mention of Kaspar and the reason it was chosen for destruction from a thousand other tiny villages—and that was where George was going. To Blanik on the anniversary of the assassination to celebrate brave, cheerful, doomed Kaspar, if the nation wouldn't.

The trip from the capital wasn't long, and George wasn't alone. Even fifty-five years later, tourists still made the trip to the annihilated village and its resurrection. Many came out of curiosity, many because their ancestors had emigrated from the old country and across the world, a few because they had lived in exile since the war and the pilgrimage was part of coming home, and one, George knew at once, for the same reason he had.

George had been in the rebuilt village some hours, wandering through and wondering where Kaspar might have lived, and wondering if the new village was really anything like the village Kaspar had remembered in the dark of the *Halifax*, when he saw the short, compact man with the erect bearing, walking stick, and slight limp.

"Sir?" George said. It was automatic, even after fifty-five years.

The man didn't turn around.

"Captain Montagu?"

The man turned. He saw George, and his face was polite and friendly, maybe recognizing a countryman, but mystified. "I'm sorry, do we—?"

"George Russell, sir. On the *Halifax*? The night we dropped them? The replacement—"

"The boy. Of course. George, yes." It wasn't exactly recognition on the former captain's face as much as memory. "How stupid of me. Especially here and now, eh? I presume you're making the same journey backward in time."

"Yessir. I thought it only proper. The least I could do for them."

"Quite."

"They did it, sir, didn't they? They won. They accomplished the mission."

"That they did," Montagu said, and, oddly, turned to let his gaze slowly take in as much of the rebuilt village as they could see from where they stood.

"I wonder if any of the houses look like Kaspar's real house?"

"I expect they tried, George. Well, it's been very nice to meet you again after so long. You didn't remain in the service after the war, or anything like that, eh?"

"No, sir. I'm a solicitor. Or I was. In Birmingham," George told him. "Sir, I never—"

"I did, you know. Stay in the service, I mean. Retired as colonel, actually. Well—"

". . . I never did know exactly what happened after they jumped. I've always wondered. How they did it. Who actually shot him. What happened to them. Why there's no monument."

"Ah, yes." Montagu nodded slowly. "Well, I suppose I can help you there. As much as anyone can who wasn't there on the ground. Shall we sit over there? This leg is a terrible nuisance. Well, I'll begin, as they say, at the beginning . . ."

BELOW THE CLOUDS A light snow had been blowing, and they missed their drop area by forty miles, landing less than five miles from the capital city. But at least they hadn't dropped into the castle courtyard of SS headquarters in the city. They landed in a winter field frozen solid, injuring Lucifer's ankle and damaging the transmitter. But their weapons, and the codes and extra crystals, survived with them.

The dirt was too frozen to successfully bury the parachutes, but Kaspar located a shallow quarry where they could hide them under piles of rocks. They slept in a barn that night, taking turns on watch. There was no way to be sure if the farmer who owned the barn was a patriot, an ordinary man afraid to become involved, a collaborator, or even a German from a family long settled in the country but still German.

In the morning they made their way to the capital city and the addresses they had been given by SOE as safe houses where they would get help. Two of them turned out to be useless, and old Nick took a flesh wound from a local policeman in escaping from one of them. The third proved to be secure, the home of a member of an underground resistance unit. But the Nazis now knew a trio of at least partisan fighters if not parachutists were in the city, and the resistance unit had been holed up and inactive for months because of the highly efficient and draconian antiresistance measures of the butcher.

They would have to move faster than they had planned or wanted, with less local help, and with two of them injured.

The resistance unit managed to spirit them safely across the city to a secure hideout near the castle. A local doctor treated Old Nick's flesh wound and pronounced it no danger, but informed them Lucifer's ankle needed at least a month's rest. Kaspar managed to radio SOE in London for advice and wasn't happy with SOE or London's response.

London: "Butcher's methods unlikely to become less draconian with time. SOE urges you proceed with all prudent speed. Moving swiftly is always safest course under clandestine conditions."

Kaspar: "Glad team safety such a high London priority. Will proceed with prudent assassination."

Fortunately, the resistance group, while forced to ground and for the most part out of action by the SD (SS intelligence service) and Gestapo, knew every detail of the butcher's daily routine. So did almost everyone else in the city. In particular, they knew his exact route between house and headquarters, and the security measures he used, which were essentially none. An open car and a driver. This wasn't only a matter of personal arrogance and bravado, or intended to impress Hitler with his courage above all the Führer's other high-level subordinates, although those were both important considerations to the butcher, but a political judgment that by showing no fear of his forced subjects he intimidated them.

Whatever the reasons, it was a fatal mistake, and Kaspar, Old Nick, and Lucifer took full advantage of it.

Their first task was to survey the daily route. This was assigned to Lucifer because he knew his native city best, and because his limp would make him seem less dangerous, and explain why he had to walk slowly and rest frequently. Old Nick cleaned and prepared the Sten guns and bombs. Kaspar conferred with the heads of various resistance groups and planned the team's escape after the success of the assassination.

The escape would not be simple or easy. A car was impossible in the occupied city, so they would be on foot or bicycle. It was finally arranged that each would attempt to reach a different safe house, abandon the attempt if they were closely pursued or in any way felt observed. If they all safely reached their assigned safe house, they would be spirited out of the city to hideouts in rural areas, and, eventually, be picked up by the RAF.

If one or all failed to reach his safe house, then they would each try to make their way alone to Kaspar's village where they would rejoin, contact the resistance, and resume the original escape plan.

Anyone who could do neither would be totally on his own and would survive however he could. With or without help.

None of the alternatives was simple or reassuring, and they all knew each could go wrong in a hundred ways at a thousand different points at any given instant.

Lucifer finally chose the best spot along the route for the attempt. It was a turn in the road where a bus stop would have enough waiting passengers to give them some reason for standing and waiting, and some panic and confusion afterward to impede immediate pursuit, in the off chance that there were other German soldiers, uniformed ORPO police, or local police in the area.

The turn was sharp, and would require the driver to slow the car significantly. It was also uphill, which meant the driver could not immediately speed up again if either the butcher or he happened to spot them. Depending on how much the car slowed to turn the sharp bend, the driver could even have to shift gears to make the hill.

Finally, there was significant cover among trees on the slopes of a park along the road to hide the lookout and give him time to warn the shooters to be ready.

Kaspar and Old Nick decided the attempt should be made in the morning as the butcher drove to work, rather than in the evening when he returned. He could be counted on to go to work, and by his usual route, almost 100 percent, but not to return the same way and at the same time each day. Too many matters could come up to prevent him from returning directly home at the normal time, and then they would have no way of knowing which route he would take or from where. They would be forced to attack outside his personal residence, which was, unlike the car, well guarded.

Lucifer would be the lookout, Kaspar the shooter, and Old Nick would have the bombs.

The day came. None of them slept well the night before, and neither did their hosts. Then it was the hour to leave. They shook hands with their fellow patriots, some of them muttered a brief prayer, and the men of Purple stepped out into the chilly early spring morning of their native country. They climbed onto their bicycles, and pedaled away in different directions.

The instant they vanished around their corners, the resistance group packed up and left the safe house. They would not return. Succeed or fail, sooner or later the SD and Gestapo would find out where the assassins had come from that morning. They would separate and make their way to various other groups. For them, the RAF would not come to pick them up. Not until the war was over and won. If it was won.

Arriving at the sharp curve by different routes, Purple took up their positions. It was 0845 hours. If the butcher were on time, he would arrive within twenty minutes.

Lucifer climbed the hill in the park and settled among the trees with his white square of cloth for signaling.

Kaspar took his place inside a grove of trees on the far side of the street from the tram stop where he could expose the Sten gun without it being immediately seen from the car.

Old Nick settled among the few sleepy passengers waiting for the next tram to come up the hill, clutching his briefcase.

At 0855 a tram started up the hill from below.

0900: A white flash high on the park hillside.

0902: The open touring car appeared, gaining on the climbing tram, two figures in the front seat and the rear seat empty. Exactly as Purple had been told the butcher so arrogantly traveled through the city every day, defying the citizens or the fates to harm him.

The citizens and the fates might not have, but he hadn't calculated SOE and London into the equation.

0905: The open car, with its chatting driver and passenger, caught up to the tram at the sharp turn and passed to its right.

Kaspar instantly ran out of his cover toward the front of the tram, flicking the safety off the Sten gun.

Passengers exited the tram, and those at the stop stood to move into the street. They jumped back as the SS driver blared his horn and the touring car passed between them and the tram, the butcher in his SS general's uniform eyeing them all coldly.

His gaze may have rested for a second on Old Nick as his hand came out of the briefcase with the bomb. If it did, or not, no one would ever know, but the butcher barked a quick order to the driver, who swerved the car and Old Nick's bomb fell short, the explosion shattering the tram windows and sending everyone screaming but missing the car.

Then the arrogant butcher made his second major mistake. He ordered the driver to stop and stood clawing at his pistol as the touring car emerged from behind the tram.

Kaspar was there with his Sten gun.

The butcher may have died in the first burst. The driver in the second. The touring car sat where it had stopped, the driver slumped over the wheel, the Nazi butcher draped dead over his own windshield . . .

GEORGE FELT HIS FACE flush with excitement. "My God, how magnificent. What courage they had, what daring. Did you ever have a moment like that, Colonel? A part of the history of your country forever."

"They were certainly brave," ex-Colonel Montagu agreed. "Some of the finest men I knew the whole time I worked for SOE. Heroes, certainly. But history . . . ?" He again gazed around the village with that odd expression. "You wanted to know what happened to them, didn't you?"

"I know they died," George said sadly.

Montagu didn't seem to hear him. "After Kaspar shot the butcher and the driver, they ran for their bicycles. The tram passengers were frozen. Then there was a distant police whistle. Someone had heard the bomb, if not the shots. Most of the tram passengers immediately decided they wouldn't go to work that day, and disappeared. Some ran to help the wounded butcher and his driver, called out to others to get help, even stopped passing drivers to take the victims to the hospital. A few men pursued Kaspar and Old Nick, trying to capture them for the Germans. Two others attacked and fought with the pursuers.

"Kaspar and Lucifer made it to their safe houses and started along the underground route to where they would hide until the RAF could pick them up, or they could stay hidden for the rest of the war. Old Nick wasn't as lucky. He bicycled straight into that whistle-blowing local policeman. Like the Vichy police, they worked for the collaboration government, and the man shot Old Nick. Old Nick killed him, but by then the ORPO were on their way, and he had to give up on his safe house and escape any way he could.

"His wound was bad, he had to find a doctor, and the doctor turned him in. The SD and Gestapo went to work on him. The resistance couldn't get Kaspar and Lucifer out of the capital—the manhunt was too severe, too extensive, and too tight. They had to hole up in one of the secure houses inside the city. Old Nick knew that as soon as he was identified, and there were many of his countrymen who could and would identify him, his family would all be killed. He belonged to the minority ethnic group that had always felt the majority group disdained them. He told the Nazis where the secure houses were.

"Kaspar, Lucifer, and the resistance people were discovered. Kaspar tried to shoot his way out, and was killed. Lucifer and the others committed suicide rather than be captured. Old Nick worked for the SD against other parachutists SOE sent until he was accidentally killed by the Nazi ORPO police in a raid. The Nazis murdered and deported more than five thousand local Jews, executed at least five thousand of the professionals and intelligentsia of the country in reprisal, and wiped this village from the earth."

Montagu stopped and again surveyed the rebuilt village. But George could tell by his eyes he wasn't seeing the resurrected village, he was seeing the destroyed village, hearing the volleys of gunfire, the screams of the women and children. George tried to hear those horrors himself and thought of Old Nick, the staunch one who wouldn't hear defeatist talk, wouldn't think of calling the assassination off.

"How could he do it? Old Nick? Turn in his friends, betray his country."

"To save himself and his family."

"That's despicable," George raged.

"That depends on which you consider more valuable, George, the person or the tribe," the former colonel said. "Unless he helped, they would murder his family, and in the end Old Nick put people over politics. I think Kaspar would have understood."

"Do you understand, sir?"

"Yes, I understand," the old SOE man said. "You wondered, I'm sure, why there are no monuments to Purple in the country? Why they've never been honored. Why there's no celebration of the assassination. After all, they did kill the first high Nazi official to die by enemy hands." That odd expression on his face again. "The answer is politics. The reprisals were so savage the nation never really resisted again. What resistance the butcher hadn't destroyed, the assassination did. They did not become a tiger, the Germans were too strong, and London and Moscow were too far away to really help.

"For the Nazis nothing changed. But the exile government in London was made much stronger. For them the assassination was a great political success. But they were safe in London while the nation at home suffered terribly, and after the war the exiles didn't want any attention to be drawn to the horrors of the reprisals the assassination had made happen. For a long time, because of the assassination, there was no love between those who remained at home and those who went into exile. No one wanted to remember the assassination or Purple."

George was silent for a time. Then he let his gaze roam across the restored village and thought of the firing squads and cattle cars to Treblinka. "That's so sad, isn't it? They were so brave, so heroic, and yet what they did was perhaps bad for their country in the end."

"The world can be complicated, George."

"I suppose it can. Still," he said, feeling the excitement of that flight, of being part of a moment bigger than himself, "we Brits did accomplish our mission that night, didn't we?"

"Oh, we accomplished our mission, George. For us it was a complete success."

"We did help kill the butcher. The only high Nazi ever killed in office."

"The butcher?" The old SOE captain shook his head. "We didn't care about the butcher, George. Whitehall, the War Office, SIS, SOE, none of us gave a bloody damn about the butcher. Except for Hitler, one Nazi big shot was the same as another. They'd replace the butcher in a heartbeat. He wasn't our mission."

"Then, what was?" George wondered, mystified, and yet—

"The reprisals, George. We wanted the reprisals. The more savage the better. And that's what we got. We got Blanik. We'd expected horrors, but never an entire village of five hundred people wiped from the face of the earth. We couldn't believe our luck. The jackpot, as they say in America. World opinion, George. More allies, more aid for our cause. Make the Nazis look such utterly inhuman monsters that they had to be defeated. Worked like a charm, too. All kinds of fundraising in America and the Commonwealth, eh. Great success."

George was silent longer this time. Then he said, "You're not here to honor them, are you, sir. You're here out of guilt."

"Guilt?" Montagu pondered. "No, not guilt, George. We had a war to win. All of us: Britain, America, the U.S.S.R., all the governments in exile. We would all have done the same, and felt no guilt. It was war."

"What then?" George asked. "An apology?"

Montagu gazed around the resurrected village one last time. "Penance, I think. Yes, call it a penance. I do this every year on this date since I retired. Come to Kaspar's village and do penance. Because, you see, he knew, George. Deep down he knew, but he came anyway. He knew, and I knew, and I want him to absolve me. Absolve us all."

Golam

JOSÉ LATOUR

I T'S DEFINITELY PERVERSE, BUT I can't resist it. Human always ends up rebelling against prohibitions and this is especially true in a profession so bizarre its greatest achievements must remain unknown. This urge was probably unleashed by neurochemical factors which the brain tries to justify in formal thought. "Death is panting behind me, Alzheimer might settle in, and some people should learn my life wasn't a total waste." Bullshit. It's just the sudden overflow of bottled-up substances.

Now I see why "recognition"—for many years a term I sneered at—has become the last incorporation to my set of values. The classics insist so much on the need of nurturing and caressing the agent's ego with appreciation and praise, you finally realize that to reach the top you should dispense with this frailty. And I did, for many years.

With the exception of five, maybe six persons, for everyone I'm a retired bureaucrat who for close to forty years commuted daily to Tel Aviv to entomb himself in concrete and pore over government statistics. I watched how my family's love, respect and admiration waned over the years and were replaced by indifference and discomfort and frustration and pity. Boredom and routine were my colors. I never traveled abroad, not even on vacation. Feeble excuses and a dislike for all things foreign were my arguments. The true reason was I wasn't allowed to. I was too valuable to be exposed to other services, which meant I knew too much.

That was the price I paid, a very low one if you consider the number of covert agents that succumbed under torture in bloodstained cells, or those who were shot or hung at dawn, or the few that were swapped after years in jail. But it's a very high price when compared to the considerable number of career officers overtly living the good life in the glittering capitals of the world while exchanging jokes with their local counterintelligence colleagues.

Two years before retirement the bug bit. I daydreamed about my moment of glory, when the Prime Minister would pin a medal on my chest. Two former PMs, plus the leaders of the other two major parties, would shake my hand and pat my shoulder in recognition. The general must have read my mind. He presented me with a gold-plated fountain pen, gave me a second-class civil service decoration in keeping with my public life story and said that, of course, he didn't have to remind me why the state's profound gratitude for my lifelong dedication to national security may perhaps be disclosed well into the next century.

A man involved for so long in the kind of deep, ultrasecret intelligence I dealt with should be encouraged to never retire, or be taken care of. Because even at seventy-five, if he's lucid, suddenly finding himself with nothing to do makes him restless. So many stories are bottled up inside him it's only a matter of time before he starts recounting them, telling his own version, getting it out of his system, as the Americans say, even if it's a shock to the system.

So, with the usual paranoia nurtured for over fifty years, I bought this Rollerpoint EF at a bookstore (NICS-2 whiz kids might have rigged my new fountain pen with a microscopic semiconductor, a transmitter, and a long-life battery to reproduce on a screen and tape the movements of the nib), stole one of my granddaughter's blank notebooks (the PC is out of the question and I shouldn't be seen buying writing paper, since I use continuous forms in my old dot-matrix printer), and today, instead of indulging in my usual study of Hebrew semantics, I begin to write this metatext supporting the notebook on the left arm of my armchair (the writing desk might have heat sensors to detect lengthy longhand sessions) with my left hand, a skill I've kept to myself.

Some of the tales I can tell are worthless by reason of their fantastic nature. Anyone in his right mind would dismiss them as outright lies should they be presented as facts. If printed as fictional stories they'll be labeled the product of a fanciful imagination. Yet I know three persons—although there may be more—who would be rendered speechless should they learn I'm writing this.

I don't know where to begin. A writer saves the most shocking pages for the end; building suspense I believe it's called. But maybe literary patterns can be altered. For instance, take the present worldwide scandal surrounding Dolly the sheep. What would happen if the international community learns about Dolly the nineteen-year-old quantum physics genius?

History teaches that James Watson and a British chap named Crick were the first to propose that a DNA molecule consists of two polynucleotide strands, each coiled in a helix, and held together by weak hydrogen bonds. History is wrong. Ozer Luria, a Polish Jew gassed in Auswitch, was the first human to formulate this and he did it in 1937, fourteen years before the American and the Briton.

Luria was a brilliant biologist. His application for immigration into the U.S. was rejected in 1928 under the influence of the Eugenics Record office, a committee claiming that America's genetic heritage would be damaged by the immigration of inferior peoples, in particular those from Eastern Europe. Infuriated, Luria devoted his supereminent brain to repudiate Francis Galton's theory of hereditary genius, reinforced at the beginning of this century with the rediscovery of Mendel's laws. Using X-rays he found the double helix—which he called the copulating serpents—and the enzymes capable of creating a matching chain of bases from a strand of DNA, with the ability to replicate itself.

Luria was dumbfounded. He left three kilograms of notes— seven years of solitary work. In the last handbook he wrote about having trespassed upon Jehova's realm. Aware of Nazi ideology and the impending doom over Europe, he buried his findings. But to his Rabbi he left directions that miraculously found us in 1943.

So we had a headstart. Our research began in 1945 under strict security in Kebara. The theoretical possibility of producing new individuals by asexual means was accepted in 1949; the first animal embryos were cloned in 1956, the first healthy puppy dog was born in 1963.

While nuclear powers devoted their fastest computers to nuclear weapons and deterrents, under the code name "Eleventh Tribe" ours churned out the sequencing of the three billion base pairs that make up the human genome, a task completed in 1993, twenty-one years after the first unimpeachable human clone was born, now a twenty-five-year-old tank commander in the Golan Heights.

Difficult to believe? Yes, I admit it is. But many educated people the world over consider us capable of this achievement. Tongue in cheek our government would deny it, a tinge of pride in the spokeperson's voice. What maybe not even the Prime Minister knows, what would probably turn against us all civilized countries and beget the disintegration of Israel, is the revelation that for the last fifteen years we've been collecting blood samples, hair, nails, saliva, sperm, skin, anything containing cells of the best brains in the world.

Husbands, wives, doctors, nurses, lab technicians, friends, hairdressers, barbers, manicurists, prostitutes, cleaning ladies, and all kinds of servants have been bought, duped, cajoled, or blackmailed into surrendering samples belonging to the greatest physicists, musicians, chemists, writers, biologists, painters, mathematicians, moviemakers, engineers, actors, and philosophers. No economists, politicians, or sociologists have been gathered. The general believes the future of mankind excludes these professions. In his view, the society that's close at hand must be governed by scientists and artists only.

As a result, six months ago we had two hundred ninety-two teenagers, six hundred seven children, and two thousand four hundred forty-four babies between two months and two years of age sprouting in the Jewish communities of ninety-three countries. Nine hundred thirty-seven women were pregnant. Infertile couples needing treatment were and are lured here. They don't have an inkling of what goes on. They are told we've combined a minor surgical procedure with a wonder drug that in 92 percent of the cases engenders a baby of the desired sex.

Full physical examinations and tests are performed while one geneticist and one anthropologist choose the world-renowned human being with the closest possible genetic compatibility and somatic resemblance. Test results and three-dimensional images of the parents are fed to the computer and it's amazing the coincidence of human and electronic recommendations on the same genius.

The woman must agree to give birth in Israel for obvious reasons. So far, the rate of congenital pathologies is the same as in natural fecundation, but social inadequacy is a corroborated fact. Science scions are the least adaptable; actors and actresses the most. The general hides from everybody that 9.2 percent of the population presents psychopathetic conditions, a very high index with respect to the rest of mankind.

"Stop," a voice ordered.

The old man who had been copying down on a notebook the contents of six typed pages complied. He carefully placed the pen on top of the notebook and raised his eyes to the huge bookcase that almost totally covered the wall ahead.

A hairy sunburned hand to his left reached over and retrieved the pen. The thin long fingers of two gloved hands coming from his right recovered the notebook and the typed pages.

The old man heaved a sigh and focused on the leather-bound volumes on the bookcase's top shelf. He wore a soiled white short-sleeved shirt, charcoal-gray slacks, and black leather lace-up shoes.

The few strands of gray hair surviving on top of his head had lost the careful arrangement that signaled the last touch of vanity. Big plastic-rimmed bifocals made his brown eyes look smaller than their actual size. Under the brilliant glare of the wrought-iron floor lamp to the left and a little behind the club chair where he sat, the old-age brown marks on his round white face and bald spots looked like repulsive insects.

"My compliments on your handwriting," Gloved Hands grace-fully said as he flipped through the notebook. The man nodded his thanks. Gloved Hands's patrician appearance was shattered by the surgical gloves and by the straight blond hair cascading down the back of a fine double-breasted dark-blue jacket, one of the three pieces of the impeccable suit by some famous designer that he donned. An inch short of six feet, the very white man had deep-set light-blue eyes, a straight nose, high cheekbones, and thin lips. Each isolated facial feature was extremely handsome; for some strange reason the aggregate wasn't.

Hairy stood on the other side of the seated old man. He wore a polo shirt, jeans, and boat shoes. An expensive deep-diver watch showed on his fuzzy left wrist. He was getting thick around the middle, had a two-day black stubble, and didn't look menacing, but the way he watched Gloved Hands brought to mind a well-trained Doberman ready to charge at his owner's command.

Gloved Hands fought off a smile as he dropped the notebook into an open briefcase on a Formica-topped coffee table by his side. Then he folded the typed pages and slid them in the inner breast pocket of his jacket. Lifting his gaze to Hairy he tilted his head to the side. The muscle nodded, approached the coffee table, shut the briefcase, grabbed its handle, and left the room.

After unbuttoning his jacket Gloved Hands eased himself on a high-backed armchair out of the lamp's cone of light, diagonally to the right of the old man. An almost unconscious stroke of his hand transferred the flowing hair to the left of the chest and then he drew from a shoulder holster a .22 LR converted SIG automatic to which a Brügger and Thomet silencer had been attached. Making himself comfortable, he crossed his legs and eased the weight of the gun by supporting the wrist on the knee.

"What do you think Mr. Chasid?" he asked.

"Yochai, please," the old man said out of habit.

Gloved Hands smiled openly. "My dear sir," he said, "we may be on different sides but I admire your gallantry and coolness under pressure."

"Thank you, Mr. . ."

"Peter."

"Thank you, Mr. Peter."

"I would greatly appreciate your views on our little stratagem."

Still looking at the bookcase the old man inclined his head to right and left, as if considering the issue from different perspectives. "Short term credibility depends on the plant," he observed at last.

"We are in full agreement." Gloved Hands said, an undercurrent of respect in his voice. "And in your calendar *short term* means . . .?"

"One week in this particular case."

"Pretty short. Would you care to elaborate?"

The old man pushed up his slipping glasses before speaking. "Well, I'm not an expert on molecular biology, but it seems to me the dates you give are unbelievable. Like cloning a human in . . . '72, if my recollection is precise. Or having completed the Human Genome Project four years ago."

"Maybe we can refine that. When did you clone your first human?"

"We haven't."

"And what are you cloning in Kebara? Lice perhaps?"

The old man ran his hands through his hair and managed some rearrangement. For the first time he smiled and fastened his eyes on Gloved Hands. "We're doing research like everybody else."

"Oh, my dear Yochai, why do Jews assume they can deceive everybody? Why do you feel so confident your secrets can't be unveiled?"

"Please, don't disappoint me," the old man said, returning his gaze to the bookcase. "I want to believe you're a worthy opponent."

Gloved Hands shook his head in slight disbelief and produced a fresh smile. "The word is you've been cloning humans for a few years now."

The old man interlaced his fingers and let both wrists rest on his thighs. "So we've heard," he said. "Zionism trying to breed superhumans of Jewish origin to conquer the world with sheer brainpower. Not a new idea, but in today's dazzling scientific environment it looks more feasible than ever. Maybe in the next century a few fools will take practical steps in that direction."

"Could we delve a little into what you termed 'short term credibility'?" Gloved Hands asked, lifting an eyebrow.

"By all means. You manage to get it published in some highly respected scientific periodical. It might confuse a lot of people initially. But the editors of this kind of publication aren't fools. They demand further substantiation and you can't provide it."

"Who says so?"

"I do. If you could I wouldn't be here."

"Dead wrong. But please proceed."

"Okay. World-class dailies won't touch it. I know because we've tried to plant much less . . . ambitious scientific disinformation and failed. So, you may have to recourse to the tabloids, which would put this on a par with the last UFO sighting."

"We have ways," Gloved Hands said confidently as three knocks were heard on the door. "Come in," he boomed.

HAIRY WHEELED IN A cart with bottles of mineral water, an ice bucket, a tea pot, a sugar bowl, glasses, teaspoons, and mugs. The old man avidly drank a glass of water served by the muscle and declined the tea. Half-jokingly Gloved Hands assured the prisoner that the infusion was free of mind-altering drugs. Laying to rest the gun by his side he backed up his contention by calmly sipping a mug full to the brim as silence reigned. When he returned the mug to the cart and recovered the gun, Hairy and the small vehicle exited.

"YOCHAI, YOUR TIME HAS come."

For a couple of seconds the old man tried to suppress his amusement, failed, and began hee-hawing. Gloved Hands scowled and the muscles at the base of his jaw bulged. The old man controlled himself. "I'm sorry," he whispered.

"Don't, please. Laughter is the best medicine."

"We couldn't agree more," the old man observed, the smile's farewell still playing on his wrinkled lips.

"Yes, I appreciate the irony of it," Gloved Hands mused as he got back on track. "You'll be seventy-six in two months, have only few years left. But look at it this way: it's payoff time. You spent the best years of your life protecting the innermost secrets of your nation. While you were cashing modest paychecks, inferior men became very rich doing business and cutting deals with the crumbs that fell from your table. Your well-stocked informational table on which, as byproducts, landed bits and pieces you passed along, like the coffee plague breaking out in Brazil. . . ."

All of a sudden the old man was wearing a very serious expression.

"Tel Aviv speculators bought futures and made a killing. Did someone send a percentage? A note of thanks? Or when you learned one week in advance of the Mexican peso's devaluation?"

"There's a mole," the old man croaked.

White Hands laughed with a vengeance. "Wouldn't that be just reciprocity?"

"You couldn't have learned any other way. Just like my left-hand writing," the old man mumbled as if to himself, eyes on the floor.

"I might comment on that if we reach an agreement. But your time has come, Yochai."

The reiteration, and the long pause after, underscored that he who laughs last laughs better.

"I'm offering you a golden future, or parachute, as the Americans say; take your pick. The people I work for are willing to provide new identities for you and the missus in the country of your choice. Three million dollars in cash will be stored in the safe-deposit box you rent, in the bank you choose, one week after the rental takes place. Round-the-clock security will be arranged free of cost as long as you live. After all this is done to your satisfaction, you write your memoirs. Your full Mossad career, no exaggerations, no lies, every word true. On the Kebara operation you write what you know, we add a few things you don't know, and that's all. The copyright is yours too, of course,"

The old man nodded gravely. "And the option?" he asked.

Gloved Hands looked pained for a second. "Oh, Yochai, c'mon, you know what the option is."

"I just wonder how you'll wrap things up, should I refuse your very generous offer."

"You were bitter for having been sidelined in your old age. The general found out through the cleaning lady you were writing something; she's an agent, you know? Under orders to surrender your notes, you killed yourself."

"This piece is your piece," Gloved Hands went on, balancing the automatic in his hand, "I've made a swap," Same cleaning lady. Thinking of her old age, she's making a little on the side. The gun, the marks on the slug and on the casing will be the right ones. Friendly hands, outraged by what happened to you and by what's going on in Kebara, photocopied the most damaging pages you wrote and leaked them to the press."

Once again the old man nodded. He lowered his eyes to the quartz watch strapped to his left wrist and observed the second hand as it swept the dial for almost a minute before perking up. "Your option story stinks, but I'm not ready to die yet, and I doubt I ever will. On the other hand, three million dollars is a lot of money. So, let's discuss some practical matters. Number one: nothing happens to my granddaughter."

"You have my word."

"I'll need more than that before making up my mind."

"Okay."

"Number two: how will we be sent abroad? My wife has a heart condition, she can't. . . . "

The old man's voice trailed off when Gloved Hands raised his hand. He slid the tip of his tongue over his lips while considering something and then glanced at the dial of his Omega. "We don't have time to go into details, but rest assured that everything has been thought out. Suffice it to say the lady taking care of your granddaughter is a witch. She can make you look ten years older or younger, make you bald as a coot or give you a shock of white hair. She has in her suitcase shoes that'll make you three inches taller. Your wife will be worked on too. Then we take passports photos and off we go. It's child's play."

The prisoner sneezed, bent forward, and pulled out a crumpled handkerchief. After wiping his nose and while returning the piece of cloth to the slack's back pocket, he spoke again. "Now I want confirmation on my granddaughter."

GLOVED HANDS PRODUCED A cellular phone from a pocket of his jacket, adjusted an earphone into his left ear and inserted the cable's opposite extreme in the phone. Uncoiling himself from the seat he approached the old man, thumbed off the gun's safety, and placed the silencer on the prisoner's right temple. "Tap out your home number and you'll find she's with your wife. She wasn't harmed. The lady just took her to an ice cream parlor before leaving her a block away from your place. But listen carefully, Yochai. If I hear anything weird, something that I judge is a code word meaning that you're acting under duress, I'll conclude you've chosen the quick way out and, much to my regret, I'll be forced to follow my orders. Okay?"

"Okay."

"Please, colonel, don't underestimate my Hebrew."

"I never underestimate men, Mr. Peter."

The prisoner punched out seven numbers. A female voice answered at the fourth ring. "Yes?"

"It's me, Nechele," the old man said.

"Thank God! Listen, Yochai. The weirdest thing happened to

Sarah. She claims she talked to you on the phone this morning . . ."

"Nechele, Nechele."

". . . and you asked her to play hooky and go with a lady . . ."

"Nechele, Nechele."

"What?"

"Where's she?"

"Right here. Watching TV."

"Is she alright?"

"Of course she's al ... Why shouldn't she?"

"Never mind. I'll explain later."

"Who's this lady that...?"

"It's a long story. How are you?"

"I'm fine."

"You sure?"

"What do you mean am I'm sure? Yochai?"

"What?"

"What's the matter with you?"

The old man chuckled. "Nothing. Except I feel horny."

"Yochai Chasid! Have you been drinking?"

"No, Nechele, no. Give my love to Sarah. Phone Mordechai and tell him Golam."

Gloved Hands pressed the trigger.

The old man recoiled, slid to the left, and tumbled down over the arm of the club chair. Through partly dislodged glasses his eyes focused on a thick leather-bound volume on the bookcase's top shelf. Amazed by his mental clarity he recalled that since adolescence, at school in his native town of Rheydt, in the Rhineland, he had been occasionally wondering for how long a severed head kept thinking after learning the history of the French revolution. He never found out but at least now he was discovering that a .22 LR slug, or at least this particular slug, did not immediately obliterate the faculties of his mind.

Vanity of vanities, all is vanity, he quoted from memory, looking at the book. The intoxicating wine of victory, of living beyond reason, of fathering healthy children. The immense vanity of being one of the very few in the know. Yes. And sorrow. *He that increaseth knowl-edge increaseth sorrow.*

The enemy had judged him well. He had been embittered by the leaks from which unscrupulous associates profited, had wanted the recognition he didn't get, had been tempted to write, had feared a putrid senility at a well-kept retirement home. *A time to be born and a time to die.* Their big misconception was to assume he would choose a few more years of uncertainty and betrayed over a swift release. They couldn't figure out he was tired of living in secrecy, paying for one hour of triumph with a thousand hours of relentless monotony. *And I hated all my labour . . . seeing that I must leave it unto the man that shall be after me. And who knoweth whether he shall be a wise man or a fool?*

The old man felt sadness carrying him away like a giant wave approaching the coastline. True, the possibility of tinkering with human nature was close at hand, something that terrified him. He had cautioned about it up to his last day on the job. Would they eventually clone humans? Would the Eleventh Tribe be more inclined to wisdom? Wouldn't they become even more vain in their superiority? *A time to break down and a time to build up.* Broken down it was. Should building start?

THE WAVE'S ROAR INCREASED. He trembled in fear when a Waffen SS company in full regalia marched along the widest street of his hometown. But suddenly this faded away and Nechele came and took him by the hand. He looked back and saw his mother telling him something that the roar wouldn't let him hear and with her hands encouraging him to keep moving. He obeyed. A warm small hand slipped into his. He looked and found it was a little girl, his youngest daughter. He turned towards Nechele and dis-covered she had been replaced by a second little girl, his eldest daughter. And he had become a small boy too; Holding hands they started running, laughing their heads off. The general watched them with compassion, his forefinger over rounded lips demanding silence. *A time to mourn and a time to dance.* The roar became deafening as a huge black cliff came closer and closer. His daughters fell behind and he could hear their childish cries asking him to return early in the evening. *A time for every purpose under heaven.*

The assassin placed the gun in the old man's right hand before taking off his gloves and leaving the room.

Spy's Fate

ARNALDO CORREA

T HE FAN STOPPED WITH a dying sound. The heat pushed aside all this time invaded the place again. He remained motionless, staring into the darkness—guilty of not jumping out of bed as soon as the electricity went off to unplug the electric cord of the refrigerator to avoid the motor coils being burned if the power went on too soon or there was a surge of high voltage on the lines. He stood at rest because he was tired, very tired. Tired of the heat in that miserable 1994 Havana summer. Tired of the sleepless nights thinking on how to solve the problems he had, waking up every time the power went off and came on. Tired of everything he had done during the last twenty years.

A month earlier he came back from Africa, where he had stayed for the last three years. He was content with the idea of finally being able to live a normal life and spending the rest of his days with his children—not children anymore—enjoying the grandchildren to come as he never did his own kids. However, his family homecoming welcome at the airport was cool and polite. His two sons, ages twenty and twenty-two, felt uneasy and inhibited and made him feel uneasy and inhibited. His daughter, seventeen, was not there to meet him; she preferred going to the beach. Two days later when she came back, she excused herself, saying, "Imagine, Dad, two days in Varadero, what a chance! As you know, Varadero is only for tourists and for the big shots' families. I hadn't had a chance to go since you took us there when I was twelve." She said it with the purpose to make him feel bad since it implied a criticism to the government. All three considered the government responsible for the many things going wrong and he seemed to be its representative to receive the complaints they had.

When he arrived at his apartment he found the three bedrooms taken, both sons living with girlfriends in two of them, and the master bedroom, now belonging to his daughter, was locked. Clearly, he did not fit into his children's plans. The worst thing was Cecilia's absence. Sitting in the living room, being treated like an embarrassing visitor, he realized that his whole past life had vanished with her death. This place was not the sweet home that filled his dreams for so many years of patient waiting in distant lands. It was a territory invaded by three hostile strangers. The small boys he always remembered taking turns wearing his boots and the tiny girl who preferred to fall asleep on his lap, grabbing firmly his left arm, had also vanished forever.

After talking with his two sons a while, he decided to make a tactical retreat to study the new situation. The first couple of days he stayed at a friend's house after saying his whole family was at the beach and he had no keys to open his home. Later, he managed to find a place in a four-story apartment house being remodeled into an office building. An old pal from the Service, now a construction foreman, authorized him to use one of the empty rooms of the building. "After we finish here there will be another house to remodel somewhere else. I can even put you on the payroll as a night watchman."

He got up from bed, completely naked as he was, and stumbled in the dark against walls and furniture searching for the electric cord that must be pulled out of the wall. Then he went to the other end of the room and opened the back door. A thrust of sea breeze, cooled by a full moon, freshened the place. "It would be heaven if this door could be kept open all night," he said to himself, but immediately thought the invitation would be accepted by all the burglars on the coast, with the sure loss of the few irreplaceable items he had there, the electric fan in first place.

There were also other disgraces to worry about: he had been dismissed from the Service where he had worked all his life. Soon after his arrival in Cuba, he had a lunch meeting with the chief of the Service and his second in command. Usually, in this type of gathering he spent all the time briefing the bosses on the highlights of his work in foreign lands. On this occasion, the chief did all the talking, mostly about the country's poor economic situation. Finally, the chief said the days of Cuba taking so active a part in helping liberation movements all over the world, even waging full-scale wars in Africa, were over. Many people had to go to civilian life. In his case he'll be transferred to the police force until he reaches retirement age in a couple of years, so he won't lose the very favorable pension of the armed forces and the Ministry of the Interior after twenty-three years in the Service. Once retired, they would like him to take a job in one of the many new enterprises being created with foreign firms, where he would have priority to pick whatever job he liked. "We need men we can trust in the key places there. Besides your pension you will have full salary and some other economical advantages those enterprises offer." The chief felt uneasy in his new salesman job. "Nothing to worry about," he kept repeating. Colonel Marcelo, second in command, stood silent as usual.

He was about to ask why he had been dumped. Nevertheless, one thing he had learned was never to ask why. If you wanted to know the reason for anything, you had to figure it out by yourself. It was true that the glorious days of Cuba as a mini-world-power had been over for quite some time, and that compelled many people to change jobs. However, not for men of his expertise, at a time when the confrontation with the United States was getting hotter by the day. The reason for his dismissal had to be something else.

He soon found out he had come back to a country very different from the one he had left. He never dreamed of so many changes. The economy seemed to be collapsing little by little after the trade and other economic relations with the Soviet Union and other Eastern European countries halted almost overnight in 1991, when the Socialist Bloc disintegrated, and the United States toughened its thirty-five-year-long war against Cuba. There was an acute shortage of everything: food, fuel, electricity, medicine, transportation. Political unrest was growing, many desperate people were trying to reach Florida at any cost to enjoy the asylum granted to Cubans by a law dating back to the sixties. In the last few months there had been armed assaults to seize small vessels from fishing enterprises and dockyards, even a passenger ferry that rendered trips from Havana Bay was highjacked several times and ended up at the bottom of the bay with quite a few people drowned inside. When this situation seemed to get out of hand, the government approved free migration in any sort of vessel. The clear objective was to force the United States, already overwhelmed by immigration from everywhere, to stop welcoming all Cubans arriving at its coasts, thus encouraging demoralizing defections and the use of force to procure vessels. Until then, all Cuban coasts were heavily guarded to suppress that type of migration. The law used to punish people captured fleeing the island with penalties of up to five years in jail; however, in the last years the surveillance had slackened, the ones caught were sent to their homes.

As soon as the new decree was known, thousands of people began to gather whatever floating material they could put their hands on to make all kinds of rafts. They hauled everything to the coast to assemble the rafts there. A lot of the launching was done around midnight when the "Terral" sets in, a wind that blows from the land toward the sea until midmorning.

From the place where he stood, he saw the shadows of people passing to and from one of the launching sites along the Havana west coast at Twenty-eighth Street in Miramar. Many times he felt curious to see the exodus, but always stopped as if he were about to look into a pestilent wound inside his own gut. That night he felt the need to see it. He put on an old pair of Levis, a bright yellow cap that glowed in the dark, a white T-shirt, and a pair of tennis shoes without socks. He only had to cross First Avenue, a block away, and walk one hundred feet on the sharp coastal coral reef. At the ruins of a small pier there were about two hundred curious bystanders and relatives of the crews getting ready to leave in two rafts. One was ready to be launched and both crews were cooperating to throw it into the water. A calm sea was beginning to ripple, pushed by a gentle breeze blowing northward from inland. He surveyed the raft with an expert eye. It was well made of six empty oil drums welded firmly together in two three-drum tandems. The framework to hold everything in place was built with four-inch steel U-beams fastened with bolts to disassemble and carry the outfit easily. Once the raft was in the water, six men boarded it and began loading the supplies. Four long oars were pulled out of the baggage and the raft began moving northward. Most of the people gathered there cheered and wished the rafters a happy journey. When the raft was about two hundred yards away from shore a sail was hoisted, the wind filled it, and the vessel gained speed. Most of the people at the coast clapped; some cried.

The next raft was very poorly made. A weak frame of wooden pieces badly nailed together enclosed a big pine box with a double bottom filled with polyurethane. He recognized one of the crew, a Negro youngster, as a friend of his elder son, who frequented his house in the past. He stepped down to the pier to get a closer look at him. The boy he remembered was now an athletic young man, as tall as he was, but his features were unmistakable.

"Andres!"

"Hello!" said the youngster without looking up, thus showing he had noticed him already.

"Are you traveling on this?"

Andres remained mute, just made a short nod with his head.

"How come, Andres? You know a Negro does not have very much future in the United States."

"What future does anybody have here?" the voice was high-pitched in anger.

He stood silent. After a while Andres faced him.

"Sorry. This is not easy, you know. However, I have to do it for my family's sake."

Andres spoke as if he were trying to convince himself. He thought it was the right moment to try again.

"Why don't we talk. Let's see what problems you have."

Andres did not answer, just turned to what he was doing before.

"Maybe I can help you. Besides, this raft will break into pieces against the first wave."

"Why don't you leave me alone?" snapped Andres, facing the man again.

"I am sure I can help you."

"If you want to help somebody, why don't you help your children? They are leaving from Cojimar now."

ON HIS WAY TO Cojimar, a small town on the coast about ten miles east of Havana, he reviewed his relationship with his children. He had been like Santa Claus—coming once a year full of presents for everyone, staying with them for a few weeks, pleasing them in all they wanted, trying to make up for so much time away. Then he would disappear again some unexpected night for another long stretch of time. Gone to somewhere, to a place that could not be known. And if it was known, could not be mentioned. In this last month, he had tried to understand what happened with them. Little by little he realized that the relationship he had kept with his family imposed tremendous hardships on them. To a point of total disaster when the economic situation of the country became so bad and his wife got ill, something she never told him or anybody in the Service until it was too late. Maybe she did not want to worry him; maybe she just gave up.

Besides the emotional stress for the youngsters to cope with a situation they were not prepared to handle, on the economic side, the purchasing power of his salary, the only income in his house, had devalued to almost nothing. The goods that could be bought at old prices in the rationing system were not enough for anybody to survive. Most of the food had to be purchased in the black market at very high prices. The value of the peso against the dollar, once about even, came down to 100 pesos for one dollar. His monthly salary, 450 pesos, could now buy very little. With this situation his daughter took the initiative. She looked through her mother's closet full of old photos and papers until she found the address and telephone number she was looking for.

He crossed Havana and reached Cojimar in less than a half hour, driving his own Lada as fast as he could. There was a crowd of more than a thousand people watching the rafts being launched. Along a large pier there were several crews busy assembling their rafts. His younger son was at the very end of the pier, already on the raft and receiving all the gear from his brother and sister. The supplies were well packed inside heavy nylon sacks, each one marked with a number in red ink, as if they had been prepared for a long time. That must have been the reason why they wanted to keep him away from the house.

He stood there not knowing what to do. He was empty, weak, looking at how the most important part of his world was running away from him.

"Can I help?"

The words stuck in his throat. He was crying for the first time since he was a child. It was a surprise for them to see him there. The two boys looked down.

"Father, you are too late!" said his daughter, looking directly into his eyes.

"A VERY IMPORTANT OFFICER from Cuban Intelligence defected to Florida in a stolen yacht," read Mr. T. S. King, head of the Cuban Section of the CIA, as he opened the envelope marked URGENT from the CIA general director, and a memo asking him to look into the matter. Mr. King knew the source of the information was very close to the high command of the Cuban Intelligence Office and the recipients of the original messages were the general director and the director of Operations of the CIA. He signed the receipt for the message and immediately called his liaison with the FBI and the immigration officers in charge of screening the Cubans arriving in Florida. The answer was that there had been no high-ranking Cuban officers of any kind among the immigrants.

Later that day, a reconnaissance plane reported the sinking of a small yacht about fifty miles southeast of Key West. Reviewing all the information that may throw some light on the matter, from the Netherlands the day before was mention of a radio call to the headquarters of a Dutch shipping company from the captain of the reefer *Silver Star*, loaded with bananas on its way to Rotterdam. The man reported a yacht being shot at by a gunboat maybe belonging to the Cuban Coast Guard. The incident took place about eleven miles northeast of Havana, very close to Cuba's territorial water limit. This may explain the probable cause for the sinking of the yacht reported by the plane.

After the incident followed a deep silence on the Cuban side, another strong, positive indication of its veracity. For some time after there was no other information about the case, so it was filed, with the preliminary conclusion that the unidentified officer could have died when his yacht sank. Maybe he was killed or wounded before, explaining why there was no call for help.

A month later a Cuban exile of the last wave was caught red-handed shoplifting in Jacksonville Beach, Florida. Once in jail the man claimed he had very important information to sell in exchange for his liberation. This statement stopped his release on bail because the county sheriff thought the man might know something very important. The prisoner claimed he had witnessed a man shoot down one of his raft partners. The sheriff filed a report. The FBI sent a detective to question the eager prisoner, who explained his story making all sorts of gestures and noises, trying to make up for his poor English. Out of all that the detective understood that a man traveling in a yacht, which was sinking, suddenly shot another man riding on the same raft the prisoner was. Later the killer jumped out of a rowboat and came with them to the raft. The FBI detective recommended that before pursuing any further investigation, psychological tests be carried out on the prisoner. He was under the impression the man was a pathological liar, maybe intoxicated after seeing too many crime fiction pictures since he came to the United States. Anyway, his report ended up in the hands of the CIA liaison who, in the absence of anything else, released it to CIA headquarters. This information, plus a recent report from Havana mentioning some gossip about a river dockyard manager being jailed and accused of collaboration with a high-ranking officer of the Ministry of the Interior, who escaped in one of the boats anchored at the yard, brought the issue to light again. Mr. King decided to send somebody who spoke fluent Spanish to interview the prisoner at Jacksonville Beach County Jail.

William T. Barter, a young man, forty-one, new at CIA headquarters but already a seasoned field officer in Latin America, was the man selected to make the inquiry. Three days later he called Mr. King, informing him that the story of the prisoner seemed to be true. He had the FBI and Florida police authorities after the alleged killer, who had disappeared two weeks earlier after he was released from the concentration camp, where most of the rafters were processed. He asked permission to pursue the investigation and to order a countrywide search warrant to find the missing man, which Mr. King granted.

For the next week, Bill Barter moved from one place to another sending his boss short notes concerning the progress of his work. The simple interview with the prisoner had become a full-scale investigation, now in its third week. During that time Mr. Barter had covered a lot of ground and spent much money; but from his reports it seemed he was on the trail of something important, so the green light to carry on was given.

Early on Monday morning of the fourth week, Mr. King, disgusted, picked up the telephone when it rang while he was shaving. Mr. Barter greeted him and said he was calling from the airport. He had just arrived from Managua, Nicaragua. The identity of the man had been disclosed and confirmed. He preferred to give Mr. King a short briefing before he wrote the final report on the case, because he needed to consult him on how to handle some sensitive issues that came up. For a reason he would explain later, he would rather talk to him outside the CIA office. Somewhat intrigued, Mr. King asked him to come to his house directly from the airport and to have breakfast with him.

"I brought back the most astonishing news for you personally," said the officer while shaking hands with his superior. Mr. King turned his back to the guest and led the way to the dining room, walking slowly, the best way to hide his lameness.

"Young man, at my age and with all I have been through, nothing astonishes me anymore."

The young man with deep blue eyes following him smiled. As he walked behind, he complimented the house's garden and the big oak tree in the backyard, a splendid landmark to locate the house in a neighborhood of houses and streets very much alike. Breakfast was already served on the dining table.

"Help yourself, and tell me this extraordinary news," said Mr. King with a slight sarcastic intonation, while he sat down with a gradual motion. A few years back a booby trap had blown off his left leg. Every so often Mr. King replaced his mechanical leg with one better and smarter, so it was not easy to notice his lameness if he moved slowly. To harmoniously match this handicap he had become a calmed man after the accident. Only on a few occasions was he his old self again, letting out the reins holding his passionate ideas spiced with the bitterness and the loneliness that had grown in him since the accident. He lived by himself in a house full of iron bars, bulletproof doors, and electronic security gadgets, another result of the incident.

Getting ready to eat now required all the attention of the young officer, Mr. Barter, who was so anxious before to communicate the news he had. After he drank the first sip of his coffee, he whispered, "The man is Roberto!"

Mr. King froze. He remained motionless, except for his left hand, holding a spoon halfway to fetch some sugar, which started to shake.

"Are you sure?"

"Dead positive! I had the hunch for a little over a week, after talking with a few Cubans in Miami, but I confirmed it last night in Managua." A silence full of the officer observing every reaction of his superior followed.

"That story is worth listening to from the beginning. Office matters can wait. Spare me no detail, Mr. Barter."

"First thing I did was to question the prisoner in Jacksonville Beach. At the time I met him, he was sorry he let out his story. In order to keep him in jail, every other day the county sheriff charged him with something else. By then he was an expert on the American judicial system after taking an accelerated course given by other inmates. He said he would tell me nothing unless he was released first. I went to the immigration office to check the files on the bird. He came in a raft with four other guys; one of them he claimed was the killer. I located his other three partners in Miami and had a friendly talk with each one separately. They did not know what I was after; they did not know their pal was in jail. None of their stories matched very well. No one mentioned anyone being killed. Therefore, I decided to get all face-to-face and put the screws to them. The county sheriff was most cooperative. So, the true story came out rather easily because the three from Miami were scared to death when I mentioned the word *deportation,* and the fourth man was more than eager to get out of jail at any price.

"Those four men plus a fifth one, now dead, left Cuba in the same raft. The second night the waves and the wind of a local thunderstorm destroyed the raft. They managed to stay together and afloat until sunrise, when they saw a yacht half sunk picking up three youngsters from another raft in distress. The yacht had a rowboat on top of the deck that was being hoisted down into the water. The men of the torn raft felt they were in a desperate situation and quickly agreed that the rowboat was their only possible salvation and swam toward it. When the five men reached the yacht three youngsters were already in the boat and the man, who turned out to be Roberto, was inside the yacht picking up his stuff. The men ganged up on the small boat. The two boys and a girl were quickly overpowered and thrown into the water. A big, husky mulatto nick-named 'El Loco' jumped to the yacht with a knife in his hand to sur-prise the man when he came out. Roberto did not come out as El Loco expected. He took a glance from a bull's-eye punch and popped out through the bow hatch, very calm and nonchalant, hands in his trouser pockets, smiling as if all that was happening was a prank. "Okay, all of you men get out of the boat. Once you are out, I'll see what can be done for you," he said.

"The mulatto decided to ignore him, thinking he was harmless. El Loco jumped right back to the rowboat and started cutting a thick rope tying the boat to the yacht. The man slowly and very gently said, "If you keep cutting that rope I will have to kill you." The mulatto said something to the man and made an obscene ges-ture. The next thing happened in a flash: the man pulled out a small pistol he had hidden in his clothes and shot the mulatto in the left eye. El Loco fell on his back, dead, not knowing what had hit him. Needless to say the other guys abandoned the boat in a hurry. Roberto told the four now very desperate men that the yacht would take more than three hours to sink. If they wanted to save them-selves they had better chop down the main sail pole with an ax lying somewhere inside the yacht. They should tie anything that floated to the pole; there were plenty of ropes around. They should also make short paddles out of the yacht's plywood. If they managed that, they could safely ride sitting on the pole. He would give them some water and food to last a couple of days and was willing to wait and guide them. He had a compass so he knew which way to go, something they surely did not know. "Take his knife; you'll need it," he said, handing them the mulatto's knife while pushing the dead body overboard. He warned that if anyone made a single hostile move he would kill all four. From that moment on, a hostile move-ment was to get closer than ten feet from him or the youngsters. He would guarantee a painless death, since he always aimed for the eyes, the surest way to get a small-gauge bullet inside a man's brain. At that range, he never missed a shot. If anyone doubted it, he was ready to give another demonstration. They all thought maybe he was bragging as a sharpshooter, but it was clear he was very capable of killing all of them.

"He kept his word. He waited until they were ready, threw a cord, and began towing the contraption put afloat, while they paddled with the oars they had managed to make. That afternoon a U.S. Coast Guard gunboat located them. When the boat was close, Roberto cut the rope, abandoned the rowboat, and joined the four men. The youngsters kept on rowing to meet the rescuers. Roberto told the scared men he was there to agree on what to tell the Americans about the incident with the mulatto. They all must say the man disappeared the night the raft was torn to pieces. Nothing should be mentioned about the yacht and the youngsters. They should say he was the carpenter who made the raft in exchange for coming with them. His name was Ramiro. The mulatto, who knew him well, had brought him into the group.

"All four men claimed that once in the camp they didn't say anything about the man because they all owed him their lives. When I tried to locate the man named Ramiro, I found he had left the camp for a job in Sarasota three weeks earlier. I drove there and found out he worked for a week and then disappeared, very excited because he was offered a good job in the copper mines in Nevada. I had the FBI conduct a search for him all over the country on murder charges, although the incident had occurred on international waters, on a foreign vessel that we did not have any jurisdiction over. His photos and fingerprints were sent to every place, but there was not a trace of information about him in the FBI, our files, or elsewhere.

"I decided to show his photos taken at the camp to some of the Cuban exiles in Miami who had been in the Cuban army or the Ministry of the Interior. Two of the men I interviewed seemed to have the idea this man had been in Africa in Cuban Intelligence in the eighties, but nobody was sure. In addition, I sent photos and fingerprints to the CIA station in Havana's U.S. Section of Interests. I received back an encouraging answer soon after: the man could be an officer named Colina who did intelligence work in Africa in the eighties. He also might have been in Nicaragua as adviser for the Sandinista army in their war against the Contras supported by the CIA. From Havana came later another report stating that there was a strong possibility this man might be the Cuban top specialist on CIA undercover actions and irregular warfare, who always worked under deep cover. Then I decided to go to Nicaragua to show his photos and question a couple of men who were very much in contact with the Cuban military personnel. It cost some money to get their cooperation, but it was worth every penny. Both have no doubts—the man is Roberto."

Mr. Barter stopped talking and started to eat his cold ham and eggs. Mr. King had eaten little. At some point in the story he lit a Cuban cigar, thus showing he was through with breakfast. He expelled the aromatic smoke away from the table and talked as if he had regained his tranquillity.

"Mr. Barter, the United States is the last place on earth for that man to come, at least as long as I live, and he knows that very well."

"Sir, Roberto was here and now is back in Cuba."

"Mr. Barter, that does not make any sense either. Why did he come here in the first place?"

"Well, sir, now comes the part of the story I wanted to tell you to see how to handle it. While I was busy looking for the man and trying to identify him, I asked an FBI detective to question the youngsters of the rowboat to make a final check on the story. It checked out very well. Nevertheless, something the FBI detective said haunted me for days: 'The kids loved this man, there was no way to avoid their praising him. At first they tried to conceal the killing of the mulatto when I pressed the point; they tried to make me believe it was self-defense. "Self-defense my eye," I told them. "This man is a cold-blooded murderer." The girl jumped at me and yelled, "You understand nothing because you haven't paid any attention to what we have told you. You were not there when this happened, but you already have a conclusive opinion on what this man did, and who is he. Out of that my conclusion, sir, is that you are a complete idiot. Let me ask you, mister, since you care so much about this mulatto son of a bitch and the other beasts, what about us? We three were on the verge of drowning. They kept kicking at our fingers every time anyone put a hand on the boat to rest. There was no place we could get a hold on the yacht because of the way it was sinking and because the waves kept throwing us against it. For how long could we resist? In what other way could he stop them from taking the boat away? He only had a little pistol this big—it seemed like a toy; it did not even make any noise when he shot it. He had to take them by surprise. Listen, man, we have thought about it and discussed the matter among ourselves a thousand times. He did the best he could do. If it was I who had had the gun there would be no fool making any inquiries here. They all would be under ten thousand feet of salty water and no one to tell about it.'" The mixture of passion, strength of character, and beauty of the girl overwhelmed the detective. He nicknamed her TNT.

"While the investigation went on, I managed to have some time free in Miami. I visited the youngsters in a house they rented on Eighteenth Street in Hialeah. I introduced myself as a member of a Catholic organization that helped young Cubans arriving in the United States. In order to aid them better I was interested to know as much as possible what their abilities, plans, and dreams were. I repeated the visit a few times. Little by little I was able to put the story of their lives together. Their mother committed suicide four months before because she was very ill and would soon die. Their father was not living with them for the last three years, he was unable to be at their mother's funeral. They always had had little relationship with him. They showed me all sorts of family photos they brought with them, but not even one of their father. They felt uneasy and afraid every time the conversation touched the subject and tried to keep him out of everything. They made a single mistake—they received many calls from an aunt living in New York. The FBI identified the woman as the sister of the man calling himself Ramiro at the camp, comparing his photos with photos when he was twelve. It was easy to get complete information on his real identity. He was born in Brooklyn in 1950. Both parents were Cubans. His father was a U.S. Navy veteran of World War II. A fanatic of the Cuban Revolution and of Fidel Castro. He left the States after the Bay of Pigs because he was deeply involved in demonstrations against the U.S. government's policy toward Cuba, and the FBI began to close in on him. His wife and a son, then twelve, followed him a few months later when they sold their belongings, and the father had an apartment in Cuba. At that time, a daughter was a senior at the university. She was engaged to be married to an American and decided to stay in the United States.

"Knowing his real name and where he was born, I searched among the new passports that had been issued in the last two months. Bingo! An attorney at law presented his birth certificate, showing that his mother delivered him at the New York Infirmary on July 17, 1950. The attorney also provided a lot of information about his life in Brooklyn and proofs he was the same person who was applying for a passport. He signed for and picked up the passport on November 2, 1994, in New York. The next thing I did was to check migration records from the date the passport was issued. He crossed the Canadian border and left Montreal on a flight to Mexico City the same day he picked up his passport, six hours before we could stop him."

"Just six hours!" Mr. King rose and walked around the table. It was easy to see his strong emotions.

"How many times have I dreamed of laying my hands on that devil. Why didn't you warn me you were after this guy? I would have put the whole Section at your disposal. I myself would have worked on that day and night. You have no idea. . . ."

There was a long silence. Mr. King slowly calmed down and sat down again. He looked older, much older, and defeated.

"His children are still here."

"Why do you say so?"

The blue-eyed man did not answer. The older man stood up again and walked around slowly, openly dragging his leg. Then he lifted his left arm and pointed a finger at Mr. Barter, saying, "I think, for the time being, you had better keep that piece of information off the record. It could filter to the Cuban exiles and might be misused. Roberto may have many enemies here. You know how savage and ruthless those Miami Cubans can be."

"Yes, sir."

The older man smiled at Mr. Barter, thinking the young man was a jewel. A little too ambitious and independent for his taste, but still a jewel.

The young man smiled, thinking his dart had hit its target.

HE HAD NEVER FELT better in his life. The small cell was cool at night. It was the beginning of November and the weather was changing in Cuba. Food was plain and scanty but he did not feel hungry because he spent little energy, most of the time sleeping or reading when he was not being questioned. Counterintelligence was handling his case, checking every detail of his recent and past history. They were very professional and careful in all they did. They had orders to work as fast as possible to decide his guilt or innocence. He knew they had to wait for information from the United States, where he had stayed for two months, to reach a final decision whether he was or wasn't a traitor. He also faced many other charges, but those charges were not important unless they became convinced he betrayed the country. If they did find him guilty and could prove it, he could be condemned to be shot dead for high treason. On the other hand, if not proven guilty but those on top were still convinced of his guilt, the other charges would be filed against him and he'd be kept in jail as long as it was legally possible. But nothing worried him, even the worst possible outcome of the investigation. He was almost in a state of grace, having regained the love of his children and restarting a relationship with his sister after thirty-two years.

In a daze, he kept reviewing in his mind everything that had happened in the last months that changed the course of his life so much. His three children spent very little time at the camp. As he recommended, they called their aunt and asked her to deposit an amount of money in a bank and to file an affidavit of support on their behalf through a lawyer without using her name. They were also instructed not to mention him to anybody, even to their aunt. They should refer to the story of the yacht as if he were a stranger they never met before. Of course, they should forget forever the attempt to steal the rowboat and the mulatto's death. They should not contact him at the camp or try to help him in any way. When he managed to get out he would call his sister and find out their address.

The first problem to solve when he reached the camp was to pass undetected through the identification screening. Off and on, he had been working mentally on that problem since he left Cuba. He put himself in the place of the American officers in charge of the job who devised the ways to question and to check the stories of thousands of immigrants. Then he decided the best way to deceive them. He would pretend he was one of the many construction workers in Havana from the eastern provinces. Eight of them worked and stayed in the house where he was sleeping. At night, after dinner, he was always invited to coffee they brought from their homeland, and to see baseball games on the black-and-white TV set they had. He asked them all sorts of questions to get information on what was going on in his own country in the new situation.

He adopted the name and life story of Ramiro Ramos, a man about his age but with much less hair, born on a farm close to the town of Velasco, Holguín province. Ramiro was the third offspring of a farmer, owner of fifteen acres devoted mainly to growing bananas, plantain, papaya, mangoes, and manioc. Ramiro never got along too well with his father and two older brothers. Besides, the three of them were enough to handle all the farmwork. As often occurs throughout the ages with younger brothers, he had to go away to earn a living. He did all sorts of jobs. For several years he cut sugar cane at harvest time not very far from his home. Later he decided to see the world, so he went to work on the Isle of Youth picking grapefruit, visited Havana, and traveled as far west as Pinar del Rio. Finally, he became a construction worker in Havana. It was a much easier job and better paid. Ramiro spent a lot of his time off searching for a single woman with her own house who accepted his companionship, to be able to move to Havana.

While he was questioned at the camp or talking with the decoys he readily detected, he told the many small stories he had heard from Ramiro, mentioning all sorts of names and excess of details. At the beginning, the officers, always in a rush, kept cutting short his longwinded answers. Finally, they quit asking him questions. After the first week he knew his story had passed.

At the beginning, only refugees with relatives or friends in the United States willing to take care of them were let out. He figured that among the Cubans in the camp, there must be thousands with nobody in the USA to back them up; there had to be a solution for those cases. Some time afterward he was offered a job as a pipe fitter's helper in Sarasota. There was plenty of work to do getting houses and hotels ready for the winter season, when a lot of wealthy older Americans flock to the warm, calm town surrounded by many stillwater lakes, with a long view to the waters of the Gulf of Mexico. He was offered five dollars an hour, six days a week, a ten-hour daily shift, with extra hours paid at time and a half. It all amounted to about $340 a week, plus room and board. He accepted the job and left the camp with a work permit and a Social Security card. His plan was to change jobs often, moving in short hops toward the frontier of Mexico or Canada, something to decide later, erasing his footprints as he moved. He decided to postpone the call to his sister until he knew his way around better, because he could not risk his real identity being known if he was under surveillance. It was in the best interests of his children and himself.

Claudia planned everything and carried it out so it was a surprise for everybody. She told her aunt that her brothers and she had decided to spend the first money they had earned going on a weekend trip to Disney World and wanted very much to meet her there. Then, she told her to get a pencil and paper and to write down the place where they would meet and the hour, and the alternative site and time in case one of the parties couldn't show up on the first date. The aunt was very anxious to meet her two nephews and her niece. When she received their first call from the camp, she wanted to come to Florida and take them right back with her. She wanted to share with them her big apartment in the middle of Manhattan. "But, from the beginning Claudia talked in a mysterious way and gave me such precise and strange instructions that I ended up feeling I was part of a conspiracy," she said laughingly when they all met.

It was an overwhelming emotion for him to see his sister together with his kids. The youngsters had gained weight, looked so well in their new outfits and happy. From the camp's information office, Claudia managed to get the address where he was working in Sarasota. She arranged there a reservation for all of them in one of the motels on the waterfront. Now in its low season, they even got a discount. After meeting their aunt, they spent the rest of Saturday seeing part of Disney World. They slept in a Best Western close to Universal Studios, and very early on Sunday morning they traveled to Sarasota to surprise him there.

That night they sat around the swimming pool of the motel. He and his sister remembered their childhood days in Brooklyn. Claudia and the boys sharpened their ears, not wanting to miss a word.

"I have always wondered what happened to the place we lived in, 677 Lincoln Place. The building had a brass plate with a date, 1905; it seemed to me so old. I remember it had four floors, two apartments on each floor. We lived on the second floor, apartment 4. Remember Irene Hands, a neighbor on other building exactly like ours? The back of her apartment and ours were ten feet apart. I was in love with Irene's sister since I was six; I wept the day she became a nun. How sweet she was!

"Much later, when I thought of the place we lived, I realized how well located it was: close to the Brooklyn Museum, Prospect Park, Botanical Garden. . . . Often comes to my mind the times Father took me to Ebbetts Field, not far away, to see the Dodgers of the fifties play! The neighborhood was sort of lower middle-class, mainly Irish immigrants. A block away was Eastern Parkway where lived many well-to-do Jewish, pretty green lawns, all well painted. . . . The dentist who straightened your teeth lived there. Going from Lincoln Place to Rodgers Avenue, there was a laundry owned by a Chinese man. We used to yell at him, 'Chinquie Charlie, Chinquie Charlie!' and he'd get mad and throw hot water at us. . . . Going the other direction, to Bedford Avenue, my mouth waters remembering George's Soda Fountain; the owner was a Greek. I always bought there my daily chocolate ration one Milky Way and one Three Musketeers for five cents apiece. Once a week, on Saturday, I treated myself with a big ice cream chocolate soda, for a quarter.

"Yes, yes, and a cheeseburger with mayonnaise and slices of tomato, to go with the soda, for another quarter."

"I liked better the taste of a burger with mustard, pickles, and onions for twenty cents. Then I could buy me a pack of potato chips, 'Cruise,' for a nickel. The bag had the image of an owl on it."

"Popcorn in the Savoy Cinema. Matinee every Saturday morning: a cowboy picture and lots and lots of cartoons."

"And the Three Stooges."

"Oh, how I hated when you started to go to school. I was already in high school at Bishop MacDonald Memorial High, and you were in Santa Teresa de Avila grammar school. I felt already a woman, wanted to go to school, and come back with friends my age; and I was stuck with you, skinny little thing eight years old."

"Come on, it was not so bad. In the back of my mind I recall you liked very much when you came to pick me up and asked Brother Gregg how I had behaved that day, how I was doing in my classes."

"You are always the same, taking people by surprise. Yes, Brother Gregg was a dream of a man. All the girls envied me because two or three times a week I had a long conversation with him about a certain little devil. . . . Oh, God, how much time has passed by! How much I have needed Mother, Father, and you! How much I have wanted to help you and now your children! Once in Italy I quit a tour in Venice because I could not think of anything else but how much you liked painting, how much you would have enjoyed being there. I started crying, felt so miserable. Why was our family ever split? . . . All this time gone forever. The neighborhood we grew up in is now the realm of junkies and thieves; nobody in his right mind dares to visit the place. The Savoy was torn down. . . . Do you really have to go back? We are your only family, we are the only ones who care for you."

AFTER A MONTH IN the custody of the Ministry of the Interior, he was released and discharged from the Service. He was now just a civilian still under investigation. Some time in the future he would have to face the charges pressed against him in a civil court. He was given back his apartment.

In no hurry to look for another job, he planned to indulge himself with a long vacation until his trial was over. In the meantime, he would have to sell some furniture and clothes or do something to get some money. He began skin-diving at the waterfront just a block away from his home almost every day. Most of the time his companion was a friend of his elder son, a youngster named Roger, who lived on Eighteenth Street. Soon after, there was a rumor in the neighborhood they were illegally spearfishing and selling the catch to foreigners that frequented the Comodoro Hotel beach, right by their hunting waters. Roger boasted they were earning as much as $80 to $100 a month each, and that should improve in tuna fish and sea bass season. However, Roger never was a reliable source of information. Some times both would spend days fixing Roger's car, a 1970 Alfa Romeo his uncle left lying around when he divorced his wife to marry a much younger woman.

Marcelo went to see him and took along a bottle of seven-year-old rum, a sign of a long and difficult talk ahead.

"Sorry we failed you. For many years Cecilia kept everything so much under control that we trusted her blindly, thinking if she was around everything was okay. We weren't able to see how many things had changed within your family when your children stopped being children, and the economic situation turned so bad. We just kept making the routine calls every month to chat a bit with Cecilia. Asking her if she needed something. Her standard reply was that everything was okay; if she needed anything it was always a simple thing to arrange: no mechanic to fix the car's brakes, someone to fix the water pump of the building. . . . She never mentioned she was ill. Little by little your kids became hostile to everything. They blamed you, they blamed us, and they blamed the government. Above all, they felt you did not care at all for them.

"We found out quite late that your sister called your daughter frequently at a neighbor's telephone and she was sending her money through third persons. There was nothing to do: it was a matter of time before your real identity became known. Nevertheless, the main thing was the drastic change in your kids' attitude. We concluded they had the final word. The only thing to do was to get you out of the game. It was too late to try anything else."

There was a long silence. Marcelo opened the bottle and served two long shots of rum in a couple of glasses. They drank the rum straight. He sensed the worst was still to come.

"Listen, man, I have another poison pill for you. Your case has become a political issue. Opinions are split. Some understand your motives and say your coming back to Cuba and your eviction from the Service close this case. However, many hard-liners want your head; they say whatever the reasons you had, you have to pay, otherwise it will create a precedent we can't afford. This country has been at war, is at war, and it seems it is going to be forever at war with the most powerful world power, and you were a soldier at the very front line. Do you get it?"

"The other day the sea almost settled that dispute. I was tangled up in a cave sixty feet deep pursuing a big fish. Almost drowned."

"You shouldn't do that sort of thing."

"When you are fishing a big one you get carried away. It is the call of the wild, something written in your genetic code since the time man lived off hunting. If I die at the bottom of the sea, promise me to publish the news in all the papers, so all my enemies will be satisfied and my soul may rest in peace."

"Promised!"

"Don't forget."

Marcelo got up, slapped his shoulder, and said, "I never forget. Call if you ever need me."

The last words were as good as gold. It meant the high command had found no trace of treason in his behavior and wanted him to keep in touch. A taste of honey on the bitter ending of his career.

A WEEK LATER, ALMOST at bedtime, he received a call from his older son with the news that Claudia had disappeared. Both brothers were at home installing a new television antenna, Claudia was in the kitchen getting ready to start cooking the evening meal. She decided to go to a grocery store just two blocks away to buy something she needed. She never came back. After thirty or forty minutes, they went after her. They searched all the places she might have been, then came back home to see if she had returned. After that, they called the police and filled a missing person's report.

His two sons were devastated. They blamed themselves for letting her go alone to the store. At the same time, they kept saying the neighborhood was safe. He tried to make them understand that those things happened, life was like that. The best thing they could do was to question all the neighbors—someone might have seen or heard something. When he hung up after an hour of talking to his sons, he thought his children were beginning to pay a very high toll for their dreams.

The next day he received a package sent from New York via DHL. It contained a photocopy of part of the front page of an old Nicaraguan newspaper with the picture of a passenger bus blown up by a mine planted by the Contras. Twenty-six injured, four killed, all civilians. He went to see Marcelo at once.

"That happened when a new CIA adviser for the Contras gave them contact mines they placed in roads mainly used by civilians.

The Nicaraguan government denounced it, and put public pressure on the Americans, but the mines kept exploding. I proposed to teach this guy a lesson. We knew where he was staying and all his movements. We had two Sandinistas infiltrated in that camp. The Saturday night we made the hit, the man was snoring loudly after drinking heavily. Since I wanted no mistakes, I myself planted a personal mine under his bed to blow up when he tried to put on his shoes the next morning. My idea was not to harm him much, just to scare him. The mattress should absorb most of the blast, at worst he would be thrown against the tin roof, but for some reason or another it blew off one of his legs. I think he woke up still drunk and he could not find his shoes. The chief here pulled my ears for taking such risks, but road mining halted. As time went on this man, Mr. Sidney King, became head of the Cuban office in the CIA. This is his revenge."

"I remember the case very well."

"My life for my daughter's. Do you understand?"

Marcelo kept silent for a moment

"This also could be an effort to recruit you. Some people here might even think this was prepared when you were there, a scheme you masterminded to deceive us."

"You are right. I thought that too."

"What are you going to do?"

"Never mind what I am going to do. I came to see what you are going to do. If the CIA uses this method against me, it is doing it against the Service."

"This has a mark of personal revenge. It is not a regular CIA move. They have to play by the unwritten rules of this game: always respect the lives of the enemy's officers. Family is sacred. If they break these rules, it becomes a jungle. If Mr. King decided to get back at you by taking your daughter as a hostage, he'll use some of the bloodiest anti-Cuba organizations to cover it up. The CIA will distance themselves as they always have. The only thing we can do is pass the word in Miami among the Cubans who serve the master:

this is eye for eye, tooth for tooth, and make sure we mean it. Besides that, through the proper channels we will ask the CIA authorities to look into this incident. I believe we are going to find receptive ears.

"Think about who really sent you this photocopy. Mr. King always said he never intended the mines to be used against civilians. It does not seem to be the way he would put the pressure on you. This might be an insider trying to warn us about the real linkage. The Cubans in charge of the kidnapping? I doubt it. Mr. King surely selected them very carefully; he doesn't make that kind of mistake."

He kept contact on the telephone with his sons daily. They wanted him there very much. Three days later the situation became a crisis: "What is stopping you, Dad? You are an American citizen. You have a valid passport. You don't need a visa; you just have to take a plane to get here. Many people have advised us on what is best to do. However, we don't know English, we don't have experience in this sort of thing. We need you here! Why don't you come and help us before it is too late?"

He called Marcelo and gave him the news.

"Somebody is putting pressure on my boys to get me over there. This seems to be Mr. King's style, all right. Do you have any news?"

Marcelo stood silent for a while, wondering if it was right to tell his friend, rather a very dear brother, the outcome of the analysis they made: if it was Mr. King's personal revenge, time was running out. An operation like that, to have the best chances to succeed, had to last only a few days. If nothing happened soon the girl had to be released or revenge would be taken on her. The psychologists who had studied Mr. King for years said the girl would pay, and they were seldom wrong.

"No, nothing new."

Early the next day he prepared himself for fishing. After he was ready he sat down at the dinner table and placed the envelope addressed to Marcelo in a visible place with a note inside: "This is the only way I see out." Roger came carrying two aqualung tanks he had filled with air the night before with a compressor he owned. He charged anyone a dollar for filling a tank.

The search for his body started in the afternoon when it was clear that he had had an accident. Roger and two professional divers surveyed all hunting waters. At that time of the year there is a strong current along the coast going northeast that must have taken his body far away, maybe into the deep waters off the island platform. The body could not float to the surface because to stay down at fifty to sixty feet he had to put on eight pounds of lead hooked to his belt. His spear gun was floating, tied by a long nylon rope to the spear anchored to a big bass head, marking the point where he must have lost consciousness. Most of the flesh of the sea bass had been eaten away by the fishes dwelling in the coral reef.

The Ministry of the Interior released an obituary to the newspapers regretting his death, caused by an "unfortunate accident." The next day the radio and television announced that his body had been found. His burial, with all honors due him, was set for the morning of the next day. Technically, his demotion and eviction from the Service had not been confirmed at the time of his death, and the high command withdrew the request. His body was brought to the funeral parlor in Calzada on K Street late in the afternoon. Some of the personnel who were searching for the body, found adrift at forty feet deep and thirty miles due east from the place he was hunting, were at the funeral and gave many details of the search. The corpse was not shown in the coffin because most of the flesh and the eyes did not exist anymore, had been eaten away by fishes. In the Institute of Legal Medicine, they identified him by his teeth. The twenty-three medals he had been awarded in Cuba and three other countries were placed in front of the coffin.

At his burial Colonel Marcelo, second in command of the Cuban Intelligence Service, delivered the last words. He praised the exemplary life of the deceased and concluded: "Whatever mistakes he made they are insignificant as compared to his proven loyalty in many difficult times, and the great deeds he accomplished in a rather short life."

Claudia returned to his home two days later. She was released the night before in Saint Louis, Missouri, and put on a train bound for Miami. When she arrived home, her brothers had everything packed. They all left Florida for a place they did not disclose.

THE THREE AUTOMOBILES ARRIVED at the house almost at the same time guided by the only big oak tree in a neighborhood with all houses and streets very much alike. The dead body of the owner, a former CIA high-ranking officer was found six days before by the police after the maid reported a suspicious silence and a dead body smell in the house. It was no secret that Mr. King had been forced to retire several months before. Since then he had been busy commencing to write his memories, seeing many influential people to complain on many things, and traveling frequently to Miami where he had old associates in the Cuban colony.

Seven men entered the house. The first to arrive was the chief of the City Police Department. The two men who followed shortly after were FBI officers. The last four to arrive a bit delayed were CIA men: the director of Operations; Mr. B. Cabot, the head of the Cuban Section; Mr. William Barter, the CIA head lawyer; W. Hiram Markovitz; and a young officer acting as liaison to the investigators of the crime.

The FBI highest-ranking officer started the meeting immediately.

"Thanks to Mr. Cabot, Mr. Barter, and Mr. Marcovitz for being here. We are sure you are going to be very helpful so we can complete our investigation much sooner. As we stated in the letter asking for this meeting, we have reached a point where we need top-level CIA cooperation.

"If we all agree, let us summarize our findings up to now: first, the killer entered the house inside the trunk of Mr. King's Mercedes-Benz. That is a very important conclusion. This point puzzled us for some time. At first, the only rational explanation seemed to be that Mr. King let the killer in himself. This house is a fortress, full of electronic alarms. To get inside, the police had to blast one of the doors, so it seemed impossible for a burglar to break in as in an ordinary house. If Mr. King had let the killer in, the whole investigation would be thrown in one direction and narrowed down quite a bit. We have now sufficient evidence to support our first conclusion: the murderer entered the house concealed in the trunk of the car.

"Second, the motive. From the beginning theft appeared to be the obvious motive. Mr. King had been cashing much of his life savings and bringing it home. At first it seemed the killer rode out of this place in Mr. King's Mercedes with close to two hundred thousand dollars, enough to pay for all his troubles and risks. Now there are evidences that point to another direction. The first question we want to ask the CIA is: Are there any grounds for another possible motive or motives as well?"

"Do you want the answer now?" asked Mr. Cabot.

"If the CIA has it now, please."

"We do not have any reason whatsoever to believe there could be another motive."

The lawyer stepped in.

"Let's put it this way: there could be endless reasons why Mr. King was killed. He took part in affairs that affected many interests and people. He was a very controversial man with a strong will. But the CIA, after careful consideration, concludes that at this moment, four months after he lost his position and thus the power to go with it, there is no other situation that we know of that might explain Mr. King's murder."

The FBI investigator continued with the same even voice, carefully selecting his words.

"Then, taking theft as a motive, the next question is, Why had Mr. King cashed so much of the money he had in stocks and bonds and transferred it to his home vault in the last months? Does the CIA know the reason?"

Mr. Barter stepped in.

"Since I was new on the job, I had to consult Mr. King on many matters. Once he told me he was going to invest most of his savings in a very profitable business in Central America where he made many influential friends while stationed there. It looks to me as if he was going to get the money out of the country in cash."

"Mr. Barter, Mr. Cabot, did you know Mr. King had been carrying out an investigation paying with his own account?"

"No, I did not," said Mr. Barter. Mr. Abbot just nodded.

"Okay, gentlemen, this is the bottom line: we have enough evidence that points out that Mr. King had been paying a lot of cash to several people, mostly Cubans working for him. In fact it looks as if he only brought home the cash needed to pay these people. Whoever did this job had a lot of inside information on the security of the house to devise probably the only way to break in. If he had this information, most likely he also knew how little money was in the vault. Was it worth it for a common burglar to go to all the trouble and risk for a few thousand dollars? That brings us back to the motive again. Maybe someone did not want Mr. King's investigations. Therefore, officially the FBI must ask the CIA to disclose the nature of this investigation, or whatever Mr. King was doing, and the identity of the people working for him."

Mr. Markovitz stopped Mr. Barter before he could answer the question:

"You just said Mr. King was doing a private investigation as a private citizen. The CIA has nothing to do with it. The CIA knows nothing about it."

"But, he started this investigation while he was in the CIA. Why is he searching all over the United States for a Cuban girl kidnapped and released some time ago? Is it true someone set him up in the CIA, as he often said? Who is Roberto?"

Mr. Cabot made a sign with his hand to stop the FBI officer.

"I am not going to answer any of those specific questions. I just want to give you our view about Mr. King's actions. As you know he was injured by a mine planted by a Cuban intelligence officer in Nicaragua long ago. This mine blew off a leg, his testicles, and half of his penis. This incident changed completely his character and his life. The field officer always hungry for action had to choose between retirement or sitting down behind a desk for eight hours a day, five days a week. At the time of the accident, we feared he would do something foolish if we forced his retirement. To our surprise, he adapted wonderfully to the new situation. He became a keen analyst—a true expert on Cuban affairs. There was nobody better for head of the Section. . . .

"A few months back the Cuban officer who caused his injuries was here in the United States for some time, then went back to Cuba. Since then, we regret to say, Mr. King lost his peace of mind completely. He dedicated himself to trying to get even with this man. We had to remove him from the CIA and distance ourselves from his bizarre behavior."

Mr. Cabot rose from his seat, indicating there were no more answers or explanations to expect from the CIA. He made a request:

"Since we are here, could you show us how Mr. King was killed?"

The chief of the city police, who had been somewhat surprised and amused watching the two giants wrestling about, led the way to the dining room. He pointed to a door opened to the garage where a Mercedes-Benz shone in the shadows.

"This is the way our men figure it happened: Mr. King stepped out of his car and walked toward the dining room, leaving the door open like that. In fact, the maid said the door remained open during the daytime. It was locked at night as a security measure. Mr. King heard or sensed somebody behind him. He took a bigger step to reach this chair, to lean on it in order to turn around faster. At the same time, he pulled out his .357 Magnum. Turning around was one of the movements most difficult for him. The intruder stood there at the door pointing his gun at him, waiting until Mr. King faced him. That is something significant, since he could have shot him many times in the back.

"The killer put a small-caliber bullet through Mr. King's left eye and into his brain. At that distance a pure-luck shot indeed."

"Wangeroog, de Schone . . ."

JÜRGEN EHLERS

WANGEROOG, THE PEARL . . .

S UCH READS THE FIRST line of a rhyme Hendrik Beukema had learned by heart at school, to remember the names of the islands of the Wadden Sea. Wangeroog or Wangerooge, as it appears on the official maps, is the easternmost of the East Frisian Islands. Hendrik was born on Vlieland, a West Frisian Island.

The West Frisian Islands belong to the Netherlands, the East Frisian Islands to Germany, the *Grodeutsches Reich*, as it is now called. The Second World War is not over yet, and the Netherlands have been occupied by German troops for almost four years. Beukema was drafted to the labor service, one of some hundred young Dutchmen who now work on Wangerooge.

Wangerooge—a pearl? Perhaps it was a pearl once, when the rhyme was written, more than a century ago. Even now, looking southward over the Wadden Sea, you might think it still is. Sea gulls and oystercatchers skim the salt marshes for food and look for nesting places. The Wadden Sea glistens in the mild April sun. The tide is up. A small vessel maneuvers through the narrow fairway, heading for Wilhelmshaven. With binoculars you can make out the name of the boat at the bow: *Joanna.*

Looking in the opposite direction, however, the eye meets the steel and concrete of coastal defenses and military installations constructed in the course of two world wars. Thus, of all the North Sea islands, Wangerooge has lost the most of its natural charm.

"Short break. Time for a cigarette!"

Only the Germans have still got cigarettes. Beukema pushes the spade into the soft dune sand and flings himself onto the grass. Originally they had come to the island as construction workers, but there is not much to be built anymore, really. Now they are digging trenches in the dunes instead, with little enthusiasm. The three Germans who control them are classified as "old and sick"; all the others are long since at the front.

Beukema gets up to have a look around. Most of the men in his group were arrested for minor offenses in the Netherlands and sentenced to labor service in Germany. One of them, Piet de Wit, is even a member of the NSB, the Dutch Nazi Party. Hendrik Beukema does not know much about the others. He is careful not to get too familiar with them. None of his comrades know why he is really here. He is an ex-radio operator of the Royal Dutch Navy, escaped to England, and brought back to Vlieland in a submarine, after having been trained as a spy. He had managed to get recruited for labor on Wangerooge. All had gone smoothly and easily. And here on the island? There is no need to sneak secretly under cover of darkness through the dunes. The island is so small, nothing much can be kept hidden anyway.

Wangerooge serves as an outpost for the naval base at Wilhelmshaven, the most important stronghold of the *Kriegsmarine* on the German North Sea coast. Only a stone's throw away, right behind him, are the gun positions of *Batterie Scharnhorst.* Nicely built positions for three 30.5 cm guns. However, there is actually just one gun. So far, Skoda has been unable to deliver the others. And now nobody believes that they will ever arrive. The war is nearly over. But not quite, not yet. Not for him. His hour is still to come. Tonight. He looks at his hands; they do not tremble.

Yesterday, London broadcast the agreed code: "Attention! To whom it concerns: The dog is barking." The six months of waiting have come to an end.

HENDRIK DOES NOT KNOW that Piet de Wit started long ago to entertain doubts about his allegiance. To him, the NSB had lost almost all its attraction. The Germans had never understood how to exploit this potential. They had not even tried. They had come as occupants, as *Herrenmenschen,* members of the master race. And the NSB bigwigs had put up with that, clicked their heels, shouted "Jawohl!," and followed whatever orders the Germans had given. Bunch of cowards! Piet had balked at that, and that is why he ended up here. The eight months of forced labor are up now, but he still cannot return home. The Germans now need every man they can get hold of.

What will happen when he eventually gets back to Holland? Will they greet him as a liberated detainee or will they prosecute him as an NSB member and put him into prison? He is twenty-seven now, he wants his share in life. But will he get it? He watches his comrades intensely and with an uneasy feeling: they do not ostracize him directly, but he certainly is not one of them either. The odd one out, even though not quite as obviously as Hendrik Beukema.

He watches the tall blond Frisian dig effortlessly, spade after spade, to deepen the trench. He cannot grasp why this man works so eagerly. Was he not an officer in the Dutch navy once? And now, by the look of it, a true friend of the Germans. The way he associates with Cordes, the building contractor, had often been ridiculed. Supposedly he is after the German's shy daughter.

De Wit is pondering the fact that there is someone more in the center of attention than he is. He will take advantage of that. Piet nudges his neighbor:

"Hendrik works like a madman," he says.

"That's what you'd better do too, you NSB man," the man returns. "After the war you'll all be finished!"

Piet swallows. Surely, it's not ill-meant, just a throwaway remark, some kind of joke, really—but menacing all the same. He pulls himself together and shakes his head. "I'm no NSB man anymore, didn't you know? I sent back my party membership book in January, by registered mail. Didn't I tell?"

His neighbor does not comment, but he seems impressed. Piet feels a little more at ease now. Only, of course, it is not true. He will have to burn the book tonight before someone discovers it.

"Looks as if Hendrik is the last Nazi around here," he mutters. Again nobody bothers to answer. But that does not matter. He must strike while the iron is hot.

EVENING. CORDES, THE BUILDING contractor, puts his papers aside and reaches for his pipe. Pointless anyway, the whole bookkeeping. Thousands of reichsmarks month after month, but there is no Reich anymore, and the money that the state owes him, he will never see. He has written it off long ago. The war is coming to an end, no doubt. But afterward there will be a golden time for building contractors, and that will make good for all his losses.

The work to complete the island's defenses is dragging along. The foreign laborers are more lax about their job, no doubt, but that would not matter too much if there were not a severe shortage of material. There is not enough gravel and cement to complete the bunkers.

A knock on the door. It is Beukema, the best of his Dutch workers. Cordes asks him in. They have met lots of times in the evenings, to have a cup of tea together and discuss the progress of their work. But tonight the Dutchman has come for a different reason. Completely calm, he unwraps something from an oily rag. Cordes hardly believes his eyes. There are tubes and other parts one would expect to find in a radio. But what Beukema assembles is a transmitter, not a receiver. Even Cordes understands that, although he knows next to nothing about technical things. He stares at his visitor.

"You must be mad," he says.

Hendrik shakes his head. "Listen! The war is coming to an end. The earlier the better for all of us. Fewer casualties, less suffering. And we will contribute to that now, you and me!"

Cordes recoils. "I am no traitor!" He sits down, breathing heavily. What can he do? The Dutchman is younger and stronger than the aging builder. Hendrik watches him closely. He stands between him and the door. Should he bolt, he would knock him down.

"Treachery," says Hendrik. "What a word! Reason is the only thing that counts. The Allies will land on Wangerooge anyway. If they can take the island in a surprise attack, probably some ten people will die. If it comes to an open battle, there will be hundreds of casualties. That is the difference. And anyway, it all comes to the same: Wangerooge will be taken."

While he is talking, his nimble hands assemble the transmitter. Small and effective. A miracle of modern technology. The tubes he had smuggled in, tightly wrapped, at the bottom of his water bottle. And the aerial? Cordes comprehends that the lightning rod that Hendrik had fixed to his roof, to do him a favor as he had said, is supposed to serve quite a different purpose.

The German awakens as if from a trance. "I am no traitor," he repeats, now with regained firmness in his voice, as if he has come to some conclusion. Hendrik gives him a sharp look, but he has no time now for further discussion. It is 8:00 P.M., his time to broadcast. Hendrik switches the radio set on and puts on the headphones. He gives his recognition signal, again and again, until London confirms. Cordes mutters something, but Hendrik cannot hear. He has begun to broadcast:

"Gun positions in Fortress Wangerooge: Scharnhorst battery: one 30.5 cm gun, untested. Graf Spee battery: wooden dummies only. Jade battery: empty. Airfield battery: four 10.5 cm guns, three in concrete bunkers . . ."

The Dutchman sees Cordes pull open the drawer of his desk and take out a large pistol—a Mauser probably. Hendrik is not prepared for that. He pulls off his headphones. "Cordes . . . ," he says placatingly. His right hand continues to transmit the Morse code.

". . . All heavy guns are assigned for fighting naval targets, facing N to NE, cannot be turned around. On the landward side favorable conditions for airborne operation. Sandy tidal flats suitable for gliders. No obstacles on that side, no land mines . . ."

If he jumped now, he would stand a chance of knocking the gun out of Cordes's hand before the old man could shoot, but he would have to topple the table, and the transmitter would be damaged. He can only hope that Cordes will not shoot. Certainly, it is not so easy to shoot a man point-blank whom you had tea with the day before. But, of course, you cannot rely on that. Keep contact, talk to the man; good heavens, say something!

"Cordes, you are done for anyway. An enemy radio transmitter in your house, they will shoot you for that. . . ."

At that moment Gerda comes in. "Stop!" she shouts. The barrel no longer points at Beukema's breast, but the situation remains tense.

"What's the matter?" Cordes shouts indignantly, without moving his eyes off Beukema. "Leave us alone!"

He jumps as his daughter puts a hand on his shoulder. "Surely, you won't shoot the father of your grandchild, will you?" Gerda says soothingly.

Cordes lowers his arm. That is too much for him. Hans, his son-in-law missing in the East since last year, and his daughter in the meantime sleeping around with this foreign worker and getting pregnant by him? By an enemy agent?

Hendrik leans back. He has broadcast his message and is waiting for the reply. He knows nothing of a child. Did Gerda lie in order to save him? He looks at her.

"It is true," she says. She smiles, but it is a joyless smile. She knows that Hendrik is married back home.

The reply from England! Everything else later. Hendrik puts on the headphones and starts to write.

"Repeat message on Thursday, same time."

What does that mean? Puzzled, he stares at the radio. There it comes again.

"Repeat message on Thursday, same time."

"Message received and understood." Hendrik turns off the transmitter.

AN HOUR LATER BEUKEMA, Cordes, and his daughter are sitting together in the living room. Cordes has brought champagne from the cellar, one of the bottles Hans had sent from France after the fall of Paris. The old man had hesitated only for a very slight moment when his daughter had proposed to drink to the remarkable event.

Remarkable indeed! Cordes drinks fast, with big gulps. The champagne goes to his head. He opens a second bottle. Not cold enough, the stuff, but who cares? They are all finished, that's for sure. It is dead easy today to take a bearing of such a radio transmitter.

Hendrik is brooding over the riddle they have presented him with. What does it mean? Why don't they strike now? If they wait too long, the raid will fail. Alteration of the gun positions has already been ordered. Did he fail to convince them? Did he leave out any crucial information? No, he doesn't think so. Even the shortage of antiaircraft ammunition was mentioned. Why the same thing all over again on Thursday? Don't they know the risk he is running?

He glances over to Gerda. Four months ago they met for the first time, secretly. It was some kind of game, private, no part of his mission. And, of course, she had been lonely, just like him. He had known that at once, the first time he had met her, here in this room, when he had looked into her grave dark eyes. Now everything is over.

Gerda smiles, but really she feels more like crying. *He did not tell me the truth, not even me,* she thinks. *Slept with me, used me.* All of a sudden she regrets that her father did not shoot him, then everything would have been over. But now? A mother-to-be with two men, but none of them will ever get to see her child. Hans is dead,

she knows that for sure, and Hendrik will be gone as soon as the
war is over. Is Hendrik his real name, anyway? She doesn't know a
thing about him.

THE HEADQUARTERS ARE LOCATED in a former hotel, large and uncomfortable. And there he is, Lieutenant Commander Heinrich Fersenburg, at
the age of fifty-two a relatively old commander, to be honest. Fortress
commander without a fortress. He only came to the island in March,
and the biggest unit he had ever been in charge of before was a school
on the mainland. He was *Oberstudiendirektor,* the head master of a
grammar school. He got to know Wangerooge from some long-bygone
vacation. A holiday resort, now garnished with a few bunkers, can-
nons, and trenches. Ridiculous. Supposed to be protecting the Wilhelmshaven naval base, a base without a navy. What little there was left
of ships afloat had been transferred to the Baltic, trying to evacuate as
many refugees as possible from beleaguered Kurland and East Prussia.

Until last week he had thought the war would happen without
him, just as in 1914–18, when the aging battleship on which he
served as a young officer did not fire a single shot in combat.

Participant in the Battle of Jutland, but in the second line only.
And now again. The war is taking place on the mainland, the real
war. Heinrich Fersenburg is not keen on taking part. No, the fighting will be over, hopefully, before anybody takes notice of the
island. Or perhaps not?

On April 18, one week ago, Helgoland, the rocky bulwark in the
center of the German Bight, had been hit by an air raid. A full-scale
attack with nearly one thousand bombers on a very small target.
Pointless, unless they are planning to follow up with naval forces for
an amphibious operation, landing in Wilhelmshaven or Cuxhaven
or somewhere else on the long, virtually undefended coast. Undefended—not counting the mines. Thousands of mines in the waters
of the German Bight, which would make any attack from the sea a
high-risk operation. Why take such a risk now? The fronts are
breaking up; the war is decided.

In contrast to his men, whom he had addressed on the führer's birthday, April 20, with a strongly worded speech, he is well aware of the military situation. The Russians are fighting their way into Berlin, the Americans have taken Hannover and advanced to the Elbe River and Hamburg, and British tanks have reached Bremen. No, he doesn't believe in this war anymore. His thoughts are drifting toward the time afterward. Schools Inspector. Now that might be a possibility. He would stand a good chance. Meckenheim is dead, and von Eisleben has exposed himself politically too much to be eligible for any public office in a postwar Germany.

The teleprinter message from Wilhelmshaven he has put aside. They claim to have intercepted a broadcast from an enemy transmitter on the island. Somewhere in the village. But as the coded message was only intercepted by one station, direction-finding remains ambiguous. The line he has drawn using the coordinates given runs obliquely through the village, passing just south of his headquarters. Surely someone misunderstood one of their own radio signals.

They intend to send a unit with a direction-finding aerial to Harlesiel, to be better prepared in case of a second broadcast.

Let them. And they have sent the message on to Berlin to have it deciphered. Fersenburg doubts that they will get a reply. He looks out the window. A clear blue sky with small tufts of white cloud is stretching overhead. It is a quarter to five in the afternoon.

The telephone is ringing. The army lines are still intact, fortunately.

"Headquarters, Fersenburg."

It is Behrends. The antiaircraft unit reports bombers approaching Wangerooge. Again. This is the third call within the last hour. Wangerooge? What does that mean? Most likely another attack on the navy base in Wilhelmshaven. What? Air alarm? Fersenburg shakes his head indignantly. "Lieutenant" Behrends! He finds it hard to suppress his aversion against that former theology student, when he replies. No alarm. No panic.

But Behrends insists. "The measurements clearly show that the bombers are heading for us, for Wangerooge!" They have all the latest radar equipment on the island, a Wassermann aerial to detect the bombers as early as they start gathering over England, a Freya for the medium range, and a Würzburg-Riese for more exact, short-distance position-finding when the planes come closer than 60 km. And now they are closer than 60 km.

In the end, Fersenburg gives in.

BY THEN IT IS too late. At 1659 two Mosquito bombers nose-dive toward the center of the island and place red target markings at an altitude of 300 meters above the abandoned airfield. A minute later, the first wave of bombers arrives. The flak opens fire. Their shots lie close. A bomber trails smoke, another explodes in midair. Two others collide and disintegrate, the debris falling into the sea. Then come the bombs. Four hundred eighty bombers drop more than six thousand bombs on an area of less than ten square kilometers. The island submerges under a cloud of smoke and dust. Within a quarter of an hour everything is over.

AS THE SMOKE DISPERSES, the island lies in ruins—the hotels and guest houses smashed, the neat little gardens plowed over, the little forest razed. Dunes, fields, and salt marshes turned into a crater landscape as bizarre as the moon's surface. And the people? *All dead*, is Hendrik's first thought when he frees himself from the debris of the camp huts. No, not all. Some are still alive. Most of them are still alive.

Cordes manages to crawl out of his ruined workshop. His daughter is badly injured. As helpers carry her away, she screams like a dying animal. White with rage Cordes digs with bare hands through the rubble. He throws blocks of masonry behind him and heaves beams aside. The upper floor of the house has collapsed; part of the ceiling is dangling menacingly above him. He ignores the danger. It takes him hours before he finds what he is looking for: trembling from exhaustion he gets onto his feet, ragged, scratched, his arms blood-covered, but in his hand the Mauser pistol, loaded and ready. Woe betide you, Hendrik, liar, traitor, murderer! Cordes makes for the Dutch workers' camp. He must take revenge right now.

"Hey, Cordes, what are you up to with that shooter?" It is Albert the baker who calls out to him across the road. His house has survived, almost undamaged. Cordes shows no reaction, he hastens on. But a moment later he realizes that people are staring at him. He stops running and pushes the gun in his belt. Nobody needs to see what he is up to. They might try to stop him otherwise.

Nobody stops him. He gets to the Dutch camp, finds it devastated by the bombs. He demands to see Hendrik, shouts for him like mad, but he cannot find him. The huts have been hit by several bombs; there are numerous dead and wounded. Nobody knows where Hendrik Beukema is. And nobody cares. Cordes would continue to look for him throughout the night and the better part of the following day, until he breaks down, completely worn out. He is taken to some relatives on the mainland at the first opportunity. His daughter he will never see again.

HENDRIK, TOO, ACTS LIKE a madman. "Repeat message on Thursday, same time!"—they knew it all the time, those pigs, and they didn't give a damn that the island was brimming with civilians and workers from abroad, one of them their own agent! All pointless. No elegant raid, no fighting with rapier but with a sledgehammer. Flatten it all totally. And then perhaps a report about the results. So many guns destroyed, so many bunkers wrecked. But spare us the details of the women and children torn to pieces or buried alive.

In the village they dig for survivors with bare hands. Hendrik makes himself useful. He is strong. He manages to clear the entrance to the cellar of a destroyed house. Now he can hear the wailing from down there. Blindly he thrusts forward. He cannot escape the falling beam. Helping hands drag him out of the rubble. Alive, but with his leg broken, over and out. Nothing to be done about it. He has to seek treatment in the field hospital. That saves his life for today.

While they are carrying him away he hears the guns of Neude-
ich battery firing at aircraft. Amazed, he realizes that it gives him
satisfaction. With regard to the military situation, the air raid was
a failure. "Fortress Wangerooge" still exists.

THE NEXT DAY ALL heavy guns are back and ready for action. But
there is no more action. The island is handed over to the Allies without a fight after the end of the war. Not by Fersenburg, however. He
died in the rubble of the headquarters, one of approximately three
hundred casualties of the air raid—half of them foreign workers.

Hendrik has to stay at the field hospital, his leg in plaster. Someone gave him flowers to thank him for his efforts in rescuing his
family. He had forced a smile and at the same time gritted his teeth
on considering the gruesome double role he had played in that
event. He had intended to save lives, not to destroy them. Now he
has to ask himself if he did not bring death over the island instead.

He cannot know that the planned landing on Wangerooge had
been abandoned weeks ago. The island had seemed too strong.
Hendrik's long-prepared mission had become useless.

THROUGH THE FOLLOWING DAYS Hendrik lives as if in a trance. Three
days after capitulation Canadian troops come to Wangerooge. The
Wehrmacht is disarmed; the Nazis will be dismissed. There is
nobody here anymore who might be interested in prosecuting an
allied spy. It is all over.

The foreigners are free to leave the island. Hendrik stands at the
stern of the *Joanna* and watches the distance between him and the
island grow. Sea gulls screech and glide slowly past. In vain, the food
they hope for is not provided. Hendrik is oblivious to the birds. He is
absorbed in thinking about Gerda. Nobody told him that she is dead.
He will never know.

Hendrik does not hear the men murmuring behind him. They
are going home, at last! But the voices behind him get more agitated.

Hendrik starts when someone shouts, "Traitor, overboard!" It is Piet, the ex-NSB man, who probably wants to gain some points. Hendrik turns around, tries to evade the attack—too late. Strong fists get hold of him and push him against the railing. In vain he beseeches the men to listen. He is an officer, an allied secret agent, can't they grasp that? He cannot prove it now, but nobody is listening anyway.

"Stop this nonsense!" he shouts, now in panic, and he hits out, but they are too many. He can taste blood on his lips, his own blood, and then he goes down. As they heave him over the rail he thinks for a moment that he might reach the island by swimming, it is no more than a kilometer away. But he is not a good swimmer, the fight has weakened him, and his plastered leg drags him down. His corpse will later be washed ashore and buried on Wangerooge.

THE JOANNA IS HEADING for Delfzijl. Piet has rid himself of his past, at last. Nobody can call him a goon of the Nazis anymore. He can relax.

The voyage drags along for more than a day. When eventually the Dutch coast comes into sight, almost all the men are sleeping below deck. That is when the Joanna hits a drifting mine in the Ems estuary. She sinks instantly. Although other boats are nearby, only seven men are rescued, twenty-seven drown. One of them is Piet.

ALL THIS IS LONG forgotten. There are no guns on Wangerooge anymore. In case you are planning to spend your holidays there, you will certainly enjoy the imposing North Sea coastal landscape. The salt marshes are turned into bird sanctuaries and part of the new Wadden Sea National Park. The dunes are covered in grass and buckthorn. In this charming landscape here and there you will come across small depressions and ponds, very picturesque, some partly covered with sedges and rushes. Most of the ponds are rather small and quite circular.

Wangeroog, the pearl . . .

What You Don't Know

STUART M. KAMINSKY

P ACKNER HAD NEVER SLEPT in a more comfortable bed. And the view from the windows leading out to the small balcony was overwhelmingly beautiful—the line of snow-covered mountains in the not-very-great distance, the valley of white dotted with chalets and the small, ancient town with its houses huddled in the middle. The inn sat on a hill high over the valley and since the snow and weather were perfect for skiing, all thirty-five rooms were occupied.

It was an ideal location for what Packner had to do today. His name was not really Packner. He had used many names.

He slept in a pair of orange-and-blue University of Illinois shorts and no shirt. He slept with his own portable lock on the door. He slept with a Charter Arms .38 Undercover Blue Revolver on the nightstand within very easy reach. Others in his profession would have thought this a particularly inefficient weapon given the options, but Packner had shot his first man—actually a woman—with such a weapon. It was almost like sleeping with a comforting stuffed animal nearby.

For the work he had to do in the morning, however, he had brought a new .40 Smith & Wesson with a ten-shot magazine. The weapon was small, easy to hide, with only a three-and-a-half-inch barrel, and it had little recoil. Modification to almost completely silence the weapon had been difficult and expensive, but Packner would have paid far more for an efficient, reasonably quiet weapon like this that would fit easily into a pocket or a hiding place.

Packner always awoke twice during the night, at 2:10 and 4:13 or within seconds of those times. It had come naturally. At those two times he surveyed the room he happened to be in and, if something seemed wrong, he arose, took his weapon, and found somewhere else to sleep, somewhere in a dark corner he had picked out when he had first entered the room. Whether the room was in a hotel, a home, or in a supposedly "safe" house, the procedure was the same.

Every morning he awoke at 6:15, showered, shampooed, shaved, and put on the clothes he had selected the night before. He had become an expert at packing during the twenty-six years he had been on the move. Packner maintained an apartment nowhere. Whatever he needed, he bought, and except for very infrequent and carefully arranged visits he stayed away from home. He always gave his shoes and clothing to the Salvation Army when he was through with them. He saved nothing.

Packner's face had changed as he grew older. It had also changed twice as a result of plastic surgery. The face in the mirror had been his for seven years. He rather liked it. It was a ruggedly handsome face, the face of a former athlete with neatly trimmed auburn hair. It was the last face he planned to have. In his infrequent returns home, his father had eventually grown to accept the new image of his son.

Shaved and showered now, Packner put on his black chino slacks and black turtleneck cotton shirt. Over that he put his black sport jacket. On his feet were black cotton socks and black Rockport shoes. He thought he looked every inch the well-dressed spy.

Packner put the .38 in the holster under his jacket. He was ready to go, to face what promised to be the most interesting morning of his life.

He removed his lock from the door and put it in a drawer. He did not bother to use any of the elaborate electronic devices to check on whether anyone entered his room while he was out. The people he was dealing with would know how to bypass all of them. Instead, he used the simplest of all detection devices, a hair from his own head, loosely attached to the door. If anyone entered, the hair would fall. Even if the intruder knew about the hair, he or she would not know how high or low he had fixed it to the door.

He did not expect anyone to enter his room. He was dealing with other professionals who would know that he would leave nothing that would be of use to them.

Packner placed the hair, closed the door very gently, and put the "Do Not Disturb" sign on the door. Then he went down to the dining room for breakfast. The view from there was every bit as beautiful as from his room.

There were fifteen people having breakfast when he arrived. The sun was bright and the vacationers looked ready for a day of skiing. Packner could ski quite well. It was not something he was interested in doing recreationally.

He found a table for two in the rear of the room, ignored the chat around him, and ordered coffee, three pieces of toast with jam, and a bowl of fruit, making clear to the waiter that he wanted only fresh fruit even if that meant he would have only a bowl of sliced oranges. There was a basket of fresh breakfast rolls on the table, along with a plate with pats of butter and a white porcelain container of orange marmalade.

There were men, women, many languages. If he wished, he could focus on any of the nearby tables and hear what they were saying. He had no interest in doing so. Packner looked out the window and nibbled at a piece of breakfast roll he had torn off.

"I hate Switzerland," came the voice. "May I join you?"

"Of course," said Packner.

The woman sat across from him. Though he saw her rarely, the woman currently known as Sandra Freid was, as always, perfectly groomed, perfectly understated in her dress. She was nearing fifty but could easily pass for forty or less and she was darkly handsome. She wore a gray knit dress that fit her perfect body snugly. Over the dress, she wore a black designer jacket that nearly matched Packner's. Her hair was cut quite short, almost boyish, and she wore a necklace of large, perfectly matched black pearls and matching earrings.

"What are you eating?" she asked in English.

"Simple fare," he said, smiling with white capped teeth.

He motioned for the waiter, who came immediately.

"I'll have what he is having," she said.

The waiter nodded and hurried away.

"Why do you hate Switzerland?" he asked.

"How much can one ski? How much chocolate can one eat? How much courtesy and politeness can one stand?"

"It is peaceful," he said, looking out the window.

"On the surface. Look out the window. It's a postcard for tourists. And this hotel."

"Chateau," said Packner. "Or inn, if you prefer."

"Chateau Yodel," she said sarcastically, shaking her head. "These people have no history of warfare, and their army knives are known throughout the world. They are an eternally neutral nation that makes deals with monsters and engages people in our profession when it suits them. Money."

"And chocolate."

"And cough drops," she said, allowing herself a smile.

"Knives, cough drops, chocolate, and banks, all essentials of civilized humanity," he said, wiping crumbs from his fingers and putting his napkin in his lap. "They have, I have reason to believe, produced several very capable people in our profession. Thank you for coming."

"You are welcome," she said, her eyes on him, her smile apparently sincere. "Not that I had a choice."

"There are always choices," he said, looking at her.

"Not always viable ones. The others—do they have viable options I don't know about?"

"You know about the others," he said, not in the least surprised.

"I saw Tain and the big one who used to be called Montrose in the lobby when they checked in last night," she said as the food came to the table. The fruit cups included strawberries, pineapple, and blood oranges. They were fresh.

"And they saw you?" Packner asked, casually putting the grape jam he had been brought on a slice of toast.

"I wanted them to see me," she said as she lifted her delicate cup of coffee. "I assume they know as little about this as I do. I thought it was a good idea to suggest to them that I was comfortable with being seen."

"Yes," said Packner, eating slowly. "You know the room number where we will be meeting?"

"I was hoping that we would go together now after breakfast."

"Of course," he said.

"Do *you* know why we are here?" she asked, lifting a spoonful of fruit to her mouth.

"Yes," he said.

She nodded. She knew that if he wished to tell her what he knew, Packner would do so. If he did not, there was no point in asking him.

"The big man is using the name Alex Korchinski," said Packner. "Tain is still David Tain."

"And you are . . . ?"

"Still Packner, at least until we leave here."

They finished at a leisurely pace, cautiously discussing nothing. He signed the bill. She let Packner do so. It was a small matter. A big matter was obviously coming up. The woman called Sandra Freid refrained from walking too closely to Packner. That was not the role to play. It might make Tain and Korchinski suspicious should they see her coming through the door or walking down the corridor on

Packner's arm. The room itself was isolated from the rest of the inn down a corridor with no rooms on either side leading to two doors. Packner reached for the handle of the door on the left.

The meeting room that he had reserved was, as Packner had ordered, stripped down to a small, drawerless table and chair against each wall. The chairs faced the center of the room where a round wooden table rested. Atop the round table was a large wooden box with no top. A ceiling-to-floor window stood behind one of the chairs and tables. The curtain was drawn. Some sunlight came through and the overhead chandelier gave off ample supporting light.

Tain was seated behind one of the tables, the one opposite the curtained window. He wore a dark suit and conservative tie. His glasses had rectangular lenses with gold frames. Tain's mother was Swedish. His father was Chinese. At thirty-five, he was the youngest person in the room and would be taken as oldest by anyone who chanced to see them. He looked like a businessman, which was what he wished to look like. Before him on his table was a black briefcase.

"Tain," said Packner as he and the woman entered the room. "It's been a while."

Tain nodded at Sandra Freid. They had met four times in the past. Three of those times neither had acknowledged that they knew the other. On the fourth occasion they had joined to assassinate a Serbian general turned negotiator in Amsterdam.

"Two years and a month," said Tain.

"Ah, the rejected lover recalling each anguished day," she said.

Tain did not answer. All three knew that any relationship between those in their work had to be kept professional.

"You know what this is all about?" Tain asked.

"I know," said Packner, taking the chair and table with the window behind him.

Sandra Freid sat at the table to his right with the door a few paces behind her.

"You've checked the room?" Packner said.

"Yes," said Tain. "I believe we will not be overheard, but, as you know, it is impossible to be certain. If one has the proper electronic equipment . . ."

"They could probably point it in our direction from Geneva and pick up every word," said Freid.

Packner looked at his watch. It was two minutes after the designated time for this meeting.

The door opened and the man who filled the doorway looked around at the seated three and the only seat remaining. The big man wore a tailor-made navy blue suit and a white shirt with no tie. His face was unlined and youthful. His hair was gray and cut very short.

The only sign of caution was in his eyes. His face revealed nothing.

"Sorry I'm late," he said in French, not bothering to exchange polite greetings with the others.

"Apology accepted," said Packner, who had expected Korchinski to arrive even later. It probably meant that he had searched one of their rooms before coming to the gathering. It was Korchinski's way.

The big man moved to the only remaining seat.

"First," said Packner, "is English acceptable?"

No one objected.

"Second, no weapons. Weapons go in the box on that table. All of them—and Mr. Tain's briefcase."

There was a long silence as Packner rose, went to the center of the room, and placed his .38 in the box, then sat and folded his arms. Sandra Freid moved next, lifting her dress and removing a small .22 strapped between her legs.

"Why?" asked Tain.

"I'll tell you when all weapons are on the table," said Packner.

Tain looked at Korchinski, who was staring at Packner.

"Why are you in charge?" asked Korchinski, his voice a pleasant baritone.

Normally, Korchinski played the laborer, the farmer, the fool, though he had a doctorate in Romance languages and literature from

Brown University and a very private passion for the work of Proust.

"When the weapons are in the center of the room," said Packner pleasantly.

Tain and Korchinski rose together.

"The weapon you're carrying and don't forget the briefcase," said Packner.

Tain nodded and took his briefcase to the center of the room, placing it carefully on the table with his pistol on top of it. Korchinski placed his Magnum next to the briefcase and both men went back to their seats.

"Tain, do you have any objection to Korchinski opening the briefcase?"

"None."

Korchinski opened the briefcase, examined it, closed it and announced, "A few papers."

"Now," said Packner as Korchinski closed the briefcase and returned to his place, "your other weapons. We will search each other."

No one objected.

"To our right," Packner went on.

"To our left would be much better," said Tain.

Packner understood. If Packner were working with Korchinski, the big man might allow Packner to keep a weapon.

Similarly, if Packner were working with Freid, he might allow her to retain a weapon. A change in direction for the search was prudent.

"Fine," said Packner. "May I suggest we begin with a look under Mr. Tain's table."

Tain smiled, reached under the table and pulled out a pistol taped within his easy reach. It had been the real reason he had arrived early for the meeting.

"Anyone else wish to volunteer a weapon before being searched?" asked Packner.

All four in the room produced knives. Korchinski produced another pistol, a very small .22.

The search went quickly, efficiently. Musical chairs. When Sandra searched Packner, she paused between his legs. It was effective though brief. Packner then searched Korchinski, who looked at the ceiling and said nothing.

Two more knives were found. No weapons. The pile in the center of the room was now worth several thousand dollars to any arms dealer. Modifications and weapons were state of the art.

"One more search," said Tain, "of the person across from us."

Following this search, Packner sat and said, "Our Greek and Italian contacts wanted us to meet. You all know that the Kadara was shot two weeks ago."

None of the other three bothered to acknowledge that they knew. Besides, the question was clearly rhetorical.

"Supposedly, he was shot by a Kurd terrorist," said Packner. "But one of us knows that he was not."

"One of us killed the Turk?" asked Korchinski.

"There can be no doubt," said Packner. "He was killed at Yalu Bai Leef. The Kurds could not know he would be there. We knew. We knew he was there to eliminate the Turkish prime minister. We knew he had been hired by the Iranians. We knew because we were all told to stay away from Yalu Bai Leef on Monday and if any of our clients wanted us there we were to refuse the assignment."

"So," said Tain, "Lahn-Ho, North, and Martino also knew. Where are they?"

"Dead," said Packner.

He paused so the others could absorb the information.

"You have answers to the obvious questions?" asked Sandra.

Packner shrugged.

"They were killed during the past month. Professionally, very professionally. The reason may have been revenge, to eliminate competition, because the four of us and the four dead might discover something that would mean the end for one of us. Maybe all of us."

"So," said Tain. "You surmise that one of us eliminated these people and plans to eliminate others in this room?"

"Yes," said Packner. "Which is why I wanted the weapons in the center of the room. When we discover who our killer is, the three of us remaining can overpower him or her and . . ."

"The evidence is weak," said Korchinski.

"Lord, yes. Very," Packner agreed. "But there is one more thing. Our Greek contact saw it. It may be a coincidence. Our four dead fellow eliminators died in reverse alphabetical order, N, M, L, K."

"Silly," said Freid. "Coincidence."

"Those of us in this room have last names beginning G, H, I, and J," said Packner. "Our real names. Our Greek contact believes our killer knew this, saw the coincidence of last names, and whimsically decided to eliminate in reverse alphabetical order, which means I am to be next."

"I see," said Freid. "If we had our weapons, the killer could simply shoot the rest of us right now."

"Or one who is not the killer could shoot the others to protect himself," said Korchinski.

"But that would leave the impression that the survivor is the renegade," said Tain. "The Greeks and Italians would mark him for elimination."

"I would guess," said Packner, "the killer has a plan to eliminate all of us and come out covered by a story."

"I can think of several scenarios," said Korchinski. "None of which I wish to share."

"Seven of us would then be dead in a period of a little over a month," said Tain.

"Each of us has eliminated far more in our careers," said Packner.

"All right," said Korchinski. "We are here. How do we identify the betrayer?"

"I suggest," said Packner, "that each of us provide what they call an 'alibi' in America. Where were we a week ago on Monday when Kadara was killed, and can we prove it?"

There was a knock at the door. No one rose ready to leap for their weapons. If someone wanted to dispose of them, they would not be knocking.

"*Entrer*," called Packner and the door opened.

A thin, almost completely bald man with a pink face, a little mustache, and a waiter's uniform entered balancing a tray in one hand.

"*Kaffe*," said the waiter professionally, ignoring the seating arrangement and the box in the middle of the room.

"*Danke*," said Packner.

Conversation ceased while the waiter, who looked at least seventy, went from table to table offering coffee and providing milk and sugar for those who wished them. He put the two-liter pot on a trivet on the table in front of Packner and left the room.

Eyes were on Packner, waiting to see if he would drink. Packner smiled.

"Any one of us could have gotten to the waiter," he said. "I didn't order coffee, but I understand it is a regular courtesy here for business meetings."

He drank. His coffee was steaming and black. The others also worked at their drinks as Packner said, "Alibis. Alibis. Alibis. I'll begin. A week ago on Monday I was in Hong Kong to discuss an assignment for a former member of the old colonial government. I did not meet with the former member of the government but with four of his representatives, all of whom are known to you. I will provide their names and each of you is free to contact all of them or whichever ones you choose."

"It compromises your relationship with them if we contact them," said Sandra.

"Can't be helped," said Packner. "This is too important. Not only is one of us trying to kill the others, but if we fail to find out who, it will certainly result in the Italians and Greeks deciding to eliminate all four of us to be safe. Ours is not an easy profession and it is getting harder by the week. Alibis anyone?"

"I was with a friend in Rome," said Sandra. "A male friend. We had spent the weekend together at a small hotel behind the Piazza De Poppolo in the direction of the Spanish Steps. The one across from the Lion Book Store."

"The one that used to be a whorehouse," Packner said. "Thin walls."

"I can provide his name and that of a mutual friend who joined us. You will find their corroboration unimpeachable when I tell you who they are, which I want to consider for a while."

"A short while," said Packner.

"Of course," she said, picking up her coffee cup.

"I was in a city I do not wish to name," said Tain. "I also have two witnesses who can verify that I was there all day Monday."

"And you will give us the names of these two?" asked Packner amiably.

"Like our Miss Freid, I will consider it and provide the name of the city and the two people after I consider how to do so without compromising them. I think you will find them acceptable."

"That leaves . . . ," Packner began.

"I was in a meeting in the morning," said Korchinski. "One of our occasional clients in the French government. There were others present. I had lunch with them in the room where we met. Names and location of the meeting will be provided when I know it is essential."

Packner shook his head.

"It doesn't surprise me that we all have alibis and witnesses to support them," he said. "One will, however, fall after examination."

"Maybe not," said Tain. "The people vouching for any of us could be people who hired us to dispose of Kadara."

"Complicating things even further," said Sandra Freid as she finished the coffee in her cup. "Add coffee to that list of Swiss specialties I gave you at breakfast. It's very good. I think there's a drop of chocolate in it, though. Maybe more than a drop."

"Ideas anyone?" said Packner.

There was no answer.

"Well, I don't care for the idea that we might leave this room," he said, "and try to kill each other."

"It would be very odd if you did. The best of us might succeed," said Tain.

"Or the luckiest," said Korchinski.

"Well," said Sandra Freid, "this has been interesting, but I think all four of us know who killed Kadara."

"Enlighten me," said Packner.

"Why, you did," she said, looking at Packner and smiling.

"Ah," said Packner, sitting back. "And how did you come to this conclusion?"

Korchinski and Tain were listening carefully, their eyes aimed at Packner.

"Putting our weapons in the center of the room was your idea and a rather odd one," she said.

"But effective," said Packner.

"This room was your choice," she said. "You could have planted a weapon here."

"Tain searched the room before we got here," said Packner. "And found . . ."

"Nothing," said Tain.

"I'm sure you could find a way, especially if you assumed that one of us might be searching this room," she said to Packner. "You are a professional."

"Thank you," said Packner. "Go on."

"You would know that given our choice of seats," she continued, "we would avoid the seat with the window to one's back. You chose the window seat. A bullet could easily come through the glass."

"Not to mention," added Tain, "that you are perfectly outlined against the light, an easy target."

"You knew you would get that seat," said Freid.

"Conclusion?" asked Packner.

"You have a weapon hidden there in case you are revealed as the betrayer or you decide to eliminate the three of us and go into hiding."

"Sandra," said Packner. "I don't think this is going to work. Convince the others, get rid of me, and walk away from what you did, is that the plan?"

"Another problem," said Korchinski. "You gave us that ridiculous story about eliminating those in our profession in reverse alphabetical order. At least two on your list do not have real last names with the letters you indicated."

"I see," said Packner. "Might one reasonably assume that you might be lying and have no such information about real last names, that you have simply leaped behind the tumbrel that is being constructed for me, that when we leave this room we will find that I am right about the names and that your alibi does not hold?"

"It holds," said Tain. "Korchinski was with me a week ago on Monday. As was Miss Freid. Actually, we were together in Paris the entire week before and the day after when we heard of Kadara's elimination."

"A coincidence?" asked Packner, shaking his head. "A *ménage à trois* coincidence? You've gotten together and decided to give me to the pack and, may I guess, you've also agreed that when I am eliminated our fellow professionals will stop, secure that their safety is ensured by the elimination of the renegade assassin. Any more deaths of any of you and those for whom we work will know that the assassin has not been caught. Your safety would depend on the killings ceasing. If we were ever to hold a convention, it should have been last year. It seems we may be down to very few members before the morning ends."

"No," said Tain. "We each suspected you and got together to wait for you to strike again, which would prove that we were not responsible and that you were."

"You gathered us not to find the killer," said Korchinski, "but to find out what we might know and whom you might best blame."

"Those who spend their lives in conspiracy are the most likely to fall victim to conspiracy," said Packner, pouring himself more coffee. "Go on."

"There really isn't anywhere to go," said Tain as Packner shook his head and sat back, balanced on the two back legs of his chair.

His eyes turned to Korchinski, who had removed a gun from his jacket pocket. The gun was small. It was aimed at Packner, whose right hand slowly came up with the .40 Smith and Wesson that he had retrieved from under the wooden slat of the window ledge where he had placed it the night before. He had carefully, but loosely, placed the slat back so that he could tilt it up and get the Short Forty as he had just done.

Packner had never searched Korchinski. Sandra and Tain had and they had let him keep his gun.

"Impasse," said Packner, pointing his weapon at Korchinski.

"Actually, no," said Tain. "I placed my briefcase so that the left end would be facing you. Mr. Korchinski did not really search it. In the side of the case is a narrow, powerful fire projectile that will explode in flames on impact with you, the table, the window."

Packner was sure the man wasn't bluffing. Bluffing wouldn't work.

"Noise will activate the projectile," said Tain, anticipating Packner's next question. "A gunshot for example."

"I hate this technology," said Packner. "It removes so much of individual initiative from our work."

"Put your gun on the table," said Freid, "and you have a choice of accidents, skiing or climbing."

"I don't like skiing," said Packner, rising. "Someone might know. I may have mentioned it to the desk clerk when I checked in."

"Thank you," said Sandra.

"Glad to do your job for you," Packner said, rising slowly and moving as if to put his gun on the table.

They would not risk an accident scenario, Packner knew. He was too dangerous. But, they didn't want him shooting any of them.

Packner, sensing that Korchinski was about to fire, threw himself backward through the window holding his weapon tightly. Tangled in drapes, he hit the snow on his left side as the flames whooshed through the window over him. The room was on fire. Inside the room, they would be heading for the door now. He did not panic. Getting free of the drapes was not as much of a problem as it might have been. They had even protected him from the broken glass that he landed on.

He was on his feet now, knowing just what to do, just what he had planned to do should it come to this. They would be coming from both sides of the inn. They would probably leave one person in the room in case Packner tried to double back. They would come cautiously, knowing he had a weapon and used it brilliantly. Packner had a reputation. Unless he succeeded in his backup plan, that reputation and possibly his life were about to be lost.

His footprints in the snow would tell his pursuers which way he headed and they would be right behind him. Packner had no time to lay down false tracks. The slope he was on had no cover till the trees almost fifty yards away.

Another precaution Packner had taken for the morning's meeting was to have the window of the room next to the one from which he had just escaped left open. He knew there was nothing scheduled inside. Packner opened the window, climbed in, and moved toward the door to the corridor. There was no point in taking the time to lock the window behind him. His footprints in the snow would give him away. What he could do was remove his shoes.

He avoided the tables and chairs in the room, barely noticing the flip chart set up for a later meeting, and went through the door, closing it behind him.

Packner went back to the room he had leaped from, gun in one hand, shoes in the other. He put down the shoes and had to balance a need for silence with an even greater need to move quickly.

The door handle was not warm. The fire was not blazing out of control inside. He opened the door slowly, carefully trying to pick up some clue, some idea of whether someone was waiting for him and, if so, whether their attention was focused on the window.

Tain stood in the far corner, out of sight from the window but not the door. He was aiming at the window framed by burning drapes and smoldering wood. Hotel staff would be rushing in soon.

Packner fired twice. It was not totally silent but close enough. Tain turned away, his head resting for an instant in the corner as if he were a child being punished for unruly behavior, and then he slumped forward.

"Tain," Korchinski's voice came from outside the window. The drapes and the wooden frame were still blazing. Korchinski could not see in nor could Packner see out.

Packner considered answering, but he knew he could not fool Korchinski. He slipped into his shoes without tying them as Korchinski repeated louder than before, "Tain."

If he weren't suspicious already, he would be in seconds. Where was the woman? Were they both outside?

Packner ran toward the window and, for the second time in five minutes, leaped out, this time through a frame of fire.

He fired at the figure he sensed to his right and rolled over in the snow. There was a return shot, but it was four or five feet off. He must have hit Korchinski. On his stomach now, Packner fired four rapid rounds in the direction of the figure he had seen. He was only able to see what he was shooting at after the fourth shot.

Korchinski was on his knees, one hand holding his gun, the other clutching his bleeding neck. The big man tried to level his gun at Packner but he was gasping for breath and his hand was shaking. Packner considered firing again, but decided that it wasn't necessary. The big man fell forward on his face into the snow.

Where was the woman?

Packner scanned the area, sitting up as he did so. She wasn't in sight. He checked the windows of the inn, including the one still burning. Nothing. He expected nothing. Had she been there, he would be dead.

Voices from inside the burning room. They were speaking German and they had discovered the obvious, the fire and Tain's body.

Packner ran to Korchinski's body, took the gun from the dead man's hand, and replaced it with his own gun. If they checked, which he doubted they would, the local police might conclude that the dead man was responsible for Tain's death. What they might have a problem with was how Korchinski could have shot himself in the throat. By then, however, Packner would be safe.

Packner went back through the open window in the room next to that in which Tain lay dead and the voices in German grew frantic.

Seated in a chair in the far right corner was Sandra Freid, her weapon leveled at Packner, who stopped.

"You've been very busy," she said calmly.

"May I sit?"

"I don't think you'll have time for that," she said. "You are a very dangerous man."

"Give me a minute, no more, to speak," he said, every bit as calm as she was.

"One minute," she said. "You come to military attention and remain so. Any movement and . . ."

"The English hired me to kill Kadara," he said, "not the Iranians or the Iraqis. Kadara had been in London the week before and killed an English foreign diplomat. It was all very secret. The network didn't know. As for the others, I didn't kill them. I was in fact hired by the Greeks and Italians to find out who it was as I said, to find out who and to eliminate them."

"I believe you," she said. "The problem is that it doesn't make any difference. I'm the person you were looking for. I killed K, L, M, and N."

Packner laughed.

"Amusing?"

"Does it strike you that our small world is as mad as the world of the people who hire us and the world as a whole?"

"It strikes me," she said. "Your minute is up. If you plan to attempt to dive out of the window or run for the door or . . . you know the possibilities. Do it now."

Her weapon came up. She held it in two hands, arms extended.

Packner made the slightest of moves in the direction of the window and then dropped to the floor. Her gun was neither silenced nor muted. The people in the burning room heard it. One man was already dead. There had been shots fired outside; they had, perhaps, already discovered Korchinski's body. None of the four men were terribly interested in finding out who was firing these new shots. All three had a good idea that it was whoever had killed the man in the corner.

THE POLICEMAN WAS SIXTY-ONE years old. There had been only one murder in the thirty-five years he had been in the town and certainly nothing like this. The policeman had a small belly and though there was no rule that said he had to wear his uniform, Kurt Menges always did so while on duty.

"And that is what happened?" asked the policeman. "Everything?"

They were in the small chalet of the waiter who had served coffee to the four people in the inn. His name was Frederick. He did not mention the guns and briefcase in the box in the middle of the room.

Frederick had worked all of the night before. His last duty before going home had been to serve the coffee. This morning he had described the four people in the room. The policeman already knew that the dead had been registered guests and a check of their rooms revealed identification cards and passports under various names and countries. Menges would turn over everything he knew and had to the national police or security, whoever came first. He would be happy to be rid of it. Thank God, none of the dead or the missing survivor and probable murderer were citizens of this town.

A door opened and a man in a shabby suit came out.

"My son," said Frederick, "Wilhelm. He came about a month ago. I'm very proud of him. He has been saving his money for many years and, keep this a secret, he plans to buy the hotel from Dorfmann."

The man was bald like his father and even had a small mustache like his father. The similarity was unmistakable.

"I think I remember him from his last visit," said Menges.

"Pleased to see you again," Wilhelm said in German.

"And you," said Menges. "Sorry it is under these circumstances."

"Can't be helped," said Wilhelm.

"I suggest you move fast on the hotel," said Menges. "Offer a down payment. Dorfmann has been talking about selling for years. With three murders in one day, he may be ready to sell very reasonably."

"That is good advice, Wilhelm," said the waiter.

"Well," said the policeman with a sigh to indicate that his work was far from done, "I've talked to everyone at the hotel. I hope they don't ask me to talk to everyone in town. My guess is that our killer skied out out through one of the passes and is in Zurich by now."

The policeman got up and added, "I will see you when this is over. We can have a few beers and not talk. I am tired of talk. I don't ski anymore myself, but if your son wishes . . ."

"I don't ski," said the younger man. "But I have always enjoyed my visits and I look forward to finding a nice woman and making this my permanent home."

Tooth Marks

BOB MENDES

THE MALAYSIA AIRLINES JUMBO JET, destination Singapore, taxied toward the concrete ramp the size of a football field, then stopped and just sat there. Mike Burke was seated on the left row of seats, wedged between a large, round-faced Thai woman who kept nibbling nuts and an even larger Chinese man with rasping breath who was hogging the armrest. It seemed likely it was going to be an uncomfortable flight, but Burke resigned himself to his fate. A new life awaited him in Singapore.

Fifteen minutes later, the plane hadn't moved. Although the captain had made an announcement about having to wait their turn on account of the rush hour, Burke had seen several planes take off with a later departure time than theirs. He wondered what was going on.

Then the woman in the window seat leaned back a little and, peering under her double chin, he saw a mobile stairway being driven to the plane and positioned by the front cabin door. A moment later a stretch Mercedes drove onto the tarmac and moored alongside the stairway like a silver ocean liner. One of the ground crew rushed forward to hold the door open. A slim, middle-aged man wearing a navy blue blazer got out of the car. He had blond hair streaked with gray and eyes as expressionless as striped marble—the prototype of an English person of property. The much younger woman who got out after him wore a fur coat, and the diamonds in her earrings sparkled in the late afternoon sun. Burke leaned forward to see her face but the woman next to him did the same, blocking his view.

Burke leaned back and closed his eyes. Only a wealthy Englishman was arrogant enough to have a jumbo jet with a few hundred passengers and the entire crew on board wait for him for more than fifteen minutes. The woman appeared, somehow, to be of a different stamp. Her manner was artless, like Kelly's. Although he'd only caught a glimpse of her, she reminded him of Kelly.

FOR THREE DAYS NOW Burke had been staying at the Liverpool Court on Chapel Street. A good hotel with 226 rooms containing original oil paintings and Victorian furniture. But to Kelly Donegal, the woman head porter, he had still been the man in 509, a hotel guest who paid with an American Express card and didn't cause any trouble. Fred Cowes, Burke's superior at G5, decided it was time to get things moving a little.

On the morning of his fourth day, Kelly had asked him to step into her office for a moment. She had shown him a telex from American Express that said that they were canceling Michael Burke's credit card, and then she asked him how long he was planning to stay at the hotel. "I don't know exactly," Burke answered. "I'm negotiating with the local museums about the purchase of some paintings. You see, I . . ."

She was immediately on guard. "Are you an artist?" she asked and scrutinized his shirt and cuticles.

He smiled and shook his head. "No, the paintings are by Ian Slane. Slane was my best friend. He died three months ago in a bombing, in Belfast."

She touched a couple of keys on her computer. "I've read something in the paper about it," she muttered.

"Slane was an important painter, Ms. Donegal. Very popular in Ireland." Slane had been one of Sinn Fein's key figures, but Kelly Donegal probably knew more about that than he did.

She frowned. "Didn't I read something about all his paintings being destroyed in the blast?"

Burke nodded. "That's right. But these are paintings he gave to me and some other friends as presents. We're now trying to sell them for the benefit of his wife and children."

Kelly Donegal's expression softened. Still holding the telex, she was studying his bill on the computer screen. Burke had had very few extras, no expensive phone calls to the mainland, no bills for elaborate meals at the restaurant. This visibly reassured her. "Your work deserves the highest praise, Mr. Burke; but if you wish to stay without a credit card, I'll be obliged to ask you for payment in advance."

"That's a bit of a problem at the moment," Burke answered, frowning. His face lit up. "But if you like I could give you one of the paintings as security. They're worth quite a bit."

She looked over his shoulder at a somber canvas by Ernst Fuchs.

"An Ian Slane would actually look quite nice here. Where can I see the paintings?"

"In my room."

"Very well. I'll be there at eight-thirty, to look at the paintings."

She looked him straight in the eye and from that moment on he ceased to be the man in room 509 to her and became Mike Burke.

THE CABIN DOOR WAS slammed shut. Burke opened his eyes. Through a small gap between the curtains that were supposed to protect the first-class passengers from the glances of ordinary folk, he saw the wealthy Englishman ascend the stairs to the upper deck. He was followed by a flight attendant carrying the fur coat belonging to his wife or mistress across her arm. The very moment the woman herself passed it, someone closed the curtain. Burke sat up with a jerk. The woman resembled Kelly Donegal in the same way Castor resembled Pollux in the Gemini sign of the zodiac. But it couldn't be, for, after all, Kelly was dead.

SHE KNEW RIGHT AWAY which painting she wanted, an Irish fishing village with powerful contrasts. While he elaborated on the painting, she drank white wine, taking small sips. There was a faint smile on her lips as she slowly looked him over from head to toe. But when he got a little too close in the vehemence of his story, she set down her glass.

"Let's get out of here," she said. "I'd like a beer."

She took him to a pub on Lime Street with stained-glass partitions and "snob screens" that ensured that the bar staff couldn't listen in on their conversation. They drank Harp beer and as soon as they'd settled on a price for the painting they moved from the big bar, which was very busy, to the small, intimate one in the back. It was nice and dark and an old man was playing tunes from the war years on a piano. They switched to Jameson Irish Whiskey and stood close enough to each other to feel each other's body heat. Later that night—they'd both had a few—he referred to Northern Ireland as the Six Counties while Kelly only referred to Northern Ireland, so they both knew where they were. But that was all Kelly divulged about herself. Alcohol had no effect on her.

At eleven-thirty they left the pub together. In the taxi she looked at him sideways; there was that faint smile on her lips again. "Are you married?"

He shrugged his shoulders. "With the kind of work I do . . ."

She put a hand on his knee. "I understand, Mike."

Maybe she expected him to kiss her, but he just put his hand over hers and held it there. The man of *Psychological Approach* had told him she was like a dormant volcano. *Approach with caution.*

Some time later he asked: "What about the room?"

"I'll take care of it," she answered.

THE LIGHTS WERE DIMMED and most of the passengers were asleep, including the fat Chinese who was unashamedly using Burke's shoulder as a pillow. Burke had withdrawn as far as possible to the other side, which earned him a few angry looks from the woman by the window. He closed his eyes and was trying to imagine what his life would be like in Singapore, when a flight attendant tapped his shoulder. "I have a better seat for you up front, sir," she whispered.

He wormed his way to the aisle with great difficulty and followed her past the curtain, into a world of luxury. The flight attendant pointed to the wide, comfortable double chairs in the back row, which were vacant. "You can sit over there, Mr. Burke. Can I get you anything? A drink perhaps, or something to eat?"

"A whiskey please."

"Coming right up." The flight attendant tried to go but Burke blocked her path.

"Would you tell me to what I owe this honor?"

"It happens sometimes, sir. If a passenger is bothered by . . ."

"There was a fellow behind me who was well over six feet tall, sitting with his knees pulled up under his chin for lack of leg room. Are you going to offer him a seat in first class as well?"

The flight attendant's face went red. "I'm sorry, sir, of course we can't do that."

"Then why me?"

The flight attendant glanced toward the stairs just long enough to give herself away. "Perhaps there is someone on board who likes you a lot, sir." With a swift movement, she pushed past Burke and disappeared into the galley.

Burke sank into the window seat. Pensively, he moved his hand across the expensive velvet seat cover, the broad armrest between the seats. A first-class ticket cost ten times as much as one in economy. He didn't know anyone who liked him enough to even buy him a ticket on the London Underground. At the gate he'd made sure everyone else went in ahead of him and he was almost positive that there was no one on board he knew, or who knew him. There was that woman who looked like Kelly, of course. A twin sister? No. Kelly had been screened. She didn't have a sister, only a brother. And he was dead too. Even if Kelly were alive she would probably rather open a cabin door and kick him out than offer him a first-class ticket.

THERE WERE A NUMBER of small apartments intended for resident personnel on the top floor of the Liverpool Court Hotel, but they were barely in use at the time. Kelly let him have an apartment not thirty feet from her own, registering him as a decorator who was designing a new interior for the top floor and who was being given a free room as part of his payment.

Kelly helped him move his stuff into the new room. All his clothes, socks, underwear were unfolded, smoothed out, and neatly tidied away in the closet—Burke let her. To show he had nothing to hide, he put the contents of his toiletry kit on the sink in the bathroom. When, at some point, he came out of the bathroom she was shamelessly reading a letter she had found in his anorak.

"Who is Kay Parker?" she asked. "Your girlfriend? Or are you married after all."

"Kay Parker is a code name," he said.

"Giving access to what?"

"Not what. To whom. Anyone who knows the code, knows who it's about."

She returned his glance unmoved. "It doesn't mean anything to me." Again, there was that little smile on her lips, which held both a promise and a threat. "But it sounds exciting."

She dropped the letter on the bed and left the room.

He felt sure she would be back soon. She would ask Sinn Fein about him and if they gave her the right answer, she would bring him into contact with her brother. He didn't even dare think about the alternative.

THE FLIGHT ATTENDANT PUT a glass and a 50 ml bottle of Jameson Irish Whiskey on the armrest next to him and a bowl of nuts to go with it. Burke wondered if she knew this was his regular drink. According to the price list, Malaysia Airways only served Scotch. He unscrewed the top and emptied the bottle into his glass.

In the early hours, just before first light, Kelly had returned. She had brought a bottle of Jameson and poured the Dublin-bottled whiskey into port glasses. After only one sip, she had set down her glass and slowly, carefully started to undress. While they were making love she acted as though she were trying to make up for years of abstinence, but they had to be quiet because the walls between the rooms were paper-thin. Whenever she was about to come, she pulled the pillow over her face to smother her cries of delight, or bit his shoulder, leaving her tooth marks. In the three days that followed, they made love every chance they got to be alone. Her way of doing it was addictive. On the third night she told him: "I'm vouching for you with my life. If you betray me, you'll die with me." On the fourth night she took him to see her brother, the brains behind the political wing of the Irish Republican Army.

She took very elaborate precautions to keep him from knowing the way to her brother. Via the fire escape she took him to the hotel's underground garage. There, they got into a small, closed Mr. Clean van, driven by a person with long, greasy hair. In the semidarkness it was impossible to tell whether the driver was male or female. They sat on wooden crates in the back of the van and at every turn they fell against each other until he put his arm around her shoulders and they braced themselves against the car's movements together. At the start of their journey they drove through a long tunnel, so he was sure they had crossed the Mersey in the direction of Birkenhead, but in the windowless cargo area of the van it didn't take long for him to lose all sense of direction. From pure nervousness he smoked one cigarette after another, but stopped when he saw that his pack was nearly empty. He needed cigarettes for the meeting. As the journey continued, his faith in G5's tracking technique and his chances of survival dwindled.

The journey ended the way it had started, in an underground garage. Kelly told him to stay put and got out. A moment later the back door opened and her brother hoisted himself into the van. He sat down on a crate opposite Burke, without shaking hands, and declined the cigarette Burke offered him. "I'd prefer it if you didn't smoke in this confined space," he said.

Burke, who already had his lighter in his hand, switched it on and off, at the same time pushing the little spring activating the miniature transmitter. He was afraid that, because of the amount of concrete surrounding them, it might not have the necessary range. If this were the case he was well and truly sunk. But for once G5 could be proud of themselves. Even before the talks had started in earnest the garage was flooded with the glare from the headlights of their anonymous cars tearing down the ramp.

THE WOMAN CAME DOWN the stairs. She had Kelly's long legs and proud hip movement. He kept looking straight ahead, even when she meticulously folded his summer jacket, which lay on the empty chair beside him, and put it in the overhead bin. She sat down beside him, and in spite of the smell of her subtle musky scent, he kept his eyes on the projection screen at the front of the first-class cabin, as if he hoped to find an explanation for her return from the dead in the silently moving images on the screen.

"Am I disturbing you?" Her voice was husky, but he couldn't make out whether this was caused by emotion or suppressed anger.

He gave up and looked at her. "You're alive?" It sounded stupid, but it was the only thing he could think of to say.

"Barely," she said. "And you? Don't you wake up all sweaty at night because you're responsible for my brother's death?"

"Sometimes." He drank the last of his whiskey. His hand was shaking a bit when he set down the empty glass.

"Listen, Kelly. I don't feel the need to grovel; I was a cop and doing my duty. It wasn't my fault that your brother resisted so much during his arrest."

"It wasn't an arrest, it was an execution."

She was right. The G5 snipers hadn't given her brother a chance. The moment he had stepped out of the van, on their orders, they had fired point-blank at the unarmed man from three sides. It had been sheer murder. Although Burke, as an undercover cop, had seen quite a lot, he had never gotten over this.

"Aren't you afraid of what the provisionals will do to you when they catch you?" she asked.

"You learn to live with fear," he said. "But living with a guilty conscience is harder."

"Are you sure you're not bothered by a false conscience, Burke?" There was no resentment left in her voice.

"No, Kelly. I quit when I heard you had died. Those three days together . . ."

"Three days could become an eternity."

What she said could be interpreted in a lot of ways but what she meant wasn't clear from the expression on her face. "And what about you, Kelly?" he asked. "Have you finished with them as well? The Englishman, is he . . . ?"

"He was a way out. He was a frequent guest at the hotel. We're lovers." She took his hand and held it to her mouth. "I had a choice, Burke. I could either join the revolutionaries and help track you down to quench my thirst for revenge. Or . . ."

"Or?"

She bit the ball of his thumb, leaving her tooth marks visible in the flesh. "Or have Charles offer you a job in Singapore, so I could have you all to myself."

His stomach felt queazy. "Do you mean that . . . that this meeting is no coincidence?"

"No," she said. "It's no coincidence. I've just played a little trick on fate, that's all."

He wanted to ask her a million questions. How did she find him? Who had died in her place, and what did she imagine their future in Singapore would be like. He coughed.

"Kelly, the Englishman, this Charles . . ."

Kelly silenced him with a wave of her hand. "Not now. I have to get back before Charles wakes up." She opened the crocodile skin handbag on her lap and took out a small box wrapped in tissue paper. "A present," she said. "So you'll remember me when you put some on in the morning." She placed the box in his hand.

For one moment he felt oddly moved. He cleared his throat. "But what about us? How do I find you in a big city like Singapore?"

She sat with her head cocked to one side, as though she were listening to the sound of the engines. Then she got up. "I'll find you." In a second she was gone.

He opened the box and took out a shiny black flask with a gold label. It was Xeryus by Givenchy, his favorite aftershave. He sat holding the flask for a long time, slowly coming to the conclusion that something wasn't right. "I'm vouching for you with my life," she had said. "If you betray me, you'll die with me." Was Kelly a forgiving person? Someone who gave presents to the man who had had a hand in her brother's death?

Burke stared at her tooth marks, which were still visible in the ball of his thumb. No. Kelly didn't compromise. She was more like a black widow. After mating, she bit her mate to death.

He shivered.

Cautiously he sprinkled a little of the flask's contents onto his thumb and sniffed. It was Givenchy, without a doubt. He held the flask close to his ear and shook it. No sloshing. The flask was probably full to the brim. Unless . . .

His mouth became dry when another horrifying possibility occurred to him. For some minutes he sat rooted to his chair, one raw bundle of nerves, while in his mind anger and fear wrestled for priority. Then he walked to the back, taking the flask with him, and locked himself in one of the toilets.

He emptied the flask into the sink. A moment later, the entire compartment smelled of aftershave, but no more than a thimbleful of liquid came out. He peered into the bottle neck, but the black glass wasn't translucent. Could a 200 cc bottle contain enough explosives to blow up a plane, he wondered? Yes, with modern resources it could. And if the bottle contained a time fuse, it was not even worth being careful. The bomb would explode anyway. "You'll die with me," she had said.

But he couldn't imagine Kelly Donegal as a mass murderer. Even less, a martyr. He only hesitated a few seconds. He dropped the flask on the floor and before he could change his mind, he stomped it to pieces. Among the fragments there were dozens of thin plastic tubes. One of them had broken and a fine white powder had spread all over the carpet.

Burke's expression went vacant, like an open grave. He stared for some minutes at the white smudge on the carpet and tried to fool himself into believing that what he was seeing was some innocent medicine. It could be something that wasn't available in Singapore and of which Kelly had brought a supply for personal use. She had handed him the wrong package by mistake when she gave him the present.

But Burke knew he was trying to kid himself. This was no innocent medicine and Kelly had not made a mistake. He suddenly felt lightheaded and nauseous. The powder was undoubtedly some sort of stimulant, heroin perhaps. If he got caught in possession of it at the Singapore airport, he risked going to jail for life.

Someone was knocking on the door. "Sir, are you okay?" It was the flight attendant's voice.

"I'm fine, thank you."

He had to get rid of this stuff. He knew that even the slightest attempt to bring drugs into the Southeast Asian Republic of Singapore was severely punished.

Hastily, he scrabbled for the plastic tubes and threw their contents in the toilet bowl. He scraped the powder from the broken tube off the floor and wiped the carpet with wet toilet paper. After throwing everything in, he flushed the toilet. To remove every last trace of the drug, he even rinsed all the fragments and the unbroken tubes before dumping the lot in the waste bin.

He left the toilet in a cloud of aftershave. The flight attendant, who was waiting for him behind the door, showed some surprise at the smell. "I dropped my bottle of Givenchy," he explained. Suddenly, he was struck with an idea. "You sell perfumes, don't you? You wouldn't happen to have Xeryus by Givenchy in stock, would you?"

"I'll have a look in a moment, sir." The flight attendant waited until he had turned to go back to his seat before briefly inspecting the toilet facility. Ten minutes later she brought him an identical bottle of Givenchy aftershave.

BURKE HAD HAD A few more whiskeys and didn't remember much of the remainder of the flight, with the exception of the mirror image flying alongside him in the dark window. Sometimes it looked like Kelly Donegal's face, distorted with ecstasy as she reached her climax, sometimes his own, tortured by the question of whether it had been Kelly's intention to use him as a drug courier without his knowledge, or whether she had intended to betray him. If it had been her intention to send him to the galleys, his back was to the wall. He couldn't go back to England. If he did, Kelly would undoubtedly inform the provisionals of his arrival. And if he stayed in Singapore she would no doubt work out new plans to eliminate him. His only means of escape would be to ring G5 in London and turn Kelly in. But that was exactly why he had fled England and the Secret Service: he was sick of the lies and the treason, the terrorism and the intimidation.

Maybe it was just his imagination running away with him. Maybe Kelly was just having him on. Burke drank his whiskey and dozed off. The flight attendant shook his shoulder and requested him to fasten his seat belt.

After they landed in Singapore, Kelly Donegal and her English lover left the plane before any of the other passengers were allowed to exit. When Burke was finally allowed off, they had long gone. He followed the flow of passengers to customs and waited his turn. He felt his shirt getting sweaty when the customs officer inspected his passport and visa.

"Next!"

He fetched his suitcase and followed the signs to the exit for people who had nothing to declare. At the desk, one of the customs officers caught his eye and gestured for him to step closer. Keeping a straight face, Burke put his suitcase and the blue linen Malaysia Airlines overnight bag containing his hand luggage on the counter. He felt someone moving behind him and looked around. Two policemen in white uniforms, with expressionless Asian faces, had taken up position behind him. The way in which they softly tapped their night sticks in the palms of their hands made him wince.

"Nothing to declare, sir?"

"Nothing."

"No hard drugs? Heroin? Morphine? Soft drugs? Hash? Marijuana? You are aware of the consequences, should you try to bring any of these into the country?" The customs officer pointed at the posters behind him: a chain gang being led away, a sentenced prisoner wearing a black hood, standing below a gallows.

The customs officer picked up the linen overnight bag and shook the contents out onto the counter. A second customs officer, wearing gold-braid epaulettes, came over and stood next to him, putting his hand on the flask of Givenchy.

"Once again. You have nothing to declare?"

Burke just shook his head.

Gold Braid picked up a hammer and with one blow broke the flask. The liquid splashed everywhere and spread across the counter in a fragrant pool. The confusion was complete.

The customs officers argued in Chinese, raising their voices. Burke thought he heard them mention the name Kelly Donegal a few times. He didn't doubt for one second that Kelly had tipped the customs men off, and although he was so nervous his legs were shaking, he was comforted by the thought that he had outwitted her.

The customs officers were now going through the rest of his luggage. They even cut open the inner lining of his suitcase, but of course they still didn't find anything.

He was allowed to leave, with a damage claim form for the broken bottle and the torn inner lining. Lightheaded with relief, he walked on. He had walked only a few yards when he was once again plucked out of the line of passengers, this time for a body search. When the policeman produced a brown envelope out of the inner pocket of his summer jacket, he was not really alarmed, more surprised.

"Heroin," declared the gold-braid epaulettes triumphantly. "More than two hundred grams."

Burke was stunned, unable to utter a single word.

"Sorry, mate. More than a hundred grams means a one-way ticket to the gallows in Singapore."

Only now did it occur to Burke that they were serious. "You're trying to set me up!" he yelled. "There was no envelope in my pocket. You planted it there yourselves."

Gold Braid smiled nastily and shrugged his shoulders. "Take him away," he said to the two cops who had come with him.

Burke was led away, cuffed hand and foot, racking his brain over the question of how the customs officer had succeeded in putting the envelope in his inner pocket without him noticing. Not until he got outside and saw Kelly standing among the spectators next to the prison van did he understand how she had tricked him. On the plane, while she was folding his summer jacket and putting it in the overhead bin, she had hidden the envelope in his pocket. Whether he had found the powder in the Givenchy bottle or the envelope first, didn't matter. The one had diverted him from the other.

But when he passed Kelly he saw to his surprise that there were tears in her eyes. It was this image that stayed with him till the end. Even as they pulled the black hood over his head, he kept wondering whether they had been tears of joy or of sorrow.

And when the hatch opened under his feet, he felt again, be it for the last time, her teeth sinking into his flesh.

Dr. Sweetkill

JOHN JAKES

F OR THREE WEEKS NICK LAMONT heard nothing from Wilburforce. For three weeks he drank too much, stayed out too late in the clubs around Soho, and stared with eyes that grew more gritty with each successive hung-over morning at the credit notices piling up in the day's post.

Then finally, one drizzly evening when Nick had touched his last friend for a few pounds, he was forced to hang around the flat because he was broke. That was when Wilburforce rang him up.

"Kemptons Luggage has a little task for you, Nicky," Wilburforce said. Kemptons Luggage was a shadow-firm in a shadow-office. It was the cover behind which Wilburforce and his counterparts in British intelligence farmed out their nasty work to free-lances like Nick. "Of course, this is rather a take-it-or-leave-it proposition."

Nick Lamont kicked one of his expensive calfskin lounging slippers halfway across the room at the grate. He wished he could smash his fist into Wilburforce's white, narrow, no-nonsense face.

Take it or leave it. Did the bastard think he could do anything except take it after the Tenderly mess? He was nearly washed up in the trade as it was.

"I'll meet you," Nick said after a moment. "Five tomorrow at the usual place?"

"Sooner. Luncheon." Wilburforce mentioned a posh grille. "Actually, Nicky, I didn't think you'd hesitate as long as you did. I'm glad to hear you're so enthusiastic about working again."

Nick Lamont's dark-burned face turned white around the edges of the lips. "I haven't said I'd take the thing. I'll listen."

Wilburforce clucked. "Try to control that red temper of yours, please. You're hardly in favor. If you want to keep on working for the firm, you'll pick up our little—ah—sales errand and relish it."

Nick's epithet was short.

Nick had made dozens of pleasant acquaintances among the British in his years in London. Not friends, really. You never could afford friends in the trade. But Wilburforce was another case. Wilburforce disliked Americans. He disliked reasonably competent Americans like Nick even more. Nick had done some jobs well.

But now Wilburforce had no reason to conceal his antipathy. As a result of the blunder in Gibraltar, Nick's stock as a free-lance was sharply down.

Wilburforce said: "Am I to interpret that filthy language to mean you are interested?"

Across the flat on the writing desk loomed the bills. Nick wanted the new silver-gray Jag so badly he could taste it.

And there was Tenderly. Tenderly, and the gun in Nick's hand in the frowsy little room upstairs over the restaurant.

"I'll be there tomorrow," he said.

"When you arrive," Wilburforce said, "try to be civil. This is not the state of Ohio, Nicky. Nor are you the muscular hero athlete who can dictate his own contract. We shall be writing the contract this trip, and you shall accept our terms, or none at all. Good evening."

CURSING, NICK SLAMMED THE dead phone down.

He walked to the windows opening onto the terrace. Rain dribbled down the glass. When he turned round to fix a whiskey-soda from the liquor cabinet, he passed the mantel mirror. He avoided glancing into it. He knew what he would see if he did; a big, husky man now turned thirty-five, and a little heavier than he should be.

But flat in the gut. Hard. His hair was still wild, curling black, though it was turning a little gray around the ears. Occasionally his hands shook when he lit a match to a cigarette. But the eyes still had the old temper-spark on occasion.

While the London rain pelted away, he drank three whiskey-sodas and then fell into bed, hoping for no dreams. He wanted to sleep soundly, in preparation for meeting Icy-Guts, as Wilburforce was calling him behind his back.

But he dreamed.

He dreamed intensely, vividly, yet disjointedly. There was the stadium in Ohio under a crisp purple and gold late afternoon sky. The stands thundered. Women's faces shone here and there, red with screaming. Suddenly, just before he made the field goal he heard an amplifier roar, "*Nick the Kick does it again!*"

Yet at the dream-moment when his foot should have connected with the ball and sent it sailing between the uprights, he was in the room in Gibraltar.

Nick had been flown over to bring back one Wing Commander Saltenham, who had, according to the evidence, been jobbing electrostatic copies of an air defense network alarm system to a notorious middleman on Gib. Wilburforce's section wanted Saltenham quietly withdrawn from circulation, in order to subject him to extended interrogation at a country estate discreetly maintained by the section in Kent. Along with Nick had gone one of Wilburforce's own operatives, an aging, modestly attired clerk type named Arthur Tenderly.

On Gib, Nick ran Saltenham to earth in the room above the restaurant. The Wing Commander was bounding a bawdy little girl with Moorish eyes and nothing on except several cheap rings. Nick threw her out, aimed his pistol at Saltenham and told him they were departing via a special flight which would take off shortly.

Tenderly had knocked, entering with hardly a sound. The 'copter was standing by, he reported. Saltenham knew he was finished. Fear coated his cheeks with acrid sweat. Yet he had guts.

Either he would be carried out dead, he announced, or he would not go. In other words, Nick would have to use the gun. Saltenham was snide about it, too. In a physical go, even with two against one, the Wing Commander promised to knock their jawbones down their throats. He looked as though he meant it. And he had one advantage—his correct guess that Nick Lamont and Tenderly had no orders to kill.

That didn't prevent Nick from going at the man with the raw sight-end of his pistol. He charged in, trying to counter-buffalo the suspected spy with a slash of the muzzle. Arthur Tenderly disapproved of Nick's gambit. What he didn't know was that Nick had, regrettably, lost his temper under Saltenham's snide needling. Tenderly chose the moment to intervene.

He seized Nick's arm to prevent serious damage being done by the rather notorious American.

"I'm running this and I'll run it my way," Nick shouted, trying to shake Tenderly's pale, small grip off his forearm. In that moment, as Nick gave his right arm a wrench to free it, the pistol, off safety, exploded.

The Wing Commander tried to escape through the window. Nick pumped one bullet into his right calf because it was already too late to do the task without a racket. Arthur Tenderly died of a gunshot wound forty-five minutes later in the naval base hospital.

After Nick had returned to London with his prisoner, his stock had begun to decline. He was questioned, requestioned, and finally cleared. But the phone failed to ring—until tonight.

And now, in the tortured dream that brought him wide awake to hear the midnight toll of bells, he somehow still saw Tenderly at his elbow. The gun had exploded. Tenderly was falling back, aghast. Somewhere an announcer thundered, "*The Kick does it again!*"

Two more drinks managed to send Nick back into a dull, thick slumber.

AT 11:30 THE NEXT DAY he took a cab to the Castlereagh Grille.

Smoking in the cab, Nick tried to think back. Where had he gone wrong?

He had started out fine in college. All-American. Some said he was the most powerful, accurate kicker ever seen on a football gridiron. Then came the Army. A stint with Intelligence. He didn't lack brains, and he preferred to be of some damn use, instead of playing ball for one of the base squads.

His Army record hadn't been bad. Afterward, he had no trouble landing on a pro club. For three years the Kick made them stand up and yell themselves silly.

Meanwhile a taste for good living built and built. It included liquor. The liquor unlocked the temper—and that led to the awful night he wrecked four rooms in a motel. After the team failed to renew his contract, he drifted to Europe. He'd grown to like a fast, expensive life. And rather quickly he found a way to earn money.

For a time he sold his services to the Allies: NATO, the French secret service twice. Then he was invited to London, with a pretty good guarantee of income as a free-lance. The work was sometimes dirty. The trade was never clean. But he enjoyed the cars and the wine and the girls the money bought. So long as he checked that temper, he was all right.

In Gib, one wild swipe of his arm had exploded a gun and killed a man. And the phone hadn't rung for a long time.

Well-dressed in a Saville Row suit and an expensive rainproof, Nick climbed out of the taxi in front of the Castlereagh Grille. He hurried inside. He didn't look like a man who was up against the fact that his luck had run out. But in the trade, you kept a hard face.

Three flights up, down a corridor, and through a succession of small private dining rooms, he came to the elegant, thick-walled chamber with steel behind every inch of patterned wallpaper. Here executives of Kemptons Luggage now and then met for "confer-ences." Here, by a dim little table lamp that threw a long shadow of the senior agent's bald head on the wall, Nick lunched with Icy-Guts.

Wilburforce picked at his chop. "Because of the Tenderly busi-ness, Nicky, you damn well may never get another assignment." He smiled. He had a gold tooth, which glowed. "Unless you take this one."

"How much is the fee?" Nick felt sarcastic. "Half the usual?"

"Twice," Wilburforce said.

Nick's scalp crawled. The jokes were over.

Thrusting aside his willow-patterned plate, Wilburforce began to speak in his flat, dry manner.

"You will be assigned a target which is a perfectly legitimate and prosperous chemical corporation near Munich. Chemotex World-wide G.m.b.h. Some of our lads working in the East, on the other side of the Curtain, have come up with the news that while the fac-tory is indeed legitimate, its department of basic research—a sepa-rate ring of the home building—is in fact a thriving laboratory doing research on nerve gas and bacteriological agents."

"Who runs the outfit?"

"The firm's director is Herr Doktor Franz Staub. We suspect he's sympathetic with the East and that, at very least, the secret labora-tory has his tacit approval. But he's small fry. The laboratory's direc-tor is much more important. His name is Yonov." Wilburforce glanced across the spotless linen, pointedly. "Dr. Genther Yonov."

An ugly memory ticked in Nick's mind. "I saw a dossier a year ago. The Athens thing. Something he'd sold. A compound. They had a code name for him."

Wilburforce nodded. "Yes, Dr. Sweetkill."

A long silence. The shadow of Wilburforce's head loomed malig-nantly on the wall.

"Dr. Sweetkill, the seller-to-all," he said at length. "Pacific yet ghastly death available on the open market. Almost uniformly, he seems to sell to the East. A filthy man. We understand Yonov has delivered to the East the formula for a new, quite deadly nerve gas code labeled Pax 11-A."

Nick lighted one of his cigarettes that cost twice as much as the ordinary kind. "And I'm supposed to do the old, formula-stealing bit?"

"Already done," Wilburforce replied. "By our lads in the East. The mechanics needn't concern you. We have Pax 11-A, right enough. But now we have another signal from Top Planning. The Yonov gas and germ factory is to be destroyed. Blown up, obliterated. This will represent a considerable setback for the other side. Years, perhaps. And you, dear Nicky, win the choice assignment. You are to penetrate the basic ·research laboratory within the Chemotex headquarters, and finish it off."

Slowly, Nick blew out smoke.

"How do I get in? Knock politely?"

Once again Nick found himself amazed by the thoroughness of Wilburforce's preparations. Despite being a bastard, the man was good. There would be a six-week training period in England. During that time Nick would be melded into the personality of Nicholas Lamont of Ridgefield, New Jersey, a young man with an impeccable record in international sales for a leading U.S. chemical firm. No relation to the American football player who enjoyed some vogue a few years ago, et cetera. N. Lamont had been hired by a man in the U.S. who was on the payrolls of both Wilburforce and Chemotex. N. Lamont would work for Chemotex in its legitimate international sales operation, and would, on a date not far away, travel to Munich to take over his new post. He would be trained by Chemotex at factory sales training sessions.

"We have the papers, we have the photos, we have everything but the man," Wilburforce said. "We even have your wife for you."

One of Nick's black eyebrows hooked up. "Wife?"

"Chemotex Worldwide treats its new employees rather royally. She will be traveling with you, all expenses paid. She's one of ours, of course. And she will not be with you," Wilburforce added rather nastily, "to gratify your sexual appetites. She will be there to aid and assist you in handling the necessary details. A man could do it alone, but a wife provides a better cover for a man your age. How you get out of the factory after you set the explosives—indeed, how you even get in to set them at all—is your affair." Wilburforce leaned forward. "Do you still want the little task, Nicky?"

Nick was cold in his mid-section. He tried to check his temper. "You hope I do."

"I hope you do. You're a smart, cheeky so-and-so. Lots of flash and brag. And there's Tenderly. He was one of my best. A lifelong friend. I hope you want it."

In the private, protected, sealed, and guarded dining room, all Nick Lamont could think about was a ridiculous stack of unpaid bills. For his guilt there was no specific symbol. It was only a feeling, heavy on his mind, never concrete except in dreams.

"I want it," Nick said. "And I'll come back in one piece."

Wilburforce dabbed his lips with a napkin. "That's doubtful. But I'm delighted you accepted all the same."

2

SIX WEEKS LATER, ON another of those dim, wet London afternoons, Nick Lamont met his bogus wife at the airfield. He had seen photos of her while he was in training. A round-hipped, slim-waisted, high-breasted girl with a pretty, though not beautiful, face. She had been trained separately. Once Nick inquired pointedly about this unusual procedure. Wilburforce fobbed him off with a reply that made no sense: the less dilly-dallying between the two of them while in training, the better they'd learn their lessons.

She wore a lavender suit, a small, wifely hat, and very little makeup.

Her diamond rings sparkled. She had a crisp, athletic stride, a pink mouth that suggested passion.

"Hello, Nicky darling," she said, kissing his cheek.

"Hello, Anne." His smile was easy. "Couldn't we have a more wifely greeting?"

"I think not." She said it low, but with a perfect smile. Something in her eyes bothered him. It was something hard and direct, which made him stop paying attention to the rather choice way her firm, high breasts thrust out.

He'd looked forward to this part of the trip even if the rest of the excursion promised to be grim. She was a damn fine-looking girl. He'd hoped they might act husband and wife in more than name. Now he was doubtful.

"I've checked my luggage aboard," the girl told him. "Including the cameras."

In the noisy, aseptic terminal, Nick chilled again. The cameras were the explosives.

They strolled toward the boarding area. "You don't seem overjoyed to see me," Nick said.

"Didn't Wilburforce tell you my real name?"

"No, just Anne Lamont."

"It's Tenderly." She paused, faced him. She stared directly into his eyes. "Charity Tenderly. I know what happened in Gib. He was my uncle, you see. We were both in the trade. I know his death was technically an accident. So I'll do my utmost to see that this job is a smasher." Her smile was bright and hollow. "I do want to make sure you succeed, you know."

Through the terminal came the mechanized scream of a BOAC jet taking off. Charity Tenderly—he was going to have a hell of a time thinking of her as Anne Lamont—walked a few steps ahead of him. She smiled again over her shoulder, as if beckoning for him to hurry. There was a red fury in Nick for a moment, which he quickly quelled. Then came a vast, fatalistic depression.

In the assignment of this girl to be his partner he sensed the hand of Wilburforce at work.

Destroy the factory.

And himself.

3

BELOW, THE PICTURE-BOOK prettiness of a Germany that looked unreal and untroubled gradually came up to meet them. They would land in Munich shortly. Nick tried to open the conversation again, meeting the difficult subject square on:

"Look, I know I've got a reputation for a temper but—"

The hostess was passing in the aisle. For her benefit, Charity interrupted, "Why, darling, I've grown used to your temper in all the years we've been married."

Nick's fingers closed on her wrist. "Don't play smart games. What happened was—"

"Final." She said it looking him straight in the eye. "A bullet. My uncle. But it's over. We don't want to be harping on it, not on airliners, not anywhere."

Nick momentarily forgot caution. "Why the hell did you come on this trip?"

Charity Tenderly grew quite serious. All malice was gone. "Because this kind of career—your career—is important to me. I do what I do—well, darling, not for cash, that's for certain."

"Then it's going to be all business?"

"Let's not argue, shall we? We'll be forced to stay in the same room. But there will be separate beds."

Nick scowled. The seat belt sign came on. Charity Tenderly said nothing more, only stared thoughtfully out the aircraft window.

A SMALL RECEPTION AND dinner party was scheduled for them at the colorful but rather touristy inn located in the tiny village not far from Munich. They had reached the inn via a limousine waiting at the airport courtesy of the Chemotex management. The Chemotex works itself was several kilometers from the city, and one kilometer past the village inn.

At the inn that evening, Nick and Charity dined by candlelight in company with Herr Doktor Franz Staub and several other executives of the firm.

The dinner was excellent. Nick avoided wine, concentrated on dark beer, and told a great many American jokes. Dr. Staub, an ascetic figure in a narrowly cut suit and small, gold-rimmed glasses, dry-washed his hands and nodded, pretending to understand the humor. Charity was seated between two of the sales executives who directed the European operation. She acted properly wifelike.

They were seated in a private dining room with a glass wall which overlooked the winding inn driveway. Shortly after the dinner began, a chauffeur-driven Mercedes arrived. Its occupant came in to join the group. She was tall, rather shapely, wearing a billowy out-of-season print dress and a large picture hat. Nick, a shade fuzzy with beer, was introduced.

"Permit me to present Fraulein Judith Yonov," said Dr. Staub.

Nick took the woman's hand briefly. Under the shadowy hat, her eyes were luminous, challenging. They were dark brown above a strong nose and full, brightly made-up lips. He judged her to be about thirty. She had large breasts, a low voice, pale cheeks. She seemed to wear a great deal of makeup. She did not remove her hat, even though the private dining room was dim.

"This is the young salesman from America?" Judith Yonov said in lightly accented English. "How pleasant."

"Your father—" Nick began. "I've heard the name. Research director, isn't he?"

"Yes. I am most regretful that he could not be here to share the occasion. But his projects—and Herr Doktor Staub's insistence on Chemotex competing vigorously in the world market—keep him laboring late many nights, I'm afraid."

Up his backbone Nick felt another oppressive crawling sensation. The daughter of Dr. Sweetkill. She reeked of Chanel. There was something eerie about her.

"I've heard among the competition in the States," Nick said, still trying to sound off-hand, "that your father has led Chemotex into some interesting basic research areas. I'd like to know more about that, Fraulein Yonov."

Was he pushing too hard? Across the table Charity's glance was a brief flicker of warning. Dr. Staub clinked his spoon against his demitasse, laughed politely.

"Ah, my dear young Herr Lamont. How fascinated you Americans are with all things new! Actually, the nature of our basic research program is a rather closely guarded secret. If I may put it as tactfully as possible, I am afraid that new employees are not permitted access to that area of our operations. At least not immediately. Indeed, we must insist upon heavy security to protect our patents and processes, as well as work in progress. In any case I'm certain you will be kept quite busy learning our current commercial line, and selling that in the U.S. markets."

Judith Yonov pushed one of the candle holders slightly to the side, in order to get an unobstructed look at Nick.

"Perhaps, Herr Doktor," she said, "if Herr Lamont is truly interested in product development—and he is one of the family now, so to speak—" There was a pause. "Perhaps I might talk with father and we might arrange a tour."

"The rules forbid—" Staub began.

"We shall see," Judith Yonov interrupted. Staub flushed, silent.

The smoke from his cigarette burned Nick's throat. It was plain to see who in the group had the clout. But he hadn't liked the shrewd, luminous glare of those eyes from beneath the big hat. He wished her face were not so heavily shadowed. The party was spoiled. He was sitting across the table from the daughter of a mass murderer. A concertina played a bright air in another room.

Had Wilburforce triple-crossed him? Was he somehow part of a game, the rules of which were known to every damn one of them except himself?

Or had there been a leak during preparations?

Judith Yonov had been baiting him.

Or had she?

Did she *know*?

PRESENTLY, AS DUSK FELL over the spectacular scenery outside, the party broke up. Nick would report to the Chemotex works tomorrow to begin training, Dr. Staub said. Pleasantries were exchanged all around. The sliding doors of the private chamber were rolled back. Judith Yonov excused herself and disappeared, presumably into a powder room.

Charity—he could not think of her as Anne, though he had no difficulty calling her that in public—was still chattering brightly with several of the executives. Nick discovered he was out of cigarettes. He left the room to buy some.

Going through the door into the inn lobby, he noticed a big, thick-shouldered man with a shaven head and a splayed nose. The man was emerging from the main tap room. He wore a dark uniform and highly polished boots. He had several inches on Nick, who was by no means small, at just over six feet.

The man walked unsteadily. He halted and blinked toward the party breaking up. He had a chauffeur's cap clutched in one hand. His eyes were small, and he reeked of beer.

Nick crossed the lobby, purchased his cigarettes, and was just turning round when he heard a quick, brittle exclamation of alarm. He knew the voice. Charity!

He whipped around fast. Several of the executives had gone to fetch their homburgs from the check rack. Charity had apparently walked into the lobby to wait for Nick. The big chauffeur had stumbled against her, because he was standing so close to her now, an idiot's smile on his lips.

"I think you've had too much to drink," Charity said.

"*Nein.*" The heavy man stroked her forearm. "American lady, *ja*? Very pretty. Looks pretty, feels pretty—"

Charity glanced past him, and her eyes for once were something other than cold. The man had her cornered. Nick crossed to her quickly, touched the man's shoulder.

"Beg pardon, but she's not for handling."

"Don't put hands on Rathke." The big man slobbered it, scowling.

"I'll put hands on anybody I damn please. Get away."

"Very pretty, very nice," the man called Rathke said, squeezing Charity's wrist. The girl made a face. That was all it took for the Lamont temper to crack.

His mouth wrenched as he punched Rathke hard twice in the belly. Rathke stumbled back, more surprised than injured. Nick's arm ached. His knuckles hurt. Several of the executives began to jabber. Staub bore down on them.

Thoroughly drunk and raging because of it, Rathke planted his big boots wide and swung a huge, flailing punch. It caught Nick's chin, spun him just enough to unbalance him and set off the red fury in him in earnest.

He went in fast. For a second or so, Rathke punished Nick's belly with big, brutal hands. Then Nick got through the man's guard, counterattacking the beefy German face with four fast, vicious punches. One of them slammed Rathke against the wall, brought a dribble of blood and a wild bellow of rage out of his mouth. Rathke lunged for Nick's throat—

In between the men there was a swirl of print fabric.

Judith Yonov spoke curtly in German, ordering Rathke to control himself. Rathke lowered his hands. He swiped his mouth with his uniform sleeve.

Nick was waiting. His tie was askew and he was breathing hard. But he was pleased, because he'd caught a glimpse of Charity's face.

She was irritated. He interpreted this to mean she was secretly pleased.

"Rathke, *nein!*" Judith Yonov exclaimed as the chauffer made up his mind, and shoved past her. Nick's head ached. Afterward he wasn't quite sure what had happened, but he believed Judith Yonov reached into her handbag, then touched her hand to the bare flesh of Rathke's left fist.

The man stopped. He blinked again. He took one more faltering step. With an audible swallow, he put on his cap.

The chauffeur stood docile. Blood made a thin red tracery down from the corner of his mouth.

"I do extend my deepest apologies for my chauffeur's behavior, Herr Lamont," Judith Yonov said. "He is under strict orders not to touch alcohol in any form. But I cannot watch him constantly."

Now the executives pressed close, apologizing in turn. In a moment Judith Yonov and Rathke had gone. But not before Rathke glanced back once, and gave a black scowl before sinking back into placid-featured obedience.

Nick guessed that Rathke had been subdued by some sort of needleprick. A Dr. Sweetkill special? Very likely. What a nice poison-flower Fraulein Yonov turned out to be.

As the party at last ended for good, Nick Lamont quietly cursed himself for the burst of temper. He might have handled it another way, though he couldn't think of a good one offhand. As he shook hands with Herr Doktor Staub and the others one by one, he noticed Charity watching him again. Not quite with approval, but without animosity.

That was worth it, he decided—that single look. Worth it even if Rathke did remember, caused more trouble and—God forbid—endangered the mission.

Charity said nothing about the incident as they went upstairs, however, and they slept in separate beds.

4

TWO EVENINGS LATER, NICK got a measure of satisfaction when Charity did at last mention the fight. Earlier they'd driven into Munich in a sea-blue Volkswagen, which the factory had provided for the length of Nick's training session. After a good deal of beer, a sumptuous meal, and some reasonably friendly if inane talk, they returned to the inn around midnight.

Nick flopped down on his twin bed. Charity stepped into the bathroom and closed the door. He lay sprawled, his hard chest speckled with cigarette ash as he squinted through the smoke at the black beams of the high-ceilinged room. In his mind he went over what he'd learned tied about Chemotex in his two days of attending classes.

He was being taught the company's products, its pricing policies, its distribution, and he had a crammed notebook full of scribbled facts. But the lunch periods had been more illuminating, because during those times he'd gotten to see more of the facilities. He dined in the company cafeteria with the various sales executives who were his tutors. Today Herr Doktor Staub had lunched with them too.

Nick's mind was drifting over the lunch talk about research—Staub had been guarded, as usual—when the bathroom door opened.

Charity walked out. She was applying a pink comb to her hair. Nick tried a whistle. He got little response except a nod which indicated the bathroom was his. Still, this was curious. On their first two evenings Charity had appeared ready for bed clad in hideous baggy striped pajamas of mannish cut. Tonight she had put on instead a black sleeping gown, lined so as to be opaque, but short. Her calves were tanned and attractive. The gown's front fell precisely away from the two ripe, high sharpnesses of her breasts.

"Don't get notions," Charity said. "I ripped the pajamas." With her back to him she began to hang up her daytime things.

Nick grinned. "Oh, here I thought it was the softening up for the kill."

The girl spun. "That's not particularly funny. I don't care to see anyone killed."

With a twist of his hand, Nick flicked ash into a tray. "I meant the romantic kill."

Charity's auburn hair shone by the dim lamps. "That's rather presumptuous of you, Nicky darling." The *darling* was acid.

"I thought so, too."

"Oh, you did?"

"Yes, but I'd like to know your reason," he said.

"I didn't ask to have my honor defended the other night."

"Aha!" Up he came off the bed, pointing a finger, "You're still thinking about it."

"I am not thinking about it! You're trying to imply I owe you something which—"

"Did I say that?" Nick cut in. "You said it. Been bothering you, has it?"

Charity flung back the coverlet on her bed. "Since we're getting so damn psychoanalytical, why did you tackle that big, vicious creature?" Charity raised her feet, bending her knees to slip her toes beneath the covers. The brief black gown's hem fell away for a second from the gently curving bottoms of her thighs. The view was exquisite, painful, and over virtually at once.

"Was it," Charity continued, "just another case of the Lamont temper breaking way out of bounds?"

Nick had an urge to hit her. "Listen, maybe I felt he shouldn't paw you. Did that occur to you?"

"Yes. But I really think it was guilt. Thanks anyway."

And, with a yank of the coverlet up over her bare shoulder, she turned her back toward him.

Nick closed his eyes. He saw it all again. The room in Gib. Tenderly's pale face wrenching as the accidental bullet drove into his breastbone and brought death and surprise to his failing eyes. Nick jumped up and stamped into the bathroom, where he slammed the door and ran the tap loudly so it would disturb her.

When he came out again, yanking the knot of his pajama bottoms tight to secure it, he made a quick round of the room as he did every evening, checking for hidden listening gear. Even though Charity was sitting up watching him, he avoided her eyes.

Finally he crawled into his own bed, reached for the light. Across his outstretched arm he looked at her. Strange, drawn lines pulled down the corners of her warm, pink, mouth.

"Nick, that was a bitchy thing for me to say. About the guilt, I mean."

"Forget it." Yet he was oddly aware of a new, unfamiliar intensity about her.

"No, really. You've a tough enough job ahead without me complicating it. I do understand why you hit that filthy boor. Just to be decent. There's not much forgiveness in me. I apologize. We're none of us perfect. I had a bad marriage, I ruined—well, forget that. But do accept my thanks. Also the promise of truce. Nick?"

"Truce." He snapped out the light immediately.

He didn't want to look too long at the black-wrapped swell of her breasts above the coverlet, nor speculate on what tiny but definite change had come over her.

She settled down with small murmurs and rumpling bedding noises. Nick smoked one more cigarette, staring into the dark. He tried to concentrate on what he had to do.

His sales training wouldn't last forever. The Chemotex research wing had to be destroyed. The gear was in the wardrobe, as part of their luggage. He had to transfer it to his attache case. Use it. By God, he would, and go back and shove a fragment of Chemotex's blown-up steel up Wilburforce's damn behind.

Well, he would come back.

AFTER ANOTHER TWELVE DAYS, at the beginning of the third week, Nick Lamont had learned enough—or all he could. He was ready to move.

A means of entrance to the basic research wing had to be found. This he'd learned early. He'd been studying the problem since.

The central building of Chemotex Worldwide G.m.b.h. presented a face to the one main access road. That face was all tinted blue glass and aluminum. Structurally, the building resembled the crossbar of a gigantic letter *T*. Running straight back from the crossbar was the basic research wing. It was three floors high, exactly like the main headquarters section. But all the doors leading into it from the main building were guarded during the daylight hours, alarm-rigged at night, and were, in any case, made of thick steel.

So far Nick had not even seen Dr. Genther Yonov. But he saw many of the scientist's white-coated research associates. They had their own private, treed, and sodded exercise park at the rear of the downstroke of the T. They checked in and out through a rear gate in a high, electrified fence. Their cars were parked in a small, separate pool alongside the secondary road which ran off the main one and serviced the rear compound-like area.

At noontime the scientists lunched in the fenced park much like highly educated animals. Other employees from the main building, as well as from the nearby but separate manufacturing buildings, lunched in the regular cafeteria. And so far as Nick could tell, there was no fraternization between those who labored for Dr. Sweetkill and all the rest.

At another lunch, Nick commented on the unusual arrangement.

"Necessary, necessary," Herr Doktor Staub replied, munching a morsel of bun. "Here in Germany, as in your United States, industrial espionage is not unknown. Thus we must guard our most precious commodity, our brainpower."

And crawling bottles full of bacteria for Eastern stockpiles? Nick wondered sourly.

Staub's explanation made a glib kind of commercial sense, though. The security even included the extra precaution of having the entire factory hooked into a master fire and police signal system which connected to the headquarters of the two municipal services in the nearby village.

Penetration looked next to impossible, until the night Nick became aware of Rathke's evening habits.

ON A CRISP MONDAY morning Nick was ready.

He packed his attaché case carefully. A small but potent automatic pistol was concealed inside a dummy text on chemical engineering. One large rectangular side of the case now contained jellied explosive layered between thin metal. Nick sweated as he carried this to his sales training class and gingerly opened the lid to take out his notepad.

A pair of sales engineers lectured at him all day. By evening, Nick was used to handling the case, which was good. Shortly after the works closed, he checked out the gate and walked down toward the regular employee car park.

The sun slanted low. The sea-blue roof of the waiting VW gleamed. Nick bent down to tie his shoe. Charity had been picking him up at the factory all the past week. Now, directly opposite the VW, Judith Yonov's Mercedes was parked.

Charity was leaning from the window of the VW, directing a sunny and seductive smile at the driver of the Mercedes, Rathke. The man stood against the left front fender of the smaller car, a witlessly pleased expression on his thick face.

One of the sales engineers who'd lectured Nick that day emerged from the gate. Nick used the man's presence as a pretext for a question. When they had exchanged goodnights, Nick turned round.

Sweat trickled down the back of his neck into his collar. He clutched the attaché case handle and walked between small, puttering sedans leaving the car park, to the VW. The Mercedes was pulling away along the secondary road, going around the rear of the gleaming headquarters toward the research wing.

"How did it go?" Nick asked once the VW was in gear. Charity was headed back toward the inn and the village. Smoothly she downshifted in the heavy factory traffic. "I must look the perfect bored wife," she said. "I didn't think it would work at all. But the poor beast evidently has so few brains—anyway, I was parked there as he drove past. I hailed him and apologized for your nasty behavior at the party. At first I think he was very suspicious. Then he smelled the gin I drank before I left the inn. When I petted his hand and gave him the smile business, I knew I had him. But it was crawly, touching him. He's an absolute brute."

They were speeding down the twisting road between fragrant pines. The peaked roofs of the village, gilt with sunset, appeared ahead. Nick felt obliged to say:

"Sorry to force it, but I was beginning to get desperate. Rathke's the one key. The Yonovs live inside the research wing. He takes care of the Yonovs. So he can get in and out. It was a damn godsend when I got to noticing that he came back tanked from the village every afternoon about the time the factory lets out. Have you set it up?"

Charity's pink tongue touched her coral-painted lips, nervously. "Yes, for this evening."

Nick was conscious of the keen of the wind past the car. "How?"

"I'm just to be walking somewhere on the main street after dark. He thinks I'll be waiting breathlessly because I have this fixation about large, powerful men with black boots—" She shuddered. Before Nick could say anything else, she swung the wheel of the Volks sharply.

The small tires skidded on the shoulder, shooting gravel backwards. The sedan slowed to a stop. Other factory traffic streamed by, going downhill to the village and the sunset. They were cool sitting in the shadow of great, soughing pines.

Quite unexpectedly, Charity gripped Nick's hand.

"I haven't forgotten my uncle. But don't let Rathke hurt you."

Startled, Nick hooked up his eyebrow again. "Does it really worry you?"

"Damnit, don't be flip, You're a decent sort. You really are. Maybe a little flashy and—oh, I don't know what's got into me. Is it living in the same room with you every night for two weeks running? Or—damn you, stop staring." And her arms, rough with the chic tweed of her suit jacket, came round his neck and her mouth came up firmly against his, moistening as her lips parted.

Nick thought, *This is idiotic. You're liable to be dead.*

But as he kissed her two things hit home hard. One, he'd grown fond of her. Two, in some strangely chemical way, the same thing had happened to her regarding him. Somehow it made what he had to do this evening all the worse, all the more frightening.

Yet for a moment it was all swept away as he wrapped his arms around her in the shadowy car, hugged her hard while her mouth opened and she kept murmuring between deep kisses that she was a bloody fool who ought to know better. Nick touched her left breast. He felt it shudder, harden beneath the fabric of her suit. She pulled back suddenly.

Her eyes were bright with a quick, amazed passion she could hardly believe herself. With both her hands she clasped his big-knuckled right one to her breasts.

"I'm crazy for you, Nicky." She was almost crying. "Damn fool blunder, isn't it? I hope you come back. Please come back. Please."

Then she tore away, almost angrily. She drove fast back to the village.

ON ONE HAND, NICK felt pleased that it had happened. On the other, he wished it hadn't. Having it happen made him all the more conscious of the attaché case jouncing lightly between his knees, layers of leather containing layers of steel and layers of steel sandwiching between them the jellied explosive he must use tonight.

THE CHIMES IN THE village church stroked half-past nine.

Nick waited in a dark place as a shadow in the center of the dim street—Charity, walking—turned. The shadow was outlined by the sudden bursting brilliance of headlights.

The auto slowed. Charity walked over, white-faced in the leakage from the lights. She leaned smiling toward the driver's side of the Mercedes.

Attaché case in one hand, Nick glided from the shadows. He raced the distance to the Mercedes, yanked open the door opposite the driver and slammed inside. He shoved the automatic pistol square against the side of Rathke's muscled neck.

"Drive to the factory or I kill you right now."

In the dash light glare, Rathke's lumpy face became by turns baffled, then dimly comprehending, then full of rage. Charity backed quickly away from the side of the gently humming car. Rathke cursed low, not too stupid to have failed to understand the betrayal. His immense right hand speared out through the open window.

Nick ground the muzzle deeper into the man's neck flesh.

"Put your hand back."

Rathke did. Charity was by then out of range.

"Either start this thing going or you're all done right here."

Rathke turned his head slowly, hatefully, toward Nick. Then he faced front. He engaged the automatic drive lever. Charity floated out of sight. Were there tears shining on her face? Nick dared not look round.

He changed the position of the gun so that it prodded into Rathke's ribs, while the Mercedes shot past the limits of the tiny village and up the winding road into the pines, toward the death works.

5

PERHAPS THE PROSPECT OF death made him euphoric. At any rate Nick found himself speaking in a fairly relaxed, conversational manner to Rathke as the Mercedes ground smoothly up the twisting mountain road.

"Now let me make one or two things clear before we hit the grounds, because unless you understand me, you'll try something or other and there'll be trouble. If there's any trouble, this car is going to crash and you're going to get it right along with me. Understand?"

No answer.

"I said understand?"

Rathke's peaked cap threw shadows far down over his face. His lips twitched. "*Ja.*"

"I know this much. You work for Yonov. His quarters are in the research wing. So I figure you know how to get in without triggering the alarms. If there's one single alarm, one goddam jangle of a bell, or light—anything—all you'll get for your pains is your brains smeared over the dash. If I don't do anything else I'll pull this trigger. It's all business between us as far as I'm concerned. Living or dying's up to you."

The brutish mouth worked at the corners, as if Rathke were bright enough to feel contempt for what Nick had said. It was not all business from Rathke's end. His smallish eyes held a vengeful brightness in the dash glare. He hadn't forgotten, or forgiven, the fight at the inn.

Nick had, though. He had because he had so much else to think about. For the first time in weeks, or months, or years, he didn't give much of a damn about a new Jag or anything, except getting back to Charity. And now that it mattered, he had to work doubly hard to keep the tension-edge out of his voice, the nervous spasm out of his gun hand. Those who theorized that there were no frightened men in the trade were fools.

Ahead, the bonnet lamps of the Mercedes brushed across the high steeled crosshatching of the electrified fence. Rathke made a tentative reach with his left hand for a small red button on the dash.

"What's that?" Nick said.

"Automatic signal. It will turn off and open the fence. We drive through when it opens."

"It had better do that and nothing else." Nick gestured with the gun. "Go on."

Rathke's splay finger pressed the red stud. Somewhere under the bonnet, an electronic device sang low. Abruptly the massive gates in the high fence began to swing inward like a scene done in slow-motion frames. The Mercedes slid ahead along the service road.

The gates passed on either side of Nick's field of vision. Then the black of the lawn where the research workers exercised during the day. The Mercedes rolled up to a rear door in the three-story building. Two blue fluorescent lights in an aluminum fixture over the door cast a ghastly glow. Nick had to risk passing through the lights.

"Out, *bitte*," he said, mockingly, though he wasn't feeling funny. The night had grown chill. The air bit at the bone. The pine smell all around was stingingly sweet. Rathke climbed from the car bent over, then straightened up.

"Do you know how to get inside with no noise?"

"*Ja*, I know."

"You'd better."

Carefully the chauffeur fished in his smartly tailored black uniform blouse. He produced a pair of aluminum keys which he jingled. Nick nodded for him to proceed. The attaché case weighed heavy in Nick's left hand.

Rathke slipped the first key into a lock, twisted. He withdrew
the key, inserted the second one into a lock immediately below.
Nick's senses felt raw. He was trying to listen, watch, take in more
than human senses could. At any second Rathke might be planning
to trip some alarm.

Using his shoulder, Rathke nudged the glass-and-aluminum
door inward. A long corridor stretched into a dwindling vista of
metal walls with pastel-colored office doors shut on either side.

"The pilot plant area," Nick said. "We'll go directly there."

"Then this stairway—we go up." Rathke led the way.

Footfalls had a hollow, eerie ring. Service lights burned here and
there in the stairwell. Inset in the walls Nick noticed one of the
black pulltoggle devices he had seen in the main plant. These were
the fire and police alarms which were connected to the village.

On the third floor Rathke went down a hall identical with that on
the first. It seemed endless. More of the black pull-toggle alarms were
spaced at intervals. Ahead, a steel door brightly lacquered in red
loomed. It bore *Keep Out* warnings stenciled in German, English, and
French.

When Nick asked whether the pilot plant lay beyond, he
received a grunt in reply. The big chauffeur pushed the panic-bar
and the door swung open. Rathke moved ahead, onto a kind of
steel-floored gallery with a rail. Below, for two stories, there was
emptiness crisscrossed with a weird tangle of glass piping.

Nick was starting through the scarlet door when he realized the
wrongness of it all.

The pilot plant tanks, distillation apparatus, centrifuges, were
two floors down on the cement.

Rathke had chosen to bring him into the plant on the third
level—the catwalk went all the way round the big chamber in a
square at the second level, too.

He was halfway through the door now, and Rathke was midway
between door and rail.

Nick broke stride as the notion registered that it was all wrong.

This brief hesitation was what Rathke had counted upon. Too late, Nick realized that the chauffeur's mind was less spongy than it seemed. For even as Nick's mind noted the arrangement of the pilot plant—huge windows; the chemical piping swooping up and down like big clear glass arteries in which colored liquids flowed slug- gishly—Rathke turned and rolled his shoulder down and came charging in to kill.

Nick tried to keep hold of the attaché case and get off a shot at the same time. Rathke's shoulder hit Nick violently at the waist. The attaché case dropped, slid away on the catwalk floor. Rathke lifted hard, up and over in one immensely powerful lunge. Nick tumbled down the man's back—straight at the rail and the drop over, and death.

Wildly, Nick shot out his free hand, fingers in a claw.

He caught the top of the railing, grappled for purchase, closed his fingers.

A red-purple pain hit his mind, and his arm was nearly wrenched out of place as it took the whole brunt of his body drop- ping. But he hung on. He hung by his left hand, cheek smashed against the rail's middle rung.

Rathke threw his cap away. He wiped his sleeve across his upper lip. He smoothed the front of his uniform tunic. He started walking toward the rail. His great black boots gleamed with a leather luster as he came on, nailed heels going *clang-scrape, clang-scrape* with each step.

Nick lifted his right hand with the automatic pistol in it. He hurt from hanging there by one hand, two floors above the concrete of the pilot plant floor. His face contorted as he tried to steady his trembling right hand, aim between the railing rungs.

The chauffeur leaped, closed thick fingers, twisted the gun loose. He threw it, clanging, down the catwalk floor where it slid to a stop several yards away.

Sweat formed on the palms of Nick's left hand, on the inside of his fingers by which he was hanging. That left hand began to slip.

"Is the American growing tired?" Rathke said. He drew out something long that suddenly doubled its length with a snick, and shone bright blue.

"Tired of holding on, *ja*?" Rathke continued, pointing the knife blade down at Nick's bloodless left hand clawed around the top rail. Nick struggled to get his right leg up. He managed to do it, giving himself a little extra support on the catwalk's edge.

Rathke kicked his foot away. Nick nearly dropped again. His shoulder took another bad jolt.

"Perhaps we release the fingers with a cut, one at a time," Rathke said. He brought the knife down toward Nick's middle finger knuckle.

The blade edge touched skin, broke through, went down to bone.

Nick bit his tongue to keep from yelling. Every bit of power he had left went into the frantic surge as he brought his right foot up again to the catwalk edge, tore his left hand back, out from under the knife, away from the rail.

His middle finger burned. For a moment he held onto nothing.

Then his grappling right hand caught the rail. With his left he reached up and dragged hard at Rathke's white collar, one quick, strong jerk at the point where the chauffeur's tie was knotted. And suddenly Rathke was pitching over, dumb eyes growing as he sailed past the rail, past Nick.

Rathke seemed to spiral slowly. His boots shone. Then his head struck the concrete and burst.

Something hurt Nick's ears. A deep, throaty sound. As he clambered up over the rail and stumbled across the catwalk, he realized that Rathke had yelled loudly when he went over. Yelled in wild, frantic fear.

How loudly?

Yes. There were footfalls somewhere off the second level of the pilot plant.

Nick could barely move. But he had to move. He shambled over and picked up his gun. Then he headed for the metal service stair down to the main floor.

Halfway to the bottom he passed another of the black pull-toggle devices set in the wall. He was recovering a little from the shock of the fight now. The footfalls had stopped. Had he imagined?

As soon as he set the timer on the explosives, he wanted out of the plant. He wouldn't be able to get much beyond the exercise yard before the explosives blew, however. There were night guards in the main building. They would surely catch him in the open. Some diversion, confusion, might help. But he had to plan for that now, and then move very fast.

Police or fire-fighters from the village would create the right kind of diversion, keep the guards from the main plant busy and give him a chance to escape. Nick reached up and pulled down the toggle. He hoped the alarms really rang in the village.

He went lurching on down the iron steps and out onto the pilot plant floor. Overhead the glass pipes full of liquids—and several contained smokish gasses, he saw—soared and crisscrossed so that he moved through a weird checkerboard of shadows. He ran panting past Rathke's corpse to a central place on the floor, knelt, unfastened the snaps of the attaché case.

"That will be quite all, Herr Lamont. *Quite all.*"

Nick twisted his head around. He'd been watching the corridor entrances at the back end of the research wing. Now he saw that the voice came from the opposite side entirely: an almost wholly shadowed doorway on the second level, but on the side leading into the main building.

At the railing was a woman in a dressing gown. Blurrily he recognized her as Judith Yonov. Beside her, gaunt, in an old maroon lounging jacket with black lapels, holding a pistol, was Dr. Sweetkill.

It was Dr. Genther Yonov who had spoken.

He was a tall, slope-shouldered man, mild of face and affecting a tuft of beard.

"Our apartments are on the end of the wing through which you entered," Yonov said as he headed toward the stairway. Judith followed. "We decided it might be prudent to circle around and approach from a different direction. Poor Rathke's yell carried, I'm afraid. Be so kind as to throw the pistol on the floor. Then you will stand back from the briefcase."

Feeling weary and defeated, Nick obeyed. Judith Yonov's voice was stridently sharp, bouncing back and forth across the pilot plant as she followed her father down the stairs:

"From the beginning it had all the smell of a penetration."

"Pity we had to lose Rathke to verify it," Yonov said. Like specters the two came toward him.

Judith Yonov came only partway, however. She stopped, standing back in the shadow thrown by a tall chemical mixing tank. Dr. Yonov appraised the disheveled Nick.

"I am aware," Yonov said, stroking his long scholar's nose with his free hand, "that you triggered the village alarm connections. All doors from this area are now locked, so the police cannot enter except by force. Still, they will be here. Their vans move rapidly. They should arrive at the back gate shortly. Well, I have already decharged that gate. They will have no difficulty getting in to the yard."

Nick's head pounded. What was there to say, or argue about? Yonov had him.

The man called Dr. Sweetkill was in his late fifties. He looked bright enough, but there was an odd, private-world gleam in his deeply set brown eyes.

Nick sucked in long breaths. Why the hell was Dr. Yonov so casual about the police arriving? Had he fixed them? Not all of them, he couldn't have, that wasn't possible. Nick would try talking his way out. Stupid idea, but what else was there now? The gun was gone, dropped on instructions. The attaché case lay open several yards away, near a centrifuge recessed into the concrete floor. The case was useless, too.

Dr. Yonov stepped around Nick, instructing him to turn so as to keep his face toward him.

"Who you are makes little difference, though we may learn that in a moment," Yonov said. His thin free hand reached up to a vertical pipe of steel which rose through the floor. A big but delicately balanced wheel with four metal spokes spun at his touch.

Through one of the glass pipes overhead, a whitish fume of smoke went crawling and flittering. Then it twisted and leaped as blowers took over.

"For the moment," Yonov went on, "it's quite enough to say that we have long anticipated a penetration attempt. Obviously they have sent us an amateur. Ah, you're looking at the wheel. Well, out there—" The gun waved toward the high windows which overlooked the nightblackened grass of the exercise yard. "Out there we have an underground valve system. We frequently employ it to test our experimental gasses in the open air on small animals. When there are no humans—no staff members relaxing there, of course," Yonov added with a stilted chuckle. "What you see going through that tube overhead is now being pumped down through conduits and up again through the valves scattered in the grass. If I no longer have the required cover for operating in this facility, then I might just as well leave it in grand style, wouldn't you say so, whoever you are?"

"Red light!" Judith Yonov said from the shadow. "Coming up the road fast."

"The gas mists quite easily," Yonov explained. "They'll not see, feel, taste, or smell it until they're in the midst of it. The alarm was an idle gesture on your part. I have not tried this special compound on small animals—or any animals. It will be interesting to note what happens."

Red light whirling, the police van screamed up to the gate in another ninety seconds. Men opened the gate. Others, also armed, followed the first pair across the lawn. Before any of them had reached the halfway point between the fence and the building, they had all dropped, white faces distorted, ugly.

Over the seven incredibly still bodies the revolving van light washed waves of dark red color. Nothing else moved.

"Satisfactory," Dr. Yonov murmured. "Yes, satisfactory." He smiled. "And now, dear friend, we turn to you."

6

DR. GENTHER YONOV STROKED the ball of his index finger up and down the side of his nose for a meditative moment. Nick's mind was dull, thick, struggling for some way to live, some way to even the wretched odds. Judith Yonov had not stirred from under the shadow of the huge chemical tank. She acted as if she were afraid of the light.

Yonov gave his gun hand a slight twist. The gesture seemed to indicate that he had made up his mind.

"First," he said in a conversational tone, "we had best cut off the gas flow into the yard, else we shall have half the neighborhood dead." Nimbly the man moved to the upright pipe, spun the delicately balanced wheel again. In the act of turning back around he suddenly seemed to move much faster, dancing across the concrete to hit Nick viciously across the side of the head with the pistol muzzle.

Nick stumbled. He tried to fend off the next blow, to right himself, to grab Yonov's gun. Yonov kicked hard with a high, telling kick to the small of the back.

Off balance, Nick skidded across the concrete floor. Suddenly there was nothing beneath him but a great, round circular darkness. Primitive panic brought a yell choking up in his throat.

Everything dropped away. He fell.

He hit hard, with a whanging sound and a cold, nasty smack to the side of his head. He sprawled on the bottom of one of the great stainless steel centrifuges whose upper rims were flush with the concrete floor.

Nick shook his head, crawled to hands and knees. The shadow of Yonov fell across the mirrored interior of the sunken centrifuge. Nick gauged the height up to the concrete floor as hardly more than four feet. But his arms and legs felt heavy, useless. He had to jump. He had to get up, get out of this sunken silvery dish—

Everything twisted again, distorted with pain. He came up on his feet, reached for the lip of the centrifuge. Yonov gave another of his little waves with the gun.

"Judith, please?"

A rasping click somewhere. Suddenly, beneath him, the slippery steel floor seemed to revolve.

The centrifuge was spinning.

Nick was slammed, hurled, around and around. Each time he tried to stand he was thrown helplessly further around the circular inside. Yonov's shadow flicked past, and past again.

Nick felt like he was in a fun-house device, crazy, laughable, but he could not stand up, nor grasp the concrete lip now because force hurled him always outward toward the wall.

Somehow Yonov's voice penetrated, filtering down: "Now, Herr Lamont, before I increase to the next highest r.p.m., perhaps you will tell me for whom you are working?"

Around and around everything went, sickeningly, a blur. Yonov's shadow was the only constant, black across Nick's field of vision every other second or so. Why couldn't he stand *up*?

Each time he tried he was thrown back to hit against the outer wall, revolving more swiftly now. Or was that all in his head?

Above, the next time round, a blue-shiny object glimmered. Yonov's voice as he called down alternately dinned and faded, depending upon the point to which the centrifuge had revolved.

"You are traveling slowly enough to see these objects which I have brought to the rim. Ten-gallon glass chemical vessels. I propose to kick one, then the next, then the third, down into the machine. Then I propose to throw a control which will slide the steel cover outward from its recess, completely covering you and all the broken glass. Instead of mixing up an intermediary as we do in production, I think thirty seconds with the cover closed and the glass flying into you will make a nice blend of blood and pain. Then I propose to slow the machine down again and you will have an opportunity to tell me who assigned you here."

Around and around.

The bell-shaped glass vessel was recognizable to Nick because Yonov's words had made it so. Already Nick could imagine the bits of shattered glass being whirled outward like deadly darts, at his cheeks, his wrists, his eyeballs.

"Say welcome to the first of the glass, my spy friend," said Yonov, pulling back to kick.

Glass shattering. Tinklings, crashings. There was a loud, flat report mingled with the breaking. Nick was still pinned against the wall of the spinning centrifuge. Only a moment later did he realize two peculiar things:

The centrifuge was slowing down.

And Yonov's shadow had vanished from the rim.

In a daze Nick swallowed hard, as the centrifuge came to a full stop by revolving one last time past the body of Dr. Sweetkill.

The scientist lay on his back. His mouth was open in dismay. His eyes were huge and fixed on the piping overhead. Blood bubbled out of a hole in his throat.

That had been the report Nick had heard. A shot. The huge glass vessels stood unbroken. Nick's sweat-blinded eyes finally found the source of all the sounds of shattering—a large lower pane in one of the pilot plant windows had smashed inward.

And threading a path through the litter, wrapped in an old tan trench coat that bore rips from where she'd climbed through the window, and looking pale and frightened, but with a small wicked gun in her right hand—

"My God," Nick said. "My God, Charity. My God."

"I—I thought you were down in there. I couldn't see exactly. I shot twice at the window first, to break it."

Through the night, out where the red van light still revolved, bells jangled.

"The alarms," Nick said. "The breaking glass triggered the plant alarms."

"I had to come after you," she said, her words overlapping his. "You'd told me about the police and fire bells being connected in the village. I was walking—just walking in the street, worrying about you and—" She fell against him. Then after she had buried her face for a moment, she drew back. "The police alarm rang in the station. I heard it from a block away. A van left. I came too. After I ran all the way up here, I saw all those men lying out there. All dead. I thought they would have things in control. I saw Sweetkill through the window. They do teach us how to fire one of these accurately, you know. It's part of the training."

Nick Lamont swallowed a long, sweet breath of air. His temples had stopped hurting. Things had settled into reasonable focus.

"Then we can get out of here. We can—"

"Not as you think," came her voice from the shadows, forgotten till now. "No, not as you think. The young lady's back presents a splendid target. She will please put her gun down, and turn."

Nick stared past Charity, who was frozen, trying to see in the mirrors of his eyes the source of the ugly feminine voice. Nick's belly iced again. He'd drawn a hand that looked like a lucky one at last, and now there was a trump.

Yonov's fallen gun had been retrieved by the girl who came walking out of the shadows.

Charity's fingers whitened about the trigger of her own weapon. Nick gauged the risk, then shook his head. Carefully he reached down and pried her fingers apart.

"I'll throw the gun off to the right," he said.

"Yes," said Judith Yonov. "Then the young lady will please stand to one side."

This Charity did, as Judith Yonov came all the way out of the chemical tank's shadow.

The strong nose, the full figure, the lipstick mouth were as Nick had remembered them. His mind created a beery image of a young woman hiding under a picture hat. Only this woman was not young.

Turkey-skin, all wrinkled and reddish, showed at the throat of her robe. Her hair was dyed. Her eyes veed with folds at the outer corners. Her makeup laid a hideous pink-orange patina over pale skin. She was not pretty, and she was at least Yonov's age.

"You needn't stare," she said. Nick heard false teeth clicking grotesquely. "I am not his daughter. I am his wife. But there are certain reasons why it was more secure for me to remain well hidden under large hats, in dark places." Her voice was dead level.

Only a quick glance at Yonov's red-throated corpse betrayed her contempt.

"Perhaps you might say I was his guardian. I was his contact, his link with the East, you see. I am the one who gave him a cause, a purpose for his work. Except for the affection the poor idiot felt for me, perhaps you Englishers—I suspect that's what you must be since the young lady has the sound of it in her voice—as I say, but for me, he might have sold you his little bottles instead. Well, I am not so fond of the theatrical as he was. I shall do this quickly. But with pleasure."

Again the eyes flicked bright and fanatic at the dead Sweetkill. She added: "I did not care for Genther personally. It was my duty to care for him. He was valuable. You have destroyed that value. I am duty-bound to finish what he began."

Nick stared at her. He heard the alarm bells still ringing, jangling down the night. He heard voices now, male voices, guards, shouting off in the direction of the main building. They hammered on the steel doors, unable to get in.

On the floor, perhaps a yard away, lay the attaché case.

I wonder if I can? Nick thought.

His mind went briefly black. He heard a thunder of a hundred thousand voices on a Sunday afternoon under an Ohio sky. There was no other way. It would never work but he had to try. Up came Judith Yonov's gun muzzle.

With a wide bash of his arm, Nick threw Charity out of the way and did the run.

His right foot came up with less speed but as much fluid power as in the past. *The kick! The kick!* they were screaming somewhere. His foot connected.

Judith Yonov's gun flamed, missed. He had kicked the attaché case hard but it seemed to slide forward slowly. Actually there was power in the kick. The case flew. It struck Judith Yonov in the left calf, not hard, but enough to distract her. Her gun hand jerked. A second bullet went upward.

A glass pipe burst, began to leak down viscous greenish fluid that smoked when it hit the concrete. Then, before Nick could stop her, Charity was past him, screaming like no civilized woman should scream.

Judith Yonov tried to shove her back. Charity clawed, pushed. Judith Yonov went tumbling into the centrifuge. Her foot caught the attaché case handle. Charity saw the case skitter and gave it a swift kick, almost as an afterthought.

She moved on fast, a blur of hate, of foul words. Her nails broke as she punched and punched at the centrifuge control box.

With a whine, as Judith Yonov howled down there with the case, the centrifuge began to spin.

Now guards were battering at the steel doors with what sounded like sledges. "Damn fool," Nick shouted in a rage at Charity. "The spin of that thing may detonate all the juice in the case and—"

His chest hurt. Time was pitifully short. He quit squandering time and words and bowled broadside into Charity. "*Run!*"

He drove her along with his shoulder. They tore their clothing and their flesh getting through the shattered window. The dash across the field of dead policemen was nightmarish. Nick had to pick Charity up once when she faltered. He hurled her bodily out through the open gate. Then the black tore open behind them in one blinding, thundering red cloud of detonation that hurled them forward half a dozen yards onto their faces.

On his neck, Nick felt the heat of the death works dying.

7

"WHAT A MESS," NICK said.

He was panting so hard, he was barely able to speak. "What a damned indescribable mess." He dragged tired hands over his clothes. They were covered with sap, quilled with pine needles.

He and Charity had run parallel with the winding road, all the way down to the village, while the fire vehicles roared up.

The inn was empty. All the personnel and guests were out in the narrow street, watching the furnace-hued sky. They had got in via the back stairs. Now, in the sanctuary of their room, Nick had shot home the iron bolt.

He sat heavy and tired on the bed, saying again, "A mess. We both look like things off the garbage heap."

"But we made it. "

Charity's words came out as a bare squeak. She tried to laugh about it. Nick scowled. He scowled because her tan trench coat was an untidy collection of blood spots and tears and sap stains. She looked sick, wretched, tired, and happy.

Nick said the first thing that came into his head:

"That was a stupid thing—"

Disbelief, utter fury sparked in the girl's eyes as her head came up. "What?"

"Killing the Yonov woman. Going crazy. It was a callous, dirty thing."

"Are you so blasted tired you don't know what you're saying?"

"You murdered her."

"Who told you this was dancing class anyway, you son of a bitch?" Tears were on her cheeks, tears coming fast as she balled her fists at her sides. "I seem to remember a man named Tenderly in Gib. A man you killed, and here I'd got it into my head that maybe I had to forgive you and now you pull this on me!"

She sank down.

"Don't you know why? Don't you know why I did it?"

Slowly she lifted her head to look at him. She was no longer crying out of anger:

"Because, Nick, I wanted you to live, not her."

He let out a breath which was more like a choke. The relief came. An end to the guilt. Wiped clean. Understanding seeped into his fatigue-dulled mind. He went toward her and sat beside her. New shiny-bright Jaguars no longer existed. Even Wilburforce hardly seemed worth bothering about.

Charity kissed him, hungrily, open-mouthed. He tried to show her he understood, and wanted her. He reached and fumbled at her clothing. Finally, when he had her living, round breast cupped in his fingers, feeling the warm rising life of it, there was no longer a need for fear.

"The local police, Nicky."

"Tomorrow.

"But—"

"Old Icy-Guts will fix it."

"I still worry that—"

"Please shut up."

They fell back together, tired, wanting. Soon the antidote was there for both of them, close together. The curtains of the inn room had been drawn tight when they crept in, so they never saw the red light of burning anymore in the German sky that night.

A Curious Experience

MARK TWAIN

THIS IS THE STORY which the Major told me, as nearly as I can recall it:

IN THE WINTER OF 1862–63 I was commandant of Fort Trumbull, at New London, Conn. Maybe our life there was not so brisk as life at "the front"; still it was brisk enough, in its way—one's brains didn't cake together there for lack of something to keep them stirring. For one thing, all the Northern atmosphere at that time was thick with mysterious rumors—rumors to the effect that rebel spies were flitting everywhere, and getting ready to blow up our Northern forts, burn our hotels, send infected clothing into our towns, and all that sort of thing. You remember it. All this had a tendency to keep us awake, and knock the traditional dullness out of garrison life. Besides, ours was a recruiting station—which is the same as saying we hadn't any time to waste in dozing, or dreaming, or fooling around. Why, with all our watchfulness, 50 percent of a day's recruits would leak out of our hands and give us the slip the same night. The bounties were so prodigious that a recruit could pay a sentinel three or four hundred dollars to let him escape, and still have enough of his bounty-money left to constitute a fortune for a poor man. Yes, as I said before, our life was not drowsy.

Well, one day I was in my quarters alone, doing some writing, when a pale and ragged lad of fourteen or fifteen entered, made a neat bow, and said:

"I believe recruits are received here?"

"Yes."

"Will you please enlist me, sir?"

"Dear me, no! You are too young, my boy, and too small."

A disappointed look came into his face and quickly deepened into an expression of despondency. He turned slowly away, as if to go; hesitated, then faced me again, and said, in a tone that went to my heart:

"I have no home, and not a friend in the world. If you *could* only enlist me!"

But of course the thing was out of the question, and I said so as gently as I could. Then I told him to sit down by the stove and warm himself, and added:

"You shall have something to eat, presently. You are hungry?"

He did not answer; he did not need to; the gratitude in his big, soft eyes was more eloquent than any words could have been. He sat down by the stove, and I went on writing. Occasionally I took a furtive glance at him. I noticed that his clothes and shoes, although soiled and damaged, were of good style and material. This fact was suggestive. To it I added the facts that his voice was low and musical; his eyes deep and melancholy; his carriage and address gentlemanly; evidently the poor chap was in trouble. As a result, I was interested.

However, I became absorbed in my work by and by, and forgot all about the boy. I don't know how long this lasted; but at length I happened to look up. The boy's back was toward me, but his face was turned in such a way that I could see one of his cheeks—and down that cheek a rill of noiseless tears was flowing.

"God bless my soul!" I said to myself; "I forgot the poor rat was starving." Then I made amends for my brutality by saying to him, "Come along, my lad; you shall dine with *me*; I am alone today."

He gave me another of those grateful looks, and a happy light broke in his face. At the table he stood with his hand on his chair-back until I was seated, then seated himself. I took up my knife and fork and—well, I simply held them, and kept still; for the boy had inclined his head and was saying a silent grace. A thousand hallowed memories of home and my childhood poured in upon me, and I sighed to think how far I had drifted from religion and its balm for hurt minds, its comfort and solace and support.

As our meal progressed I observed that young Wicklow—Robert Wicklow was his full name—knew what to do with his napkin; and—well, in a word, I observed that he was a boy of good breeding; never mind the details. He had a simple frankness, too, which won upon me. We talked mainly about himself, and I had no difficulty in getting his history out of him. When he spoke of his having been born and reared in Louisiana, I warmed to him decidedly, for I had spent some time down there. I knew all the "coast" region of the Mississippi, and loved it, and had not been long enough away from it for my interest in it to begin to pale. The very names that fell from his lips sounded good to me—so good that I steered the talk in directions that would bring them out: Baton Rouge, Plaquemine, Donaldsonville, Sixty-mile Point, Bonnet-Carré, the Stock Landing, Carrollton, the Steamship Landing, the Steamboat Landing, New Orleans, Tchoupitoulas Street, the Esplanade, the Rue des Bons Enfants, the St. Charles Hotel, the Tivoli Circle, the Shell Road, Lake Pontchartrain; and it was particularly delightful to me to hear once more of the *R. E. Lee*, the *Natchez*, the *Eclipse,* the *General Quitman*, the *Duncan F. Kenner*, and other old familiar steamboats. It was almost as good as being back there, these names so vividly reproduced in my mind the look of the things they stood for. Briefly, this was little Wicklow's history:

When the war broke out, he and his invalid aunt and his father were living near Baton Rouge, on a great and rich plantation, which had been in the family for fifty years. The father was a Union man. He was persecuted in all sorts of ways, but clung to his principles. At last one night masked men burned his mansion down, and the family had to fly for their lives. They were hunted from place to place, and learned all there was to know about poverty, hunger, and distress. The invalid aunt found relief at last: misery and exposure killed her; she died in an open field, like a tramp, the rain beating upon her and the thunder booming overhead. Not long afterward the father was captured by an armed band; and while the son begged and pleaded, the victim was strung up before his face. [At this point a baleful light shone in the youth's eyes, and he said, with the manner of one who talks to himself: "If I cannot be enlisted, no matter—I shall find a way—I shall find a way."] As soon as the father was pronounced dead, the son was told that if he was not out of that region within twenty-four hours it would go hard with him. That night he crept to the riverside and hid himself near a plantation landing. By and by the *Duncan F. Kenner* stopped there, and he swam out and concealed himself in the yawl that was dragging at her stern. Before daylight the boat reached the Stock Landing and he slipped ashore. He walked the three miles which lay between that point and the house of an uncle of his in Good Children Street, in New Orleans, and then his troubles were over for the time being. But this uncle was a Union man, too, and before very long he concluded that he had better leave the South. So he and young Wicklow slipped out of the country on board a sailing vessel, and in due time reached New York. They put up at the Astor House. Young Wicklow had a good time of it for a while, strolling up and down Broadway, and observing the strange Northern sights; but in the end a change came—and not for the better. The uncle had been cheerful at first, but now he began to look troubled and despondent; moreover, he became moody and irritable; talked of money giving out, and no way to get more—"not enough left for one, let alone two." Then, one morning, he was missing—did not come to breakfast.

The boy inquired at the office, and was told that the uncle had paid his bill the night before and gone away—to Boston, the clerk believed, but was not certain.

The lad was alone and friendless. He did not know what to do, but concluded he had better try to follow and find his uncle. He went down to the steamboat landing; learned that the trifle of money in his pocket would not carry him to Boston; however, it would carry him to New London; so he took passage for that port, resolving to trust to Providence to furnish him means to travel the rest of the way. He had now been wandering about the streets of New London three days and nights, getting a bite and a nap here and there for charity's sake. But he had given up at last; courage and hope were both gone. If he could enlist, nobody could be more thankful; if he could not get in as a soldier, couldn't he be a drummer-boy? Ah, he would work so hard to please, and would be so grateful!

Well, there's the history of young Wicklow, just as he told it to me, barring details. I said:

"My boy, you are among friends now—don't you be troubled any more." How his eyes glistened! I called in Sergeant John Rayburn—he was from Hartford; lives in Hartford yet; maybe you know him—and said, "Rayburn, quarter this boy with the musicians. I am going to enroll him as a drummer-boy, and I want you to look after him and see that he is well treated."

Well, of course, intercourse between the commandant of the post and the drummer-boy came to an end now; but the poor little friendless chap lay heavy on my heart just the same. I kept on the lookout, hoping to see him brighten up and begin to be cheery and gay; but no, the days went by, and there was no change. He associated with nobody; he was always absentminded, always thinking; his face was always sad. One morning Rayburn asked leave to speak to me privately. Said he:

"I hope I don't offend, sir: but the truth is, the musicians are in such a sweat it seems as if somebody's got to speak."

"Why, what is the trouble?"

"It's the Wicklow boy, sir. The musicians are down on him to an extent you can't imagine."

"Well, go on, go on. What has he been doing?"

"Prayin', sir."

"Praying!"

"Yes, sir; the musicians haven't any peace of their life for that boy's prayin'. First thing in the mornin' he's at it; noons he's at it; and nights—well, *nights* he just lays into 'em like all possessed! Sleep? Bless you, they *can't* sleep; he's got the floor, as the sayin' is, and then when he once gets his supplication-mill agoin' there just simply ain't any let-up to him. He starts in with the bandmaster, and he prays for him; next he takes the head bugler, and he prays for him; next the bass drum, and he scoops *him* in; and so on, right straight through the band, givin' them all a show, and takin' that amount of interest in it which would make you think he thought he warn't but a little while for this world, and believed he couldn't be happy in heaven without he had a brass band along, and wanted to pick 'em out for himself, so he could depend on 'em to do up the national tunes in a style suitin' to the place. Well, sir, heavin' boots at him don't have no effect; it's dark in there; and, besides, he don't pray fair, anyway, but kneels down behind the big drum; so it don't make no difference if they *rain* boots at him, *he* don't give a dern—warbles right along, same as if it was applause. They sing out, 'Oh, take a walk!' and all sorts of such things. But what of it? It don't faze him. *He* don't mind it." After a pause: "Kind of a good little fool, too; gits up in the mornin' and carts all that stock of boots back, and sorts 'em out and sets each man's pair where they belong. And they've been throwed at him so much now that he knows every boot in the band—can sort 'em out with his eyes shut."

After another pause, which I forbore to interrupt:

"But the roughest thing about it is that when he's done prayin'— when he ever *does* get done—he pipes up and begins to *sing*. Well, you know what a honey kind of voice he's got when he talks; you know how it would persuade a cast-iron dog to come down off of a doorstep and lick his hand. Now if you'll take my word for it, sir, it ain't a circumstance to his singin'! Flute music is harsh to that boy's singin'. Oh, he just gurgles it out so soft and sweet and low, there in the dark, that it makes you think you are in heaven."

"What is there 'rough' about that?"

"Ah, that's just it, sir. You hear him sing

'Just as I am—poor wretched, blind'—

just you hear him sing that once, and see if you don't melt all up and the water come into your eyes! I don't care *what* he sings, it goes plum straight home to you—it goes deep down to where you *live*—and it fetches you every time! Just you hear him sing

'Child of sin and sorrow, filled with dismay,
Wait not till tomorrow, yield thee today;
Grieve not that love
Which, from above'—

and so on. It makes a body feel like the wickedest, ungratefulest brute that walks. And when he sings them songs of his about home, and mother, and childhood, and old memories, and things that's vanished, and old friends dead and gone, it fetches everything before your face that you've ever loved and lost in all your life—and it's just beautiful, it's just divine to listen to, sir—but, Lord, Lord, the heartbreak of it! The band—well, they all cry—every rascal of them blubbers, and don't try to hide it, either; and first you know, that very gang that's been slammin' boots at that boy will skip out of their bunks all of a sudden, and rush over in the dark and hug him! Yes, they do—and slobber all over him, and call him pet names, and beg him to forgive them. And just at that time, if a regiment was to offer to hurt a hair of that cub's head, they'd go for that regiment, if it was a whole army corps!"

Another pause.

"Is that all?" said I.

"Yes, sir."

"Well, dear me, what is the complaint? What do they want done?"

"Done? Why, bless you, sir, they want you to stop him from *singin'*."

"What an idea! You said his music was divine."

"That's just it. It's *too* divine. Mortal man can't stand it. It stirs a body up so; it turns a body inside out; it racks his feelin's all to rags; it makes him feel bad and wicked, and not fit for any place but perdition. It keeps a body in such an everlastin' state of repentin', that nothin' don't taste good and there ain't no comfort in life. And then the *cryin'*, you see—every mornin' they are ashamed to look one another in the face."

"Well, this is an odd case, and a singular complaint. So they really want the singing stopped?"

"Yes, sir, that is the idea. They don't wish to ask too much; they would like powerful well to have the prayin' shut down on, or least-ways trimmed off around the edges; but the main thing's the singin'. If they can only get the singin' chocked off, they think they can stand the prayin', rough as it is to be bullyragged so much that way."

I told the sergeant I would take the matter under consideration. That night I crept into the musicians' quarters and listened. The sergeant had not overstated the case. I heard the praying voice pleading in the dark; I heard the execrations of the harassed men; I heard the rain of boots whiz through the air, and bang and thump around the big drum. The thing touched me, but it amuse me, too. By and by, after an impressive silence, came the singing. Lord, the pathos of it, the enchantment of it! Nothing in the world was ever so sweet, so gracious, so tender, so holy, so moving. I made my stay very brief; I was beginning to experience emotions of a sort not proper to the commandant of a fortress.

Next day I issued orders which stopped the praying and singing. Then followed three or four days which were so full of bounty-jumping excitements and irritations that I never once thought of my drummer-boy. But now comes Sergeant Rayburn, one morning, and says:

"That new boy acts mighty strange, sir."

"How?"

"Well, sir, he's all the time writin'."

"Writing? What does he write—letters?"

"I don't know, sir; but whenever he's off duty, he is always pokin' and nosin' around the fort, all by himself—blest if I think there's a hole or corner in it he hasn't been into—and every little while he outs with pencil and paper and scribbles somethin' down."

This gave me a most unpleasant sensation. I wanted to scoff at it, but it was not a time to scoff at *anything* that had the least suspicious tinge about it. Things were happening all around us in the North then that warned us to be always on the alert, and always suspecting. I recalled to mind the suggestive fact that this boy was from the South—the extreme South, Louisiana—and the thought was not of a reassuring nature, under the circumstances. Nevertheless, it cost me a pang to give the orders which I now gave to Rayburn. I felt like a father who plots to expose his own child to shame and injury. I told Rayburn to keep quiet, bide his time, and get me some of those writings whenever he could manage it without the boy's finding it out. And I charged him not to do anything which might let the boy discover that he was being watched. I also ordered that he allow the lad his usual liberties, but that he be followed at a distance when he went out into the town.

During the next two days Rayburn reported to me several times. No success. The boy was still writing, but he always pocketed his paper with a careless air whenever Rayburn appeared in the vicinity. He had gone twice to an old deserted stable in the town, remained a minute or two, and come out again. One could not pooh-pooh these things—they had an evil look. I was obliged to confess to myself that I was getting uneasy. I went into my private quarters and sent for my second in command—an officer of intelligence and judgment, son of General James Watson Webb. He was surprised and troubled. We had a long talk over the matter, and came to the conclusion that it would be worthwhile to institute a secret search. I determined to take charge of that myself. So I had myself called at two in the morning; and pretty soon after I was in the musicians' quarters, crawling along the floor on my stomach among the snorers. I reached my slumbering waif's bunk at last, without disturbing anybody, captured his clothes and kit, and crawled stealthily back again. When I got to my own quarters, I found Webb there, waiting and eager to know the result. We made search immediately. The clothes were a disappointment. In the pockets we found blank paper and a pencil; nothing else, except a jackknife and such queer odds and ends and useless trifles as boys hoard and value. We turned to the kit hopefully. Nothing there but a rebuke for us!—a little Bible with this written on the flyleaf: "Stranger, be kind to my boy, for his mother's sake."

I looked at Webb—he dropped his eyes; he looked at me—I dropped mine. Neither spoke. I put the book reverently back in its place. Presently Webb got up and went away, without remark. After a little I nerved myself up to my unpalatable job, and took the plunder back to where it belonged, crawling on my stomach as before. It seemed the peculiarly appropriate attitude for the business I was in.

I was most honestly glad when it was over and done with.

About noon next day Rayburn came, as usual, to report. I cut him short. I said:

"Let this nonsense be dropped. We are making a bugaboo out of a poor little cub who has got no more harm in him than a hymn book."

The sergeant looked surprised, and said:

"Well, you know it was your orders, sir, and I've got some of the writin'."

"And what does it amount to? How did you get it?"

"I peeped through the keyhole, and see him writin'. So, when I judged he was about done, I made a sort of a little cough, and I see him crumple it up and throw it in the fire, and look all around to see if anybody was comin'. Then he settled back as comfortable and careless as anything. Then I comes in, and passes the time of day pleasantly, and sends him on an errand. He never looked uneasy, but went right along. It was a coal fire and new built; the writin' had gone over behind a chunk, out of sight; but I got it out; there it is; it ain't hardly scorched, you see."

I glanced at the paper and took in a sentence or two. Then I dismissed the sergeant and told him to send Webb to me. Here is the paper in full:

> Fort Trumbull, *the 8th.*
> COLONEL *I was mistaken as to the caliber of the three guns I ended my list with. They are 18-pounders; all the rest of the armament is as I stated. The garrison remains as before reported, except that the two light infantry companies that were to be detached for service at the front are to stay here for the present— can't find out for how long, just now, but will soon. We are satisfied that, all things considered, matters had better be postponed un—*

There it broke off—there is where Rayburn coughed and interrupted the writer. All my affection for the boy, all my respect for him and charity for his forlorn condition, withered in a moment under the blight of this revelation of cold-blooded baseness.

But never mind about that. Here was business—business that required profound and immediate attention, too. Webb and I turned the subject over and over, and examined it all around. Webb said:

"What a pity he was interrupted! Something is going to be postponed until—when? And what is the something? Possibly he would have mentioned it, the pious little reptile!"

"Yes," I said, "we have missed a trick. And who is 'we' in the letter? Is it conspirators inside the fort or outside?"

That "we" was uncomfortably suggestive. However, it was not worthwhile to be guessing around that, so we proceeded to matters more practical. In the first place, we decided to double the sentries and keep the strictest possible watch. Next, we thought of calling Wicklow in and making him divulge everything; but that did not seem wisest until other methods should fail. We must have some more of the writings; so we began to plan to that end. And now we had an idea: Wicklow never went to the post office—perhaps the deserted stable was his post office. We sent for my confidential clerk—a young German named Sterne, who was a sort of natural detective—and told him all about the case, and ordered him to go to work on it. Within the hour we got word that Wicklow was writing again. Shortly afterward word came that he had asked leave to go out into the town. He was detained awhile and meantime Sterne hurried off and concealed himself in the stable. By and by he saw Wicklow saunter in, look about him, then hide something under some rubbish in a corner, and take leisurely leave again. Sterne pounced upon the hidden article—a letter—and brought it to us. It had no superscription and no signature. It repeated what we had already read, and then went on to say:

> *We think it best to postpone till the two companies are gone. I mean the four inside think so; have not communicated with the others—afraid of attracting attention. I say four because we have lost two; they had hardly enlisted and got inside when they were shipped off to the front. It will be absolutely necessary to have two in their places. The two that went were the brothers from Thirty-mile Point. I have something of the greatest importance to reveal, but must not trust it to this method of communication; will try the other.*

"The little scoundrel!" said Webb; "who *could* have supposed he was a spy? However, never mind about that; let us add up our particulars, such as they are, and see how the case stands to date. First, we've got a rebel spy in our midst, whom we know; secondly, we've got three more in our midst whom we don't know; thirdly, these spies have been introduced among us through the simple and easy process of enlisting as soldiers in the Union army—and evidently two of them have got sold at it, and been shipped off to the front; fourthly, there are assistant spies 'outside'—number indefinite; fifthly, Wicklow has a very important matter which he is afraid to communicate by the 'present method'—will 'try the other.' That is the case, as it now stands. Shall we collar Wicklow and make him confess? Or shall we catch the person who removes the letters from the stable and make *him* tell? Or shall we keep still and find out more?"

We decided upon the last course. We judged that we did not need to proceed to summary measures now, since it was evident that the conspirators were likely to wait till those two light infantry companies were out of the way. We fortified Sterne with pretty ample powers, and told him to use his best endeavors to find out Wicklow's "other method" of communication. We meant to play a bold game; and to this end we proposed to keep the spies in an unsuspecting state as long as possible. So we ordered Sterne to return to the stable immediately, and, if he found the coast clear, to conceal Wicklow's letter where it was before, and leave it there for the conspirators to get.

The night closed down without further event. It was cold and dark and sleety, with a raw wind blowing; still I turned out of my warm bed several times during the night, and went the rounds in person, to see that all was right and that every sentry was on the alert. I always found them wide awake and watchful; evidently whispers of mysterious dangers had been floating about, and the doubling of the guards had been a kind of endorsement of those rumors. Once, toward morning, I encountered Webb, breasting his way against the bitter wind, and learned then that he, also, had been the rounds several times to see that all was going right.

Next day's events hurried things up somewhat. Wicklow wrote another letter; Sterne preceded him to the stable and saw him deposit it; captured it as soon as Wicklow was out of the way, then slipped out and followed the little spy at a distance, with a detective in plainclothes at his own heels, for we thought it judicious to have the law's assistance handy in case of need. Wicklow went to the railway station, and waited around till the train from New York came in, then stood scanning the faces of the crowd as they poured out of the cars. Presently an aged gentleman, with green goggles and a cane, came limping along, stopped in Wicklow's neighborhood, and began to look about him expectantly. In an instant Wicklow darted forward, thrust an envelope into his hand, then glided away and disappeared in the throng. The next instant Sterne had snatched the letter; and as he hurried past the detective, he said: "Follow the old gentleman—don't lose sight of him." Then Sterne scurried out with the crowd, and came straight to the fort.

We sat with closed doors, and instructed the guard outside to allow no interruption.

First we opened the letter captured at the stable. It read as follows:

> HOLY ALLIANCE *Found, in the usual gun, commands from the Master, left there last night, which set aside the instructions heretofore received from the subordinate quarter. Have left in the gun the usual indication that the commands reached the proper hand—*

Webb, interrupting: "Isn't the boy under constant surveillance now?"

I said yes; he had been under strict surveillance ever since the capturing of his former letter.

"Then how could he put anything into a gun, or take anything out of it, and not get caught?"

"Well," I said, "I don't like the look of that very well."

"I don't either," said Webb. "It simply means that there are conspirators among the very sentinels. Without their connivance in some way or other, the thing couldn't have been done."

I sent for Rayburn, and ordered him to examine the batteries and see what he could find. The reading of the letter was then resumed:

> *The new commands are peremptory, and require that the MMMM shall be FFFFF at 3 o'clock tomorrow morning. Two hundred will arrive, in small parties, by train and otherwise, from various directions, and will be at appointed place at right time. I will distribute the sign today. Success is apparently sure, though something must have got out, for the sentries have been doubled, and the chiefs went the rounds last night several times. W. W. comes from southerly today and will receive secret orders—by the other method. All six of you must be in 166 at sharp 2 A.M. You will find B. B. there, who will give you detailed instruction, Passwords same as last time, only reversed—put first syllable last and last syllable first.*

REMEMBER *XXXX. Do not forget. Be of good heart; before the next sun rises you will be heroes; your fame will be permanent; you will have added a deathless page to history.* AMEN.

"Thunder and Mars," said Webb, "but we are getting into mighty hot quarters, as I look at it!"

I said there was no question but that things were beginning to wear a most serious aspect. Said I:

"A desperate enterprise is on foot, that is plain enough. Tonight is the time set for it—that, also, is plain. The exact nature of the enterprise—I mean the manner of it—is hidden away under those blind bunches of M's and F's, but the end and aim, I judge, is the surprise and capture of the post. We must move quick and sharp now. I think nothing can be gained by continuing our clandestine policy as regards Wicklow. We *must* know, and as soon as possible, too, where '166' is located, so that we can make a descent upon the gang there at 2 A.M.; and doubtless the quickest way to get that information will be to force it out of that boy. But first of all, and before we make any important move, I must lay the facts before the War Department, and ask for plenary powers."

The dispatch was prepared in cipher to go over the wires; I read it, approved it, and sent it along.

We presently finished discussing the letter which was under consideration, and then opened the one which had been snatched from the lame gentleman. It contained nothing but a couple of perfectly blank sheets of notepaper! It was a chilly check to our hot eagerness and expectancy. We felt as blank as the paper, for a moment, and twice as foolish. But it was for a moment only; for, of course, we immediately afterward thought of "sympathetic ink." We held the paper close to the fire and watched for the characters to come out, under the influence of the heat; but nothing appeared but some faint tracings, which we could make nothing of. We then called in the surgeon, and sent him off with orders to apply every test he was acquainted with till he got the right one, and report the contents of the letter to me the instant he brought them to the surface. This check was a confounded annoyance, and we naturally chafed under the delay; for we had fully expected to get out of that letter some of the most important secrets of the plot.

Now appeared Sergeant Rayburn, and drew from his pocket a piece of twine string about a foot long, with three knots tied in it, and held it up.

"I got it out of a gun on the waterfront," said he. "I took the tompions out of all the guns and examined close; this string was the only thing that was in any gun."

So this bit of string was Wicklow's "sign" to signify that the "Master's" commands had not miscarried. I ordered that every sentinel who had served near that gun during the past twenty-four hours be put in confinement at once and separately, and not allowed to communicate with any one without my privity and consent.

A telegram now came from the Secretary of War. It read as follows:

> Suspend habeas corpus. Put town under martial law. Make necessary arrests. Act with vigor and promptness. Keep the department informed.

We were now in shape to go to work. I sent out and had the lame gentleman quietly arrested and as quietly brought into the fort; I placed him under guard, and forbade speech to him or from him. He was inclined to bluster at first, but he soon dropped that.

Next came word that Wicklow had been seen to give something to a couple of our new recruits; and that, as soon as his back was turned, these had been seized and confined. Upon each was found a small bit of paper, bearing these words and signs in pencil:

EAGLE'S THIRD FLIGHT
REMEMBER XXXX
166

In accordance with instructions, I telegraphed to the Department, in cipher, the progress made, and also described the above ticket. We seemed to be in a strong enough position now to venture to throw off the mask as regarded Wicklow; so I sent for him. I also sent for and received back the letter written in sympathetic ink, the surgeon accompanying it with the information that thus far it had resisted his tests, but that there were others he could apply when I should be ready for him to do so.

Presently Wicklow entered. He had a somewhat worn and anxious look, but he was composed and easy, and if he suspected anything it did not appear in his face or manner. I allowed him to stand there a moment or two; then I said pleasantly:

"My boy, why do you go to that old stable so much?"

He answered, with simple demeanor and without embarrassment:

"Well, I hardly know, sir; there isn't any particular reason, except that I like to be alone, and I amuse myself there."

"You amuse yourself there, do you?"

"Yes, sir," he replied, as innocently and simply as before.

"Is that all you do there?"

"Yes, sir," he said, looking up with childlike wonderment in his big, soft eyes.

"You are *sure*?"

"Yes, sir, sure."

After a pause I said:

"Wicklow, why do you write so much?"

"I? I do not write much, sir."

"You don't?"

"No, sir. Oh, if you mean scribbling, I *do* scribble some, for amusement."

"What do you do with your scribblings?"

"Nothing, sir—throw them away."

"Never send them to anybody?"

"No, sir."

I suddenly thrust before him the letter to the "Colonel." He started slightly, but immediately composed himself. A slight tinge spread itself over his cheek.

"How came you to send *this* piece of scribbling, then?"

"I nev—never meant any harm, sir!"

"Never meant any harm! You betray the armament and condition of the post, and mean no harm by it?"

He hung his head and was silent.

"Come, speak up, and stop lying. Whom was this letter intended for?"

He showed signs of distress now; but quickly collected himself, and replied, in a tone of deep earnestness:

"I will tell you the truth, sir—the whole truth. The letter was never intended for anybody at all. I wrote it only to amuse myself. I see the error and foolishness of it now; but it is the only offense, sir, upon my honor."

"Ah, I am glad of that. It is dangerous to be writing such letters. I hope you are sure this is the only one you wrote?"

"Yes, sir, perfectly sure."

His hardihood was stupefying. He told that with as sincere a countenance as any creature ever wore. I waited a moment to soothe down my rising temper, and then said:

"Wicklow, jog your memory now, and see if you can help me with two or three little matters which I wish to inquire about."

"I will do my very best, sir."

"Then, to begin with—who is 'the Master'?"

It betrayed him into darting a startled glance at our faces, but that was all. He was serene again in a moment, and tranquilly answered:

"I do not know, sir."

"You do not know?"

"I do not know."

"You are *sure* you do not know?"

He tried hard to keep his eyes on mine, but the strain was too great; his chin sunk slowly toward his breast and he was silent; he stood there nervously fumbling with a button, an object to command one's pity, in spite of his base acts. Presently I broke the stillness with the question:

"Who are the 'Holy Alliance'?"

His body shook visibly, and he made a slight random gesture with his hands, which to me was like the appeal of a despairing creature for compassion. But he made no sound. He continued to stand with his face bent toward the ground. As we sat gazing at him, waiting for him to speak, we saw the big tears begin to roll down his cheeks. But he remained silent. After a little, I said:

"You must answer me, my boy, and you must tell me the truth. Who are the Holy Alliance?"

He wept on in silence. Presently I said, somewhat sharply:

"Answer the question!"

He struggled to get command of his voice; and then, looking up appealingly, forced the words out between his sobs:

"Oh, have pity on me, sir! I cannot answer it, for I do not know."

"What!"

"Indeed, sir, I am telling the truth. I never have heard of the Holy Alliance till this moment. On my honor, sir, this is so."

"Good heavens! Look at this second letter of yours; there, do you see those words, 'Holy Alliance'? What do you say now?"

He gazed up into my face with the hurt look of one upon whom a great wrong had been wrought, then said, feelingly:

"This is some cruel joke, sir; and how could they play it upon me, who have tried all I could to do right, and have never done harm to anybody? Someone has counterfeited my hand; I never wrote a line of this; I have never seen this letter before!"

"Oh, you unspeakable liar! Here, what do you say to this?"—and I snatched the sympathetic-ink letter from my pocket and thrust it before his eyes.

His face turned white—as white as a dead person's. He wavered slightly in his tracks, and put his hand against the wall to steady himself. After a moment he asked, in so faint a voice that it was hardly audible:

"Have you—read it?"

Our faces must have answered the truth before my lips could get out a false "yes," for I distinctly saw the courage come back into that boy's eyes. I waited for him to say something, but he kept silent. So at last I said:

"Well, what have you to say as to the revelations in this letter?"

He answered, with perfect composure:

"Nothing, except that they are entirely harmless and innocent; they can hurt nobody."

I was in something of a corner now, as I couldn't disprove his assertion. I did not know exactly how to proceed. However, an idea came to my relief, and I said:

"You are sure you know nothing about the Master and the Holy Alliance, and did not write the letter which you say is a forgery?"

"Yes, sir—sure."

I slowly drew out the knotted twine string and held it up without speaking. He gazed at it indifferently, then looked at me inquiringly. My patience was sorely taxed. However, I kept my temper down, and said, in my usual voice:

"Wicklow, do you see this?"

"Yes, sir."

"What is it?"

"It seems to be a piece of string."

"*Seems*? It is a piece of string. Do you recognize it?"

"No, sir," he replied, as calmly as the words could be uttered.

His coolness was perfectly wonderful! I paused now for several seconds, in order that the silence might add impressiveness to what I was about to say; then I rose and laid my hand on his shoulder, and said gravely:

"It will do you no good, poor boy, none in the world. This sign to the 'Master,' this knotted string, found in one of the guns on the waterfront—"

"Found *in* the gun! Oh, no, no, no! do not say *in* the gun, but in a crack in the tompion—it *must* have been in the crack!" and down he went on his knees and clasped his hands and lifted up a face that was pitiful to see, so ashy it was, and wild with terror.

"No, it was *in* the gun."

"Oh, something has gone wrong! My God, I am lost!" and he sprang up and darted this way and that, dodging the hands that were put out to catch him, and doing his best to escape from the place. But of course escape was impossible. Then he flung himself on his knees again, crying with all his might, and clasped me around the legs; and so he clung to me and begged and pleaded, saying, "Oh, have pity on me! Oh, be merciful to me! Do not betray me; they would not spare my life a moment! Protect me, save me, I will confess everything!"

It took us some time to quiet him down and modify his fright, and get him into something like a rational frame of mind. Then I began to question him, he answering humbly, with downcast eyes, and from time to time swabbing away his constantly flowing tears:

"So you are at heart a rebel?"

"Yes, sir."

"And a spy?"

"Yes, sir."

"And have been acting under distinct orders from outside?"

"Yes, sir."

"Willingly?"

"Yes, sir."

"*Gladly*, perhaps?"

"Yes, sir; it would do no good to deny it. The South is my country; my heart is Southern, and it is all in her cause."

"Then the tale you told me of your wrongs and the persecution of your family was made up for the occasion?"

"They—they told me to say it, sir."

"And you would betray and destroy those who pitied and sheltered you. Do you comprehend how base you are, you poor misguided thing?"

He replied with sobs only.

"Well, let that pass. To business. Who is the 'Colonel,' and where is he?"

He began to cry hard, and tried to beg off from answering. He said he would be killed if he told. I threatened to put him in the dark cell and lock him up if he did not come out with the information. At the same time I promised to protect him from all harm if he made a clean breast. For all answer, he closed his mouth firmly and put on a stubborn air which I could not bring him out of. At last I started with him; but a single glance into the dark cell converted him. He broke into a passion of weeping and supplicating, and declared he would tell everything.

So I brought him back, and he named the "Colonel," and described him particularly. Said he would be found at the principal hotel in the town, in citizen's dress. I had to threaten him again, before he would describe and name the "Master." Said the Master would be found at No. 15 Bond Street, New York, passing under the name of R. F. Gaylord. I telegraphed name and description to the chief of police of the metropolis, and asked that Gaylord be arrested and held till I could send for him.

"Now," said I, "it seems that there are several of the conspirators 'outside,' presumably in New London. Name and describe them."

He named and described three men and two women—all stopping at the principal hotel. I sent out quietly, and had them and the "Colonel" arrested and confined in the fort.

"Next, I want to know all about your three fellow-conspirators who are here in the fort."

He was about to dodge me with a falsehood, I thought; but I produced the mysterious bits of paper which had been found upon two of them, and this had a salutary effect upon him. I said we had possession of two of the men, and he must point out the third. This frightened him badly, and he cried out:

"Oh, please don't make me; he would kill me on the spot!"

I said that that was all nonsense; I would have somebody nearby to protect him, and, besides, the men should be assembled without arms. I ordered all the raw recruits to be mustered, and then the poor, trembling little wretch went out and stepped along down the line, trying to look as indifferent as possible. Finally he spoke a single word to one of the men, and before he had gone five steps the man was under arrest.

As soon as Wicklow was with us again, I had those three men brought in. I made one of them stand forward, and said:

"Now, Wicklow, mind, not a shade's divergence from the exact truth. Who is this man, and what do you know about him?"

Being "in for it," he cast consequences aside, fastened his eyes on the man's face, and spoke straight along without hesitation—to the following effect:

"His real name is George Bristow. He is from New Orleans; was second mate of the coast-packet *Capitol* two years ago; is a desperate character, and has served two terms for manslaughter—one for killing a deckhand named Hyde with a capstan-bar, and one for killing a roustabout for refusing to heave the lead, which is no part of a roustabout's business. He is a spy, and was sent here by the Colonel to act in that capacity. He was third mate of the *St. Nicholas* when she blew up in the neighborhood of Memphis, in '58, and came near being lynched for robbing the dead and wounded while they were being taken ashore in an empty woodboat."

And so forth and so on—he gave the man's biography in full. When he had finished, I said to the man:

"What have you to say to this?"

"Barring your presence sir, it is the infernalist lie that ever was spoke!"

I sent him back into confinement, and called the others forward in turn. Same result. The boy gave a detailed history of each, without ever hesitating for a word or a fact; but all I could get out of either rascal was the indignant assertion that it was all a lie.

They would confess nothing. I returned them to captivity, and brought out the rest of my prisoners, one by one. Wicklow told all about them—what towns in the South they were from, and every detail of their connection with the conspiracy.

But they all denied his facts, and not one of them confessed a thing. The men raged, the women cried. According to their stories, they were all innocent people from out West, and loved the Union above all things in this world. I locked the gang up, in disgust, and fell to catechizing Wicklow once more.

"Where is No. 166, and who is B. B.?"

But *there* he was determined to draw the line. Neither coaxing nor threats had any effect upon him. Time was flying—it was necessary to institute sharp measures. So I tied him up a-tiptoe by the thumbs. As the pain increased, it wrung screams from him which were almost more than I could bear. But I held my ground, and pretty so on he shrieked out:

"Oh, *please* let me down, and I will tell!"

"No—you'll tell *before* I let you down."

Every instant was agony to him now, so out it came:

"No. 166, Eagle Hotel!"—naming a wretched tavern down by the water, a resort of common laborers, longshoremen, and less reputable folk.

So I released him, and then demanded to know the object of the conspiracy.

"To take the fort tonight," said he, doggedly and sobbing.

"Have I got all the chiefs of the conspiracy?"

"No. You've got all except those that are to meet at 166."

"What does 'Remember XXXX' mean?"

No reply.

"What is the password to No. 166?"

No reply.

"What do those bunches of letters mean—'FFFFF' and 'MMMM'? Answer! or you will catch it again."

"I never *will* answer! I will die first. Now do what you please."

"Think what you are saying, Wicklow. Is it final?"

He answered steadily, and without a quiver in his voice:

"It is final. As sure as I love my wronged country and hate everything this Northern sun shines on, I will die before I will reveal those things."

I tied him up by the thumbs again. When the agony was full upon him it was heartbreaking to hear the poor thing's shrieks, but we got nothing else out of him. To every question he screamed the same reply: "I can die, and I *will* die; but I will never tell."

Well, we had to give it up. We were convinced that he certainly would die rather than confess. So we took him down, and imprisoned him under strict guard.

Then for some hours we busied ourselves with sending telegrams to the War Department, and with making preparations for a descent upon No. 166.

It was stirring times, that black and bitter night. Things had leaked out, and the whole garrison was on the alert. The sentinels were trebled, and nobody could move, outside or in, without being brought to a stand with a musket leveled at his head. However, Webb and I were less concerned now than we had previously been, because of the fact that the conspiracy must necessarily be in a pretty crippled condition, since so many of its principals were in our clutches.

I determined to be at No. 166 in good season, capture and gag B. B., and be on hand for the rest when they arrived. At about a quarter past one in the morning I crept out of the fortress with half a dozen stalwart and gamy U.S. regulars at my heels, and the boy Wicklow, with his hands tied behind him. I told him we were going to No. 166, and that if I found he had lied again and was misleading us, he would have to show us the right place or suffer the consequences.

We approached the tavern stealthily and reconnoitered. A light was burning in the small barroom, the rest of the house was dark. I tried the front door; it yielded, and we softly entered, closing the door behind us. Then we removed our shoes, and I led the way to the barroom. The German landlord sat there, asleep in his chair. I woke him gently, and told him to take off his boots and precede us, warning him at the same time to utter no sound. He obeyed without a murmur, but evidently he was badly frightened. I ordered him to lead the way to 166. We ascended two or three flights of stairs as softly as a file of cats; and then, having arrived near the farther end of a long hall, we came to a door through the glazed transom of which we could discern the glow of a dim light from within. The landlord felt for me in the dark and whispered to me that that was 166. I tried the door—it was locked on the inside. I whispered an order to one of my biggest soldiers; we set our ample shoulders to the door, and with one heave we burst it from its hinges. I caught a half-glimpse of a figure in a bed—saw its head dart toward the candle; out went the light and we were in pitch darkness. With one big bound I lit on that bed and pinned its occupant down with my knees. My prisoner struggled fiercely, but I got a grip on his throat with my left hand, and that was a good assistance to my knees in holding him down. Then straightway I snatched out my revolver, cocked it, and laid the cold barrel warningly against his cheek.

"Now somebody strike a light!" said I. "I've got him safe."

It was done. The flame of the match burst up. I looked at my captive, and, by George, it was a young woman!

I let go and got off the bed, feeling pretty sheepish. Everybody stared stupidly at his neighbor. Nobody had any wit or sense left, so sudden and overwhelming had been the surprise. The young woman began to cry, and covered her face with the sheet. The landlord said, meekly.

"My daughter, she has been doing something that is not right, *nicht wahr*?"

"Your daughter? Is she your daughter?"

"Oh, yes, she is my daughter. She is just tonight come home from Cincinnati a little bit sick."

"Confound it, that boy has lied again. This is not the right 166; this is not B. B. Now, Wicklow, you will find the correct 166 for us, or—hello! where is that boy?"

Gone, as sure as guns! And, what is more, we failed to find a trace of him. Here was an awful predicament. I cursed my stupidity in not tying him to one of the men; but it was of no use to bother about that now. What should I do in the present circumstances?— that was the question. That girl *might* be B. B., after all. I did not believe it, but still it would not answer to take unbelief for proof. So I finally put my men in a vacant room across the hall from 166, and told them to capture anybody and everybody that approached the girl's room, and to keep the landlord with them, and under strict watch, until further orders. Then I hurried back to the fort to see if all was right there yet.

Yes, all was right. And all remained right. I stayed up all night to make sure of that. Nothing happened. I was unspeakably glad to see the dawn come again, and be able to telegraph the Department that the Stars and Stripes still floated over Fort Trumbull.

An immense pressure was lifted from my breast. Still I did not relax vigilance, of course, nor effort, either; the case was too grave for that. I had up my prisoners, one by one, and harried them by the hour, trying to get them to confess, but it was a failure. They only gnashed their teeth and tore their hair, and revealed nothing.

About noon came tidings of my missing boy. He had been seen on the road, tramping westward, some eight miles out, at six in the morning. I started a cavalry lieutenant and a private on his track at once. They came in sight of him twenty miles out. He had climbed a fence and was wearily dragging himself across a slushy field toward a large old-fashioned mansion on the edge of a village. They rode through a bit of woods, made a detour, and closed upon the house from the opposite side; then dismounted and skurried into the kitchen. Nobody there. They slipped into the next room, which was also unoccupied; the door from that room into the front or sitting room was open. They were about to step through it when they heard a low voice; it was somebody praying. So they halted reverently, and the lieutenant put his head in and saw an old man and an old woman kneeling in a corner of that sitting-room. It was the old man that was praying, and just as he was finishing his prayer, the Wicklow boy opened the front door and stepped in. Both of those old people sprang at him and smothered him with embraces, shouting:

"Our boy! Our darling! God be praised. The lost is found! He that was dead is alive again!"

Well, sir, what do you think! That young imp was born and reared on that homestead, and had never been five miles away from it in all his life till the fortnight before he loafed into my quarters and gulled me with that maudlin yarn of his! It's as true as gospel.

That old man was his father—a learned old retired clergyman; and that old lady was his mother.

Let me throw in a word or two of explanation concerning that boy and his performances. It turned out that he was a ravenous devourer of dime novels and sensation-story papers—therefore, dark mysteries and gaudy heroisms were just in his line. Then he had read newspaper reports of the stealthy goings and comings of rebel spies in our midst, and of their lurid purposes and their two or three startling achievements, till his imagination was all aflame on that subject. His constant comrade for some months had been a Yankee youth of much tongue and lively fancy, who had served for a couple of years as "mud clerk" (that is, subordinate purser) on certain of the packet-boats plying between New Orleans and points two or three hundred miles up the Mississippi—hence his easy facility in handling the names and other details pertaining to that region. Now I had spent two or three months in that part of the country before the war; and I knew just enough about it to be easily taken in by that boy, whereas a born Louisianian would probably have caught him tripping before he had talked fifteen minutes. Do you know the reason he said he would rather die than explain certain of his treasonable enigmas? Simply because he *couldn't* explain them!—they had no meaning; he had fired them out of his imagination without forethought or afterthought; and so, upon sudden call, he wasn't able to invent an explanation of them. For instance, he couldn't reveal what was hidden in the "sympathetic ink" letter, for the ample reason that there wasn't anything hidden in it; it was blank paper only. He hadn't put anything into a gun, and had never intended to—for his letters were all written to imaginary persons, and when he hid one in the stable he always removed the one he had put there the day before; so he was not acquainted with that knotted string, since he was seeing it for the first time when I showed it to him; but as soon as I had let him find out where it came from, he straightway adopted it, in his romantic fashion, and got some fine effects out of it. He invented the "Gaylord"; there wasn't any 15 Bond Street, just then—it had been pulled down three months before. He invented the "Colonel"; he invented the glib histories of those unfortunates whom I captured and confronted him with; he invented "B. B."; he even invented No. 166, one may say, for he didn't know there was such a number in the Eagle Hotel until we went there. He stood ready to invent anybody or anything whenever it was wanted. If I called for "outside" spies, he promptly described strangers whom he had seen at the hotel, and whose names he had happened to hear. Ah, he lived in a gorgeous, mysterious, romantic world during those few stirring days, and I think it was *real* to him, and that he enjoyed it clear down to the bottom of his heart.

But he made trouble enough for us, and just no end of humiliation. You see, on account of him we had fifteen or twenty people under arrest and confinement in the fort, with sentinels before their doors. A lot of the captives were soldiers and such, and to them I didn't have to apologize; but the rest were first-class citizens, from all over the country, and no amount of apologies was sufficient to satisfy them. They just fumed and raged and made no end of trouble! And those two ladies—one was an Ohio Congressman's wife, the other a Western bishop's sister—well, the scorn and ridicule and angry tears they poured out on me made up a keepsake that was likely to make me remember them for considerable time—and I shall. That old lame gentleman with the goggles was a college president from Philadelphia, who had come up to attend his nephew's funeral. He had never seen young Wicklow before, of course. Well, he not only missed the funeral, and got jailed as a rebel spy, but Wicklow had stood up there in my quarters and coldly described him as a counterfeiter, nigger-trader, horse-thief, and firebug from the most notorious rascal-nest in Galveston; and this was a thing which that poor old gentleman couldn't seem to get over at all.

And the War Department! But, oh, my soul, let's draw the curtain over that part!

NOTE: I showed my manuscript to the Major, and he said: "Your unfamiliarity with military matters has betrayed you into some little mistakes. Still, they are picturesque ones—let them go; military men will smile at them, the rest won't detect them. You have got the main facts of the history right, and have set them down just about as they occurred."
M.T.

Winds of Change

JOHN LUTZ

L AST NIGHT WHEN I was with my wife I accidentally spoke your
name."

Alison didn't answer David immediately. Slanted sunlight blasted
from between the clouds in the California sky and glinted off the
highly polished gray hood of her 1936 Chevy convertible. Tommy
Dorsey's band was playing swing on the dashboard radio. The car
was five years old, but Alison regarded it as if it were the newest
model. She had only recently been able to afford such a luxury.

"What was your wife's reaction?" she asked at last, shifting gears
for a steep grade in the twisting road.

David threw back his handsome head, his blond hair whipping
forward in the turmoil of wind, and laughed. "None. She didn't
understand me, I'm sure. There's so much she doesn't understand
about me."

Alison didn't caution him to be more discreet, as she usually
did. She seemed lulled by their motion through the warm, balmy
evening. Her long auburn hair flowed gracefully where it curled

236

from beneath the scarf that covered her head and was knotted beneath her chin. She knew that she and David were an enviable young couple in her sleek convertible, speeding along the coast road in mountainous Big Sur Country, with the shaded, thick redwood forest on their right and the sea, charging the shore and crashing sun-shot against the rocks on their left.

He extended a long arm and languidly, affectionately, dragged his fingertips across the shoulder of her wool sweater. She felt her heart accelerate at his touch.

"My wife doesn't know you're a spy," he said.

Alison turned her head toward him and smiled. "Let's hope not."

She braked the convertible, shifted gears again, and pulled to the side of the highway. Then she drove up the narrow, faintly defined dirt road that led to their usual picnic place. Within a few minutes, the car was parked in the shade of the redwood trees of smaller variety that grew in that wild section of California.

She got the wicker picnic basket from the trunk, watching David's tall, lanky frame as he quite carefully spread the blanket on the grass. David was a methodical person, which was why he was good at his job; he had a talent and fondness for order. Alison stopped and deftly straightened the seams of her nylons, then joined him.

Alison Carter and David Blaine both worked at Norris Aircraft Corporation just north of Los Angeles. Alison was a secretary and David the chief of security. The people who were paying Alison for information about the top-secret XP25 pursuit plane had advised her to strike up an acquaintance with the plant security chief. If she were caught, the relationship would be a valuable insurance policy.

Of course Alison had followed their advice. She believed everything they told her. She had been barely eighteen when Karl Prager had first approached her, had first become her lover. Nineteen when their affair was over and she was in too deeply as an informer ever to hope she might get out.

Not that it had bothered Alison to sell "industrial information." Oh, she knew she was working for the Germans, actually, but what difference did that make? It wasn't as if America was at war. Politics didn't interest Alison in the slightest, and the money Karl paid her more than doubled her meager salary earned as a secretary.

Alison hadn't had to think of a way to meet David. Her rather extravagant habits, considering her salary, prompted him to ask her some routine questions one day. When she'd told him she was the beneficiary of her late father's will, he'd believed her.

They'd seen each other again, after business hours, despite the fact that David was married. Apparently he and his wife, Glenda, were having difficulties. For Alison, the business of seducing the shy and precise David Blaine quickly became pleasure. And by the time he found out she was violating company rules, he was willing to overlook her transgressions.

On Saturdays, David would often give Glenda an excuse, that probably even she didn't believe, and he and Alison would drive up the coast road in Alison's convertible and picnic with sandwiches and champagne in their private, lover's hideaway.

ALISON SAT DOWN BESIDE David on the blanket. She untied and removed her head scarf, plucking out the bobby pins helping to hold it in place. Through the trees, the undulating blue-green sea was barely visible, but she could hear its enigmatic whisper on the rocky beach.

David paused in unwrapping the sandwiches. He dug into his shirt pocket and handed Alison a folded sheet of paper patterned with scrawled numbers. "Here," he said casually, "these are the performance specifications you asked for."

The figures represented the data on the experimental plane's latest test flight. Alison accepted the paper with a smile and slipped it into a pocket of her skirt. She knew that David took the business of revealing company information no more seriously than she did. He didn't know to whom she was giving the information—probably he assumed it was a rival aircraft manufacturer—and he didn't care. It was his love affair that was important to him, that had consumed his very soul, and not dry columns of figures that meant nothing except to an aeronautical engineer. He knew he'd be fired if the company found out about Alison and him, but he could always get another job of some sort. And he'd still have Alison.

After they'd eaten the ham sandwiches and finished the champagne, David looked at her with his level blue eyes. His head was resting in her lap, and she was stroking his fine blond hair that was just beginning to thin at the crown of his head. Alison had thought the first time she saw David that he looked very much like movie star Richard Widmark.

"There's so much I want to say to you today," he told her.

"Not now," she said, bending her body and kissing him on the lips. "Let's not talk now."

As usual, David saw her point of view, and agreed with it.

An hour later, in the purpling twilight, Alison lay on her back and watched a plane drone high overhead in the direction of the sea. A U.S. Navy plane, she noted, on a routine nighttime training mission.

David was asleep beside her, his deep, regular breathing merging with the sounds of the plane and the eternal sighing of the sea. Though her body was very still alongside his sleeping form, Alison's mind was tortured and turning.

Not that she had any real choice. Her time of choices was over. She wished David had never told her about speaking her name in front of his wife. But he had. And Alison knew that he might speak her name again in the wrong circumstances, even if tomorrow he still saw things her way.

Quietly, she rose from the blanket and fished in her straw purse for her key ring. She walked to her car, the tall grass tickling her bare feet and ankles, thinking *tomorrow, tomorrow . . .*

She unlocked and opened the car's trunk, and left it open as she returned to stand over David. She was holding a small revolver that she'd gotten from the trunk, the gun they had given her.

Alison didn't want to miss where she was aiming, didn't want to hurt him more than necessary. She did love him.

She knelt beside David, placing the gun barrel inches from his temple, and glanced in all directions to make certain they were alone. In the sudden chill breeze rushing in from the ocean, she drew in her breath sharply and squeezed the trigger.

The crack of the gun seemed feeble in the vastness of mountains and sea.

Alison sat with her eyes clenched shut until the sound of David moving on the blanket ceased. Then, still not looking at him, she returned to the car and got a shovel from the trunk.

She wrapped David's still body in the blanket and dragged it deeper into the forest. She began to dig.

In a very few hours, halfway around the world, a signal would be given, and the Japanese would attack Pearl Harbor. War would immediately be declared, not only against Japan but against Germany and Italy as well. The rules of the game Alison was being forced to play would abruptly change. Who knew if David would have been willing to continue to play if the stakes were real? Who could say what else he might have accidentally let slip to his wife? Alison knew that much more than her job, and perhaps a criminal record, depended on David's silence now. Her survival was at stake.

As she cast loose earth over the huddled, motionless form in the blanket, Alison didn't realize she was burying a ring in David's pocket, the engagement ring he had intended to give her when he awoke. The ring with her initials engraved inside the band. The ring wrapped loosely in a copy of the letter he had written to his wife, confessing everything and explaining why he was leaving her.

Alison worked frantically with the shovel, feeling her tears track hotly down her cheeks. At least David's war was over. He was at peace. Her war was just beginning, and look what it had already forced her to do.

She would be one of the first to realize why hers was a losing cause.

Two Fishers

GUY DE MAUPASSANT

P ARIS WAS BLOCKADED—FAMISHED—at the point of death. Even the sparrows on the housetops were few and far between, and the very sewers were in danger of becoming depopulated. People ate anything they could get.

Monsieur Morisot, watchmaker by trade, was walking early one bright January morning down the Boulevards, his hands in the pockets of his overcoat, feeling hungry and depressed, when he unexpectedly ran into a friend. He recognized Monsieur Sauvage, an old-time chum of the riverside.

EVERY SUNDAY BEFORE THE war Morisot used to start at daybreak with his bamboo fishing rod in his hand, his tin bait and tackle box upon his back. He used to take the train to Colombes, and to walk from there to the Island of Maranthe. No sooner had he arrived at the river than he used to begin to fish and continue fishing until evening. Here every Sunday he used to meet Monsieur Sauvage, a linen-draper from Paris, but stout and jovial withal, as keen a fisher-man moreover as he was himself.

Often they would sit side by side, their feet dangling over the water for half a day at a time and say scarcely a word, yet little by little they became friends. Sometimes they never spoke at all. Occasionally they launched out into conversation, but they understood each other perfectly without its aid, for their tastes and ideas were the same.

On a spring morning in the bright sunshine, when the light and delicate mist hovered over the river, and these two mad fishermen enjoyed a foretaste of real summer weather, Morisot would say to his neighbour: "*Hein!* not bad, eh?"

And Sauvage would reply: "I know nothing to beat it."

This interchange of sentiments was quite enough to engender mutual understanding and esteem.

In autumn, toward evening, when the setting sun reddened the sky and cast shadows of the fleeting clouds over the water; when the river was decked in purple; when the whole horizon was lighted up and the figures of the two friends were illumined as with fire; when the russet-brown of the trees was lightly tinged with gold, and the trees themselves shivered with a wintry shake, Monsieur Sauvage would smile at Monsieur Morisot and say: "What a sight, eh?"

And Monsieur Morisot, without even raising his eyes from his float would answer: "Better than the Boulevards, *hein!*"

THIS MORNING, AS SOON as they had recognized each other they shook hands warmly, quite overcome at meeting again under such different circumstances.

Monsieur Sauvage sighed and murmured: "A nice state of things."

Monsieur Morisot, gloomy and sad, answered: "And what weather! Today is New Year's Day." The sky, in fact, was clear, bright, and beautiful.

They began to walk along, sorrowful and pensive. Said Morisot: "And our fishing, eh? What times we used to have!"

Sauvage replied: "When shall we have them again?"

They went into a little café and had a glass of absinthe, and then started again on their walk.

They stopped at another café for another glass. When they came out again they were slightly dazed, like people who had fasted long and then partaken too freely.

It was lovely weather; a soft breeze fanned their faces. Monsieur Sauvage, upon whom the fresh air was beginning to take effect, suddenly said: "Suppose we were to go!"

"Go where?"

"Why, fishing!"

"But where?"

"To our island, of course. The French outposts are at Colombes. I know Colonel Dumoulin; he will let us pass through easily enough."

Morisot trembled with delight at the very idea: "All right, I'm your man."

They separated to fetch their rods.

An hour afterwards they were walking fast along the high road, towards the town commanded by Colonel Dumoulin. He smiled at their request but granted it, and they went on their way rejoicing in the possession of the password.

Soon they had crossed the lines, passed through deserted Colombes, and found themselves in the vineyard leading down to the river. It was about eleven o'clock.

On the other side the village of Argenteuil seemed as if it were dead. The hills of Orgremont and Saumons commanded the whole country round. The great plain stretching out as far as Nanterne was empty as air. Nothing in sight but cherry trees, and stretches of grey soil.

Monsieur Sauvage pointed with his finger to the heights above and said: "The Prussians are up there," and a vague sense of uneasiness seized upon the two friends.

The Prussians! They had never set eyes upon them, but for months past they had felt their presence near, encircling their beloved Paris, ruining their beloved France, pillaging, massacring, insatiable, invincible, invisible, all-powerful, and as they thought on them a sort of superstitious terror seemed to mingle with the hate they bore towards their unknown conquerors. Morisot murmured: "Suppose we were to meet them," and Sauvage replied, with the instinctive gallantry of the Parisian; "Well! we would offer them some of our fish for supper."

All the same they hesitated before venturing into the country, intimidated as they were by the all-pervading silence.

Eventually Monsieur Sauvage plucked up courage: "Come along, let's make a start; but we must be cautious."

They went through the vineyard, bent double, crawling along from bush to bush, ears and eyes upon the alert.

Only one strip of ground lay between them and the river. They began to run, and when they reached the bank they crouched down among the dry reeds for shelter.

Morisot laid his ear to the ground to listen for the sound of foot-steps, but he could hear nothing. They were alone, quite alone; gradually they felt reassured and began to fish.

The deserted island of Maranthe hid them from the opposite shore. The little restaurant was closed, and looked as if it had been neglected for years.

Monsieur Sauvage caught the first gudgeon, Monsieur Morisot the second. And every minute they pulled up their lines with a little silver object dangling and struggling on the hook. Truly, a miraculous draught of fishes. As the fish were caught they put them in a net which floated in the water at their feet. They positively reveled in enjoyment of a long-forbidden sport. The sun shone warm upon their backs. They heard nothing—they thought of nothing—the rest of the world was as nothing to them. They simply fished.

Suddenly a smothered sound, as it were underground, made the earth tremble. The guns had recommenced firing. Morisot turned his head, and saw above the bank, far away to the left, the vast shadow of Mont Valerien, and over it the white wreath of smoke from the gun which had just been fired. Then a jet of flame burst forth from the fortress in answer, a moment later followed by another explosion. Then others, till every second as it seemed the mountain breathed out death, and the white smoke formed a funeral pall above it.

Monsieur Sauvage shrugged his shoulders. "They are beginning again," he said.

Monsieur Morisot, anxiously watching his float bob up and down, was suddenly seized with rage against the belligerents and growled out: "How idiotic to kill one another like that."

Monsieur Sauvage: "It's worse than the brute beasts."

Monsieur Morisot, who had just hooked a bleak, said: "And to think that it will always be thus so long as there are such things as Governments."

Monsieur Sauvage stopped him: "The Republic would not have declared war."

Monsieur Morisot in his turn: "With Kings we have foreign wars, with the Republic we have civil wars."

Then in a friendly way they began to discuss politics with the calm common sense of reasonable and peace-loving men, agreeing on the one point that no one would ever be free. And Mont Valerien thundered unceasingly, demolishing with its cannonballs French houses, crushing out French lives, ruining many a dream, many a joy, many a hope deferred, wrecking much happiness, and bringing to the hearts of women, girls, and mothers in France and elsewhere, sorrow and suffering which would never have an end.

"It's life," said Monsieur Morisot.

"Say rather that it's death," said Monsieur Sauvage.

They started, scared out of their lives, as they felt that someone was walking close behind them. Turning round, they saw four men, four tall, bearded men, dressed as servants in livery, and wearing flat caps upon their heads. These men were covering the two fishermen with rifles.

The rods dropped from their frightened hands, and floated aimlessly down the river. In an instant the Frenchmen were seized, bound, thrown into a boat, and ferried over to the island.

Behind the house they had thought uninhabited was a picket of Prussian soldiers. A hairy giant, who was sitting astride a chair, and smoking a porcelain pipe, asked them in excellent French if they had had good sport.

A soldier placed at the feet of the officer the net full of fish, which he had brought away with him.

"Not bad, I see. But we have other fish to fry. Listen, and don't alarm yourselves. You are a couple of French spies sent out to watch my movements, disguised as fishermen. I take you prisoners, and I order you to be shot. You have fallen into my hands—so much the worse for you. It is the fortune of war. Inasmuch, however, as you came through the lines you are certainly in possession of the password. Otherwise you could not get back again. Give me the word and I will let you go."

The two friends, livid with fear, stood side by side, their hands nervously twitching, but they answered not a word.

The officer continued: "No one need ever know it. You will go home quietly, and your secret will go with you. If you refuse it is death for you both, and that instantly. Take your choice."

They neither spoke nor moved.

The Prussian calmly pointed to the river and said: "Reflect, in five minutes you will be at the bottom of that water. I suppose you have families."

Mont Valerien thundered unceasingly.

The two Frenchmen stood perfectly still and silent.

The officer gave an order in German. Then he moved his chair farther away from the prisoners, and a dozen soldiers drew up in line twenty paces off.

"I will give you one minute," he said, "not one second more."

He got up leisurely and approached the two Frenchmen. He took Morisot by the arm and said, in an undertone: "Quick! Give me the word. Your friend will know nothing. I will appear to give way."

Monsieur Morisot did not answer.

The Prussian took Monsieur Sauvage aside and said the same thing to him.

Monsieur Sauvage did not answer.

They found themselves once more side by side.

The officer gave another order; the soldiers raised their guns.

By accident Morisot's glance fell upon the net full of fish on the ground a few steps off. A ray of sunshine lit up their glittering bodies, and a sudden weakness came over him. "Good-bye, Monsieur Morisot," replied Monsieur Sauvage. They pressed each other's hands, trembling from head to foot.

"Fire," said the officer.

Monsieur Sauvage fell dead on his face. Monsieur Morisot, of stronger build, staggered, stumbled, and then fell right across the body of his friend, with his face turned upwards to the sky, his breast riddled with balls.

The Prussian gave another order. His men dispersed for a moment, returning with cords and stones. They tied the stones to the feet of the dead Frenchmen, and carried them down to the river.

Mont Valerien thundered unceasingly.

Two soldiers took Morisot by the head and feet. Two others did the same to Sauvage. The bodies swung to and fro, were launched into space, described a curve, and plunged feet first into the river.

The water bubbled, boiled, then calmed down, and the little wavelets, tinged with red, circled gently towards the bank.

The officer, impassive as ever, said: "It is the fishes' turn now."

His eye fell upon the gudgeon lying on the grass. He picked them up and called out: "Wilhelm." A soldier in a white cap appeared. He threw the fish towards him.

"Fry these little animals for me at once, while they are still alive and kicking. They will be delicious."

Then he began smoking again.

The Little Green Book

JACK RITCHIE

T HE OLD MAN SIGHED. "Amador is dead, too?"

"Yes," I said. "And yet he almost succeeded. He killed two of the General's guards before he was shot down."

The old man sat down on the bench beside the mountain hut. "Tell me how it went."

"I took the motor bus to the capitol and went to where Amador lives with his parents," I said.

"When I arrived we had several glasses of wine, for there was still an hour before the General's ceremony."

The old man frowned slightly, for he does not drink.

"Amador needed some courage," I said. "I thought it was for the best that he drink a little. I do not think that a little wine did harm. He did not fail because of that."

The old man waved a hand slightly. "Go on."

"I gave him the revolver," I said. "And then I went alone to the church which overlooks the Presidential Square. I climbed to the tower where I could watch what would happen. There were many

248

people in the square and on the platform with the General there were foreigners who people say advise the General."

The old man nodded. "It has happened in other countries."

"There were speeches to mark the opening of the new military road," I said. "From the tower I could not see Amador in the crowd. I did not see him at all until it happened." I paused for a moment and then went on. "When the General rose to say his words, I heard the gunshots and saw the two guards fall. And then I saw Amador—for just one moment. He had almost reached the top of the platform when the machine guns fired. And then it was over. Amador was dead."

The old man rubbed his eyes.

"How many have we lost? Cajal, Molinos, Gondomar?"

"And Evariste," I said. He spoke tiredly. "I had almost forgotten. I am an old man and I forget."

"It does not matter," I said.

"They were not patriots. They did what they did for money."

The old man shook his head. "You are too harsh. The money I gave them does not replace their lives."

We looked silently down the mountain. Below us lay the border and beyond that the north and freedom. There were wire fences and guards, but one could get through if one knew the way.

Once again I asked, though I knew what his answer would be. "Why do you not leave? Why do you not go where you are safe?"

The old man smiled faintly. "So many of my kind have fled across the border vowing that they would remember the homeland. But once they were gone and safe, they were content to live and forget. No, I cannot leave my country's soil. My place is here."

In the days before the General came to power, the old man had been one of the great land owners. In the mornings he would ride his horse among the fields and the workers, and when he returned in the evening he would not have seen one-tenth of what he owned.

The estates are broken up now and each family has been allotted twenty acres. The peasants seem content, though there are shortages and there is talk that soon each man's twenty acres will be taken away again to create a commune such as they have in many parts of the country. But that is talk which no one chooses to believe.

The old man stared at his folded hands. "We must find some-one else."

I looked to where the sun had almost set. "I think that the time has now come for me to do what we know is necessary."

The old man looked up. "No. I cannot allow you to go. If there were some guarantee that you would succeed, then perhaps I might. But if you failed, then I would be alone. I could do nothing anymore." He rose and patted my shoulder. "You are my eyes and my ears. I cannot leave this hut. I must hide here. If my face were seen, it would be the end. Many people still believe in the General."

It had been six months since I had turned the mountain path and seen the old man for the first time. I had been hunting for the small deer of this region, for since the General has come there is little meat in my village.

He had been ragged and bearded and yet I had known who he was, for he had once been president of the Republic and his picture had been on the walls of every schoolroom.

He had raised his hands when I pointed the gun and had waited, Perhaps to be shot.

I had stood there and wondered what to do, for in times such as these one must protect oneself. To allow a man such as he to go free— to escape—could be dangerous if it were ever known.

I do not know what I might have done, but then the rains came— swiftly and heavily as they do in the season—and we had taken refuge in the hut.

And I had let him talk, for there was nothing else to do until the rains ceased, and he had spoken of freedom and country and what must be done by patriots.

When the rains stopped, I had shared my food with him, for he was hungry, and we came to an agreement.

Now the old man's eyes were tired. "We must go on. We must not fail again."

"No," I said. "The General must die."

For a moment doubt seemed to cross his face. "Does it do any good to kill this one man?"

"He is the General," I said.

He smiled sadly. "You are simple and direct. But if we kill this one man, will it change things? Is this new movement more than just one man? Will the General be replaced by someone who is worse?"

"I do not know," I said. "But we must hope that what we do is right."

He nodded slowly. "Yes. We must do something. Whatever we can." He took several weary breaths. "I sit here and know nothing of what occurs in our country. Without a radio or even newspapers it is difficult to know what the people really want."

I spat upon the ground. "The newspapers are not worth reading. They are all about the General and how much his people love him."

We were silent and then the old man said again, "Now we must find someone else. Someone who will be more successful than Amador."

"Yes," I said. "I will go to the capital tomorrow."

It was almost dark now. I bade the old man goodbye and went down the path to the village where I sleep.

I returned to the hut on the mountain three days later.

The old man had been hiding in the brush, but he came out when he saw that it was only me.

"You have found someone?" he asked.

"Yes," I said. "Guerrero is his name. He is a man who drinks. Who brawls. But he is a man of great physical courage and will do much for money."

The old man frowned. "Can we trust such a one as that? Will he risk death?"

"He does not plan to die," I said. "He is very expert with a rifle."

The old man gave that thought. "Do you think he will succeed?"

"Yes," I said. "I think he will succeed."

The old man took the little green book from his pocket and wrote. He tore the paper from the book along the dotted lines. "Ten thousand," he said. "You will remind Guerrero that this check is good. Not in this country, of course, but across the border where I still have lands and money. Will he know how he can get the money?"

"He will know," I said. "Like the others."

Down the mountainside, at the turn in the path, I waved to the old man and then continued on my way.

Cajal. Molinos. Gondomar. Evariste. Amador. And now Guerrero. I smiled.

They were but names and I had taken them from the air. The men did not exist and never had.

How much money did the old man still have?

But perhaps I should not be greedy.

This time when I crossed the border to cash the check, I thought I would remain there.

The Story of a Conscience

AMBROSE BIERCE

C APTAIN PARROLL HARTROY STOOD at the advanced post of his
picketguard, talking in low tones with the sentinel. This post
was on a turnpike which bisected the captain's camp, a half-mile in
rear, though the camp was not in sight from that point. The officer
was apparently giving the soldier certain instructions—was perhaps
merely inquiring if all were quiet in front. As the two stood talking,
a man approached them from the direction of the camp carelessly
whistling, and was promptly halted by the soldier. He was evidently
a civilian—a tall person, coarsely clad in the homemade stuff of
yellow-gray, called "butternut," which was men's only wear in the
latter days of the Confederacy. On his head was a slouch felt hat,
once white, from beneath which hung masses of uneven hair, seemingly unacquainted with either scissors or comb. The man's face was
rather striking; a broad forehead, high nose, and thin cheeks, the
mouth visible in the full dark beard, which seemed as neglected as
the hair. The eyes were large and had that steadiness and fixity of
attention which so frequently mark a considering intelligence and a

will not easily turned from its purpose—so say those physiogno-
mists who have that kind of eyes. On the whole, this was a man
whom one would be likely to observe and be observed by. He carried a walking stick freshly cut from the forest and his ailing
cowskin boots were white with dust.

"Show your pass," said the Federal soldier, a trifle more imperi-
ously perhaps than he would have thought necessary if he had not
been under the eye of his commander, who with folded arms looked
on from the roadside.

" 'Lowed you'd rec'lect me, Gineral," said the wayfarer tranquilly,
while producing the paper from the pocket of his coat. There was
something in his tone—perhaps a faint suggestion of irony—which
made his elevation of his obstructor to exalted rank less agreeable to
that worthy warrior than promotion is commonly found to be.
"You-all have to be purty pertickler, I reckon," he added, in a more
conciliatory tone, as if in half-apology for being halted.

Having read the pass, with his rifle resting on the ground, the soldier handed the document back without a word, shouldered his
weapon, and returned to his commander. The civilian passed on in
the middle of the road, and when he had penetrated the circumja-
cent Confederacy a few yards resumed his whistling and was soon
out of sight beyond an angle in the road, which at that point entered
a thin forest. Suddenly the officer undid his arms from his breast,
drew a revolver from his belt and sprang forward at a run in the same
direction, leaving his sentinel in gaping astonishment at his post.
After making to the various visible forms of nature a solemn promise
to be damned, that gentleman resumed the air of stolidity which is
supposed to be appropriate to a state of alert military attention.

CAPTAIN HARTROY HELD AN independent command. His force con-
sisted of a company of infantry, a squadron of cavalry, and section of
artillery, detached from the army to which they belonged, to defend
an important defile in the Cumberland Mountains in Tennessee. It
was a field officer's command held by a line officer promoted from

the ranks, where he had quietly served until "discovered." His post was one of exceptional peril; its defense entailed a heavy responsibility and he had wisely been given corresponding discretionary powers, all the more necessary because of his distance from the main army, the precarious nature of his communications and the lawless character of the enemy's irregular troops infesting that region. He had strongly fortified his little camp, which embraced a village of a half-dozen dwellings and a country store, and had collected a considerable quantity of supplies. To a few resident civilians of known loyalty, with whom it was desirable to trade, and of whose services in various ways he sometimes availed himself, he had given written passes admitting them within his lines. It is easy to understand that an abuse of this privilege in the interest of the enemy might entail serious consequences. Captain Hartroy had made an order to the effect that anyone so abusing it would be summarily shot.

While the sentinel had been examining the civilian's pass the captain had eyed the latter narrowly. He thought his appearance familiar and had at first no doubt of having given him the pass which had satisfied the sentinel. It was not until the man had got out of sight and hearing that his identity was disclosed by a revealing light from memory. With soldierly promptness of decision the officer had acted on the revelation.

TO ANY BUT A singularly self-possessed man the apparition of an officer of the military forces, formidably clad, bearing in one hand a sheathed sword and in the other a cocked revolver, and rushing in furious pursuit, is no doubt disquieting to a high degree; upon the man to whom the pursuit was in this instance directed it appeared to have no other effect than somewhat to intensify his tranquility. He might easily enough have escaped into the forest to the right or the left, but chose another course of action—turned and quietly faced the captain, saying as he came up: "I reckon ye must have something to say to me, which ye disremembered. What mout it be, neighbor?"

But the "neighbor" did not answer, being engaged in the unneighborly act of covering him with a cocked pistol.

"Surrender," said the captain as calmly as a slight breathlessness from exertion would permit, "or you die."

There was no menace in the manner of this demand; that was all in the matter and in the means of enforcing it. There was, too, something not altogether reassuring in the cold gray eyes that glanced along the barrel of the weapon. For a moment the two men stood looking at each other in silence; then the civilian, with no appearance of fear—with as great apparent unconcern as when complying with the less austere demand of the sentinel—slowly pulled from his pocket the paper which had satisfied that humble functionary and held it out, saying:

"I reckon thi' 'ere parss from Mister Hartroy is—"

"The pass is a forgery," the officer said, interrupting. "I am Captain Hartroy—and you are Dramer Brune."

It would have required a sharp eye to observe the slight pallor of the civilian's face at these words, and the only other manifestation attesting their significance was a voluntary relaxation of the thumb and fingers holding the dishonored paper, which, falling to the road, unheeded, was rolled by a gentle wind and then lay still, with a coating of dust, as in humiliation for the lie that it bore. A moment later the civilian, still looking unmoved into the barrel of the pistol, said:

"Yes, I am Dramer Brune, a Confederate spy, and your prisoner. I have on my person, as you will soon discover, a plan of your fort and its armament, a statement of the distribution of your men and their number, a map of the approaches, showing the positions of all your outposts. My life is fairly yours, but if you wish it taken in a more formal way than by your own hand, and if you are willing to spare me the indignity of marching into camp at the muzzle of your pistol, I promise you that I will neither resist, escape, nor remonstrate, but will submit to whatever penalty may be imposed."

The officer lowered his pistol, uncocked it, and thrust it into its place in his belt. Brune advanced a step, extending his right hand.

"It is the hand of a traitor and a spy," said the officer coldly, and did not take it. The other bowed.

"Come," said the captain, "let us go to camp; you shall not die until tomorrow moring."

He turned his back upon his prisoner, and these two enigmatical men retraced their steps and soon passed the sentinel, who expressed his general sense of things by a needless and exaggerated salute to his commander.

EARLY ON THE MORNING after these events the two men, captor and captive, sat in the tent of the former. A table was between them on which lay, among a number of letters, official and private, which the captain had written during the night, the incriminating papers found upon the spy. That gentleman had slept through the night in an adjoining tent, unguarded. Both, having breakfasted, were now smoking.

"Mr. Brune," said Captain Hartroy, "you probably do not understand why I recognized you in your disguise, nor how I was aware of your name."

"I have not sought to learn, Captain," the prisoner said with quiet dignity.

"Nevertheless I should like you to know—if the story will not offend. You will perceive that my knowledge of you goes back to the autumn of 1861. At that time you were a private in an Ohio regiment—a brave and trusted soldier. To the surprise and grief of your officers and comrades you deserted and went over to the enemy. Soon afterward you were captured in a skirmish, recognized, tried by court-martial, and sentenced to be shot. Awaiting the execution of the sentence you were confined, unfettered, in a freight car standing on a side track of a railway."

"At Grafton, Virginia," said Brune, pushing the ashes from his cigar with the little finger of the hand holding it, and without looking up.

"At Grafton, Virginia," the captain repeated. "One dark and stormy night a soldier who had just returned from a long, fatiguing march was put on guard over you. He sat on a cracker box inside the car, near the door, his rifle loaded and the bayonet fixed. You sat in a corner and his orders were to kill you if you attempted to rise."

"But if I asked to rise he might call the corporal of the guard."

"Yes. As the long silent hours wore away the soldier yielded to the demands of nature: he himself incurred the death penalty by sleeping at his post of duty."

"You did."

"What! You recognize me? You have known me all along?"

The captain had risen and was walking the floor of his tent, visibly excited. His face was flushed, the gray eyes had lost the cold, pitiless look which they had shown when Brune had seen them over the pistol barrel; they had softened wonderfully.

"I knew you," said the spy, with his customary tranquility, "the moment you faced me, demanding my surrender. In the circumstance it would have been hardly becoming in me to recall these matters. I am perhaps a traitor, certainly a spy; but I should not wish to seem a suppliant."

The captain had paused in his walk and was facing his prisoner. There was a singular huskiness in his voice as he spoke again.

"Mr. Brune, whatever your conscience may permit you to be, you saved my life at what you must have believed the cost of your own. Until I saw you yesterday when halted by my sentinel I believed you dead—thought that you had suffered the fate which through my own crime you might easily have escaped. You had only to step from the car and leave me to take your place before the firing squad. You had a divine compassion. You pitied my fatigue. You let me sleep, watched over me, and as the time drew near for the relief-guard to come and detect me in my crime, you gently waked me. All, Brune, Brune, that was well done—that was great—that—"

The captain's voice failed him; the tears were running down his face and sparkled upon his beard and his breast. Resuming his seat at the table, he buried his face in his arms and sobbed. All else was silence.

Suddenly the clear warble of a bugle was heard sounding the "assembly." The captain started and raised his wet face from his arms; it had turned ghastly pale. Outside, in the sunlight, were heard the stir of the men falling into line; the voices of the sergeants calling the roll; the tapping of the drummers as they braced their drums. The captain spoke again:

"I ought to have confessed my fault in order to relate the story of your magnanimity; it might have procured you a pardon. A hundred times I resolved to do so, but shame prevented. Besides, your sentence was just and righteous. Well, Heaven forgive me! I said nothing, and my regiment was soon afterward ordered to Tennessee and I never heard about you."

"It was all right, sir," said Brune, without visible emotion; "I escaped and returned to my colors—the Confederate colors. I should like to add that before deserting from the Federal service I had earnestly asked a discharge, on the ground of altered convictions. I was answered by punishment."

"Ah, but if I had suffered the penalty of my crime—if you had not generously given me the life that I accepted without gratitude you would not be again in the shadow and imminence of death."

The prisoner started slightly and a look of anxiety came into his face. One would have said, too, that he was surprised. At that moment a lieutenant, the adjutant, appeared at the opening of the tent and saluted. "Captain," he said, "the battalion is formed."

Captain Hartroy had recovered his composure. He turned to the officer and said: "Lieutenant, go to Captain Graham and say that I direct him to assume command of the battalion and parade it outside the parapet. This gentleman is a deserter and a spy; he is to be shot to death in the presence of the troops. He will accompany you, unbound and unguarded."

While the adjutant waited at the door the two men inside the tent rose and exchanged ceremonious bows, Brune immediately retiring.

Half an hour later an old Negro cook, the only person left in camp except the commander, was so startled by the sound of a

volley of musketry that he dropped the kettle that he was lifting
from a fire. But for his consternation and the hissing which the
contents of the kettle made among the embers, he might also have
heard, nearer at hand, the single pistol shot with which Captain
Hartroy renounced the life which in conscience he could no
longer keep.

In compliance with the terms of a note that he left for the officer
who succeeded him in command, he was buried, like the deserter
and spy, without military honors; and in the solemn shadow of the
mountain which knows no more of war the two sleep well in
long-forgotten graves.

A Demon in My Head

JEAN-HUGUES OPPEL

A KIND OF TRIBUTE TO JIM NISBET

RAIN AGAIN.
Stanley turns up the collar of his raincoat. Brushes off a drop of water from his nose.

It rained yesterday. It was already raining the day before, and the day before that. Stanley is resigned to it now: ever since he set foot in France it rained, rained all over the country, from east to west and north to south, just to please everyone. Not the kind of torrential rainfall that sometimes inundates the countryside, nor even sudden and repeated showers, but an obsessive spray of continuous drizzle, falling all day long, from dawn till dusk, stopping only for a few brief hours just before daybreak. Stanley is not really certain, though, since dawn is when he sleeps. Rather, when he tries to sleep. When the pain almost disappears from his head. And while dozing in a semiconscious state, he doesn't want to take the chance of waking up completely by going to see whether he's right or wrong through the window of the hotel room.

Hotel rooms, that is. A new one every night. Never the same one twice. A change every day, wherever he may be, registering under a new identity each time. Stanley is his real first name, but his real last name is known only to his employers and himself. As it once was to his parents, a long time ago. To his colleagues, he's Franklin—Stanley Franklin. Which means that some of them foolishly call him Frank, or Franky. Or Stan if they're paying much attention, and feeling friendly. His father always called him Stan, or "the little asshole," when he'd had too much to drink. Stanley doesn't remember being called "Stan" that often. He can hardly even remember his mother who died from cancer just after his third birthday. But he does remember a shitload of aliases, so many fictitious entities who all suffered from migraines after the pain woke up again in his brain.

When he works in France he chooses French undercover names, to make checking in to a hotel easier. European laws offer interesting possibilities for people like him. Stanley has a whole set of false IDs, the main problem being to present the right one after introducing himself to the receptionist. National ID cards are easier to forge than passports, another reason he disguises himself as a citizen of the country he's in and whose language he speaks fluently without an accent. France. Italy. Spain. And all the Anglo-Saxon countries, naturally. Though he's never been able to master London's cockney accent convincingly enough.

The wind rises—then dies out immediately. A sort of ridiculous fart. An atmospheric incident. The sky is not today going to blow clear all its clouds, that are heavy as lead and recklessly covering everything, even erasing the horizon line on the open sea. The salty waters look like slate. There's not a single shadow in the whole landscape, that's completely drowned in the obstinate grayness. The port town emerges from a bed of dirty wet cotton.

Saint-Malo.

The Britanny coast. The port from which Jacques Cartier set sail and discovered Canada (five centuries later than the Vikings), the beaches full of tourists, the ramparts enclosing the inner city within their huge walls. For the Malouins of old stock, the walled-in city center is the only part that rightly deserves the name of Saint-Malo. Those who were born outside the ramparts are considered mere additions to the city, like extra pockets patched onto a pair of trousers. Even if they do know how to pay their respects to the bars of the Rue de la Soif, the Street of Thirst. Stanley is standing on top of the ramparts, his coat drenched. This morning, when he woke up, he decided to buy himself a hat, an imitation oilcloth one, a la Indiana Jones, that doesn't make his face look too bad. The hat keeps his head cool (an idea that's probably purely psychosomatic) lightening the harshness of the migraines—when they happen.

More and more frequently.

Out of caution, Stanley saw a doctor when the first symptoms appeared, and after he had excluded the idea of it being due to just hangovers. The doctor didn't pay much attention and prescribed the usual light treatment. After swallowing buckets of aspirin and paracetamol tablets, and following a drastic no-booze diet without any results, he decided to go into overdrive and get a brain scan. All the while he was careful not to leak anything to his employers about his problem. Nothing showed up in the scan. No blood clots, not a trace of a tumor, benign or malignant. The machine's screen showed only the image of a normal, healthy brain. The symptoms persisted, though, sporadically, before again turning into the same familiar painful demon. So he tried every medical test available; and again, nothing showed up anywhere. The inside of Stanley Franklin's skull remains a scientific mystery.

And a heavy burden to its bearer.

Who now checks his watch. Barely fifteen minutes left before the appointment. Stanley heaves a sigh, and looks ahead. This part of the city's fortified ramparts overlook two docks separated by a drawbridge. Stanley's glance mechanically registers the front of the closed casino, extending into a huge block of buildings, among which are a meeting hall and a luxury hotel. He walked past the hotel when he entered the city center. He never stays in that type of establishment, unless the job demands it. He slept in a cheaper hotel, the Antinea, quite far from the ramparts, on the

Chaussée du Sillon (the Furrow Roadway) that runs along the Great Beach—on the odd-numbered side of the street, a good three-quarters of a mile walk for anyone careless enough not to study a map of Saint-Malo before deciding where to stay. Stanley could have taken a cab, but he preferred to walk along the sea. To air out his head.

An old boat dating back to the days of sailing ships is moored at the nearest dock. A perfectly restored schooner. Despite the rain, some kind of party is going on. An extended, booze-filled lunchtime trying to ease into the evening cocktail hour. Stanley can see people on the deck, bottles passing from hand to hand, and he can almost hear the clinking of glasses. The schooner is moored in front of a long prefabricated building, outside of which men are putting up a tent with blue and white stripes. At the top of the central pole, there is already a flag bearing the emblem of the national French radio network. Stanley has read in the local press that a literary festival is due shortly to take place there. A well-established cultural event, yearly renewing the theme of travel, be it authentic or imaginary. Travel through words and fiction.

His presence there is no fiction. It's real. It may even be glamorous, like some fiction, but the dead bodies he's left in his professional wake are made of flesh and blood, not paper.

Stanley doesn't have to look at his watch again to know that the moment has arrived. He leaves the ramparts, goes down a steep flight of stairs, and comes to a narrow street packed with restaurants. He had lunch in one of them that served Brittany-style pancakes and that was trying to appear like an authentic traditional local place, but only came off looking like a tourist trap. He had a real treat there, nevertheless. He even allowed himself a whole mug of bubbling dry cider, that fortunately didn't go to his head. With his taste buds still nostalgic about the lunch, Stanley slowly walks up the street (its pedestrians driven away by the rain) and crosses a little square where several cafés are crushed together. He goes to L'Univers, connected to the hotel of the same name.

Bretons are said to be stubborn: though it's been raining for ages, every morning the bistros around the square set their tables and chairs outside with sunshades and plastic-covered menus, while catering to their customers inside, where it's warm and dry, only to pack away the whole rain-soaked paraphernalia at dusk and begin again the next day with admirable obstinateness. L'Univers is no exception.

Under the awning of the hotel porch, Stanley removes his dripping hat and shakes it before entering the bar. He goes straight to the deepest recesses of the room, chooses a table for two set apart from the others, sits down after taking his raincoat off and orders a glass of white wine from the waiter, then puts his elbows on the table, waiting for the man who should not be long now.

The man appears. He more or less repeats Stanley's whole ceremony, with one added element: Stanley's hands were free, but the man who just came in is clenching a leather briefcase with a combination lock. He puts the case between his legs as he sits down. When his glass of wine is served, he waits until the waiter is away to start to speak, finally.

"Prelude . . ."

". . . to a scream," completes Stanley.

He'd rather have blurted out ". . . to the afternoon of a faun," but that's not the password. The guy opposite him acknowledges receipt of the message by a single quick blink.

"Philip Royce," the guy introduces himself.

His identity is as phony as François Guérin, the name Stanley chose to use when he checked in at the hotel the day before. No reason to introduce himself now: his mere presence there, in front of a glass of white wine, and the speaking of these simple words are better than any calling card.

"When did you arrive?" asks Royce.

"Yesterday. As scheduled."

"That's what I expected, of course. It was only a way to break the ice. Okay, the rest of the job will be as easy as anything."

Royce extends his arm, as if to gesture to the port vista beyond the walls.

"At the far end of the Duguay-Trouin dock, Terre-Neuve—Newfoundland Wharf—there's a cargo ship. Yellow—you can't miss it. It's called *Ulysses,* easy to remember."

"A suspicious cargo?"

"Normally suspicious."

"Keyser Söze?" Stanley adds ironically.

Royce does not smile, either because he hasn't understood the pun or because he hasn't seen the movie. Or because he has absolutely no sense of humor.

"The *Ulysses* is registered under the Panamanian flag. . . ."

"Not very original, that."

"Don't interrupt me. The owner's Greek, charters it out occasionally to a Taiwanese guy. The captain's from Cyprus, crew the Philippines. Certain containers are being transported undercover for a Dutch company. . . . Put a torpedo through the hull of that ship, and you'll see a walkout of the majority of the delegates of the General Assembly of the United Nations!"

Royce does have something of a sense of humor. But Stanley doesn't laugh.

"Am I supposed to sink the cargo ship?"

"No. You're supposed to take care of the person who's boarding it tonight, at 12:15 precisely."

Royce looks down at the briefcase wedged between his ankles.

"Combination Omega."

Stanley nods. He knows that type of briefcase; what they carry via the diplomatic pouch, the various combinations for opening them. He also knows what taking care of someone means in his line of work. The nodding of his head triggered the pain in his brain, a shot of burning fire that makes him wince and put his hand to his temple.

Royce raises his eyebrow.

"You feeling all right?"

"I'm fine, thanks!" Stanley shoots back, turning his wince into a smile.

A tense little smile. Royce blinks, for a fraction of a second. The kind of staring look of the man in charge, on the lookout for the slightest weakness in his collaborators. Stanley studies the well-fed American sitting in front of him, full of confidence both in himself and the star-spangled banner, his freshly manicured nails, his suit, soberly cut but obviously expensive, with matching tie. After his recruitment on the campus of a prestigious university, Royce became the perfect image of a product of Langley's executives school, the kind of man to walk in every morning—and not without emotion—over the CIA emblem decorating the tiled floor of the Agency sanctuary. Had he been born twenty years earlier, he would have most certainly chosen a career in the army, first West Point, then the command of a crack unit, his head filled with dreams of glory in action, to finally end up at the Pentagon speculating over sophisticated imagery and useless war games. Had his brain cells been a little more on the democratic side, he would be teaching mathematics or philosophy at North Carolina State University at Raleigh. Raleigh or elsewhere, but to Stanley North Carolina feels right: traces of a moderate southern drawl still linger at the end of Royce's sentences.

"The usual equipment?" continues Stanley.

"Yeah."

"Infrared scope?"

"Better. A light-intensifying scope. Ratio of 16 and no grain."

"Silencer?"

"Sound-muffler. Noisier, but the shooting's more accurate. I don't have to tell you, of all people . . ."

"Ammo?" Stanley cuts in.

"Standard. Hollow points."

"It's an execution then."

"I'd rather use the word *elimination.*"

A shadow of a smile on Royce's lips.

"A clean-cut job, at precisely 12:15. The target won't be alone, but easily recognizable. A woman. Here's her picture. Take a close look."

Stanley carefully studies the photograph that Royce is showing him. The hair is ash blond, the face relatively common, slanting eyes and thin lips. Royce turns the snapshot over to a second photo glued to the back that shows the woman standing, so Stanley can memorize the height, size, and proportions; in short, the general appearance of the target.

The photograph disappears back into Royce's pocket.

"The men with her are there to ensure her safety. A minimum of four guys, maybe more. Should another woman be present to put us off the track—though it's not likely—go for both."

Royce speaks in a dry, neutral voice, as if listing a series of obvious facts. Though he doesn't really know why, Stanley feels like asking who the target is, and why it's to be eliminated. He knows he'll be told it's none of his business, but he can't help it. Curiosity nags him, another little demon trying to compete with the one responsible for his headaches.

"Who's the woman?"

"None of your business."

Serves him right. Royce didn't raise his voice; he merely showed his disapproval by staring at Stanley, killing him with his glare.

"I shouldn't . . ."

Royce looks as if he didn't hear a thing.

"Once the job's done, go back to your hotel and wait for new instructions. You'll be called on the cellular phone. That's it."

Royce stands up. The briefcase remains at his feet on the floor; he pushes it back a little farther under the table with the toe of his shoe before wheeling around and leaving the bar without looking back. He hadn't touched his glass of wine. Neither had Stanley.

Stanley uses his feet and a clever series of ankle movements to recover the briefcase. The pain has returned to his head, where it settles for good.

It won't leave him till nightfall.

There's nothing he can do but let go and get on with it while looking for another place to stay for the night. Stanley decides to choose an even cheaper hotel than the Antinea, a few streets off the sea, near a cemetery. Stanley likes hotels near cemeteries; the neighbors don't make much noise. And anyway, he'll be closer to the train station. He came to Saint-Malo by rail, he'll leave the same way or by another way, depending on his instructions. He just hopes he won't have to use a car. Stanley doesn't drive unless he absolutely has to—not since the day a violent headache nearly threw his secondhand Chevy under the trailer wheels of a thirty-ton Kenworth. It was the first car he'd ever owned and he'd bought it cash with his first paychecks. He'd chosen the station wagon expecting to fill it with a wife, dog, and kids, before the hazards of his profession condemned him to celibacy.

If the guy who called himself Royce had got in the easy way, Stanley's entry to the CIA was almost by accident. He hadn't been to high school, and he'd started his emancipated adult life doing a series of menial jobs usually reserved for American teenagers—part-time pocket money gigs, like newspaper boy, flipping hamburgers in a greasy spoon, and gas station attendant. Then he slowly but surely changed his ways and got into petty juvenile crimes, shitty jobs but easy money, until he was soon confronted with the ultimate alternative: a lifetime sentence at the state penitentiary (with a possible one-way ticket out on death row) or joining the army. The big cop who questioned him after a dumb burglary—a dinky little botched-up job—had been very clear, and some leftover lucidity had thrown Stanley into the army barracks when he left jail on parole. That's where people realized he was pretty good at target-shooting and hand-to-hand combat, and was no dumber than anybody else, and had no political beliefs whatsoever. A blank page, as it were, with a virgin brain that a clever mentor would know how to fill up. The providential instructor came from Langley, appreciated Stanley's physical capacities and, above all, the virgin and malleable wax of his brain. He became convinced that, properly trained, Stanley would be a perfect recruit for the Agency—which turned out to be true. With no specific talents except his extraordinary fists, an eagle eye, and his naive patriotism, Stanley became an excellent field agent, though he was limited to "action" missions. With most of his time spent abroad, this chaotic existence definitely excluded the family life he dreamed of. From one-night stands to brief affairs, the emptiness of the Chevy persisted, went on and on, until the day a violent headache . . . His headaches may have started a little bit earlier, sure, though even today Stanley is unable to say precisely when.

But he lives with it.

At Stanley's request, the receptionist of his new hotel is only too pleased to provide him with aspirin, all the while giving him directions to the nearest drugstore. In his room with the curtains drawn, Stanley swallows a few tablets with a glass of water, as a matter of form, more to set his mind at rest than for any real good it might do him. Royce's briefcase is lying on the bed. Open.

Apart from a cellular telephone operating on reserved frequencies, the briefcase contains the different parts of an automatic rifle, a Steyr AUG A1. The usual stuff. High power combined with light weight. Stanley slowly puts the various elements together. Checks the light-intensifying scope, the breech, the positioning of the cartridges in the thirty-round magazine, to be shot one by one or fully automatic like a machine gun. He adjusts the sound-muffler on the mouth of the barrel. Lifts the now-complete rifle to his shoulder and aims it at his own reflection in the mirror hanging above the desk near the double bed. He pins himself in the middle of the forehead through the crosshairs. His index finger lightly touches the trigger. That might be the way to kill the demon, but he wouldn't be there to know. Stanley smiles, takes the rifle apart, and carefully puts its elements back into the briefcase.

And leaves for dinner.

NO MORE RAIN.

Stanley had left his hat in his room and exchanged his raincoat for a more convenient pilot's jacket. As good things always come in pairs, his headache faded at dusk and soon disappeared altogether. He went to the nearest restaurant, where he ate only a main dish of grilled turbot with French green beans, and decided to pass the time over a cup of verbena tea instead of a dessert. He drank only water during the meal and took a good dose of aspirin just in case (probably as superfluous as before) before leaving the table. The briefcase stayed with him throughout the meal.

Now he's waiting.

Quai de Terre-Neuve (Newfoundland Wharf). At the far end of the Duguay-Trouin dock, with the lights of the walled-in city just in front of it, their reflection in the water merging with the lights of the dock illuminated by dim old lampposts every thirty yards or so. Only the minimum regulation-required lights illuminate the *Ulysses,* so one can only guess at its shape in the night rather than see it clearly outlined. The wharf itself is under the glare of two big flood-lights attached to the front of a warehouse, but as if on purpose, their large beams do not actually reach the yellow hull of the ship with the black line painted along its side diagonally two-thirds of the way down from the bow. Stanley has positioned himself under one of the big floodlights: he is lying flat on his stomach on a stack of containers, an easy climb. Should he be spotted during the oper-ation, anyone looking up toward him will be dazzled by the glare. Stanley knows his job.

Royce's briefcase sits near him, the Steyr lying on the lid, now complete with its magazine and a cartridge in the chamber. Stanley has checked the light-intensifying scope and adjusted its brightness level. He has modified the backsight and adapted it to the shooting angle, grabbing the opportunity to study the cargo deck. No one vis-ible. Stanley could see everything as if in broad daylight in heavily contrasted black and white, and his eye had to reaccustom itself to the darkness of the night once it had left the scope to see again the dark shape of the ship, its regulation lights, a faint greenish glow in the deserted pilothouse, probably the dimmed light of a radar screen. The diagonal stripe across the yellow hull is the gangway ladder that the target is to climb up to get aboard. The scope has defined its minutest details. Stanley has it lined up right on it, within the range of the rifle, allowing for a good safety margin in order to hit the target and get away from the scene once the job is done.

The demon wakes up just after midnight. Awaking from his dormant state, or more precisely: a wave of heat creeps through his skull and Stanley stiffens. When it starts that way, slow and easy, he knows what follows. Knows that the pain will lodge its fangs in his brain and he'll have to live with it while he's shooting—until the day he won't be able to anymore and will have to confess everything to his employers, asking them to retire him from action, praying all the while they believe him when he tells them the symptoms only appeared recently. So that they will not try to check back and realize he'd been lying all along; an agent who lies over a single detail lies over the rest of it, that's the Agency creed. In which case, a devoted colleague will take care of Stanley. The noise of an engine, on the wharf.

Slowly approaching car, beams low. It's 12:12 and 38 seconds on Stanley's watch. A $5,000 chronometer can't be wrong: the target is early. Stanley doesn't like it. Punctuality is common ground for allies and enemies alike. The car is long and black, and slows to a stop near the gangway ladder in front of the cargo ship. Just enough room left over to make a U-turn; had it stopped a little farther on, it would have been blocked by an enormous mooring post and would have to maneuver, wasting precious seconds. The driver knows his job.

Neutral. Engine still on, idling. A man gets out of the car, passenger side. Stands near the door, his back to the ship. Stanley slowly picks up the Steyr.

The man's eyes sweep over the wharf, slowly, in a circular pan shot over 180 degrees. He then turns toward the ship, looks up at the dimly lit pilothouse. He can make out a capped figure through the porthole. Motionless. It's 12:13. Stanley raises the rifle to his shoulder and unlocks the safety catch, riveting his eye to the scope and activating the light intensifier.

The wharf is as if in broad daylight. The long car is a Renault Safrane, limo model. Bulletproof, naturally. Tinted windows. The man is tall and broad-shouldered, a square jaw, a square head with a crew cut. The pain shows its teeth in Stanley's brain.

A second man gets out of the car, from the back seat this time, same side. A clone to the other in height, bulk, and the dark suit with a bulging jacket: they're two of a kind, caricatures of body-guards. It's 12:14 and a few seconds. Stanley's index finger fits the curve of the trigger snugly as if caressing a clitoris. A third muscle man, identical to the other two, gets out of the Safrane on the side opposite the ship, and stands in the sight line. The target will come out behind him and the invisible driver will stay at the wheel, unless the whole quartet is just a bunch of incompetents.

12:15. On the dot.

The inside of Stanley's head is on fire—the rest of his body, a block of ice. His index finger, a comma made of steel, wouldn't bend under the weight of an anvil. The target gets out of the car, ship side. The third muscle man doesn't cover her completely. A woman indeed. The only woman in the group.

The general appearance fits. Unfortunately, her hair is hidden under a scarf—but the sunglasses are uncalled for and reassure Stanley. The rifle's crosshairs are pinned on the middle of the scarf. The three bodyguards quickly surround the woman and lead her toward the gangway ladder, staying as close to her as possible. Stanley aims now at the second man's temple. It doesn't worry him a bit: the target is behind the man and will have to step aside to get aboard. The ladder is too narrow to be climbed up by two people abreast, so Stanley will have her whole climb to make sure he doesn't miss his target.

The car is already making a U-turn on the wharf, in one fast, impeccable maneuver. The capped figure has left the pilothouse and suddenly appears on the deck, walking toward the group of four at the bottom of the ladder. The group breaks up. The sight catches up with its target. A lock of blonde hair is visible under the scarf.

Stanley fires. Once. The sound-reducing device muffles the det-onation—the demon roars in his brain. The barrel of the Steyr sweeps over the ladder diagonally, briefly stopping three times. Three times only—each time with a pressure on the trigger. The three bodyguards collapse, one after the other. The last one falls over the body of the target. The capped figure has disappeared behind the ship's rail. The driver jumps out of the car, a gun in his hand. Stanley has already left the top of the pile of containers.

It's 12:16.

At 12:17, the Steyr has been taken apart and carefully put away inside the briefcase, the Omega combination scrambled, the cellular phone clipped to Stanley's belt. Stanley takes a shortcut to reach the seaside and goes back to his hotel by making a long detour. At this time of night, few pedestrians walk the streets, but on the Chaussée du Sillon, along the Great Beach, now that the rain has stopped, he can see passersby still out admiring the rising tide slowly devouring the endless tongue of sand, before going to the port where the action is for a last drink. Stanley walks, he's not in a hurry, his lips are dry; salty fresh air blows in from the ocean. His legs move automatically, like mechanical devices, and his head is burning. In his hand, the briefcase is heavy as lead.

The hotel receptionist is at his desk and bids him good night with just the right amount of servility. Stanley goes upstairs, thinking the night was indeed very good for him, if not for everyone. He opens the door, enters the dark room; closes the door behind him and locks it before switching on the light. An old habit.

"Under the sign of the razor . . ."

". . . the damned don't die," Stanley finishes mechanically.

Jumping only once it's done. The bedside lamp goes on, revealing a man sitting in the only armchair of the bedroom. The man has red hair, with pale freckles and almost green eyes with a trusting look in them. He smiles, a Beretta pistol in his hand. A pistol he puts away in its armpit holster, in a natural movement.

"Good reflexes," he says.

"You're the new instructions?" Stanley grumbles.

"I am."

"The cellular phone was just a decoy?"

"The usual equipment, nothing more. First, I have to take it back."

Stanley gives him the briefcase. And the cellular phone he has unclipped from his belt.

"Omega combination."

The man nods. He places his fingers on the digits of the lock, opens the briefcase, puts the phone in its place, closes the lid, scrambles the lock—and looks up at Stanley.

"Then I've got to make my report. You used a little overkill tonight . . ."

Stanley stiffens, unable to repress his anger.

"I was being watched on the port?!"

"Not watched, assisted, there's a difference, isn't there? Don't be so touchy; it's standard procedure. Nothing personal."

"And you followed me afterward, I imagine, since you're here."

"These things happen, when the job is important."

"The job was important?"

"It's none—"

"—of my goddamned business! I know!" Stanley snaps back. "A thinking spy is a dead spy, I know the story."

"You're not a spy, you're an agent," the red-haired man corrects him, in a gently scolding tone. "Spies are the ones in the opposing camp . . ."

"And what is the opposing camp, these days?"

The man stares at him, shocked.

"You're joking, I hope?"

"I'm joking," Stanley blurts out, clenching his teeth.

A short silence. The red-haired man looks down at Stanley. Sniffles, as if from a nervous tic.

"I'm perfectly willing to believe you; you just did an excellent job. But you didn't go at it lightly. . . . What was going on in that head of yours?"

"A demon," Stanley whispers.

"What did you say?"

"Nothing. . . . I just thought I'd do my best to cover my retreat. I . . . improvised. Was . . . was I wrong?"

"It's not for me to decide." The red-haired man sighs. "I just have to deliver my report . . . objectively. You know what I mean? Anyway, you're to be debriefed the day after tomorrow at 4:00 P.M., usual place, and you'll have the opportunity to explain yourself. In detail. Those are the new instructions."

"And . . . that's it?"

The man stands up. Grips the handle of the briefcase and walks to the door.

"That's it. Were you expecting anything else?"

"No."

"Good-bye, then."

The red-haired man leaves the room.

Once on his own, the door locked again, Stanley opens the curtains of the window. Overview of the crosses of the cemetery. A big black dog wanders among the gravestones. Stanley refuses to see a symbol in it. The inside of his head is roaring like a burning forge. The completed task hasn't brought him any relief. Far from it. It's as if the demon were actually condemning him for the job done, and well done as jobs go: four hits, direct hits each time, before anybody could even react, on moving targets and at a distance—except that Stanley was supposed to hit only once, as he had just been reminded. The pain swells in his head, and he has to fight it back; looking for a reassuring image to buffer it.

The image of the target comes naturally. Not a reassuring one at all.

The blonde woman. One more trophy to add to his list of successes. Stanley smiles with difficulty—like a razor blade splitting his mouth. It's none of his business. He doesn't know who she was; he'll never know; he doesn't have to know. All the same, the need to know has become stronger, growing through the years—ever since Stanley's points of reference had disappeared, collapsing with the

Wall, and the hereditary enemy whose elimination was a duty and sufficed to nourish his primary patriotism, without a second thought. The demon had already begun to nibble at his brain, of course, but Stanley could easily satisfy his wicked appetite: Good against Evil, the Truth being engraved in the marble of the White House. But today, as they say, a new world order has arrived; hence new missions—except that no one had ever thought of reprogramming the underlings whose functions were to carry them out successfully without asking questions, as they used to. But for Stanley, nothing is quite what it used to be: the malleable wax of his brain is not virgin anymore. Stanley has learned to think, even if he does not understand—and he *does* ask himself questions. Stanley is in doubt. Stanley would like to know whether he executes (sorry, eliminates) a surviving defender of the red vermin, a fanatic terrorist, or a simple shit disturber to the neoliberalism.

Stanley would actually like to give a name to the demon devouring the inside of his head. . . .

Guilt?

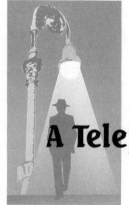

A Telephone Call Too Many

CARMEN IARRERA

M Y HUSBAND IS BACK earlier than usual. Roving the living room, he is fretful, rearranging the knickknacks again and again, as he always does when something is going wrong for him.

This mania of his makes me mad, but I pretend not to notice it. I don't want to start another quarrel. I don't want it at all, because I myself am nervous too.

No, maybe it's not nervousness. It's just anxiety, with a vein of anger.

Okay, okay, the poor man is back early because he's got a cold and he feels stuffed, his head disturbed, he himself not able to concentrate on his work. But why doesn't he stop touching those knickknacks? Why doesn't he go elsewhere, in his study for example, letting me read my book in peace?

Read? Liar, I could even hold this book upside down, and I wouldn't notice it. What I am actually doing is . . .

"I'll get it."

He raises the receiver before I could even move my hand. Yet the telephone is here, near my elbow.

"Hallo? . . . Hallo? . . . They hung up."

The telephone is the one on the confidential line, a number known only by my husband's staff, by the services and, of course, by the White House. It's a line impossible to control. John and I are the only two people in the house who even touch it.

John is looking at the receiver in his hand. He is incredulous, as he would be if someone called him stupid.

And could the famous John Marvin, from the great Marvin family, be stupid? He graduated from the university very young, with high marks and honors. He's having a very successful career in the diplomatic service, going from London to Peking to Paris. Plus, he's now ambassador in Colombia, an assignment of great responsibility and delicacy, considering our government's action against the drug trade.

As far as I am concerned, I'd prefer to live in Paris. Here in Bogotá, if you don't invent something to do, you run the risk of being stifled with boredom.

John is still looking at the telephone, puzzled.

It is clear that this evening he is out of sorts.

But we cannot avoid going to the party, so I must get ready. My hair will be a problem, as usual. It is unamenable, just like me.

We are almost ready to go when the telephone starts ringing again. John is checking the knot of his tie in the hall mirror. There is a telephone there too, on the console. He answers on the first full ring.

"Hallo? . . . Hallo? . . . They hung up again. What a pain."

He is speaking with that unconcerned countenance he shows when he doesn't want to look nervous. He undoes the knot and ties it again. I think the tie looked better before.

The party is not as boring as I supposed. The self-service approach allows me to leave discreetly some tiresome guests, mostly that pedantic German ambassador that at formal dinners always sits at my side; I don't know why.

A chat about the weather with the English ambassador's wife. A glass of vodka, which will cost me at least a full diet day, with the Russian military attaché. A thousand shining smiles given here and there before I can call my duty done. For the rest of the party it will be enough to let them admire me. It's not too difficult, for them or for me.

From time to time I look at my husband. John is still a handsome man. Tall, elegant, noble bearing. Surely the white hair of his temples doesn't take away his glamor.

He is hiding well the uneasiness he felt at home, especially now that he is arousing great interest giving notice that the vice president will soon come to Bogotá. Funny to see how they are all so excited for the visit of that silly man: I suspect that everybody is as bored as I am.

MY HUSBAND IS PUTTING his key into the lock of our apartment when the telephone begins to ring.

The ring goes on insistently, hardly muffled by the thickness of the door. John fumbles with the key, but succeeds in opening the door and lifting the receiver in the middle of a ring.

"Hallo? Hallo? Damn!"

Another hang-up. John is sure to have clearly heard the click.

All the charm he has displayed during the party has vanished. He is very pale. He drops onto the sofa and asks me for a whiskey. He drinks it greedily. I lightly touch his forehead. It is burning. I am afraid this cold and fever will keep him home for a while.

THE ROUTINE OF THE house is turned topsy-turvy. My husband ill in bed means a lot of people everywhere in our living quarters, his secretary established in our room, the telephone always ringing. Not the private one, the other.

I have noticed—and it's made me curious and upset—that this morning, before the secretary came in, John had removed the receiver of the telephone he has on the night table so as to keep the line busy. He did it on purpose, because I replaced it once, and ten minutes later it was as before.

It is clear John doesn't want that telephone ringing when there is somebody else in the room. To say it better, he doesn't want somebody to notice the reaction he has when the caller hangs up on him. I know my husband well. Yes, I know him very well, but not so well as to understand why he is reacting so excessively.

Come evening, when the house is quiet once more, John cradles the receiver. And, immediately, the telephone starts ringing again.

John is nearer than I. He grasps the telephone maniacally. This matter is beginning to make me nervous.

"Hallo? Damn! Who is speaking?"

He slams down the receiver so violently he makes me jump. I can see him panting, and he is deeply pale. He notices me observing him. I try to joke. I say that maybe it's somebody that is after me, and that John scares him. My husband looks at me so fixedly that I have the unpleasant feeling he doesn't see me. Maybe he hasn't even heard what I've said. His hand is still clamped on the receiver. All this is very strange. Strange and unpleasant too.

JOHN HAS HAD A very bad night. He has rolled over a thousand times and has drunk all the bottle of water he had on the side table. Because of the fever, of course, but his tossing and turning haven't let me sleep, either, and this morning everything is again as yesterday. The house full of people going to-and-fro, the bedroom turned into an office, the preparations for the visit of the vice president, the never-ending discussions between my husband and his staff about who to invite and who not to invite to the party we will give in his honor, the "normal" telephone that goes on ringing and ringing.

While the private one is silent. It has been taken off the hook again by my husband who, in order not to be noticed, is looking at it as he were a watchdog. I ask myself why those calls without answer upset him so much. He cannot be so jealous. He isn't capable of that . . .

Anyhow, I have had enough of it.

John has no fever anymore, but today is Sunday, and so he remains at home. He avails himself of the opportunity to rest a little on the sofa in the living room, watching TV, under the plaid blanket . . . near the telephone. My husband is still pale, too much so for it to be from a temperature he hasn't got anymore. I must understand why he's so strained. I observe John, looking for the right words to ask him what is going on, but then the telephone starts ringing again.

This time I am nearer than he and faster. My hand is already on the receiver, but my husband snatches it from my fingers.

"Hallo? Hallo? Who's there? Damn!!"

I am irritated, even disconcerted. I cannot understand why he concentrates so doggedly on the telephone, why he doesn't allow me to answer it. And I am beginning to be worried too. John has slammed down the receiver so violently that all the unpleasant things I was going to tell him have stuck in my throat. I stare at him without speaking. His forehead beads with sweat, and his own stare is glassy and lost.

We keep silent for a long time. He is also staring without seeing at the images on the television screen. I am staring without seeing at the words printed on the pages of my book.

Later the telephone rings again, persistently. John gazes at it with hate, then makes a convulsive movement, yanking the wire, pulling the plug from the wall. Just a moment and we hear the ring in the bedroom.

John gets paler then ever. Jumping to his feet, he runs into the bedroom and yanks out that plug too.

It isn't enough. Now the one in the hall drills into our brains. John gets hold of the receiver this time, throwing it against the wall. Then he stumbles back into the living room and falls groaning on the sofa.

I look at him, dumb, and dismayed. I don't recognize my own husband. Where is that quiet, measured, controlled man? Where is that diplomat, so sagacious, so careful, who never lets slip a word, an action, that is less than perfect?

His rash fury lasted only moments, but I feel as if I am staring at him for an endless time. . . .

He raises his head slowly. His stare is empty.

"Sorry . . ."

I sit down slowly too, as if a sudden movement could break that strange tense atmosphere that permeates the room.

"Sorry. . . . I realize I must give you an explanation."

The words come out with trouble. And with more trouble he tells me everything else. I listen to him without breathing, my back crushed against the back of the sofa.

My husband, John Marvin, the ambassador of the United States to Colombia, is a spy. This is the first thing I understand. The only thing, as his words knock in vain against the deaf barrier of my disbelief.

My head is buzzing, I feel sick. I pluck up my courage and try to follow what he is saying. I know he will not say it twice.

At first I hear him in flashes, then I begin to understand. I understand everything. He is asking me to forgive him. He says that he made a mistake, that he has been blackmailed, that he surrendered. That he has betrayed his country, our country.

And now, those calls . . .

He tells me that "they" are tormenting him, on purpose. That "they" want to provoke him beyond measure, to break down his nerves in order to ask him more, and more. Only God knows what, by now.

It is impossible . . . the calls . . . I cannot believe what I am hearing. I burst out with a hysterical laughter, then I burst into tears.

I don't sleep a wink the whole night, but I don't want to remember all the things he put into my mind, either. The thousand thoughts that flooded my brain and broke my heart.

My husband is a spy.

Enough. It has been difficult, but I made up my mind: I will never touch that telephone again. I'll let it ring. I'll let John answer. He agrees. He is even grateful for the relative serenity with which I have reacted to his confession, but he's too tense to ask himself what the consequences could be. For the moment I will behave as ever, the perfect wife of the perfect ambassador. Later on, if my nerves will permit, I'll decide what to do.

At home I feel stifled. I go out on any excuse. John, on the contrary, stays there, near the telephone. And there I find him when I come back two hours later.

He looks at me with an anguished face and tells me that "they" have called, and hung up, three times, I am sure that soon or later his nerves will shatter.

We decide to have the private line number changed. We don't lack for pretexts. He will ask for it tomorrow, at work. Because, fever or not, calls or not, he must arrange everything for the vice president's visit. And everything means everything: from the decision of how many escort cars they need at the airport to the list of the guests at the gala party, from the schedule of the official meetings to the schedule of the confidential ones, from the choice of the menu to the choice of the flowers for the vice president's wife, from the selection of the better slum to visit, to the removal of the light blue color that the vice president hates from everywhere, especially the towels in the bathrooms.

Next week will be terrifying.

THE LAST TWO DAYS have been relatively quiet. This morning, going out, John has even summoned his old smile. But this evening, when he closes the door behind him, I immediately understand that he is upset again.

"In my office too! Today they called me twice and hung up! In my office! It's unbelievable!"

I pour him a glass of whiskey even before he asks for it, and then I pour another one for myself. Neither am I serene. . . .

The ring of the telephone makes me spill some whiskey on the furniture.

John and I stare at each other. In his eyes I see disbelief, then the dull shade of anguish again.

"It's impossible . . . it's been only two days . . . only two days since the number was changed!

I tell him it may be the White House, or the services. . . . But my words sound forced. It's the third time the telephone rings, the fourth . . .

"Hallo! Hallo! *Hallo!*"

His lips are trembling. He puts down the receiver. His hands are trembling too.

I feel something near pity for him.

THE CALLS—DRIPPING LIKE water on a softstone—go on day after day. My husband is nearly unrecognizable. The embassy's doctor, who is a dear friend, noticed that something is wrong and insisted on examining him. He found John very tired, practically worn out. He said he needs immediate rest, but that he understands perfectly his unavoidable engagements. He has given him a heap of tranquilizers, and another of stimulants, making my husband promise that after the vice-presidential visit he will have a long, quiet holiday on the beach, far away from politics, far away even from this hostile and difficult country.

By now his evenings at home are marked only by waiting for those spasmodic, threatening calls. I am very tense too. The telephone ring has become a painful pang in my brain. I don't know how long I'll be able to stand it, but I must hold out. I have resolved to. I cannot do otherwise.

John has lost all his strength. When, this evening, the telephone rings for the thousandth time, I see him take the receiver in a very slow, enfeebled movement.

"Hallo? . . . Yes."

His voice has changed its tone. It's sharp, attentive. John draws himself up, tense like a taut rope, almost near the breaking point.

"Yes, it's me. . . . No, I am alone. What do you want from me? . . . *What?*"

He flares up, then his face loses every drop of blood. John is again flabby, inert on the sofa.

"No, it's not so simple. . . . No. . . . Yes, I understand . . . I understand what you are asking. . . . Yes, okay. . . . Okay, I'll see. Call me back tomorrow evening. . . . No, maybe it won't be necessary."

He hangs up.

I know, I feel that now my face is nothing more than an anxious mask, ugly to behold. It has to be like the one that John is raising toward me. I don't say a word.

"Pour me a whiskey, please. A double."

The neck of the bottle clinks against the glass. I feel an indescribable strain. Now everything depends on my husband's reaction.

The stout whiskey dose doesn't return any color to his complexion. It remains ashen-gray. He speaks again, very slowly.

"They want to participate at the party in honor of the vice president. They want to come here to the embassy with an invitation. . . . Do you understand what that means?"

I nod.

"The vice president is coming here to support the fight against the drug trade. The relationship between our country and this one is very strained now. Sorry, you know it perfectly, I don't need to explain it to you. They . . . they are twisted, but I understand what they want to do. They want to come here, to the party, with an invitation signed by me and . . . and dope or poison or maybe even kill the vice president in his own embassy. Oh, my God, my God . . ."

I can hardly breathe. It has happened. My husband is no longer himself. These calls have driven him out of his mind. He is destroyed, unrecognizable even to me.

"I cannot allow it," he says in a whisper. "I cannot."

Then he takes a long, deep breath and stands up. He gives me a kiss on my forehead, stumbles into his studio and locks the door behind him.

I grasp the bottle and drink from it.

Two endless minutes later, during which I feel my blood pounding in my temples. There is a shot.

The shot I was waiting for.

My husband, the spy, has killed himself. He has decided to exit the scene in the old-fashioned way, as a gentleman.

I LIE DOWN ON the sofa, motionless. I don't feel anything. No emotions, just a horrible void. I don't know how long I remained here, lost into this void.

The telephone rings. It's not threatening anymore. I know who is calling. I have always known it, since that first call John answered only because he'd gotten a cold and was home at an unusual hour. Three or four calls without an answer were enough to persuade my husband that "they" were threatening him, wanted to force his hand, to break his nerves. So began that terrible agitation that made him confess to betraying our country. Then everything started to collapse around me. Everything . . .

Yes, I know perfectly well who is calling. It's the U.S. military attaché.

My lover.

Sometimes life is strange. My lover, hanging up three or four times one after another as soon as he heard my husband's voice, had unintentionally shaken his guilty conscience and gotten him to confess the wickedness he had done.

That discovery has devastated me, has removed any meaning from every moment of my marriage, has torn my life to pieces.

I went out on an excuse, I ran to my lover, and I told him everything. I had to.

When I worked for the services, in Washington, he was my boss. I swore to him I'd serve, above everything else, my president and my country.

With him I looked for a solution to that horrible situation. With him I devised the stratagem to break John's nerves for good. To drive him to take the only step that would prevent anybody ever discovering he had betrayed his own oath. And, above all, that would surely stop him from betraying again.

So my lover's calls followed mercilessly, one on another until, finally, the blackmail one.

We knew very well that, although he was a traitor, my husband would never hand the vice president over to some killer. It was logical that, in the presence of such an insane demand, my husband would exit the scene, would kill himself. People of his class behave like that.

THE BLOODY TELEPHONE GOES on ringing. But I don't want to answer. I am not able to.

I am tired. Much too tired.

The Ant Trap

HOWARD ENGEL

M Y NAME IS MAX SCHUR. If the name seems familiar, you may be a keen reader of European papers and magazines. Maybe you saw the piece I did in *Stern* on the *Gastarbeiters*, the immigrant Turks in Berlin, or a photo-article in *Paris Match* called "Brando's Island." I'm the senior writer for a bunch of Euro-centered magazines and have appeared, less frequently, in leading American publications as well. There was an article in the *Atlantic* about the Falasha, the black Jews of Ethiopia, last December. The *New York Times Magazine* recently printed a piece I did about the *Ringstrasse* here in Vienna.

What I wanted to tell you about was the curious thing that happened here about a month ago to a man of my acquaintance. I knew him as Kruger. Josef Fliess, my editor at *Stern,* knew him as Sachs. He was a character one was always walking into. As conspicuous as a beached whale, every morning and afternoon he sat in the bar of the Hotel Sacher doing crosswords. The table was always the same table and the drink in front of him was always drowning in melted ice. He was a leftover figure from the old days. Back then, he might have been away from the city for weeks at a time, showing up again in his usual place with a sunburned nose or a new attaché case. Now he was always there in the same shabby suit and sweat-stained hat hung on the bentwood coat stand.

Kruger—I'll call him that to keep things simple—found his English newspapers in a dusty kiosk that specialized in foreign papers and pornography not far from the hotel. He preferred the *Times,* because he needed the challenge of the Everyman, but any paper would do. If the English papers were late, he would solve *"Les sept erreurs"* in *France-Soir*, bending over the page, lost in utter contemplation of the two images.

He drank steadily, but was never drunk. The management was never embarrassed by his behavior. Occasionally, he would fold and refold his paper as though it were a copy of some important treaty, and place it carefully in an inside pocket before getting up from his chair and walking slowly to the *toiletten* in the lobby. At lunch he bought a *Nusskipferl* or a chocolate *Sacher Torte* and ate it without showing any sign of relish. At such times he sipped a *grossen braunen* or an *espresso*.

Kruger's face was a map of broken roads leading nowhere. His forehead remained clear and high, but there was no color in his features. It was as though he had been forgotten on the table in the act of selling his blood. His nose was straight, even aristocratic, a point of pride with him in this polyglot cesspool, although the stubble on his chin and the untrimmed mustache led to speculation among the waiters about a tiny flat or *Mansarde* under the eaves in the north end: cold water and rusting razor blades staining the enameled metal of the *lavoir.*

Herr Kruger seldom had the privacy of his table at the Sacher violated by a visitor, unless he had run out of cigarettes. When that happened, he would cast about for a more provident neighbor and invite him to join him. One violator of Kruger's peace was a sweating American broadcast-journalist with a Bogart trenchcoat and a tape recorder. Kruger said nothing in answer to the questions the reporter asked. The American held the microphone close to Kruger's silent mouth in vain. After a quarter of an hour, he went away unsatisfied.

Vienna had changed. It was no more the Vienna of the fifties, or even of the eighties, than it was the old imperial city of Franz Josef. In her five hundred years, Vienna continued to astonish the *amateurs* of her diversity. Half the baroque bordello of light opera and half the chilly hausfrau, saving the vegetable water, Vienna had come to the end of another century with a subtle new look. The *Ringstrasse* could have been one of the *grands boulevards* in Paris. The *Prater* had finally been cleansed of all traces of Carol Reed and Orson Welles. The city still thrived on business of all kinds: legal, semilegal, and the usual. From my very first day here, a country boy with a provincial journalism diploma, the city always reminded me of the tram that brought me here: durable, gritty, corrupting, and late.

Without doubt the old trade in illegal currencies and documents was still taking place. Exchanges of papers and money continued to be made in the *Herrn*. The odd arrest was made as the *Gendarmerie* descended, "acting upon 'information' " as the newspapers reported the next day. Even the Hotel Sacher was not proof against such official invasions onto the terrace or into the bar. Two drug dealers were swept away by the *polizei* one afternoon not fifteen steps from Kruger's gin and lime. The loud, two-note *folgeton* siren retreating down the street did not bother him. It wasn't the police Kruger feared.

Six months earlier, when spring was stirring the chestnut trees into rusty blossoms, Kruger had had another visitor. He had been walking toward the Sacher from his flat near the *Naschmarkt*, not far from the *Staatsoper,* when a stranger in English tweeds fell into step with him. Kruger stopped in his tracks, until the other took his arm and steered him toward a bench facing the *Karlskirche*. They spoke for some time, or at least the man in tweeds talked and Kruger listened. No plume of vapor came from his mouth into the morning air.

It was generally understood that Kruger was a spy. Vienna knew all about spies and spying, had added to the literature in both fact and fiction. In the old days they went about it quite openly. Swedish Ingrid, who was neither Swedish nor named Ingrid on her Russian passport, played the embassy circuit, especially when there were visiting Americans in town. There was another, a Eurasian, who pretended that what she was looking for was an American husband. That was her cover story. In fact, unknown at the time to her employers in Hanoi, she was indeed looking for an American husband, and vanished from the scene when she found one. Josef, my friend at *Stern's* Vienna bureau, the editor I mentioned, had had a post card from her with a picture of the tallest building in Omaha or Lincoln in Nebraska. Kruger wasn't the only washed-up operative that I saw in a day. I could name six or seven who regularly sat at a table in the *Stammcafé* and another six or seven on the *Mariahilferstrasse*. But spies and espionage were a drug on the market. There wasn't an editor in town interested in a story about the underground of agents and counteragents. To hear them talk, it was a bore that was, in the words of Bill Solly, the Canadian songwriter: "un-to-be-thought-upon, un-to-be-said."

But that was before Kruger's spectacular end, which I mean to tell you about.

After his first appearance, the man in tweeds came again. I saw the two of them walking in front of the opera or sitting in a café. Only once did I see him at the Sacher. He had ordered rice pudding of all things, and the waiter was none too eager to please. I asked Josef about the man in tweeds. Fliess knew everybody. He could get you opera tickets or a Polish telephone number or a piece of the Berlin wall if you wanted it bad enough and had the money.

"You mean the Englishman?" I nodded. I had gone to Josef's office at *Stern* and he had taken me across the street to a place where journalists from *Kronenzeitung* and other papers traded gossip. "You're talking about Bill Brydon, once known as the greatest master spy of the century. You may know him as Victor Penney.

He reorganized the anti-Soviet counterintelligence center in London after Philby found it convenient to try a change of air.

"They call your Englishman—the man in tweeds—the 'Bad Penny' in the *London Daily Express*," Josef continued. "They say that he ran a bigger network than that Cambridge crew ever did." Here he paused, looking at me over his cup. "But, why is it, Max, that I suspect you know all of this already?"

"But I've never written—"

"I'm not talking about writing, Max. Those pale blue eyes of yours look far too innocent."

I grew quite hot suddenly. My necktie needed adjusting. "If you're suggesting—"

"Calm yourself. I'm an old friend. Remember?"

"What happened after 1989?"

"They were shut down. Both sides slammed the doors. Penney and his wife went to visit Philby in Moscow—were there when he died, in fact—and lived there for a time in a cold-water flat. Since she left him, he's been at loose ends. No jobs for the boys nowadays. Certainly not for our 'Bad Penny'—not from either side of the street. The Cold War had been good to Penney and to his network— people like Sachs—the man you call Kruger—and the rest of them. They were all tainted by what they'd been."

"Now you're getting melodramatic, Josef."

"Oh, Penney can travel more now. He has historic immunity: much better than the diplomatic kind. He's even lectured in Texas of all places. He's become untouchable, a celebrity, an icon from the past."

"What's he to do now? Nobody will ever trust him again."

"Such people don't live forever."

"But you just said . . ."

"People have accidents. It happens every day."

"Are you suggesting—?"

"Now who's being melodramatic? No. There will be no contract put out on Mr. Penney. Nor do I imagine him shooting himself in a back room somewhere. He's not the type. But short of a miracle, he has disappeared from the world stage."

Josef paid for my coffee. It was his way of showing off that he had stopped being freelance and could afford to live in a first-floor apartment. There is no better friend than a useful one. We walked together a little ways. He stopped at a chemist's to buy some ant traps. "They have invaded my apartment," he said. "Driving my wife insane."

"I should buy some as well," I said. "It's the spring. My kitchen is full of them."

Before we parted, he gave me an assignment that took me to the morgue at the *Pressehaus* that same afternoon. While I was there, I pulled out all I could find about Victor Penney and the other notorious double agents of the Cold War years. For operations that were all clandestine and reflected so badly on the governments involved, I was surprised to find so much material. There was an indirect connection linking him to the sale of seven Mi-24 helicopter gunships made to the Tigray People's Liberation Army in Ethiopia. Under another name, Densher, he was managing the Emperor Haile Selassie's arms purchases from three of the biggest weapons manufacturers. Earlier, he was distributing free Kalashnikovs in Madagascar, Mozambique, and Mauretania through the agency of a Cuban cat's-paw named Ortega. In his prime, as Josef told me, he ran a dozen agents between Bucharest and Lisbon. In one history of the Kim Philby defection, I read about the "Bad Penny" on almost every other page. He'd been Philby's heir apparent; the uncrowned prince of SIS.

Penney was meticulous in selecting, recruiting, indoctrinating, and training his people. He made sure that each was loyal to him personally before the faceless MI6 came into it. He was clever enough to make sure that each of his agents worked only one side of the street. I can see how working with double agents could grow complicated. Playing both sides against the middle could be and had been the most dangerous of games. That Penney got out with his life after it became known, after the unmasking of Burgess, MacLean, and then Philby, that he was talking to people at a high level in the KGB as well as running agents for the firm, is a fair measure of the man's intelligence and gamesmanship.

But what was he doing here? Why was he looking up his old colleague? With all covers blown, with the Cold War itself a dated theme for fiction, what was he up to? That's what I decided I wanted to find out.

I discovered what he was up to far more quickly and more directly than I could have dreamed. Not two days later, Kruger called me over to his table, and, for the first time in the history of the Sacher, he bought me a beer. You can imagine the expression on the waiter's face. I looked for the empty packet of cigarettes, but the one on the table was nearly full. When a first and then a second *Schwechater* had vanished, Kruger left off speaking about the Baroque glories of the old imperial city and got down to cases. He began by complimenting my rise in my profession. He made an awkward flatterer and was quite aware of it. He continued by reminding me of some small services I had done him in the past, things I do not retail around Vienna these days. I thought that it was shaping up into an extortionate demand for money in exchange for silence about those same small services. I tried not to move in my chair, not to be taken in by this superannuated fraud. Then, quite out of the blue, he asked me if I missed the excitement of the old days. Was I available for a new assignment? Naturally, I let him continue, only showing my interest by my silence.

"Max, a job has come up. It's right up your alley. The terms will be better than in the old days, but everything else will be familiar ground."

"What sort of job?"

"As usual, you're being premature. Let's, for the sake of argument, say that it has to do with the three newcomers in NATO. I'm not saying that *that's* the job, but it's in that ballpark, as the Americans say. Would you be interested? Have you two weeks to spare? Is your passport in order?"

I confess that I was caught off guard. It was as though he had swept the tablecloth from the table without dislodging a single parfait glass. "You know the drill," he said. "I'll say no more at present, but if you wish to hear more, meet me at the café across from the Freud Museum at 1830 on Friday. Bring your tooth-brush."

I knew the museum in the *Berggasse,* that steep old street to be avoided when there was ice in the streets. I remembered interviewing the curator at number 19 for an article in the *Herald Tribune's* Paris bureau. The café I knew less well. It attracted tourists. I couldn't remember when I last sat at one of its marble-topped tables.

Kruger got up; he didn't offer his hand and was gone before I could easily catch my breath. As I watched his retreating back weaving through the crowd, I firmly decided to hear more, to keep the appointment.

But that was the night I met the woman I shall call Barbara Ployer. I have not used her real name, since I would not like to bring harm to one who inadvertently did me such a good turn. She said she was a pianist who had given a recital the previous night at the *Kleinen Konzerthaussaal.* I hadn't gone to hear her, but I met her late at night walking alone along the *Wienfluss* near the Hilton. If it hadn't been for the heavy traffic, it would have been a highly romantic meeting. She was young, a native *Wienerin,* and still somewhat excited by what I guessed had been a triumphant *début.* I suggested a drink and we went to a nearby bar. After that we found a cellar—blue lights, a jazz group, someone doing "My Funny Valentine" on alto sax—and then a succession of fleeting images. We were in a restaurant not much better than a *beisel* at one point; I remember the reflection of lights in the water. Later there was a hotel room, something rather American with room service and Klimt reproductions glinting metallically in the light from the bathroom. Then the pleasures of the flesh formed a cinematic montage of sensations one after the other. I remember the blue veins on the inside of her arms, the cadence of her conversation and have no recollection at all of what either of us said. I think she said something unpleasant about Horowitz and something funny about Gould. I remember her laugh and the way she twisted my hand while laughing

When the world stood upright again, she was gone and the time of my appointment in the *Berggasse* had passed. I had wakened in a room not far from my own apartment. I had no idea whose it was, and left, without taking down the flat number or even the address. I needed a bath and found one as quickly as possible. When I checked my pocketbook, I was not surprised to discover that my money was gone. Gradually, some details of the past twenty-four hours floated back to me, fragments, flotsam for some Proust's delectation. There were dark shadows under my eyes and the taste of tobacco in my mouth as I managed the razor around a welt on my cheekbone that I had never seen before.

Out in the light of day, I bought a clutch of newspapers and tried to recapture the time that I had lost. I rejoiced in finding the tobacconist still on my corner, and the newspaper kiosk in its usual place across the street. Against a hording, I saw a listing of coming and recently past events scheduled at the *Kleinen Konzerthaussaal*. I couldn't find the name of the woman I'd spent the night with. A program of *lieder* and art songs had been scheduled on the evening in question. No recitals by pianists of either sex.

In hopes of finding Kruger, I went to the Sacher. A double espresso failed to revive me. The schnaps was more effective. I remember wondering how he would treat my excuse for missing our appointment. I didn't imagine that he put much stock in romantic encounters. I couldn't even imagine him taking pleasure in my lost pocketbook.

An item below the fold in the front page of the *Kronenzeitung* sobered me. The short piece told how eight people had been found in a station wagon pulled from *der Alten Donau* near *Kaisermühlen* late the preceding afternoon. The eight bodies had apparently been executed with a shot in the back of the head, Soviet-style. There was little more to report other than the identities of those of the bodies that were known. One was Kruger. Had it not been for Barbara Ployer, one might very well have been mine.

Unaccountably, I found myself thinking of Josef's invasion of black ants. There is a patent poison available at most chemists' in Vienna, and, for all I know, throughout the rest of the civilized world, that is designed to rid the purchaser of such an invasion. I had intended to buy some. This poison does not merely kill the invading horde, but, when the bait is carried back into the nest, it kills the whole colony. I have watched the stunned invaders carrying their wounded comrades back to the nest. I have tried to justify my quarrel with the ants crawling up the pipes of my hot water heater, with the extermination of ants who had never crossed my threshold. One should not allow oneself to become sentimental about the extermination of unwanted insects.

Non-Interference

JANWILLEM VAN DE WETERING

To Dingjum?" Adjutant Grijpstra of the Amsterdam Municipal Police asked. "That's a long way off, Sergeant. That's in the North. You sure?" He looked at Sergeant De Gier suspiciously. De Gier's tall, wide-shouldered body sprawled behind his dented desk with his feet propped up on its top, between files not arranged neatly. Sunlight glinted off his pistol's butt and barrel, protruding from a well-worn shoulder holster that contrasted crudely with the sergeant's spotless, tailored blue shirt. De Gier smiled innocently, showing strong white teeth and sparkling, oversized, soft brown eyes. His moustache, model cavalry officer, previous century, was swept up neatly under his long straight nose and high cheekbones supporting a noble brow, supporting thick brown curls in turn.

"Sure," the sergeant said. "I think we should go to Dingjum. It'll be a nice day today, we have just been supplied with a new car, Dingjum is a pleasant little town, set in unspoiled country, we'll drive along Holland's longest and neatest dike, with the sea on one side and a lake on the other, we'll watch birds, sails on the horizon, interesting cloud formations—the car has a sunroof, we can drive and watch the sky in turns—I think I'm sure it's a lovely idea."

Adjutant Grijpstra sighed. His hands, clasped on a steadily rising and receding round belly, covered by a pinstriped blue waistcoat, gently unhooked their fingers and rose in feeble protest. "Dingjum is some sixty miles outside of our territory, Sergeant. We're specialists, members of the celebrated Murder Brigade, we only move for specific and urgent reasons. Whatever could demand our presence in the little rural town of Dingjum?"

Sergeant De Gier withdrew his feet and jumped up in one extended, graceful and lithe, powerful movement. He found a newspaper on a filing cabinet and handed it to the gray-haired solid adjutant, still at ease in his swivel-chair on the other side of the small gray-painted room. "Front page news. Absorb its contents. *Fresh contents.* This happened less than a week ago."

Grijpstra read. He mumbled. "A *Chinese* businessman? In *Dingjum?* An *arrow* into his throat? While watering exotic plants in a *greenhouse?*"

The sergeant poured coffee from a thermos-flask into paper cups. "Exotic is right."

Adjutant Grijpstra put the newspaper down and reached for the coffee. "Thanks. I still fail to see what we could do in Dingjum. There's State Police out there. We would interfere. They might not like that."

"We're never liked," Sergeant De Gier said, contentedly slipping behind his desk again. "However, there might be an exception. Lieutenant Sudema is in charge of the local station; you remember the lieutenant?"

"Yes," Grijpstra said. "That was a while ago. I didn't care for all the tomato salad he made us eat."

"And we gave Lieutenant Sudema the credit for our solution," De Gier said gently. "We always do when we can. We're not so bad, Adjutant."

"Oh, but we are," Grijpstra said. "We disturb the peace of our esteemed colleagues. We did that time. The lieutenant didn't exactly welcome us. And we had a legal excuse then; we don't have one now. We found a corpse in Amsterdam that lived, when still alive, in Dingjum. We pursued a hot trail. We're pursuing nothing now."

"I sort of like going after nothing," the sergeant said softly. "Oh, come on now, Grijpstra. An arrow in a millionaire's throat, and the millionaire is a Chinese who officially resides in the Fiji Islands but who somehow owns a capital villa here, and who originated in Taiwan, and who has married one of our former beauty queens, and who owns a factory of computer parts that he doesn't manage; it's all in the article; that's a lot of nothing that adds up nicely."

"Where?" Grijpstra said, looking at the paper again. "Ah. The tale continues on page three. Let's see." He turned pages, holding the paper up to get a better look at the dead man's wife. "Why does she wear a tiny two-piece bathing suit? Ah, that was her prize-winning outfit. Some years ago. Still a bit of a girl then, though definitely sexy. A woman now, eh what? A most attractive woman?"

"You bet," De Gier said. "You'd meet her, if we would go to Dingjum. Don't you want to meet with a mature beauty queen?"

"Nah," Grijpstra said.

"You do," De Gier said. "And more than I. You've repressed your lusts; there's an evil power in you, pushing its tentacles through your flimsy defenses. You'd go a long way to be able to meet a sex symbol in her dainty flesh. Maybe *she* shot that arrow? If the Chinese dead man was a millionaire? The couple has no children. Wouldn't the lady make a first-class suspect? You could manipulate her, ask her tricky questions, prod her luscious soul, wiggle, finger, feel . . ."

"What's with you?" Grijpstra asked furiously.

"Spring," De Gier whispered. "Spring brings out romantic desire in me. It's a good spring now and we could go for a drive."

Grijpstra pulled himself free of his desk and swiveled his chair. His short legs, in trouserpipes that were rather badly rumpled, and sagging socks and shoes that hadn't been recently polished, scissored slowly. "Yeh," Grijpstra said. "Never mind your romantic needs for now. A Chinese multimillionaire living off the fat of our land, and officially residing in the Fiji Islands, what does that lead to?"

"Non-payment of taxes," De Gier said. "Easy question, easy answer. It also points to extreme cleverness."

The adjutant's heavy body made another complete turn, while a steady sun ray highlighted his short silver hair. "How so?"

"Our corpse," De Gier said, "the former Lee Dzung, married one of this country's certified beautiful women. Why? To kill a whole flock of fat ducks with one broadside of his foreign gun. He doesn't pay taxes in Holland, right?"

"Right," Grijpstra said. "In Fiji, tax would be nominal. But Dzung is active in business here. His factory produces high-priced products."

"Now then, Adjutant. Dzung is our guest, he flies in and out, and when he's here he has a beautiful villa, it says so in the article, surrounded by a park, which is owned by his wife, and he owns his wife."

"Yes," Grijpstra said. "If Dzung owned property here he would have to become a resident and pay Dutch income taxes. A diabolic way out that would satisfy human greed, and Dzung picked the best looking wife the country could provide, doubly attractive to him for she is of another race. Long-legged, full-bosomed, golden-haired." Grijpstra studied the photograph again, grunting with pleasure. "A dirty boy's dream. The answer to all his hidden filthy desires."

"You're so Calvinistic," De Gier mused. "Maybe you become overexcited when you contemplate that perfect and inviting shape, but why should Dzung?"

"It's natural," Grijpstra said. "Aren't Chinese Confucianists? Confucianism preaches a strict code of morals, an impossible system that automatically produces pleasurable guilt." Grijpstra grinned. "Show me a Chinese beauty queen and my feelings of forbidden lust will be doubled, too. Now suppose I could marry her, and put her in a pagoda, and spend a few months a year with her in a, to me, exotic setting, and have expert foreigners produce my pricy gadgets, and make tax-free profits . . . for that's another point here . . ." the adjutant's blunt forefinger poked in the direction of De Gier's immaculate shirt—". . . if the Dingjum factory is owned by a mother company in far-off Fiji, full profits can be channeled there."

De Gier got up, reaching for a silk scarf of a delicate baby-blue color that went well with his indigo shirt. "Shall we go?"

"Whoa," Grijpstra said.

De Gier knotted his scarf, tucking it neatly into his collar.

"An excuse, Sergeant?" Grijpstra pleaded. "We do need an excuse."

De Gier scratched his strong chin. "Yep. Let's see now. About a month ago a bum fell into the Emperor's Canal. The water police fished him out last week. Remember?"

"Yagh." The adjutant grimaced.

"You're telling me," De Gier said. "I almost fainted when they brought that mess in."

Grijpstra looked stern. "You fell into my arms. Was the bum connected to the North?"

"If he wasn't he is now," De Gier said. He opened a drawer and found a disheveled file. "No, right. He was from the North. We haven't checked the death properly yet. An accident probably, the man was an alcoholic, but he could have been pushed. He will have relatives in the North and we can check with the register of his place of birth, which is, let's see now, the town of Dokkum."

"Close enough to Dingjum," Grijpstra said. "Then on the way back, remembering all that tomato salad Lieutenant Sudema made us eat, when we consulted him on that other case . . ."

". . . we sort of casually drop in and ask how the lieutenant has been doing of late."

"Adjutant Grijpstra," Lieutenant Sudema said. "How nice to see you. And Sergeant De Gier. What a pleasant surprise." The lieutenant, splendidly uniformed, saluted his colleagues. He stood between two plane trees, artfully cut so that their branches framed his station, housed in a medieval brick cottage with a pointed gable that carried a stone angel, grasping for a trumpet that had been missing for a century or so. "Amazing. I haven't seen you for a year, a Chinese businessman is most mysteriously murdered here, and you pop up, on a lovely day like this. Out of the blue." The lieutenant pointed at the sky. "It is a nice day, today, don't you think?"

"Happened to pass by," Adjutant Grijpstra said. "We were checking the register in Dokkum regarding a dead drunk at our end and . . ."

"Dokkum is south of here, of course," the lieutenant said. "Close to the highway. But you came up another ten miles just to say hello."

"How's your wife?" De Gier asked.

"You came to see my wife?" Lieutenant Sudema asked. "I see. You're a bachelor, and from Amsterdam, of course; a wicked city, in our provencial eyes that is. Free sex hasn't exactly penetrated here. My wife is well, Sergeant. You did make quite an impression on her the last time you darkened our doorstep. Would you like to meet her again? She's at work now but she'll be back later today. You could wait."

De Gier scratched his right buttock. "You're making him nervous," Grijpstra said. "I've known the sergeant some ten years by now and he's quite shy with women. They'll have to attack him to get anywhere and they'll have to be single."

"My wife isn't single," Lieutenant Sudema said.

"I know," De Gier said. "I was merely inquiring whether Gyske is in good health."

"You're not interested in my murder?"

"He is," Adjutant Grijpstra said, "and so am I. Any progress?"

The lieutenant asked his guests in and found comfortable chairs. A constable brought coffee. He was sent out again to bring in two bags of large fresh tomatoes from the lieutenant's private crop. Sudema discussed tomatoes for a while, and their diseases. The lieutenant's tomatoes were disease-free but that was only because . . .

"Right," Grijpstra mumbled from time to time. "You don't say," Sergeant De Gier murmured once in a while.

"So Mr. Lee Dzung was shot dead with an arrow was he?" Grijpstra asked.

"So we thought," Sudema said.

"He wasn't?" De Gier asked.

"No," Lieutenant Sudema said. "If it had been all arrow, the case might have been hard to crack. There are these newfangled crossbows now, with telescopes; horrible weapons I'll have you know, and all over the place. I thought it had to be one of those. There was an article about crossbows in the *Police Gazette* that I had happened to read, and some of the weapons make use of small darts. When I saw the corpse, some metal protruded from the wound, sharp and gleaming, so I thought it was a dart. But you know what it really was?"

"Do tell." The sergeant sat forward in his chair.

"A . . ." the lieutenant opened a drawer in his desk and checked with his notebook, ". . . what was it called now; right, here, a *shuriken*."

"A what?" Grijpstra asked.

"Metal disc," De Gier said. "Shaped like a star with a hole in the middle. A *shuriken* isn't shot but thrown. A very deadly weapon, Adjutant, when it flies from the hand of a trained assassin."

The lieutenant pushed his chair back. "So, you see, the case is out of my hands. Are you ready for lunch? The local pub still serves its famous lambchops with the local tomato salad, made out of my tomatoes, of course. I trust you'll be my guests?"

They walked along a country lane, shaded by tall elms. The lieutenant and the sergeant strode along and the adjutant panted, bringing up the rear.

"Why is the case out of your hands?" Grijpstra asked, wheezing between words.

The lieutenant waved airily. "State Security took over. As soon as the pathologist dug up that, what was it now?"

"*Shuriken*?" De Gier asked.

"Right, as soon as we found that a bizarre Far Eastern weapon had been used, we drew our conclusion. Mr. Dzung manufactures a new type of computer chip, that holds more information better, and is capable of programming computers in a most superb way. He makes them in Taiwan. Now he also makes them here. Why? Eh?"

"Why?" De Gier asked.

"You don't know?" Lieutenant Sudema stopped in his tracks. The adjutant bumped into him. De Gier caught them both. "No," De Gier said.

"Is Taiwan close to Russia?" Sudema asked. "Listen, Sergeant, that part wasn't clear to me, either; all I knew was that some outlandish weapon was used, so the killer wasn't Dutch. Mr. Dzung is Chinese. The killer probably, too. Two Chinese visited here last week. I enquired at Mr. Dzung's factory and the manager, a Dr. Haas, tells me that the other Chinese had argued with Mr. Dzung, in Chinese, of course, so he didn't know what about. He assumed that the other Chinese wanted something that Mr. Dzung wouldn't give. An assurance perhaps. That's what the conversation sounded like. Much shouting back and forth."

"Taiwan is friendly with America" Grijpstra said.

Lieutenant Sudema clapped his hands. "Right, you're so right. The State Security chaps, called in by me, working overtime, in the weekend and all, telexed with the CIA. It was all clear at once. Dzung manufactures special computer chips in Taipeh—that's the capital of Taiwan—with American know-how, and with his own, too, for Dzung was a genius and came up with considerable improvements that he patented at once. Those chips may not be sent to Russia, though it's easier to send stuff to Russia from here than from Taiwan."

"And the two Chinese that came to yell at Dzung?" the sergeant asked.

"Assassins," the lieutenant whispered. "*Ninjas*. Ever heard of them? The most dangerous killers on Earth. They could have killed Dzung straight off but they were good enough to warn him first. Dzung didn't listen. So?" The lieutenant stood on one leg, produced a transparent object from his trouser pocket, swung his body from the hip and let go of the object. "*Zip!*"

"*Wow*," De Gier said, "Ninjas in Dingjum. Throwing a *shuriken*, Tssssshhh!"

"Nah," Grijpstra said.

"You don't believe it?" Lieutenant Sudema asked. "I'm sorry to hear that. I wouldn't believe it at first, either, because, let's face it, Adjutant, we're staunch Dutchmen here, very limited in our outlook and ways. We don't throw exotic razor-sharp steel stars at each other. The very idea. But why wouldn't some nasty outside fellow throw a *whatdoyoucallit* on Dutch territory? It's a big bad world out there and it does interfere with us at times. We may as well face that."

"You really don't believe in the lieutenant's theory?" De Gier asked Grijpstra. "If a *shuriken* was found in Mr. Dzung's throat, then somebody threw it."

"Not a ninja," Grijpsira said. "Ninja, indeed. Ridiculous. One of these black-hooded chaps that slither about on slippers? A ninja in Dingjum would be as conspicuous as a man from Mars."

"I didn't see the Chinese," the lieutenant said. "State Security is making an effort, but they won't catch them; so much is sure. Those ninjas got out of the country immediately after they had fulfilled their contract. Slipped across the border to Germany, flew out of Frankfurt—so State Security presumes."

"Crazy," Grijpstra said.

Lieutenant Sudema towered over the adjutant and glared down from under the visor of his immaculate cap. "So what else, colleague?"

Grijpstra looked up. "His wife, maybe? Did you interrogate his wife?"

Sudema marched on. De Gier loped along next to him. Grijpstra hobbled behind. The lieutenant turned. "That poor girl had a bad deal; she's better off now. Dzung didn't turn out to be a nice man. Do you know that he wouldn't even let her out of his grounds? He treated her something terrible, like a slave almost, as his sex object; she was just another possession. Everything was in her name, the car, the house, but he kept her short. Wouldn't even pay for driving lessons."

"So the pathetic doll did pretty good out of that murder," De Gier said brightly.

Sudema flapped a hand. "Makes her a suspect, sure. You don't think I didn't see that? Listen, Sergeant. Mr. Dzung got killed at 11:05 A.M.; a gardener saw him fall. At that moment, Mrs. Dzung was in the basement, operating a laundry machine, being assisted by a maid. She's not good at sports. She was nowhere near."

"I would like to see the location," Grijpstra said. "After lunch of course. I wouldn't miss your tomato salad. Eh, De Gier? Remember that tomato salad? With that delicious dressing? Made with herbs from the lieutenant's lovely wife's very own garden?"

MRS. DZUNG STOOD IN the open doorway. De Gier gaped. Grijpstra stepped back in abject wonder. Mrs. Dzung looked even better than in the photograph they had studied. She was tall, very tall, but perfectly proportioned. She was also well-dressed, in tight leather dark trousers and a flowing white blouse. Her long hair wasn't blond but gold, and as fine as the rays in a spider's web, and luxurious, cascading down her supple shoulders. Her large eyes were sparkling blue and seemed semi-transparent, with the pure color reaching inward, attracting the observer into their unfathomable depths. Her nose was finely chiseled and her lips full, though tight in contour. They parted to smile down at her audience. "Hello, Lieutenant."

Sudema introduced his companions. Mrs. Dzung was called Emily, she said in a voice that vibrated pleasantly, soothingly, De Gier thought; there was a motherly quality to the woman though she still had to be quite young, in her early twenties, no more. De Gier felt that he wanted to be lifted up and pressed into those giant breasts, turned upside down like a cat that is cuddled, a large tomcat that will purr and meanwhile reach out with a sly paw, pushing gently, kneading firmly, begging for a kiss from those supple and moist lips.

"Minny to my friends," the vibrating voice murmured.

"I'm your friend," De Gier said. He felt very friendly. He would hold her hand and they would jog along friendly beaches, past a friendly sea, and then run up a dune and be really pally between the wildflowers and the waving grass.

"My colleagues," Lieutenant Sudema said, "would like me to show them around your garden. This must be painful to you, Minny, you don't have to come along."

"Come back for tea," Mrs. Dzung said. "I'll have it ready on the rear terrace." Her eyes met De Gier's, expressing a special invitation. "Yes," De Gier said, "oh, yes, for sure!"

"She likes you," Sudema said as he took them to the greenhouse. "She likes me, too. We're as tall as she. She told me she doesn't like looking down on men. I'm married."

"Dzung was small-sized?" Grijpstra asked.

"Fat, too." Sudema's face showed some degree of well-meant pity. "She told me pudgy men turn her off completely."

De Gier nodded. "Fat men have a hard time. Drag all that weight around while available women turn away. Lonely, heavy . . ."

"Who's fat?" Grijpstra asked. "Tell me, is the factory's director, this Dr. Haas you mentioned, fat? Dzung didn't run his company, right? He couldn't because he isn't a resident here. There must be somebody else in charge. Is that fellow fat?"

"Dr. Haas?" Sudema thought. "He's sort of regular."

"Tall?"

"Regular," the lieutenant said again. "Ordinary looking, even though he's got all these PhDs in science and all, but likable nevertheless, I thought. The State Security fellows had a long talk with him, they were rather impressed."

"Why?" De Gier asked. "You just described him as regular. Regularity is hardly impressive."

"Looks don't always matter, Sergeant."

Grijpstra patted Sudema's shoulder. "I'm glad you say that. That's the sergeant's trouble, he doesn't penetrate beyond the outside layer. Like with that lady just now. Did you see him gape? Biased De Gier could never consider her as a suspect. She immediately, because she happens to look fertile and warm, changes into some sort of goddess in his immature mind. When there are beautiful people around, I may as well forget about De Gier. He becomes a dead weight that I have to drag around. Disgusting. Quite."

"That lady is no suspect," the lieutenant said sternly.

"Why are we standing here?" De Gier asked. "That's the greenhouse over there. This is some garden by the way." He looked around. "Just look at the placement of these rocks. Makes you think you're surrounded by mountains. Very foreign."

"Exactly," the lieutenant said. "The ninja feller was hiding here, behind this little artificial hill. He crouched down, waiting for Dzung to move about in the greenhouse over there. Because of the warm weather, the windows were open, but as you can see the view is somewhat obstructed by all those flowering plants in there. The killer waited patiently, right here."

"Orchids," De Gier said. "Lee Dzung was growing beautiful orchids. This is an elegant place. Maybe Chinese heaven looks like this. Wasn't he smart, this Mr. Dzung?"

"Okay," Sudema said. "Dzung was moving about inside the greenhouse. The killer is waiting for his chance. He throws the . . . hmmm . . . well, he threw it, jumped over that outside wall and was gone. Nobody saw him. The gardener was on the other side of the greenhouse. He heard Dzung fall."

"Yeh," Grijpstra said. "Smart is the word. But Dzung got killed. He got outsmarted. Pity, really. I like a man to get away with the whole thing. Just think: No taxes. Immense profits. Flies in and out in first-class airplanes. Has this wonderful woman in what he considers an exotic foreign country. Plays about in surroundings that must be ideal to Chinese taste."

"As you say," Sudema said. "Dzung flew in and out. There's a Lear Jet in Amsterdam Airport, now, registered in Fiji."

"I wonder if Dzung made a will," Grijpstra said.

"Who cares?" De Gier asked. "He's subject to Dutch law. Minny is legally married to the deceased so she inherits the house and whatever else he owns in Holland."

"Dzung would have known that, wouldn't he?" Grijpstra asked. "He probably has other wives."

"Mistresses more likely," De Gier said. "He had to marry here so that he could have this heaven in Minny's name. If he was smart, he wouldn't marry unless he had to." De Gier turned around. "What's the place worth? Just check that palace. Terraces, spires, three stories. Well-furnished, I'm sure."

"Nothing but the best," the lieutenant said. "There's a Chinese wing, toward the other side, stocked with treasures. Screens and paintings and sculptures and what not. Most outlandish. Minny took me on a tour."

"A tour . . ." De Gier said, "maybe I could ask her . . ."

"None of that." Grijpstra's heavy finger poked at the sergeant's stomach. "There will be no flirtation with a suspect."

"Ah." Sudema smiled benignly. "No interference, of course. I'm taking you around, showing you this and that, discussing theories, analyzing suspicions, but this case is closed; to you, and to me, too. State Security took over."

Minny called from the terrace. "Tea is ready."

De Gier noticed that his hostess had changed into a modest dress, and that her long hair was done up in a simple bun. There was faint makeup accentuating her large eyes, that threw him a penetrating glance from behind darkened lashes. "Poor Lee," Minny said. "He always enjoyed himself so much, wandering about in his gown, fussing with the plants, creating the illusion of a river by spreading all those pebbles. Do you know that he brought a truckload of oval pebbles in and then put them down parallel, one by one? See it there? It's coming out between those two little hills, like a stream rushing out of mountains? He explained it to me; he was such an artist."

"In Chinese?" Grijpstra asked.

"In English," Minny said.

"You speak good English?"

"Some," Minny said. "I was learning."

"Did your husband often go to his factory in Dingjum?" Grijp-stra asked.

Minny arranged her long slender legs, pulling up her skirt a little, then dropping it again. De Gier shivered.

"Are you cold?" Minny asked, her soft eyes expressing concern about the sergeant's involuntary shudder.

"Just impressed by your beauty," De Gier said kindly. "Did your husband take an interest in his product? Computer chips was it? Some advanced line of specialized mint goods?"

"You should see that factory," Minny said. "Everything is auto-mated. The chips manufacture chips. The machines hum day and night and Dr. Haas watches them from a glass cage stuck to the ceil-ing. Dr. Haas used to visit here from time to time and they'd work with a computer that Lee rigged up on the third floor. It was linked to the factory. Lee hardly ever went out."

"You know Dr. Haas well?"

"He'd come over for dinner."

"Often?"

"Yes," Minny said. "Too often, and always so late. I like to have dinner early but Haas worked until eight o'clock at night. I got bored. Chips and computers, that's what my husband and Haas always talked about. It's another language. Other languages bore me, too."

"Would you show me that stone river?" De Gier asked. "I'm fas-cinated. So Mr. Dzung personally arranged a million pebbles so they would look like wavelets; how poetic."

"There's a real stream on the other side of the house," Minny said, "and quite a large pond. Lee was breeding goldfish. Some are so beautiful, with all sorts of blended colors and many-finned tails."

De Gier saw the stone river first, and picked up some pebbles. He followed his hostess down a path around the main building of the estate and squatted at the side of a pond. Minny sat next to him on an ornamental rock. "Can you make pebbles bounce off water?" De Gier asked. "I used to be good at that when I was a kid. Maybe I can still do it." He threw a pebble with a clumsy twist of his wrist. It ricocheted once and sank.

"That wasn't so good," Minny said. "Let me try, too."

All Minny's pebbles splashed and disappeared. "Maybe they aren't the right pebbles," De Gier said, staring discreetly at Minny's slim ankles. "Were you really happy with Lee?"

He thought she moved closer, for her hand almost touched his. "Yes," Minny said. "I like older men. My father left my mother when I was small so I'm probably frustrated. Lee was over forty."

"I'm thirty-nine," De Gier said.

She straightened her dress down her legs. "You look younger."

"I'll be forty next month." The sergeant got up and extended a hand. She held on to him and allowed herself to be lifted. They walked along and reached a lawn that stretched to the far fence. A tennis ball had been left on the path. "That's Poopy's ball," Minny said. "Poopy is my terrier. Lee didn't like the dog; it would dig holes in all his funny gardens. Poopy is staying with my sister now."

De Gier picked up the ball and ran out to the lawn. "Catch." She jumped but the ball whizzed by her and hit the house. It came bouncing back. De Gier put up a slow hand and missed it, too.

Grijpstra and Sudema appeared. "Come and see me sometime," Minny said into the sergeant's ear. "It gets lonely here. But please, phone me first."

"Sure," De Gier smiled. "Thank you for the tea," he said loudly. "And for letting us see the gardens. I envy you."

A maid came out of the mansion to tell Minny that the laundry machinery in the cellar wasn't working properly again. Minny said good-bye and disappeared into the house.

"Let's go, Sergeant," Grijpstra ordered briskly. De Gier glanced over his shoulder. "Just a minute." He ran back to the side-garden and picked up Poopy's ball. Released from a swing of De Gier's long arm, it hit a wall and came shooting back. He caught it without effort.

"Are you coming?" Grijpstra bellowed.

De Gier dug in his pocket and produced a pebble. The pebble was flung at the pond's surface and bounced off, and again, and again, in long graceful curves.

The sergeant came running back.

Grijpstra frowned. "Childish!"

"Heh, heh," said De Gier.

"TELL ME EVERYTHING," SERGEANT GRIJPSTRA said, as he waved at Sudema who was saluting them from under the plane trees that guarded his station. The lieutenant had begged to be excused for a while. His tomatoes needed their daily attention. He would be available again a little later in the day. De Gier drove around the corner, parked the VW, lit a cigarette, and reported on his recent adventure.

"Okay," Grijpstra said. "You've got something there, but that business about phoning her first means nothing. Maybe there's no lover as yet in Minny's life. Women hate being surprised by an erotic enthusiast suddenly appearing at the door. Minny is attractive but a quarter of her beauty is clothes, make-up, perfume, and what not. She wants to smack you with the full 100 percent of her oversized dazzle; and to work that up may take her an hour."

"Wow," De Gier said.

"Beg pardon, Sergeant?"

"She's beautiful," De Gier said. "A Viking Queen. You know, you meet this absolutely stunning woman and you somehow manage to wake up next to her in the morning, and you kiss her awake and you wait for the heavenly wisdom flowing out of that lovely shape, and it isn't there?"

"I have no idea what you're talking about," Grijpstra said. "I live a quiet life. I paint tasteless pictures on my days off. Now, what are you saying?"

"That," De Gier said, "I don't think Minny will be disappointing."

Grijpstra withdrew into a disagreeable silence.

"I'm," De Gier said dreamily, "telling you that Minny is capable of murder. She inspires me." He grinned at the adjutant. "To do good things, of course. But then I'm a good guy. Now, what if she was involved with a bad guy, a ninja? Wouldn't she inspire him to do evil?"

Grijpstra moved his back against his seat, grunting softly. "Yeh. Maybe. So she can't throw pebbles and she can't catch balls. Why? She must have tried some sports. All schools have games. She looks athletic."

"Did you notice that her left eye tends to drift somewhat?" De Gier asked. "She may have trouble focusing, especially when she's tired. These last days must have been a strain."

"Let's go," Grijpstra said. "We stayed in a hotel in Dingjum once, that time we were here before. An old-fashioned inn. Think you can find it again?"

The innkeeper remembered the two Chinese visitors who came for Mr. Dzung. "Mr. Wang and Mr. Tzu. Their full names and addresses are in the register; let me look them up."

"You checked their passports?" Grijpstra asked.

The innkeeper nodded. "I always do."

De Gier noted the names and addresses on his pad. Both Chinese originated in Taipeh.

"They were older men," the innkeeper said. "Quite pleasant."

"Athletic?" De Gier asked.

The innkeeper laughed. "Not really. I have a mini golf course in the back and they puttered about; they weren't too good."

"And where did they go from here?"

"Let's see now," the innkeeper said. "Wait a minute. Maybe I do know. They phoned Philips Electronics; I remember because they couldn't find the right number and there was some trouble with the operator, it seemed. I helped them out. They were supposed to meet someone there and we couldn't locate the fellow, but they did talk to him in the end."

"So you think they left for Philips Headquarters from here?"

"Yes," the innkeeper said. "I remember now. They had a rented car and my wife helped them to trace a route on the map."

"Can we use the phone?" De Gier asked. "It would help if you remembered the name of the man at Philips."

De Gier dialed. "Sir? A Mr. Wang and a Mr. Tzu, are they still around?"

He listened. "They're in Amsterdam now?" He thanked his informant and replaced the phone.

"BACK AGAIN?" SUDEMA ASKED. "I thought I was rid of you. I beg your pardon. Always happy to entertain colleagues, of course. Especially when they don't interfere. You wouldn't be interfering, would you now?"

"You know, Lieutenant," Grijpstra said, "I do admire you. You said that Minny wasn't a suspect and, by jove, she isn't."

"Not a direct murder suspect," De Gier said. "No, sir!"

"And you did express doubts about those two Chinese," Grijpstra said. "You and I both know what State Security is like. A bunch of old dodderers wandering about their Victorian offices looking for a lost slipper. They actually managed to come out here?"

"Briefly," Sudema said. "They talked to Dr. Haas and wrote their report. They also checked out some shipments of chips that were sent to Germany and probably reached Moscow."

"And what is Dr. Haas going to do, now that his boss is dead?"

Sudema rolled a cigarette and studied its ends. He tapped the cigarette on his desk. "Yes, Adjutant, I know. I'm perhaps not quite as foolish as you city slicker chaps may be thinking. There could be a possible connection there. Minny has talked to her lawyer and it seems pretty clear that the factory is now hers. It may be an affiliated company to the Fiji tax-free head office, and linked to Taipeh, but according to Dr. Haas, all the patents are in Lee Dzung's name and Minny will probably inherit them outright, too."

De Gier rolled a cigarette, too, and imitated Sudema's careful treatment of the ends. "If that lawyer knows his job, Minny stands a chance of getting hold of all Dzung's assets."

Sudema blew a little smoke to the station's rustic ceiling and admired its age-old beams. "Minny didn't kill Dzung."

Grijpstra peeled a cigar out of plastic. "You know, Lieutenant, I would just love to watch you while you make monkeys out of State Security. I could never stand seeing those nincompoops waste the taxpayers' money. Do you have any idea about the size of their budget?"

"I saw the Mercedes limousine they parked in front of this station," Sudema said. He hit the desk. "Do you know that they wouldn't eat at our restaurant here? They said they didn't care for tomato salad. They actually preferred to go back to Amsterdam and some fancy bodega. It took them three and a half hours to get back here again."

"I think we should go and see Dr. Haas sometime," De Gier said, "and perhaps you can come along, Lieutenant. I know how busy you are but this might be worth it. As an officer you don't need us to sign the final report with you. We weren't really here, anyway; we were just passing through as we happened to be in the neighborhood."

"I do," Sudema said, "sometimes read the weekly magazines. We're dealing with Taiwan Chinese. You mentioned that Dzung was a smart guy. I agree. The Taiwan authorities probably squeezed Dzung in Taipei. Imagine—here's a genius who comes up with a superb product and he makes an immense profit. Who runs Taiwan? Generals and so forth, corrupt warlords who escaped from the communist mainland. So Dzung thinks of a way in which he can have his noodles with sauce and eat them, too. Maybe he sold his stuff from here to Russia out of spite."

"How did he get Minny?" Grijpstra asked.

"My guess is as good as yours, Adjutant."

"Let the sergeant guess." Grijpstra pushed De Gier's shoulder. "Share your knowledge of the world, De Gier."

"Me?" De Gier looked up. "Escort service, I would imagine. Dzung came here, he set up his operation with Dr. Haas. He probably found

Haas through some technical paper. All these top-notch scientists correspond, meet at congresses, get together on schemes. Haas introduced Dzung to an organization that rents out attractive females. Dzung selected the very best. Haas suggested marriage and Minny was willing. She preferred to be legal."

Sudema rolled another perfect cigarette. "Yes, I think so, too, and there may be some risk there: Minny obviously benefits by her husband's death. Dr. Haas does not. For one thing, he's married and has some kids. He strikes me as a scientist, not as a businessman. Dzung is the genius, not Haas. And . . ." Sudema was admiring the beams of his ceiling again, "let's face it, Dutchmen aren't killers. The Taiwanese are. If Dzung was selling superchips to the Russians, the Americans would lean on the generals of Taipeh. . . ."

"Who would send thugs, ninjas, lithe louts trained in bizarre murderous methods," Grijpstra said, sucking his cigar contently. "The CIA must be pleased that Dzung caught that steel star in his neck. But I still think all this is very far-fetched. Now what if there were no assassins? Not from Taipeh anyway? Now suppose you could prove that? Wouldn't that be great? A feather in your hat?"

"I think I could help," De Gier said.

"Please do," the lieutenant said, "I'm very fond of feathers." Grijpstra got up. "I could save you some time. You drive to Amsterdam with my sergeant and I'll visit this Dr. Haas. When you come back you can tie things tip."

"You wouldn't interfere now?" Sudema asked. "Right, Adjutant?"

"Never," Grijpstra said. "Just tell me where I can find the good doctor."

"You're not coming through very clearly," the operator at the radio room of Amsterdam Municipal Headquarters said.

De Gier frowned at the small microphone in his hand. "As long as you can hear me. I'm looking for a Mr. Tzu and a Mr. Wang, staying in a hotel in Amsterdam; could you check which hotel I should go to and let me know within the next half hour?"

"Will try. Over and out."

The VW was speeding along the Great Dike and approaching the capital. Sudema had been watching swans on the lake. He glanced at De Gier's handsome profile. "Shouldn't we call for an arrest team? I'm a fairly good shot but my book on martial arts says that a good thrower of . . . what the hell, what do you call those things again?"

"*Shuriken*, Lieutenant?"

"Right. That a good thrower of those damned things can fling a dozen in no time at all. It'll be like a barrage from an automatic rifle."

"Nah," De Gier said.

"Suit yourself," Sudema said. "I hear you won the prizes at the national police unarmed combat contest this year. Can you catch those *whatdoyoucallums*?"

"Forget unarmed combat," De Gier said. "Nothing beats a gun. Make sure that they can't reach you with any part of their bodies and shoot to kill in case of doubt. Don't complain and explain later. Self-defense is still a good excuse." He grinned at the lieutenant. "Don't worry about the present situation, though."

"You're pretty sure, eh, Sergeant?"

"I don't think Wang and Tzu are assassins," De Gier said. "If I did, I would probably ask for assistance. I'm not really a hero, you know. I have to go home and feed my cat. There're some books I'd still like to read, and perhaps I'll meet a lady sometime who'll look like Minny."

"Not Minny herself? I think you'd be welcome."

"Wouldn't that be nice?" De Gier asked. "And wander about in that exotic abode the morning after? Breakfast on the terrace? If she really baked those cookies that came with the tea herself, she'll be a good cook, too."

The lieutenant smiled happily. "And she isn't a dumb blonde, either."

"Intelligence goes both ways," De Gier said. The radio crackled.

"Sergeant De Gier?"

"Right here."

"Your parties are staying at the Victoria Hotel. We checked with the desk and they are in their room. Should I tell them to expect you?"

"Please," De Gier said. He pushed the microphone back under the dashboard.

"We aren't being silly now?" Sudema asked. "If we are, I might want to phone my wife."

De Gier unhooked the microphone. "Headquarters? De Gier again. Please phone the State Police station at Dingjum, Friesland, and tell the constable to phone Lieutenant Sudema's wife to tell her that her husband may be late for dinner."

"Thanks," Sudema said.

DE GIER SHOOK HANDS; Lieutenant Sudema saluted.

"Please sit down," Mr. Wang said.

"Cup of tea?" Mr. Tzu asked. He poured. The four men raised their cups and smiled politely at each other.

"We're sorry to hear about Mr. Dzung's death," Wang said. "Very sorry. To die in a foreign country is unpleasant experience. Perhaps his body can go home, yes?"

"If a request is made," Sudema said, "I'm sure we would be happy to oblige. To be murdered is also an unpleasant experience."

"Very sad," Tzu said. Tzu stooped; a hearing aid hid in the tufted white hairs sprouting from his ear. He also wore thick glasses. Wang's belly rested comfortably on his thighs. Wang would be a little younger than Tzu.

"We represent Mustang Electrics," Wang said. "We deal in advanced computer technology. Mr. Dzung and Dr. Haas are known to us and we thought that Dzung might help us to do business with Philips, on commission, of course."

"Or take over our idea," Tzu said, "for money, but he wasn't interested. So, instead, we made contact with Phillips directly."

"Successfully?" De Gier asked.

"Hopefully," Wang said.

"Likely," Tzu said. "Very likely, yes; our suggestions were well received."

"We hear," De Gier said, smiling apologetically, "that you and Mr. Tzu did, eh, disagree with Mr. Dzung while visiting him in Dingjum? There was, perhaps, some expression of anger during your brief get-together?"

"Hmm?" Wang asked. He spoke in Chinese to Tzu. Tzu shook his head.

"No," Wang said. "Not at all. It's very rude to be angry with a business relation. Besides, it doesn't pay."

Tzu polished his glasses with the tip of his tie. "Now, who would have told you that Dzung and us had disagreement?"

De Gier reached absent-mindedly for his teaspoon but his movement was awkward and the spoon slithered across the table into Wang's lap. The sergeant apologized.

"Hmm?" Wang asked.

"Sorry, sir, I dropped my spoon on your side."

Wang picked up the spoon with some effort, as he had to bend down. He gave it back.

"Talking about Dr. Haas," De Gier said, "you say you knew him. Dr. Haas was in Taiwan, perhaps?"

Tzu nodded. "Oh yes, for many years. Quite an expert on things Chinese. Very bright, this Dr. Haas."

"Like what things Chinese?" Lieutenant Sudema asked.

Tzu replaced his glasses. "Chinese table-tennis. He was very good. He beat my twice-removed nephew, an expert in Kung Fu."

"Kung Fu equates with table-tennis?" De Gier asked.

Wang smiled. "No."

"Many-sided man, this Dr. Haas," Tzu whispered.

De Gier smiled over the rim of his cup. "And what are you doing in Amsterdam now?"

Wang smiled broadly. "Very little, Sergeant. Bit of a holiday. The negotiations with Philips were straightforward, no time was wasted, so now we waste it here, a few days of . . ."

"Museums," Mr. Tzu said.

"Museums, Sergeant," Wang nodded enthusiastically.

322 JANWILLEM VAN DE WETERING

De Gier got up. "I hope you're enjoying your stay in the city." He stumbled as he went to shake Mr. Tzu's hand. Mr. Tzu tried to move away but bumped heavily against a chair. Sudema steadied De Gier's sliding body.

"I'm sorry," De Gier said.

"My fault entirely," Tzu said, smiling.

GRIJPSTRA WAS WAITING AT the State Police station. De Gier bounded through the door. "That didn't take long did it? Did you see Dr. Haas?"

"I did," Grijpstra said. "Lieutenant Sudema? Sir?"

Sudema snapped to attention. "Yes, Adjutant, at your orders. I hope we didn't hold you up."

"Lieutenant," Grijpstra said heavily, "why didn't you tell me that Dr. Haas has an alibi?"

Sudema slid behind his desk and threw his cap at a hook attached to the wall. The cap missed the hook. "I didn't? I thought I had."

De Gier sat down. "A good alibi?"

"Pretty good, Sergeant." Grijpstra smiled sadly. "We may have wasted time and effort. What were your Chinese ninjas like?"

"They never threw any steel stars, I would think." De Gier stretched. "Boy, I'm surprised we weren't caught for speeding. A hundred miles an hour all the way up that wonderful straight dike. Wasn't that fun, Lieutenant?"

"Yes," Sudema said. "I rather agree with your sergeant, Grijpstra. Maybe Wang and Tzu are excellent actors but I would think they're what they say they are, businessmen trying to make a profit and, at present, have a little holiday in sexy Amsterdam."

"They're clumsy," De Gier said. "Definitely no sportsmen. Unco-ordinated movements and entirely unaware of their physical positions. They couldn't drop a brick on a rabbit in a trap."

"Could Dr. Haas do better?" Sudema asked.

Grijpstra arranged his hands on his stomach and slid a little further down in his chair. "Yes."

"You tested him?" De Gier asked.

"Dr. Haas," Grijpstra said ponderously, "is an agile athlete. A fly buzzed by him and he caught it with two fingers, without paying much attention. I threw him my lighter and he plucked it from the air. I bumped him on the staircase and I swear he was ready to do a somersault and drop to the landing below on his feet."

"But he didn't throw a *shuriken* at Mr. Dzung?" De Gier asked. "Isn't that hard to believe?"

"Wasn't Dzung killed at eleven-o-five A.M. last Friday morning?" Grijpstra asked.

"Yes," Sudema said brightly.

"At that time, Dr. Haas claims he was in his office and," Grijpstra said as he raised a menacing finger, "he produced two witnesses to prove that fact." His finger dropped to accuse Sudema. "You never told me that."

"The beeper stuff?" Sudema asked. "State Security believed it. Why shouldn't it?"

"So why didn't you tell me?"

"I forgot," Sudema said. "Adjutant, you're in the country now. We're all bumpkins here, vegetating in rustic retardation."

Grijpstra's hand became a fist that shook and trembled. "No, sir. You didn't believe that beeper stuff yourself and you're testing me now. Am I right? Confess."

Sudema bowed his head. "I believed the alibi at the time, but later I wondered, and when you came here to shine your dazzling light, I thought I might not mention the detail to see what you might make of it."

"What beeper stuff?" De Gier asked.

"Bah," Grijpstra said. "You know about beepers, Sergeant. A gadget you keep in your pocket and it beeps when you're wanted. So you run along and find out what you're wanted for. They use beepers at Dzung's computer factory. Some of the employees wander about and may be out of reach of a phone, so they get beeped and respond."

"At eleven A.M. last Friday, Dr. Haas beeped two of his wandering employees?" De Gier asked.

"And they both answered by phone," Grijpstra said. "They made use of inside phones connected to Dr. Haas's center of command. He spoke to them, gave them instructions, listened to their comments, commented on their comments—there were conversations. Both employees confirm that fact. Dr. Haas provided himself with a very nice alibi, all right."

"Can you crack it?" Sudema asked. "Dr. Haas was very confident when State Security questioned him as to his whereabouts at the time of Dzung's death. Too confident, maybe?"

"Now the lieutenant tells us," Grijpstra complained.

"You weren't here at the time," Sudema said.

"Grijpstra?" De Gier asked. "Can you crack that alibi or not? If you can't, we're going home. I've got to feed my cat sometime. She's waiting for me at my apartment right now."

Grijpstra took off his coat and waistcoat. He linked his fingers behind striped suspenders and began to pace the floor. Sudema stared.

"He's thinking," De Gier said. "Would you like to help? Are you wearing suspenders?"

"Are you?" Sudema asked.

"I'm not," De Gier said, "but maybe you can lend me a pair."

Sudema opened a wardrobe, took a pair of suspenders from his spare uniform, and passed it to De Gier. De Gier snapped them to his trousers. He nodded to the lieutenant. Lieutenant Sudema took off his uniform jacket and slid his hands behind the narrow strips that kept up his pants. "Like this? You are both crazy! Am I humoring you properly?"

"When conventional methods fail," De Gier said, "and time presses, we explore the beyond. You don't mind dancing a little now, do you?"

"Oh shit," Sudema said. "Do I have to?"

"*Think*," Grijpstra roared, interrupting his self-induced trance. "*Think, if you please.*"

"*Think*," shouted De Gier.

"Think," squeaked the lieutenant.

They walked in a circle, chanting "Think," Grijpstra sonorously, De Gier in a normal voice, and the lieutenant in a falsetto. The constable from the office next door came in to see if everything was all right. The contemplators ignored him. The constable withdrew, whistling his disbelief. He whistled rhythmically, in time with the chant.

Grijpstra skipped his feet at every fourth measure. De Gier did likewise. The lieutenant imitated his examples. The dance didn't take long. Grijpstra stopped at his chair and sat down. De Gier dropped down on the next chair. Sudema hopped behind his desk.

"That must have done it," Grijpstra said. "You first, Sergeant. Did anything occur?"

"Let's hear the lieutenant," De Gier said. "Our method is new to him and may have worked spectacularly on his unsuspecting brain. What thoughts popped up, sir?"

"I thought," Sudema said dreamily, "that Dr. Haas is a computer expert. He analyzes what goes on in normal communication, then apes it with his machines. All communication can be analyzed and classified."

"Foreseen?" Grijpstra asked. "Programmed into a phone at proper intervals?"

"But," De Gier said, "not when the communication is too complicated. The number of possible responses to a given question is fairly large, and one response to one question wouldn't even satisfy a numbskull of State Security. There would have to be several responses, and responses to the responses, and proper timing of them all."

"Ah," Sudema said. He patted the top of his desk. "Ah. Now I know what bothered me when Dr. Haas presented his alibi. Both workers who were willing to swear that they had communicated with him, proving thereby that Haas was in his office, were numbskulls."

"Are numbskulls employed by a factory turning out superchips for advanced computers?" De Gier asked.

Sudema waved a hand. "The two witnesses were of the fetch-and-carry variety. They open and close heavy boxes, put

326   JANWILLEM VAN DE WETERING

them on trucks, or take them off trucks, as the case may be; that sort of thing. They were usually busy outside the main building, running about between storage sheds; that's why they carried beepers."

"So," Grijpstra said, "Dr. Haas would give them simple commands. First he beeps them. They run to the nearest phone and dial the chief's number. He answers. 'Hello.' "

"Yes," De Gier said, "and the man says, 'Hi boss, it's me, Frank,' and Haas says, 'Hi Frank, would you carry box X from storage station Z,' and Frank says, 'There are no more boxes X, boss.' "

"Right," Sudema said, "and Haas says, 'Sure Frank, there's still a box X in shed A, in the rear.' "

Grijpstra rubbed his hands. "Yes. But Frank might be saying more than he is expected to say; the message becomes longer, and if Haas gives a pre-recorded answer, it cuts into what Frank has to say and Frank becomes bewildered."

Sudema rubbed his hands, too. "And Frank wasn't right? Frank testified to me and the State Security yoyos that he was conducting a normal conversation with Dr. Haas while that very same Dr. Haas, our athletic friend who kills flies on the wing between thumb and finger, was throwing a—what do you call it again?"

"*Shuriken*?" De Gier asked.

"Yep," Sudema nodded vigorously. "No matter, however. Dr. Haas holds PhDs in science. He must have used a device that wouldn't permit his pre-recorded messages, commands, orders, to get into the phone before the line was void of Frank's response."

Lieutenant Sudema sighed. "Pretty tricky."

De Gier shrugged. "Isn't Dr. Haas supposed to be a wizard? He's got a factory filled with tricky equipment. Surely it won't be too difficult for him to devise a gadget that wouldn't let the recorded messages out before Frank could finish phrasing his simple comments?"

Grijpstra rubbed out his soggy cigar butt. "Listen, Lieutenant, Frank and the other witness who holds up Dr. Haas's alibi are predictable men. Dr. Haas was their boss so they wouldn't gab too much at him. First he gives them an order, then they say that it can't be done. Haas knows that, beforehand. He has manipulated the situation. His device waited for Frank, or the other feller, to stop talking, and then released another pre-recorded message in Dr. Haas's voice. He tells them that they are mistaken and that they *can* obey his order if they do this or that. They say 'Yes, Sir,' and hang up. Thinking back, it may seem to them that they had quite a conversation."

De Gier checked his watch. "It's getting late. Minny says that Dr. Haas likes to work late, but he may, by now, be ready to leave his office. Are we doing something? If not, I'd rather go back. I've got to feed my cat."

"Would you," Grijpstra asked Sudema, "own one of those mini-cassette players that also records?"

Sudema jumped up, rushed across his office, yanked the door open and pointed accusingly at the constable reclining behind his desk. "Ha!"

The constable was listening to his cassette player, connected to his ears by tiny phones. "Give," Sudema barked, holding out his hand. "And find me a spare tape."

He ran back. "Here you are, Adjutant."

Grijpstra explained. Sudema applauded. "Clever," De Gier said, raising his eyebrows. "Amazing. You thought of that yourself?"

"Sit in the corner there," Grijpstra said, "and fill up that tape. You may not be equipped with a lot of furniture upstairs but you are a good actor."

De Gier spoke into the cassette recorder. Grijpstra put on his waistcoat and jacket. Sudema practiced fast draws with his pistol.

"Now," Grijpstra said. "That sounds fine. Return the lieutenant's suspenders and go talk to the constable. Make sure that he knows what to do."

Sudema's gun was stuck again in its holster. He yanked it free. "Pow!" He pointed it at a cupboard. He shook his head. "Can't we give this thing a little time? I could call in an arrest team."

"Nah," Grijpstra said.

"GENTLEMEN," DR. HAAS SAID. "I was just on my way out. You might not have caught me."

"You're using the right verb," Grijpstra said in a cold, menacing voice. "You're under arrest, sir. Anything you say from now on we'll most definitely use against you. Isn't that right, Lieutenant?"

"Absolutely," Sudema said. "You're ordered, Dr. Haas, to return to your office forthwith. I, a ranking officer of the State Police, accuse you of foully murdering your employer, Lee Dzung. A despicable deed for which you will be tried in due course."

"You're joking," Dr. Haas said bravely. He looked at De Gier.

De Gier arranged his face into an expression of stern contempt.

"Sergeant," Grijpstra said, "you can go outside and guard the building."

De Gier turned and left.

"Now," Sudema said, "let's not waste time. Back to your office, sir, where you can confess to your heinous crime."

Dr. Haas sat down in his office. The lieutenant and Grijpstra looked at him expectantly. "Are you crazy?" Dr. Haas said. "What are you trying to do? What is this charade? Me kill my good friend Lee? My beneficent employer?"

"Your alibi is not good," Sudema barked. "You never fooled us, I'll have you know. Anyone can turn rings around State Security, dear sir. Espionage? Foreign killers? Selling of contraband killing machines to the red devils lurking nearby? Ha!" Sudema laughed harshly for a while.

"You're dealing with the Police now," Grijpstra said. "The State Police. The lieutenant saw through your ruse from the start."

Dr. Haas smiled. "Really, Adjutant. I can prove to you that quite a lot of equipment left this factory with a dubious destination. I warned Lee many a time. I'm sorry he died, of course, but he had it coming. Believe me, the Taiwanese Secret Service doesn't play around. You underestimate our State Security, too. Once they know what was on, they wisely decided not to pursue the matter."

Grijpstra peeled a cigar. He looked up. "Bah. Really, Dr. Haas. I'm a police officer, too. Your true motivations can be spelled out easily enough. What were you after? Money? How to get it? Well now . . . ?"

Grijpstra sucked smoke. "Well now, my crafty doctor, you seduced poor Minny, arranged to divorce your wife, promised Minny you would marry her, planned to procure Dr. Dzung's millions that way."

"*What would I want with Minny?*" Dr. Haas shouted.

"Leaving out the pornography," Sudema said quietly, "we know exactly what you'd like to do to the hapless girl. A sex object framed in pure gold?"

Dr. Haas folded his arms. "I do have an alibi, Lieutenant. You've heard it before and the judge will hear it, too. I beg you, for your own sake, not to make an idiot of yourself."

The phone rang. Dr. Haas picked it up. "Who? Sergeant De Gier? Who's Sergeant De Gier?"

The voice on the phone said he was the tall man with the magnificent moustache whom Dr. Haas had just met.

"I see," Dr. Haas said. "What do you want? I'm busy."

The voice said that he wanted Dr. Haas to confess to killing Lee Dzung, a multimillionaire, so that he could marry Mrs. Dzung and collect the multimillions.

"You're out of your poor mind," snarled Dr. Haas.

The voice on the phone said that he was out of the phone, and that, in fact, he was coming into Dr. Haas's office.

De Gier walked into the room. "See?"

Dr. Haas looked at De Gier.

The voice on the phone said that it was surprising, was it not? How could Dr. Haas be speaking to Sergeant De Gier on the phone while Sergeant De Gier was standing right before him? Now wasn't that weird?

Dr. Haas slammed down the phone.

Silence filled the office.

"How did you do that?" Dr. Haas finally asked.

"You know how," Lieutenant Sudema said darkly. "Same way you fabricated your alibi. We don't have your advanced equipment so we used my constable to make the call and to activate the recorder at the appropriate moments. The device you have around will be tracked down by experts. Should be easy enough. Your proof will be destroyed."

Dr. Haas hid his face in his hands.

"Or you can show it to us now," Grijpstra said kindly. "It'll shorten your agony, poor man."

"You pathetic asshole," De Gier said kindly. "Minny doesn't love you anyway. You would have lost without our non-interference. What a risk to take." The sergeant spread his hands. "You really think she would go for you? She thinks you're boring. What a senseless rigmarole you set up. You merely did her a service that she planned you to perform. You really think Minny would hand you the loot?"

"Poor sucker," Sudema whispered.

"She abused you," Grijpstra said, nodding sadly.

Dr. Haas dropped his hands. "Minny loves me as much as I love her. I liberated that poor innocent girl. We'll be happy together forever after."

"Yes?" De Gier asked. "You were planning to see her tonight?"

Dr. Haas glared at the sergeant.

Grijpstra jumped up. "*At what time?*" Grijpstra roared. He sat down heavily again. "Not that it matters, as she won't be seeing you. Even at such short notice, with Mr. Dzung turning in his recently dug grave, she's soliciting another lover."

"Not you," Sudema said helpfully. "Oh, no!"

"Impossible!" Dr. Haas grabbed the phone. De Gier's hand grabbed the doctor's wrist. "Allow me, sir," De Gier said. "I'll make that call. What's her number?"

Dr. Haas mumbled the number. De Gier dialed. "Minny?" De Gier asked shyly. "It's me, Rinus De Gier. The sergeant you played ball with this afternoon. Remember?"

"Oh, Rinus," Minny moaned.

Grijpstra sneaked up to the phone. He pressed a button on its side. Minny's voice became audible to all parties concerned.

"Of course I remember," Minny said weakly.

"I was wondering," De Gier said. "I'm supposed to stay in Dingjum tonight. Not on what I came to see you about this afternoon, that's all over now. I was just wondering . . ."

"Oh, do come," Minny said. "That would be nice. I'm so lonely in this big house. Could you see me in an hour or so? I do want to receive you in style."

Grijpstra smiled gleefully at Sudema. Sudema winked back. Dr. Haas listened with round eyes.

"I'll be there," De Gier said. "Good-bye, dear Minny."

"Good-bye, Rinus," Minny said softly. "Thanks for calling."

De Gier replaced the phone.

Grijpstra rubbed his hands while looking at the doctor. "See? You got trapped in your own greed. She has no use for you now that Mr. Dzung's vast wealth is available to her. She'll have the time of her life with more attractive men."

"You may be smart, Doctor," Lieutenant Sudema said, "but your looks are regular, to say the least. You really thought that a beauty queen would fall for you?" Sudema laughed harshly.

The phone rang. Dr. Haas picked it up. Minny's voice once again penetrated to the far corners of the office. "Haas? Listen Haas, something has come up. I don't want to see you tonight. Okay?"

"But Minny," Haas said. "Please, we have an appointment; there's so much to discuss; our future . . ."

"What future?" Minny asked shrilly. "Perhaps you should never come to see me again. If you do, you might be in trouble."

"*Minny?*" Dr. Haas shrieked. The phone clicked dryly.

"Now, make your confession," Sudema said briskly. "Let's get this over with."

Dr. Haas looked at the blotter on his desk. His face became calm. His deeply recessed eyes behind the gold-rimmed spectacles began to sparkle.

A smile pushed up the corners of his thin lips.

"What's up?" Grijpstra asked.

"If you won't talk," Sudema said, "I have to remind you that you are under arrest. Please stand up, turn and face the wall with your hands above your head. Spread your legs, Dr. Haas. I have to frisk you now."

Dr. Haas smiled. "Just a minute, Lieutenant. Let's go through this again. What did I do?"

"You killed a man, Doctor," Sudema said.

"I exterminated a dangerous criminal," Dr. Haas corrected. "A flaw in our society who supplied the enemy with lethal machinery that will be used to do away with the free world. I also removed an alien sadist who beat up one of the most beautiful women with a whip split in seven thongs. I saved both democracy and a rare specimen of local female beauty. Is that a crime?"

"Sure," De Gier said. "Undemocratic, too. Did you ask for a vote?"

Dr. Haas kept smiling. "You're such a joker, Sergeant. Allow me to finish my plea. If you arrest me, nothing is gained and much will be lost. Maybe Minny will get the present available loot, and good luck to her, I say. Dzung's wealth will soon be replaced. I have, together with the wicked alien, developed an almost unimaginable improvement that will make intercontinental missiles all-seeing. Only I know how these inventions work. Let me go free and I will set up a fresh company that will control patents I can apply for alone. All three of you will be my partners. Your investment only involves your friendship and, in return, I'll hand over 10 percent of the shares. My millions will soon be made. I assure you, the profits of our new venture will be immense."

"And Minny?" Sudema asked.

"Who cares about Minny?" Dr. Haas asked.

"Have her." Dr. Haas presented Minny to De Gier on the palm of his hand. "You're so clever, Sergeant, maybe you can marry her, too. It would be nice if you can bring in some of our present equipment. It will save me some time."

"Won't Minny be a problem?" De Gier asked.

"How could she be, Sergeant? It was she who suggested I do away with Lee. As an accomplice, she'll have to stay mum."

"A bribe?" Sudema asked. Grijpstra kicked him gently. "Ah," Sudema said, "Well, maybe not."

"You wouldn't want to see Minny waste away in jail," De Gier said, "would you, Lieutenant?"

Sudema grinned helpfully. "Absolutely not, But only 10 percent for me and you get Minny, too . . ."

"Weren't you married?" De Gier asked. "Of course, you could ignore that illusionary bond—not too often, of course—and if you happened to share a growing experience with my wife, and if I was away that evening, spending a million here or there . . ."

The lieutenant's left eyelid trembled nervously. "You mean you wouldn't mind?"

"I spent my formative years in Amsterdam," De Gier said.

Dr. Haas looked up. "Let's be serious, gentlemen." He turned to De Gier. "And would you mind sitting down, Sergeant? You make me nervous. When I was in the Far East, I practiced some of the martial arts, and if there's one thing I learned it was the art of always being aware. Now, let's go through this again. I'm a scientist, too, and my mind is trained to make optimal use of any available situation." He smiled at his audience. "For mutual benefit, of course; it's the object of science to make this a better world. I could raise my offer to 15 percent to the lieutenant and adjutant and nothing extra for the sergeant provided he marries Minny. If not . . ." the doctor made an appeasing gesture, ". . . well, that's fine, too. The sergeant gets 15 percent, too. Money, and a lot of it, will flow in either case."

"You *are* a businessman," Grijpstra said. "We were misinformed."

"Interesting," Sudema said.

De Gier moved toward a chair. "I agree. Shall we call it a deal? The sooner I can free myself from my tedious present routine . . ." He looked at Dr. Haas. The doctor wasn't paying attention. De Gier turned and leaped. Grijpstra's gun pointed at Dr. Haas. Sudema was still trying to yank his pistol free.

Both Dr. Haas's hands fled under his jacket. "*Hey!*" shouted De Gier. His flat hands hit the doctor's wrists. One came back and flew out again, this time against the doctor's chin. The doctor tumbled out of his chair and De Gier fell on top of him. The sergeant's nimble hands quickly frisked the doctor's body. De Gier got up, holding several metal stars in each hand.

Dr. Haas was coming to. Sudema gave up trying to get to his pistol, rotted the suspect over, yanked his arms to the rear, and connected them with handcuffs.

THE CONSTABLE WAS WAITING at the State Police station. He waved his cassette recorder. "Did I do all right?"

"Splendid job," Sudema said. "Now you know why I allowed you to listen to Beethoven during office hours. I knew your gadget would come in handy one day. Lock up this suspect, Constable. Be careful, he's a dangerous gent."

"Well," De Gier said, "we'd better drive back while there's still light. We can watch the cormorants land on the lake at sunset. Didn't we have an instructive day? I thank you, Lieutenant, for showing us the way you work."

"What about my report?" Sudema asked.

"You don't need us for mere paperwork," Grijpstra said. "Suspect will provide you with a detailed confession. You made the arrest. There's circumstantial evidence; those star-shaped discs, for instance."

"We don't want to interfere," De Gier said. "Are you coming, Grijpstra?"

Sudema blocked the door. "We still have to catch Minny."

"She's all yours," De Gier said. "Bring her in, confront her with Dr. Haas. They'll yell at each other. Their mutual accusations will add up to evidence. That's all normal routine."

"But she's waiting for you, dolled up and all." Sudema patted the sergeant's shoulder. "You bring her in, Sergeant, after you've reaped your reward. Your chief and I will be at my house, having a late supper."

"I have to go," De Gier said. "I'm really not very good with women. My cat is female, too; she wipes the floor with me. I might release your suspect and interfere with your case."

"Don't want to interfere with your routine here, sir," Grijpstra said, pushing the lieutenant gently aside. "Thanks for the lunch. Your tomato salad was very tasty."

Charlie's Game

BRIAN GARFIELD

W HEN I TURNED THE corner I saw Leonard Ross going into Myerson's office ahead of me. By the time I reached the door I heard Ross say, "Where's Charlie?"

"Late. As usual. Shut the door."

Late. As usual. As far as I could remember—and I have phenomenal recall—there had been only one time when I had been late arriving in Myerson's office and that had been the result of a bomb scare that had grounded everything for three hours at Tempelhof. His acidulous remark had been a cheap shot. But then that was Myerson.

Ross was shutting the door in my face when I pushed in past him and kicked it closed. Ross said, "Hello, Mr. Dark."

Myerson only glanced up from the desk. Then he went on pretending to read something in a manila file folder. I said, "Welcome back, Charlie," in an effort to prompt him but he ignored it and I decided to play his silly game, so I dropped my raincoat across a chair and squeezed into one of the tubular steel armchairs and perused the photos on the wall, waiting him out.

The room was stale with Myerson's illegal Havana smoke; it was a room that obviously was unnerving to youngsters like Leonard Ross because among Myerson's varied and indeterminate functions was that of hatchet man. Any audience with him might turn out to be one's last: fall into disfavor with him and one could have a can tied to one's tail at any time, Civil Service or no Civil Service; and as junior staff, Ross had no illusions about his right to tenure. I had none myself: I was there solely at Myerson's sufferance, but that was something else—he could fire me at any time he chose to but he was never going to choose to because he needed me too much and he knew it.

His rudeness meant nothing; that was what passed for amiability with Myerson. I gave Ross a glance and switched it meaningfully toward a chair and finally Ross sat down, perched uneasily on the edge of it.

The view from Myerson's window isn't terribly impressive. An enormous parking lot and, beyond it, a hedgerow of half-wilted trees. Here and there you can see the tops of the high-rises around Langley.

Finally he closed the file and looked at me. "You're late."

"Would you care for a note from my mother explaining my tardiness?"

"Your sarcasms seldom amuse me."

"Then don't provoke them."

"You are," he said, "preposterously fat."

"And you are a master of the non sequitur."

"You disgust me, do you know that?" He turned to young Ross. "He disgusts me. Doesn't he disgust you?"

Ross made embarrassed gestures and I said, "Don't put the kid on the spot. What's on?"

Myerson wasn't in a particularly savage mood, obviously, because he gave up trying to goad me with no more prompting than that. He tapped the manila folder with a fingertip. "We've got a signal from Arbuckle."

"Where's Arbuckle?"

"East Africa. You really ought to try to keep up on the postings in your own department."

Ross explained to me, "Arbuckle's in Dar-es-Salaam."

"Thank you."

Ross's impatience burst its confines and he turned to Myerson: "What's the flap, then?"

Myerson made a face. "It distresses me, Ross, that you're the only drone in this department who doesn't realize that words like *flap* became obsolete sometime before you were born."

I said, "If you're through amusing yourself maybe you could answer the young man's question."

Myerson squinted at me; after a moment he decided not to be affronted. "As you may know, affairs in Tanzania remain sensitive. Especially since the Uganda affair. The balance is precarious—a sort of three-sided teetertotter: ourselves, the Soviets and the Chinese. It would require only a slight upheaval to tip the bal—"

"Can't you spare us the tiresome diplomatic summaries and get down to it?"

Myerson coolly opened the file, selected a photograph, and held it up on display. "Recognize the woman?"

To Ross I suppose it was only a badly focused black-and-white of a thin woman with attractive and vaguely Oriental features, age indeterminate. But I knew her well enough. "Marie Lapautre."

"Indeed."

Ross leaned forward for a closer look. I imagine it may have been the first time he'd ever seen a likeness of the dragon lady, whose reputation in our world was something like that of John Wesley Harding in the days of gunslingers.

"Arbuckle reports she's been seen in the lobby of the Kilimanjaro in Dar. Buying a picture post card," Myerson added drily.

I said, "Maybe she's on vacation. Spending some of the blood money on travel like any well-heeled tourist. She's never worked that part of the world, you know."

"Which is precisely why someone might hire her if there were a sensitive job to be done there."

"That's all we've got? Just the one sighting? No evidence of a caper in progress?"

"If we wait for evidence it could arrive in a pine box. I'd prefer not to have that sort of confirmation." He scowled toward Ross. "Fidel Castro, of course, has been trying to persuade Tanzania to join him in leading the Third World toward the Moscow sphere of influence, but up to now the Nyerere regime has maintained strict neutrality. We have every reason to wish that it continue to do so. We want the status to remain quo. That's both the official line and the under-the-counter reality."

Ross was perfectly aware of all that, I'm sure, but Myerson enjoys exposition. "The Chinese aren't as charitable as we are toward neutralists," Myerson went on, "particularly since the Russian meddlings in Angola and Ethiopia. The Chinese want to increase their influence in Africa—that's confirmed in recent signals from the Far East. Add to this background the presence of Marie Lapautre in Dar-es-Salaam and I believe we must face the likelihood of an explosive event. Possibly you can forecast the nature of it as well as I can?"

The last question was addressed to me, not Ross. I rose to meet it without much effort. "Assuming you're right, I'd buy a scenario in which Lapautre's been hired to assassinate one of the top Tanzanian officials. Not Nyerere—that would provoke chaos. But one of the others. Probably one who leans toward the Russian or Chinese line."

Ross said, "What?"

I told him, "They'd want to make the assassination look like an American plot."

Myerson said, "It wouldn't take any more than that to tilt the balance over toward the East."

"Deal and double deal," Ross said under his breath in disgust.

"It's the way the game is played," Myerson told him. "If you find it repugnant I'd suggest you look for another line of work." He turned to me: "I've booked you two on the afternoon flight by way of Zurich. The assignment is to prevent Lapautre from embarrassing us."

"All right." This was the sum of my response; I didn't ask any questions. I pried myself out of the chair and reached for my coat.

Ross said, "Wait a minute. Why not just warn the Tanzanians? Tell them what we suspect. Wouldn't that get us off the hook if anything did happen?"

"Hardly," Myerson said. "It would make things worse. Don't explain it to him, Charlie—let him reason it out for himself. It should be a useful exercise for him. On your way now—you've barely got time to make your plane."

BY THE TIME WE were belted into our seats Ross thought he had it worked out. "If we threw them a warning and then somebody got assassinated, it would look like we did it ourselves and tried to alibi it in advance. Is that what Myerson meant?"

"Go to the head of the class." I gave him the benediction of my saintly smile. Ross is a good kid: not stupid, merely inexperienced. He has sound instincts and good moral fibre, which is more than can be said for most of the Neanderthals in the Company. I explained, "Things are touchy in Tanzania. There's an excess of suspicion toward *auslanders*—they've been raided and occupied by Portuguese slave traders and German soldiers and British colonialists and you can't blame them for being xenophobes. You can't tell them things for their own good. Our only option is to neutralize the dragon lady without anyone knowing about it."

He gave me a sidewise look. "Can we pin down exactly what we mean by that word 'neutralize'?"

I said, "Have you ever killed a woman?"

"No. Nor a man, for that matter."

"Neither have I. And I intend to keep it that way."

"You never even carry a piece, do you, Charlie?"

"No. Any fool can shoot people."

"Then how can we do anything about it? We can't just ask her to go away. She's not the type that scares."

"Let's just see how things size up first." I tipped my head back against the paper antimacassar and closed my eyes and reviewed what I knew about Marie Lapautre—fact, rumor, and legend garnered from various briefings and shoptalk along the corridors in Langley.

She had never been known to botch an assignment.

French father, Vietnamese mother. Born 1934 on a plantation west of Saigon. Served as a sniper in the Viet Minh forces at Dienbienphu. Ran with the Cong in the late 1960s with assignments ranging from commando infiltration to assassinations of village leaders and then South Vietnamese officials. Seconded to Peking in 1969 for specialized terrorist instruction. Detached from the Viet Cong, inducted into the Chinese Army and assigned to the Seventh Bureau—a rare honor. Seconded as training cadre to the Japanese Red Army, a terrorist gang. It was rumored Lapautre had planned the tactics for the bombings at Tel Aviv Airport in 1975. During the past seven or eight years Lapautre's name had cropped up at least a dozen times in reports I'd seen dealing with unsolved assassinations in Laos, Syria, Turkey, Libya, West Germany, Lebanon, and elsewhere.

Marie Lapautre's weapon was the rifle. At least seven of the unsolved assassinations had been effected with long-range fire from Kashkalnikov sniper rifles—the model known to be Lapautre's choice.

She was forty-five years old, five feet four, one hundred and five pounds, black hair and eyes, mottled burn scar on back of right hand. Spoke five languages, including English. Ate red meat barely cooked when the choice was open. She lived between jobs in a seventeenth-century villa on the Italian Riviera—a home she had bought with funds reportedly acquired from hire-contract jobs as a freelance. Five of the seven suspected assassinations with Kashkalnikovs had been bounty jobs and the other two probably had been unpaid because she still held a commission in Peking's Seventh Bureau.

We had met, twice and very briefly; both times on neutral ground—once in Singapore, once in Teheran. In Singapore it had been a diplomatic reception; the British attaché had introduced us and stood by watching with amusement while we sized up each other like rival gladiators, but it had been nothing more than a few minutes of inconsequential pleasantries and then she had drifted off on the arm of a Malaysian black marketeer.

The files on her were slender and all we really knew was that she was a professional with a preference for the 7.62mm Kashkalnikov and a reputation for never missing a score. By implication I added one other thing: if Lapautre became aware of the fact that two Americans were moving in to prevent her from completing her present assignment she wouldn't hesitate to kill us—and naturally she would kill us with proficient dispatch.

THE FLIGHT WAS INTERMINABLE. I ate at least five meals. We had to change planes in Zurich and from there it was another nine hours. I noticed that Ross was having trouble keeping his eyes open by the time we checked into the New Africa Hotel.

It had been built by the Germans when Tanganyika had been one of the Kaiser's colonies and it had been rebuilt by Africans to encourage business travel; it was comfortable enough and I'd picked it mainly for the food, but it happened to be within easy walking distance of the Kilimanjaro, where Lapautre had been spotted. Also, unlike the luxurious Kilimanjaro, the New Africa had a middle-class businessman's matter of factness and one didn't need to waste time trying to look like a tourist.

The change in time zones seemed to bewilder Ross. He stumbled groggily when we went along to the shabby export office that housed the front organization for Arbuckle's soporific East Africa station.

A fresh breeze came off the harbor. I've always liked Dar; it's a beautiful port, ringed by palm-shaded beaches and colorful villas on the slopes. Some of the older buildings bespeak a dusty poverty, but the city is more modern and energetic than anything you'd expect to find near the equator on the shore of the Indian Ocean. There are jams of hooting traffic on the main boulevards. Businessmen in various shadings: Europeans, turbaned Arabs, madrassed Asians, black

Africans in tribal costumes. Now and then a four-by-four lorry growls by carrying a squad of soldiers, but the place hasn't got that air of police-state tension that makes the hairs crawl on the back of my neck in countries like Paraguay and East Germany. It occurred to me as we reached Arbuckle's office that we hadn't been accosted by a single beggar.

It was crowded in among cubbyhole curio shops selling African carvings and cloth. Arbuckle was a tall man, thin and bald and nervous; inescapably he was known in the Company as Fatty. He had one item to add to the information we'd arrived with: Lapautre was still in Dar.

"She's in room four-eleven at the Kilimanjaro but she takes most of her dinners in the dining room of the New Africa. They've got better beef."

"I know."

"Yeah, you would. Watch out you don't bump into her there. She must have seen your face in dossiers."

"We've met a couple of times. But I doubt she'd know Ross by sight."

Ross was grinding knuckles into his eye sockets. "Sometimes it pays to be unimportant."

"Hang onto that thought," I told him. When we left the office I added, "You'd better go back to the room and take the cure for that jet lag."

"What about you?"

"Chores and snooping. And dinner, of course. I'll see you at breakfast. Seven o'clock."

"You going to tell me what the program is?"

"I see no point discussing anything at all with you until you've had a night's sleep."

"Don't *you* ever sleep?"

"When I've got nothing better to do."

I watched him slouch away under the palms. Then I went about my business.

THE BREAKFAST LAYOUT WAS a nice array of fruits, juices, breads, cold cuts. I had heaped a plate full and begun to consume it when Ross came puffy-eyed down to the second-floor dining room and picked his way through the mangoes and sliced ham. He eats like a bird.

The room wasn't crowded; a sprinkling of businessmen and a few Americans in safari costumes that appeared to have been tailored in Hollywood. I said mildly to Ross when he sat down, "I picked this table at random," by which I meant that it probably wasn't bugged. I tasted the coffee and made a face; you'd think they could make it better—after all they grow the stuff there. I put the cup down. "All right. We've got to play her cagey and careful. If anything blows loose there won't be any cavalry to rescue us."

"Us?"

"Did you think you were here just to feed me straight lines, Ross?"

"Well, I kind of figured I was mainly here to hold your coat. On-the-job training, you know."

"It's a two-man job. Actually it's a six-man job but the two of us have got to carry it."

"Wonderful. Should I start practicing my quick draw?"

"If you'd stop asking droll questions we'd get along a little faster."

"All right. Proceed, my general."

"First the backgrounding. We're jumping to a number of conclusions based on flimsy evidence but it can't be helped." I enumerated them on my fingers. "We assume, one, that she's here on a job and not just to take pictures of elephants. Two, that it's a Seventh Bureau assignment. Three, that the job is to assassinate someone—after all, that's her principal occupation. Four, that the target may be a government leader here, but not Nyerere. We don't know the timetable so we have to assume, five, that it could happen at any moment. Therefore we must act quickly. Are you with me so far?"

"So far, sure."

"We assume, six, that the local Chinese station is unaware of her mission."

"Why should we assume that?"

"Because they're bugging her room."

Ross gawked at me.

I am well past normal retirement age and I'm afraid it is not beneath me to gloat at the weaknesses of the younger generations. I said, "I didn't waste the night sleeping."

He chewed a mouthful, swallowed, squinted at me. "All right. You went through the dragon lady's room, you found a bug. But what makes you think it's a Chinese bug?"

"I found not one bug but three. One was ours—up-to-date equipment and I checked it out with Arbuckle. Had to get him out of bed; he wasn't happy but he admitted it's our bug. The second was American-made but obsolescent. Presumably placed in the room by the Tanzanian secret service—we sold a batch of that model to them about ten years ago. The third mike was made in Sinkiang Province, one of those square little numbers they must have shown you in tech briefings. Satisfied?"

"Okay. No Soviet agent worth his vodka would stoop to using a bug of Chinese manufacture, so that leaves the Chinese. So the local Peking station is bugging her room and that means either they don't know why she's here or they don't trust her. Go on."

"They're bugging her because she's known to freelance. Naturally they're nervous. But you're mistaken about one thing. They definitely don't know why she's here. The Seventh Bureau never tells anyone anything. So the local station wants to find out who she's working for and who she's gunning for. The thing is, Ross, as far as the local Chinese are concerned she could easily be down here on a job for Warsaw or East Berlin or London or Washington or some Arab oil sheikh. They just don't know, do they?"

"Go on."

"Now the Tanzanians are bugging her as well and that means they know who she is. She's under surveillance. That means we have to act circumspectly. We can't make waves that might splash up against the presidential palace. When we leave here we leave everything exactly as we found it, all right? Now then. More assumptions. We assume, seven, that Lapautre isn't a hipshooter. If she were she wouldn't have lasted this long. She's careful, she cases the situation before she steps into it. We can use that caution of hers. And finally, we assume, eight, that she's not very well versed in surveillance technology." Then I added, "That's a crucial assumption, by the way."

"Why? How can we assume that?"

"She's never been an intelligence gatherer. Her experience is in violence. She's a basic sort of creature—a carnivore. I don't see her as a scientific whiz. She uses an old-fashioned sniper's rifle because she's comfortable with it—she's not an experimenter. She'd know the rudiments of electronic eavesdropping but when it comes to sophisticated devices I doubt she's got much interest. Apparently she either doesn't know her room is bugged or knows it but doesn't care. Either way it indicates the whole area is outside her field of interest. Likely there are types of equipment she doesn't even know about."

"Like for instance?"

"Parabolic reflectors. Long-range directionals."

"Those are hardly ultrasophisticated. They date back to World War II."

"But not in the Indochinese jungles. They wouldn't be a part of her experience."

"Does it matter?"

"I'm not briefing you just to listen to the sound of my dulcet baritone voice, Ross. The local Chinese station is equipped with parabolics and directionals."

"I see." He said it but he obviously didn't see. Not yet. It was getting a bit tedious leading him along by the nose but I liked him and it might have been worse: Myerson might have sent along one of the idiot computer whiz-kids who are perfectly willing to believe the earth is flat if an IBM machine says it is.

I said, "You're feeding your face and you look spry enough but are you awake? You've got to memorize your lines fast and play your part perfectly the first time out."

"What are you talking about?"

ACCORDING TO PLAN ROSS made the phone call at nine in the morning from a coin box in the cable office. He held the receiver out from his ear so I could eavesdrop. A clerk answered and Ross asked to be connected to extension four-eleven; it rang three times and was picked up. I remembered her voice right away: low and smoky. *"Oui?"*

"Two hundred thousand dollars, in gold, deposited to a Swiss account." That was the opening line because it was unlikely she'd hang up on us right away after that teaser. "Are you interested?"

"Who is this?"

"Clearly, Mademoiselle, one does not mention names on an open telephone line. I think we might arrange a meeting, however. It's an urgent matter."

Ross's palm was visibly damp against the receiver. I heard the woman's voice: "For whom are you speaking, *M'sieur?*"

"I represent certain principals." Because she wouldn't deal directly with anyone fool enough to act as his own front man. Ross said, "You've been waiting to hear from me, *N'est-ce-pas?*" That was for the benefit of those who were bugging her phone; he went on quickly before she could deny it: "At noon today I'll be on the beach just north of the fishing village at the head of the bay. I'll be wearing a white shirt, short sleeves; khaki trousers, and white plimsolls. I'll be alone and of course without weapons." I saw him swallow quickly.

The line seemed dead for a while but finally the woman spoke. "Perhaps."

Click.

"Perhaps," Ross repeated dismally, and cradled it.

DRIVING US NORTH IN the rent-a-car he said to me, "She didn't sound enthusiastic, did she. You think she'll come?"

"She'll come."

"What makes you think so?"

"Without phone calls like that she wouldn't be able to maintain her standard of living."

"But if she's in the middle of setting up a caper here—"

"It doesn't preclude her from discussing the next job. She'll come."

"Armed to the teeth, no doubt," Ross muttered.

"No. She's a pro. A pro never carries a gun when he's not on a job—a gun can get you into too much trouble if it's discovered. But she's probably capable of dismantling you by hand in a hundred different ways so try not to provoke her until we've sprung the trap."

"You can be incredibly comforting sometimes, you know that?"

"You're green, Ross, and you have a tendency to be flip and you'd better realize this isn't a matter for frivolous heroics. You're not without courage and it's silly to pretend otherwise. But don't treat this thing with childish bravado. There's a serious risk you may end up facedown in the surf if you don't treat the woman with all the caution in the world. Your job's simple and straightforward and there's nothing funny about it—just keep her interested and steer her to the right place. And for God's sake, remember your lines."

WE PARKED OFF THE road and walked through the palms toward the edge of the water. The beach was a narrow white strip of perfect sand curving away in a crescent. There was hardly any surf. At the far end of the curve I saw a scatter of thatched huts and a few dilapidated old piers to which were tethered a half dozen primitive outrigger fishing boats. It was pleasantly warm and the air was clear and dry: the East African coast has none of the muggy tropicality of the West one. Two small black children ran up and down the distant sand and their strident voices carried weakly to my ears. The half mile of beach between was empty of visible life. A tourist-poster scene, I thought, but clearly a feeling of menace was preoccupying Ross; I had to steady him with a hand on his shoulder.

Out on the open water, beyond a few small boats floating at anchor, a pair of junks drifted south with the mild wind in their square sails. A dazzling white sport-fisherman with a flying bridge rode the swells in a lazy figure-eight pattern about four hundred yards offshore; two men in floppy white hats sat in the stern chairs trolling lines. Beyond, on the horizon, a tramp prowled northward— a coaster: Tanga next, then Mombasa, so forth. And there was a faint spiral of smoke even farther out—probably the Zanzibar ferry.

I put my back to the view and spoke in a voice calculated to reach no farther than Ross's ears: "Spot them?"

Ross was searching the beach. "Not a soul. Maybe they didn't get the hint."

"The sport fisherman, Ross. They've got telescopes and long-range microphones focused on this beach right now and if I were facing them they'd hear every word I'm saying."

That was why we'd given it several hours' lead time after making the phone call. To give the Chinese time to get in position to monitor the meeting.

"They've taken the bait," I said. "It remains to be seen whether the dragon lady will prove equally gullible."

Ross was carrying the rifle and I crooked a finger and he gave it to me. We were still in the palms, too shadowed for the watchers on the fishing boat to get much of a look at us. I slid back into the deeper shadows and watched Ross begin to walk out along the beach, kicking sand with his toes. He had his hands in his pockets but then thought the better of that and took them out again and I applauded him for that—he was making it obvious his hands were empty.

I saw him look at his watch. It was eleven fifty-five. *Don't get too nervous, Ross.* He walked out to the middle of the crescent of sand and stood there looking back inland and I had some idea what he was going through: trying to ignore the fishing boat a quarter of a mile behind him, trying to talk himself out of the acute feeling that someone's telescopic crosshairs were centered between his shoulder blades.

I watched him begin to walk around in an aimless little circle —perhaps he felt they'd have a harder time hitting a moving target. He hadn't much to worry about, actually; they had no reason to take potshots at him—they'd be curious, not murderous—but perhaps Ross was no longer in a state of mind where logic was the ruling force. I trusted him to do his part, though. I knew a little about him. He'd come right into the Company after college, seeking adventure and challenge, and if he'd been worried by the stink of the Company's growing notoriety he'd balanced it with a naive notion that the Company needed people like him to keep it clean. Mainly what I knew about him was that Joe Cutter gave him very high marks and there's nobody in Langley whose judgment I'd sooner trust than Joe's. This caper should have been Joe's by rights—it was more in his line than mine, I'm more of a troubleshooter and rarely get picked for front-line counter-espionage capers because I'm too visible—but Joe hates Myerson even more than I do and he'd managed to get himself posted out to the Near East away from Myerson's influence.

I heard the putt-putt of an engine and watched a little outboard come in sight around the headland and beat its way forward, its bow gently slapping the water, coming at a good clip. Ross saw it too—looked at it, then looked away, back into the palm trees— probably wondering when the woman would show up. He hadn't yet realized she was already here. I saw him do a slow take and turn on his heel again. Then we both watched the outboard come straight in onto the beach.

It was the dragon lady and she was alone at the tiller. She tipped the engine up across the transom, jumped overside and came nimbly ashore, dragging the boat up onto the sand a bit. Then she turned to look at Ross across the intervening forty yards of sand. I had a good view of her in profile. Ross was trying to meet her stare without guile. Her eyes left him after a bit and began to explore the trees. I didn't stir; I was in among a cluster of palm boles and the thing she'd spot first would be movement.

She made a thorough job of it before she turned toward Ross. She walked with lithe graceful strides: petite but there was nothing fragile about her. She wore an *ao dai*, the simple formfitting dress of Indochina; it was painted to her skin and there was no possibility she could have concealed a weapon under it. Perhaps she wore it for that reason.

Ross didn't move. He let her come to him. It was in his instructions.

I was near enough to hear them because the offshore breeze carried their voices to me.

"Well then, *M'sieur*."

"The money," Ross began, and then he stopped, tongue-tied.

Christ. He'd forgotten his lines.

"*Oui?*"

He looked away from her. Perhaps it was the glimpse of the white sport boat out there that galvanized him. I heard him speak clearly and calmly. "The money's on deposit and we have the receipt and the numbered account book. If you do the job you'll be given both of them. Two hundred thousand American dollars in gold. That works out to something over half a million Swiss francs at the current rate."

She said, "I would need a bit more information than that."

"The name of the target, of course. The deadline date by which the assignment must be completed. More than that you don't need." Ross kept his face straight. I had a feeling he was feverishly rehearsing the rest of his lines.

She said, "You've left out one thing."

"I don't think so, Mlle. Lapautre."

"I must know who employs me."

"Not included in the price of your ticket, I'm afraid."

"Then we've wasted our morning, both of us."

"For two hundred thousand dollars we expected a higher class of discretion than you seem inclined to exercise." It was a line I had drilled into him and apparently he hadn't liked it—it went against his usual mode of expression—but I had insisted on the precise wording, and now she responded as I'd said she would: it was as if I'd written her dialogue as well as Ross's.

She said, "Discretion costs a little more, M'sieur, especially if it concerns those whom I might regard as my natural enemies. You *are* American."

"I am. That's not to say my principals are."

> *The thing is, Ross, you don't want to close the door, you want to keep her talking. String her along, whet her curiosity. She's going to insist on more information. Stall. Stretch it out. Don't give her the name of the target until she's in position.*

Casually Ross put his hands in his pockets and turned away from her. I watched him stroll very slowly toward me. He didn't look back to see if she was following him. He spoke in a normal tone so that she'd have trouble hearing him against the wind if she let him get too far ahead of her. "My principals are willing to discuss the matter more directly with you if you agree to take the job on. Not a face-to-face meeting, of course, but one of them may be willing to speak to you on a safe line. Coin telephones at both ends—you know the drill."

It was working. She was trailing along, moving as casually as he was. Ross threw his head back and stared at the sky. I saw what she couldn't see—Ross wetting his lips nervously. "The target isn't a difficult one. The security measures aren't too tough."

"But he's important, isn't he? Visible. Otherwise the price would not be so high."

It was something I hadn't forecast for him and I wasn't sure Ross would know how to handle it but he did the right thing: he made no reply at all. He just kept drifting toward the palms, off on a tangent from me now, moving in seemingly aimless half circles. After a moment he said, "Of course you weren't followed here." It was in the script.

"Why do you think I chose to come by open boat? No one followed me. Can you say the same?"

Position.

Ross turned and she moved alongside. She had, as I predicted, followed his lead: it was Indochinese courtesy, inbred and unconscious—the residue of a servile upbringing.

She stood beside him now a few feet to his right; like Ross she was facing the palm trees.

Ross dropped his voice and spoke without turning his head; there was no possibility the microphones on the boat would hear him. I barely caught his words myself, and I was only about thirty feet downwind of him. "Don't speak for a moment now, Mademoiselle. Look slightly to your right—the little cluster of palm trees."

She was instantly alert and suspicious; I saw her face come around and I stirred a bit and it was enough to make her spot me. Then I leveled the rifle, aiming down the sights.

In the same guarded low voice Ross said, "It's a Mannlicher bolt action with high-speed ammunition. Hollowpoint bullets and he's an expert marksman. You'd stand no chance at all if you tried to run for it." Ross kept stepping back because I'd told him not to let her get close enough to jump him and use him for a shield. Yet he had to stay within voice range because if he lifted his tone or turned his head the fine-focus directional mike on the sport fishing boat would pick up his words immediately.

I saw her shoulders drop half an inch and felt relief.

> *If she doesn't break for it in the first few seconds she won't break at all. She's a pro and a pro doesn't fight the drop.*

"You're in a box, Mlle. Lapautre. You've got one way to get out of it alive. Are you listening to me?"

"Certainly."

"Don't try to figure it out because there are parts of it you'll never know. We're playing out a charade, that's all you need to keep in mind. Play your part as required and you'll walk away alive."

"What do you want, then?"

It was evident that her cool aplomb amazed Ross, even though I'd told him to expect it.

I knew she couldn't have recognized me; most of me was behind one of the palms and all she really could see was a heavyset fellow with a rifle. Because of the angle I was hidden completely from the view of those on board the sport fishing boat. All they'd be able to tell was that Ross and Lapautre were having a conversation in tones too low for their equipment to record. They'd be frustrated and angry but they'd hang on hoping to pick up scraps of words that they could later edit together and make some sense out of.

Ross answered her, *sotto voce*: "I want you to obey my instructions now. In a moment I'm going to step around and face you. The man in the trees will kill you if you make any sudden move, so pay attention. . . . Now I'm going to start talking to you in a loud voice. The things I say may not make much sense to you. I don't care what you say by way of response—but say it quietly so that nobody hears your answers. And I want you to nod your head 'yes' now and then to make it look as if you're agreeing with whatever proposition I make to you. Understand?"

"No," she said. "I do not understand."

"But you'll do as I say, won't you."

"I seem to have little choice." She was looking right at me when she said that.

"That's good enough. Here we go."

Then Ross stepped off to the side and made a careful circle around her, keeping his distance, looking commendably casual. He started talking midway around: "Then we've got a deal. I'm glad you agreed to take it on."

He stopped when he was facing her from her port bow. The woman didn't speak; she only watched him. Ross enunciated clearly and I appreciated that; we both were mindful of the shotgun microphone focused on his lips from four hundred yards offshore.

"I'm glad," he said again. "You're the best in the business, I think everybody knows that."

Her lip curled ever so slightly: an expression exquisite in its subtle contempt. "And just what is it I'm supposed to have agreed to?"

Ross nodded vigorously. "Exactly. When you talk to my principals you'll recognize the Ukranian accents immediately but I hope that won't deter you from putting your best effort into it."

"This is absurd." But she kept her voice right down. I was aiming the thing straight at her heart.

"That's right," Ross said cheerfully. "There will be no official Soviet record of the transaction. If they're accused of anything naturally they'll deny it, so you can see that it's in your best interests to keep absolutely silent."

"This is pointless. Who can possibly benefit from this ridiculous performance?"

"I think they'll find that acceptable," Ross said. "Now then, about the target. He must be taken out within the next twelve days because that's the deadline for a particular international maneuver the details of which needn't concern you. The target is here in Dar-es-Salaam, so you'll have plenty of time to set up the assassination. Do you recognize the name Chiang Hsien?"

She laughed then. She actually laughed. "Incredible."

Ross managed to smile. "Yes. The chief of the Chinese station in Dar. Now there's just one more detail."

"Is that all? Thank goodness for that."

Ross nodded pleasantly. "Yes, that's right. You've got to make it look as if it's the work of Americans. I'd suggest you use an American rifle. I leave the other details in your hands, but the circumstantial evidence must point to an American plot against the Chinese people's representative. You understand?"

"Is that all then?"

"If you still want confirmation I'll arrange for a telephone contact between you and my principals. I think that covers everything, then. It's always pleasant doing business with a professional." With a courtly bow—he might have been Doug Fairbanks himself—Ross turned briskly on his heel and marched away toward the trees without looking back.

I watched the woman walk back to her open boat. The junks had disappeared past the point of land to the south; the outriggers were still tethered in the water by the village; the coastal steamer was plowing north, the Zanzibar ferry's smoke had disappeared—and the two whitehatted men in the stern of the sport fishing boat were packing up their rods and getting out of their swivel chairs. The dragon lady pushed her boat into the surf, climbed over the gunwale, made her way aft and hooked the outboard engine over the transom. She yanked the cord a few times. It sputtered and roared; and she went chugging out in a wide circle toward the open water, angling to starboard to clear the headland.

When she'd gone a couple hundred yards Ross came through the trees beside me and said, "What happens now?"

"Watch." I smiled at him. "You did a beautiful job, you know."

"Yeah, I know I did."

I liked him for that. I hate false modesty.

The sport fisherman was moving, its engines whining, planing the water: collision course. Near the headland it intercepted the little open outboard boat. The woman tried to turn away but the big white boat leaped ahead of her and skidded athwart her course.

"That skipper knows how to handle her," Ross commented without pleasure.

With no choice left, the woman allowed her boat to be drawn alongside by a long-armed man with a boathook. One of the men in the stern—one of the two with white hats—gave her a hand aboard. She didn't put up a struggle; she was a pro. I saw them push her toward the cabin—they went below, out of sight, and then the two boats disappeared around the headland, one towing the other.

Ross and I walked back to the car; I tossed the rifle into the back seat—we'd drop it off at Arbuckle's. It wasn't loaded. If she'd called our bluff I'd have let her run for it. (There's always another day.)

I said, "They'll milk her of course, but they won't believe a word of it. They've got the evidence on tape and they won't buy her denials. They wouldn't believe the truth in a thousand years and it's all she's got to offer."

Ross leaned against the car, both arms against the roof, head down between his arms. "You know what they'll do to her, don't you. After they squeeze her dry."

I said, "It'll happen a long way from here and nobody will ever know about it."

"And that makes it right?"

"No. It adds another load to whatever we've already got on our consciences. If it makes you feel a little better it's a form of justice— think of the people she's murdered. She may survive this, you know. She may come out of it alive. But if she does she'll never get another job in that line of work. Nobody'll trust her again."

"It hasn't solved a thing," he complained. He gave me a petulant little boy look. "They'll just send somebody to take her place, won't they? Next week or next month."

"Maybe they will. If they do we'll have to deal with it when it happens. You may as well get used to it, Ross—you play one game, you finish it, you add up the score and then you put the pieces back onto the board and start the next game. That's all there is to it—and that's the fun of it. As long as you stay lucky there's always another game."

Ross stared at me. "I guess there is," he said reluctantly.

We got in the car and Ross turned the key. I smiled briefly, trying to reassure him. The starter meshed and he put it in gear. He said with sudden savagery, "But it's not all that much fun for the losers, is it."

"That's why you should always play to win," I replied.

Ross fishtailed the car angrily out into the road.

Betrayed

JOHN D. MACDONALD

I T WAS AN INDIAN summer afternoon in mid-October—Sunday afternoon. Francie had gone back to the lab, five miles from the lakeside cabin, but Dr. Blair Cudahy, the Administrator, had shooed her out, saying that he was committing enough perjury on the civil service hours-of-work reports without having her work Sundays, too.

And so Francie Aintrell had climbed back into her ten-year-old sedan and come rattling over the potholed highway back to the small cabin. She sat on the miniature porch, her back against a wooden upright, fingers laced around one blue-jeaned knee.

Work, she had learned, was one of the anesthetics. Work and time. They all talked about the healing wonder of time. As though each second could be another tiny layer of insulation between you and Bob. And one day, when enough seconds and minutes and years had gone by, you could look in your mirror and see a face old enough to be the mother of Bob, and his face would remain young and unchanged in memory.

But she could look in the wavery mirror in the little camp and touch her cheeks with her finger tips, touch the face that he had loved, see the blue eyes he had loved; the black hair.

And then she would forget the classic shape of the little tragedy. West Point, post–World War II class. Second Lieutenant Robert Aintrell. One of the expendable ones. And expended, of course, near a reservoir no one had ever heard of before.

KIA. A lot of them from that class became KIA on the record.

When he had been sent to Korea, she had gone from the West Coast back to the Pentagon and applied for reinstatement. Clerk-stenographer. CAF 6. Assigned to the District Control Section of the Industrial Service Branch of the Office of the Chief of Ordinance.

And then they send you a wire and you open it, and the whole world makes a convulsive twist and lands in a new pattern. It can't happen to you—and to Bob. But it has.

So after the first hurt, so sharp and wild that it was like a kind of insanity, Francie applied for work outside Washington, because they had been together in Washington, and that made it a place to escape from.

Everyone had been sweet. And then there had been the investigation. Very detailed, and very thorough. "Yes, Mrs. Aintrell is a loyal citizen. Class A security risk."

Promotion to CAF 7. "Report to Dr. Cudahy, please. Vanders, New York. Yes, that's in the Adirondacks—near Lake Arthur. Sorry the only name we have for that organization is Unit 30."

And three miles from Vanders, five miles from the lake, she had found a new gravel road, a shining wire fence at the end of it, a guard post, a cinder-block building, a power cable marching over the hills on towers, ending at the laboratory.

She had reported to Blair Cudahy, a fat, little, mild-eyed man. She could not tell, but she thought that he approved of her. "Mrs. Aintrell, you have been approved by Security. There is no need, I'm sure, to tell you not to discuss what we are doing here."

"No, sir," she had replied. "I quite understand."

"We are concerned with electronics, with radar. This is a research organization. The terminology will give you difficulty at first. If we accomplish our mission here, Mrs. Aintrell, we will be able to design a nose fuse for interceptor rockets which will make any air attack on this continent—too expensive to contemplate."

At that, Cudahy hitched in his chair and turned so that he could glance over his shoulder at an enlarged photograph of an illustration Francie remembered seeing in a magazine. It showed the fat red bloom of the atom god towering over the Manhattan skyline.

Cudahy turned back and smiled. "That is the threat that goads us on. Now come and meet the staff."

Most of them were young. The names and faces were a blur. Francie didn't mind. She knew that she would straighten them out soon enough. Ten scientists and engineers. About fifteen technicians. And then the guards and housekeeping personnel.

The bachelor staff lived behind the wire. The married staff rented cabins in the vicinity. Dr. Blair Cudahy's administrative assistant was a tall, youngish man with deep-set quiet eyes, a relaxed manner, a hint of stubbornness in the set of the jaw. His name was Clinton Reese.

After they were introduced, Cudahy said, "I believe Clint has found a place for you."

"Next best thing to a cave, Mrs. Aintrell," Clint Reese had said. "But you have lovely neighbors. Mostly bears. You have a car?"

"No, I haven't," she said. His casual banter seemed oddly out of place when she looked beyond his shoulder and saw that picture on Cudahy's office wall,

"I'll take you to the local car mart and we'll get you one."

Cudahy said, "Thanks, Clint. Show her where she'll work and give her a run through on the duties, then take her out to that place you rented. We'll expect you at nine tomorrow morning, Mrs. Aintrell."

Clint took her to her desk. He said, "Those crazy people you met are scientists and engineers. They work in teams, attempting different avenues of approach to the same problem. Left to their own devices, they'd keep notes on the backs of match folders.

Because even scientists sometimes drop dead, we have to keep progress reports up to date in case somebody else has to take over. There are three teams. You'll take notes, transcribe them, and keep the program files. Tomorrow I'll explain the problems involved in the care of madmen. Ready to go?"

They stopped at Vanders and picked up her luggage from the combination general store and bus depot. Clint Reese loaded it into the back of his late model sedan. He chattered amiably all the way out to the road that bordered the north shore of Lake Arthur.

He pulled off into a small clearing just off the road and said, "We'll leave the stuff here, in case it turns out to be a little too primitive."

The trail leading down the wooded slope toward the lake shore was hard-packed. At the steepest point there was a rustic handrail. When Francie first saw the small cabin, and the deep blue of the lake beyond it, her heart seemed to turn over. Bob had talked of just such a place. A porch overlooking the lake. A small wooden dock. And the perfect stillness of the woods in mid-September.

The interior was small. One fair-sized room with a wide, built-in bunk. A gray stone fireplace. A tiny kitchen and bath.

Clint Reese said, in the manner of a guide, "You will note that this little nest has modern conveniences. Running water, latest model lanterns for lights. Refrigerator, stove heater, and hot-water heater all run on bottled gas. We never get more than eight feet of snow, so I'm told, and you'll have to have a car. The unscrupulous landlord wants sixty a month. Like?"

She turned to him smiling. "Like very much."

"Now I'll claw my way up your hill and bring down your bags. You check the utensils and supplies. I laid in some food, on the gamble that you'd like it here."

He came down with the bags, making a mock show of exhaustion. He explained the intricacies of the lanterns and the heaters, then said that he'd pick her up in the morning at eight-fifteen.

"You've been very kind," she said.

"Dogs and children go wild about me. See you tomorrow."

After he had disappeared around the bend of the trail, she stood frowning. He was her immediate superior, and he had acted totally unlike any previous superior in the Civil Service hierarchy. Usually they were most reserved, most cautious. He seemed entirely too blithe and carefree to be able to do an administrative job of the type this Unit 30 apparently demanded.

But she had to admit that he had been efficient about the cabin. And so, on a mid-September afternoon, she had unpacked. The first thing she took out of the large suitcase was Bob's picture. She could imagine him saying, "Baby, how do you *know* there aren't any bears in those woods? Fine life for a city gal."

"I'll get along, Bob," she told him. "I promise you, I'll get along."

And with his picture watching her, she unpacked and cooked, and ate, and went to bed in the deep bunk, surrounded by the pine smell, the leaf rustle, the lap of water against the small dock.

The work had been very hard at first, mostly because of the technical terms used in the reports, and also because of the backlog of data that had piled up since the illness of the previous girl. During the worst of it, Clint Reese found ways to make her smile. He helped her in her purchase of the ten-year-old car.

The names and faces straightened out quickly, with Clint's help. Gray chubby young Dr. Jonas McKay, with razor-sharp mind. Tom Blajoviak, with Slavic slanting merry eyes, heavy-handed joshing, big shoulders. Dr. Sherra, lost in a private fog of mental mathematics and conjecture.

Francie had pictured laboratories as being gleaming, spotless places full of stainless steel, sparking glass, white smocks. Unit 30 was a kind of orderly, chaotic jumble of dust and bits of wire and tubing and old technical journals stacked on the floor in wild disarray.

She soon caught the hang of their verbal shorthand, learned to put in the reports the complete terms to which they referred. McKay was orderly about summoning her. Tom Blajoviak found so much pleasure in dictating that he kept calling for her when he found nothing at all to report. Dr. Sherra had to be trapped before he would dictate to her. He considered progress reports to be a lot of nonsense.

With increasing knowledge of the personalities of the three team leaders came a new awareness of the strain under which they worked. The strain made them sometimes irritable, sometimes childish. Dr. Cudahy supervised and coordinated the technical aspects of the lines of research, treading very gently so as not to offend. And it was Clint's task to take the burden of all other routine matters off Cudahy's shoulders, so that he could function at maximum efficiency at the technical supervision at which he excelled.

It had been a very full month, with little time for relaxation. Francie sat on the porch of the cabin on the October Sunday afternoon, realizing how closely she had identified herself with the work of Unit 30 during the past month.

With the Adirondack tour season over, most of the private camps were empty. There were only a few fishermen about. She heard the shrill keening of the reel long before the boat, following the shoreline, came into view through the remaining lurid leaves of autumn.

A young girl, her hair pale and blond, rowed the boat very slowly. She wore a heavy cardigan and a wool skirt. A man stood in the boat, casting a black-and-white plug toward the shallows, and reeling it in with hopeful twitches of the rod tip. The sun was low, the lake still, the air sharp with the threat of coming winter. It made a very pretty picture. Francie wondered if they'd had any luck.

The boat moved slowly by, passing just ten feet or so from the end of the dock, not more than thirty feet from the small porch. The girl glanced up and smiled, and Francie instinctively waved. She remembered seeing them in Vanders in the store.

"Any luck?" Francie asked.

"One decent bass," the man said. He had a pleasant weather-burned face.

As he made the next cast Francie saw him slip. As the girl cried out he reached wildly at nothingness, and fell full length into the lake, inadvertently pushing the boat away from him. He came up quickly, looked toward the boat, then paddled toward the end of Francie's dock. Francie ran down just as he climbed up onto the dock.

"That must have been graceful to watch," the man said ruefully, his teeth chattering.

The girl bumped the end of the dock with the boat. "Are you all right, dear?" she asked nervously.

"Oh, I'm just dandy," the man said, flapping his arms. "Row me home quick."

The blond girl looked appealingly at Francie. "If it wouldn't be too much trouble. I could row home and bring dry clothes here and—"

"Of course!" Francie said. "I was going to suggest that."

"I don't want to put you out," the man said. "Darn fool stunt, falling in the lake."

"Come on in before you freeze solid," Francie said.

The girl rowed quickly down the lakeshore. The man followed Francie in. The fire was all laid. She touched a match to the exposed corner of paper, handed him a folded blanket from the foot of the bunk.

"That fireplace works fast," she said. "Get those clothes off and wrap yourself up in the blanket. I'll be on the porch. You holler when you're ready."

She sat on the porch and waited. When the man called she went in. She put three fingers of whiskey in the bottom of a water tumbler and handed it to him. "Drink your medicine."

"I ought to fall in the lake oftener! Hey, don't bother with those clothes!"

"I'll hang them out."

She put his shoes on the porch, hung the clothes on the line she had rigged from the porch corner to a small birch. Just as she finished she saw the girl coming back, rowing strongly. Francie went down and tied the bow line, and took the pile of clothes from her, so that she could get out of the boat more easily.

"How is he?" the girl asked in a worried tone.

"Warm on the inside and the outside, too."

"He wouldn't want me to tell you this. He likes to pretend it isn't so. But he isn't well. That's why I was so worried. You're being more than kind."

"When I fall out of a boat near your place I'll expect the same service."

"You'll get it," the girl said.

Francie saw that she was older than she had looked from a distance. There were fine lines near her eyes, a bit of gray in the blond temples. Late twenties, possibly.

The girl took the clothes, put out her free hand, "I'm Betty Jackson," she said. "And my husband's name is Stewart."

"I'm Francie Aintrell. I'm glad you—dropped in."

Francie waited on the porch again until Betty came out. "He's dressed now," Betty said. "If we could stay just a little longer—"

"Of course you can! Actually, I was sort of lonesome this afternoon."

They went in. Francie put another heavy piece of slabwood on the fire. Stewart Jackson said, "I think I've stopped shivering. We certainly thank you, Miss Aintrell."

"It's Mrs. Aintrell. Francie Aintrell."

She saw Betty glance toward Bob's picture. "Is that your husband. Francie?"

"Yes, he—he was killed in Korea." Never before had she been able to say it so flatly, so factually. "That's tough."

Stewart Jackson looked down at his empty glass. "That's tough. Sorry I—"

"You couldn't have known. And I'm used to telling people." She went on quickly, in an effort to cover the awkwardness. "Are you on vacation? I think I've seen you over in town. "

"No, we're not on vacation," Betty said. "Stewart sort of semiretired last year, and we bought a camp up here. It's—let me see—the seventh one down the shore from you. Stew has always been interested in fishing, and now we're making lures and trying to get a mail-order business started for them."

"I design 'em and test 'em and have a little firm down in Utica make up the wooden bodies of the plugs," Stewart said. "Then we put them together and put on the paint job. Are you working up here or vacationing?"

"I'm working for the Government," Francie said, "in the new weather station." That was the cover story which all employees were instructed to use—that Unit 30 was doing meteorological research.

"We've heard about that place, of course," Betty said. "Sounds rather dull to me. Do you like it?"

"It's a job," Francie said. "I was working in Washington and after I heard about my husband, I asked for a transfer to some other place."

Jackson yawned. "Now I'm so comfortable, I'm getting sleepy. We better go."

"No," Francie said meaning it. "Do stay. We're neighbors. How about hamburgers over the fire?"

She saw Betty and Stewart exchange glances. She liked them. There was something wholesome and comfortable about their relationship. And, because Stewart Jackson was obviously in his mid-forties, they did not give her the constant sense of loss that a younger couple might have caused.

"We'll stay if I can help," Betty said, "and if you'll return the visit. Soon."

"Signed and sealed," Francie said.

It was a pleasant evening. The Jacksons were relaxed, charming. Francie like the faint wryness of Stew's humor. And both of them were perceptive enough to keep the conversation far away from any subject that might be related to Bob.

Francie lent them a flashlight for the boat trip back to their camp. She heard the oars as Betty rowed away, heard the night voices calling, "Night, Francie! Good night!"

Monday she came back from work too late to make the promised call. She found the flashlight on the porch near the door, along with a note that said, "Anytime at all, Francie. And we mean it. *Betty and Stew.*"

Tuesday was another late night. On Wednesday, Clint Reese added up the hours she had worked and sent her home at three in the afternoon, saying, "Do you want us indicted by the Committee Investigating Abuses of Civil Service Secretaries?"

"I'm not abused."

"Out, now! Scat!"

At the cabin Francie Aintrell changed to jeans and a suede jacket and hiked down the trail by the empty camps to the one that the Jacksons had described. Stew was on the dock, casting with a spinning rod.

"Hi!" he said, grinning. "Thought the bears got you. Go on in. I'll be up soon as I find out why this little wooden monster won't wiggle like a fish."

Betty Jackson flushed with pleasure when she saw Francie. "It's nice of you to come. I'll show you the workshop before Stew does. He gets all wound up and takes hours."

The large glass-enclosed porch smelled of paint and glue. There were labels for the little glassine boxes, and rows of gay, shining lures.

"Here, it says in small print, is where we earn a living," Betty said. "But actually it's going pretty well." She held up a yellow lure with black spots. "This one," she said "is called—believe it or not— the Jackson Higgledy-Piggledy. A pickerel on every cast. It's our latest achievement. Manufacturing costs twelve cents apiece, if you don't count labor. Mail-order price, one dollar."

"It's pretty," Francie said dubiously.

"Don't admire it or Stew will put you to work addressing the new catalogues to our sucker list."

Stew came in and said, "I'll bet if the sun was out it would be over the yardarm."

"Is a martini all right with you, Francie?" Betty asked.

Francie nodded, smiling. The martinis were good. The dinner much later was even better. Stew made her an ex-officio director of the Jackson Lure Company, in charge of color schemes on bass plugs. Many times during dinner Francie felt a pang of guilt as she heard her own laughter ring out. Yet it was ridiculous to feel guilty. Bob would have wanted her to learn how to laugh all over again.

She left at eleven, and as she had brought no flashlight, Betty walked home with her, carrying a gasoline lantern. They sat on the edge of Francie's porch for a time, smoking and watching the moonlight on the lake.

"It's a pretty good life for us," Betty said. "Quiet. Stew's supposed to avoid strenuous exercise. And he's really taking this business seriously. Probably a good thing. Our money won't last forever. "

"I'm so glad you two people are going to be here all winter, Betty."

"And you don't know how glad I am to see you, Francie. I needed some girl-talk. Say, how about a picnic soon?"

"I adore picnics."

"There's a place on the east shore where the afternoon sun keeps the rocks warm. But we can't do it until Sunday. Stew wants to take a run down to New York to wind up some business things. I do the driving. Sunday, OK then?" Betty stood up.

It was agreed and Francie stood on the small porch and watched the harsh lantern light bob along the trail until it finally disappeared beyond the trees.

Sunday dawned brisk and clear. It would be pleasant enough in the sun. Francie went down the trail with her basket. When she got to the Jackson camp, Betty was loading the boat. She looked cute and young in khaki trousers, a fuzzy white sweater, a peaked ball-player's cap.

The girls took turns rowing against the wind as they went across the lake. Stewart trolled with a deep-running plug, without much success. He was grumbling about the lack of fish when they reached the far shore.

They unloaded the boat, carrying the food up to a small natural glade beyond the rocks. Stew settled down comfortably, finding a rock that fitted his back. Betty sat on another rock. Francie sprawled on her stomach on the grass, chin on the back of her hand.

Stew took a bit of soft pine out of his jacket pocket and a sharp-bladed knife. He began to carve carefully. He lifted the piece of pine up and squinted at it.

"Francie, if I'm clever enough, I can now carve myself something that a fish will snap at," he said. "A lure. A nice sparkly, dancy little thing that looks edible. "

"With hooks in it," Francie said.

He looked down at her benignly. "Precisely. With hooks in it. You stop to think of it, an organization isn't very different from a fish. Now, I'm eventually going to catch a fish on this, because it will have precisely the appeal that fish are looking for. Now, you take an organization. You can always find one person in it, if you look hard enough, that can be attracted. But then, it's always better to use real bait instead of an artificial lure."

"Sounds cold-blooded," Francie said sleepily.

"I suppose it is. Now, let's take for example, that supersecret organization you work for, Francie."

She stared at him. "What?"

"That so-called weather research outfit. Suppose we had to find bait to make somebody bite on a hook?"

Francie sat up and tried to smile. "You know, I don't like the way you're talking, Stew."

"You're among friends honey. Betty and I are very friendly people."

Francie, confused, turned and looked at Betty. Her face had lost its usual animation. There was nothing there but a catlike watchfulness.

"What is this anyway?" Francie said, laughing. But her laughter sounded false.

"We came over here," Stew said, "because this is a nice, quiet place to settle down and make a deal. Now don't be alarmed, Francie. A lot of time and effort has gone into making exactly the right sort of contact with you. Of course, if it hadn't been you, it would have been somebody else in Unit 30. So this is the stroke of midnight at the fancy-dress ball. Everybody takes off their masks."

Slowly the incredible meaning behind his words penetrated to Francie's mind. She looked at them. They had been friends—friends quickly made and yet dear to her. Now suddenly they had become strangers. Stew's bland, open face seemed to hold all the guileless-ness of the face of an evil child. And Betty's features had sharpened, had become almost feral.

"Is this some sort of a stupid test?" Francie demanded.

"I'll say it again. We are here to make a business deal. We give you something, you give us something. Everybody is satisfied," Stewart Jackson smiled at her.

Panic struck Francie Aintrell. She slipped as she scrambled to her feet. She ran as fast as she could toward the boat, heard the feet drumming behind her. As she bent to shove the boat off, Betty grabbed her, reached around her from behind, and with astonishing strength, twisted both of Francie's arms until her hands were pinned between her shoulder blades.

The pain doubled Francie over. "You're hurting me," she cried. There was an odd indignity in being hurt by another woman.

"Come on back," Betty said, her voice flat-calm.

Stew hadn't moved. He cut a long, paper-thin strip from the piece of pine. Betty shoved Francie toward him and released her.

"Sit down, honey," Stew said calmly. "No need to get all upset. You read the papers and magazines. I know that you're a well-informed, intelligent young woman. *Please* sit down. You make me nervous."

Francie sat on the grass, hugged her knees. She felt cold all the way through.

"I don't know what you expect me to do, But you might as well know that I'll never do it. You had better kill me or something, because just as fast as I can get to a phone I'm going to—"

"Please stop sounding like a suspense movie, Francie," Stewart said patiently. "We don't go around killing people. Just let me talk for a minute. Maybe you, as an intelligent young woman, have won-dered why so many apparently loyal and responsible people have committed acts of treason against their country. To understand that, you have to have an appreciation of the painstaking care with which all trusted people are surveyed.

"Sooner or later, Mrs. Aintrell, we usually find an avenue of approach to at least one person in each secret setup in which we interest ourselves. And, in the case of Unit 30, the Fates seem to have elected you to provide us with complete transcripts of all current progress reports dictated by Dr. Sherra, Dr. McKay, and Mr. Blajoviak."

Shock made Francie feel dull. She merely stared at him unbelievingly.

Stewart Jackson smiled blandly. "I assure you our cover is perfect. And I believe you have helped us along by casually mentioning your nice neighbors, the Jacksons."

"Yes, but—"

"We thought at first my boating accident might be too obvious, but then we remembered that there is nothing in your background to spoil your naiveté."

"You're very clever and I've been very stupid. But I assure you that nothing you can say to me will make any difference."

"Being hasty, isn't she?" Stewart said.

With the warm, friendly manner of a man bestowing gifts, he reached into the inside pocket of his heavy tweed jacket and took out an envelope. He took a sheet of paper from the envelope, unfolded it, and handed it to her. It was the coarse, pulpy kind of paper.

In the top right-hand corner were Chinese ideographs, crudely printed. In the top left hand corner was a symbol of the hammer and sickle. But it was the scrawled pencil writing that tore her heart in two as she read.

> Baby, they say YOU will get this. Maybe it's like their other promises. Anyway I hope you do get it. This is a crumb-bum outfit. I keep telling them I'm sick, but nobody seems to be interested. The holes healed pretty good, but now they don't look so hot. Anything you can do to get me out of this, baby, do it. I can't last too long here, for sure. I love you, baby, and I keep thinking of us in front of a fireplace—it gets cold here—and old Satchmo on the turntable and you in the green housecoat, and Willy on the mantel.

FRANCIE READ IT AGAIN and instinctively held it to her lips, her eyes so misted that Stewart and the rock he leaned against were merged in a gray-brown blur.

Bob was alive! There could be no doubt of it. No one else would know about the green housecoat, about Bob's delight in the zipper that went from throat to ankles. And they had all been wrong. All of them! Happiness made her feel dizzy, ill.

Stewart Jackson's voice came from remote distances: " . . . find it pretty interesting, at that. That piece of paper crossed Siberia and Russia and came to Washington by air in a diplomatic pouch—one that we don't have to identify. When we reported your assignment to Unit 30, our Central Intelligence ordered an immediate check of all captive officer personnel. In that first retreat after the Chinese came into it, they picked up quite a lot of wounded American personnel.

"It was quite a break to find your husband reported as killed in action instead of captured. If he'd been captured they'd never have transferred you to Unit 30, you know. So they told Lieutenant Ain-trell the circumstances and he wrote that letter you're holding. It got to you just as fast as it could be managed."

"He says he's sick!" Francie exclaimed indignantly. "Why isn't he being taken care of?"

"Not many doctors and not much medicine on the Chinese mainland, Francie. They use what they have for their own troops."

"They've got to help him!"

Betty came over, put her arm around Francie's shoulders, "I guess, Francie, dear, that is going to be up to you."

Francie twisted away from her. "What do you mean?"

"It's out of our hands," Stew Jackson said. "You can think of us as just messengers from the boys who make the decisions. They say that when, as an evidence of your good faith, they start to receive copies of Unit 30 progress reports, they will see to it that your husband is made more comfortable. I understand that his wounds are not serious. You will get more letters from him, and he'll tell you in those letters that things are better. When your services are no longer needed they will make arrangements to have him turned over to some impartial agency—maybe to a Swedish hospital ship.

"He'll come home to you, and that will be your reward for services rendered. Now if you don't want to play ball, I'm supposed to pass the word along, and they'll see that he gets transferred from the military prison to a labor camp, where he may last a month or a year. Now, you better take time to think it all over."

"How can you stand yourselves or each other?" Francie asked. "How can two people like you get mixed up in such a filthy business?"

Stewart Jackson flushed. "You can skip that holier-than-thou attitude, Mrs. Aintrell. You believe in one thing. We believe in something else. Betty and I just happen to believe there's going to be a good spot for us when this capitalistic dictatorship goes bankrupt and collapses of its own weight."

Jackson leaned forward with a charming smile. "Come on, Francie. Cheer up. And you should know that, as an individual, you certainly are not going to affect the course of world affairs by the decisions you make. As a woman, you want your husband and your happiness. The odds are that Unit 30 research will get nowhere anyway. So what harm can you do? And the people I work with are never afraid to show gratitude. Certainly your Bob won't thank you for selling him out, selling him into a labor camp."

"There's more than one way to sell Bob out."

"Sentimentality masquerading as patriotism, I'm afraid. Think it over. How about the food, Betty? Join us, Francie?"

Francie didn't answer. She stood up and walked down the shore of the lake. She sat huddled on a natural step in the rocks. There seemed to be no warmth in the sun. She looked at the letter. In two places, the pencil had torn the cheap, coarse paper. His hand had held the pencil. She remembered the marriage vows. To honor and cherish. A sacred promise, made in front of man and God.

She felt as though she were being torn in half, slowly, surely. And she could not forget that he was in danger and frighteningly alone.

She walked slowly back to Stewart and Betty. "Is that promise any good?" she asked, in a voice which was not her own. "Would he really be returned to me?"

"Once a promise is made, Francie, it is kept. I can guarantee that.

"Like they've kept treaties?" Francie asked bitterly.

"The myth of national honor is part of the folklore of decadent capitalism, Francie," Betty said. "Don't be politically immature. This is a promise to an individual and on a different basis entirely."

Francie looked down at them. "Tell me what you want me to do?" she asked.

"We have your pledge of cooperation?" Stewart Jackson asked.

"I—yes. " Her mouth held a bitter dryness.

"Before we go into details, my dear Francie, I want you to understand that we appreciate the risk you are taking. If you ever get the urge to be a little tin heroine—at your husband's expense, of course—please understand that we shall take steps to protect ourselves. We would certainly make it quite impossible for you to testify against us."

Betty said quickly, "Francie wouldn't do that, Stew." She laughed shallowly.

"Now, Francie," Stewart said softly, "I will tell you what you will do."

When they rowed away from her dock they waved a cheerful good-bye to her. Francie went in and closed the door carefully behind her, knowing that doors and bolts and locks had become useless. Then she lay numbly on the bunk and pressed her forehead against the rough pine boards. Until at last the tears came. She cried herself out, and when she awakened from deep sleep the night was dark, the cabin cruelly cold.

She awakened to a changed world. The adjustment to Bob's death had been a precarious structure, moving in each emotional breeze. Now it collapsed utterly. She was again the bride, the Francie Aintrell of the day before the telegram arrived. And as she moved about, she began, in the back of her mind, to stage the scene and learn the lines for the moment of his return, for the moment when his arms would be around her again.

She pumped up the lantern and carried it over to the table. She set it down and stood very still looking at the object. There, on the table, was one of the plugs manufactured by the Jacksons. It was a gay red lure, with two gang hooks, with yellow bead eyes.

The doors were still locked. She tried to tell herself it was purposeless melodrama, the sort of thing a small boy might do. She turned down slightly the harsh white light of the lantern and slowly walked into her bedroom.

Early next morning she parked her car behind the lab and walked in and sat at her desk. The smiling guards at the gate had a new look.

Clint Reese came out and gave her an impersonal good morning and spun the dial on the locked file for her. She took the current Sherra folder from the drawer back to her desk, found her place, continued the transcription of notes that had been interrupted on Saturday.

They would want a full report, she told herself. Not just the final three or four pages. No one watched her closely. It would be easy to make one additional carbon. She planned how she would do it. Fold the additional carbons and stick them in the blue facial-tissue box. Then take the box with her to the lavatory. There she could fold them smaller and tuck them into her bra. But she would do it with the next report. Not this one, because it was only a portion of a report.

Sherra's report took twice as long as it should have. She made continual errors. Twice Clint Reese stopped by to pick up the completed report for checking by Cudahy and each time she told him it would be ready soon. When she took it to him at last she imagined that he gave her an odd look before he went on into Cudahy's office, the report in his hand.

Big Tom Blajoviak's note was on her spindle: *Come and get it, sweetheart.*

She took her book and went toward the cubicle in the corner where there was barely room for Blajoviak and a desk.

The door was ajar a few inches. He glanced up at her and said, "Enter the place of the common people, Francie. Just because I'm not a doctor, it's no reason to—"

"Have you really got something this time, Tom? Or is it more repetition?"

"Child, your skepticism is on the uncomplimentary side. Open thy book and aim your little pointed ears in this direction. Hark to the Blajoviak."

"Honestly?"

His square strong face altered. The bantering look was gone. "At five o'clock yesterday, Francie, we began to get a little warm. Here we go." He held his copy of the last report in front of him. "This would be new main subject, Francie. I make it *Roman numeral nine*. Isolation of margin error in Berkhoff Effect. Sub A. Following the series of tests described in *Roman eight* above, one additional memory tube was added to circuit C. The rerunning of the tests was begun on October twenty-third—"

He dictated rapidly. Francie's pencil darted along the notebook lines with the automatic ease of long practice. It took nearly an hour for the dictation.

"So that's it," he said, leaning back, smiling with a certain pride.

"Not that it means anything to me, you know," she said.

"It just might, Francie. It just might mean that instead of getting fried into the asphalt, you might look out to sea and say, 'Ah' at the big white lights out there. Fireworks for the kiddies instead of a dis-integration."

She glanced down at her whitened knuckles. "Is it that impor-tant, Tom?"

"Are you kidding?"

She shook her head. "No, I just don't understand—all this."

"There was a longbow, and some citizen comes up with body armor. And then the crossbow, and so they made heavier armor. And then gunpowder, which eventually put guys into tanks. Every time, it sounded like an ultimate weapon, and each time a defense just happened to come along in time. Now our ultimate weapon is the thermonuclear missile. Everybody is naked when that baby comes whining down out of the stratosphere. So we have to stop it up there where it won't do any harm."

He paused an instant, then went on earnestly. "We can't depend on the slow reaction time of a man. We've got to have a gizmo. And now, for the first time, I think we're getting close to the ultimate interceptor. If you-know-who could find out how close we are, I'll bet they'd risk everything to try to knock us out before we could get into production on the defensive end. Cudahy wants this one fast as you can get it out, honey."

She stood up. "All right, Tom. As soon as I can get it out."

Francie went to work. She watched her hands add the extra onion-skin sheet to the copies required by office routine. At five o'clock Cudahy came out of his office to check the progress. He seemed to be concealing jubilation with great difficulty. He patted her shoulder.

"Take a food break at six, Mrs. Aintrell," he said, "and then get back to it. I'll be here, so you won't have to lock anything up."

"Yes, sir," she said in a thin voice.

Cudahy had not noticed the extra copy. But she could not risk leaving the extra copy in sight while she went to the mess hall. At five of six she took the tissue box, containing the folded sheets into the lavatory. She tucked the sheets into her bra, molding the papers into an inconspicuous curve.

She looked at her face in the mirror, ran the finger tips of both hands down her cheeks. Bob had told her she would be lovely when she was seventy.

She looked into the barren depths of her own eyes and she could hear the voice of Tom Blajoviak: "Fireworks for the kiddies instead of disintegration. Knock us out before we could—"

Francie Aintrell squared her shoulders and walked out of the lavatory. She took her red shortcoat from the coat tree.

Clint Reese sat on the corner of a desk, one long leg swinging. He said, "Remind me to put all my black-haired women in red coats."

She found that she was glad to see him. His lighthearted manner made the lab work seem a little less important, made her own impending betrayal a more minor affair. And she sensed that during the past month Clint had grown more aware of her. A subtle game of awareness and flirtation would make her forget what she was about to do—or almost forget.

She said, "If you want to see a woman eat like a wolf, come on and join me."

He put on his wool jacket. "I'll take care of all the wolflike characteristics around here, lady."

They walked to the small mess hall. Wind whined around the corner of the building and they leaned into it.

"And after the dogs are gone, we can always boil up the harness," he said.

She heard the false note in her own laughter. They shut the mess-hall door against the wind, hung up their jackets. They filled their trays, carried them back from the service counter to a table for two by the wall. Clint Reese sat down and shut his eyes for a moment. She saw a weariness in his face that she had not noticed before.

Reese smiled at her. "Now make like a wolf," he said.

She had thought she was hungry, but found that she couldn't eat.

"OK, Francie," he said. "Let's have it.

She gave him a startled look. For once there was no banter in his voice, no humor in his eyes.

"What do you mean?" she asked him.

"As official nursemaid to all personnel, I keep my eyes open. Something has been worrying you all day."

"Then make some jokes, and cheer me up, why don't you?"

He was grave. "Sometimes I get tired of jokes. Don't you?"

"Aren't you a little out of character, Mr. Reese? I thought you were the meringue on the local pie."

He looked through her and beyond her. "Perhaps I am. Tonight, my girl, I am lonesome and in a hair-taking-down mood. Want to see my tresses fall?"

"Sure," she said.

He took a sip of his coffee, set his cup down. "Underneath this tattered shirt beats the heart of a missionary."

"No!"

"And perhaps a fool. I own a tidy little construction business. I was making myself useful, and discovering that I had a certain junior-executive-type flair for the commercial world, when the Army put its sticky finger in the back of my collar and yanked me off to the wars. I was flexing my obstacle-course muscles on Okinawa when they dropped those big boomers on the Nipponese.

"Now get the picture. There I was as intrigued by those big boomers as a kid at the country club on the night of the fourth. *Siss boom, ah!* A big child at heart. Still thinking I was living in a nice, cozy little world. I was in one of the first units to go to Japan. I wangled a pass and went to Hiroshima. It was unpretty. Very."

In the depths of his eyes she saw the ghosts that he had seen.

"Francie, you can't tell another person how it is to grow up in one day. I wandered around in a big daze, and at the end of the day I had made up my mind that this was a desperate world to live in, a frightening world. And it took me another month to decide that the only way I could live with myself was to try to do something about it.

"When they gave me a discharge I turned the management of the company over to my brother and went to school to learn something about nuclear physics. I learned that if I studied hard I'd know something about it by the time I was seventy-three, so I quit. What resource did I have? Just that little flair for administration, the knack of getting along with people and keeping them happy and getting work done.

"So I decided to be a dog-robber for the professional boys who really know what the score is. By being here I make Cudahy more effective. Cudahy in turn makes the teams more effective.

"And now, I understand, we're beginning to get someplace. Maybe because I'm here we get our solution a month sooner than otherwise. But if it were only twenty minutes sooner, I could say that I have made a contribution to something I believe in."

Francie felt a stinging in her eyes. She looked away from him, said huskily, "I'm just a little stupid I guess. You seemed so—casual, sort of."

He grinned. "With everybody going around grinding their teeth, you've got to have some relief. If I landed in a spot full of clowns I'd turn into the grimmest martinet you ever saw. Any administrative guy in a lab setup is a catalyst. So let's get back to the original question, now that you've made me prove my right to ask it. What's bothering you Francie?"

She stood up so abruptly that her chair tilted and nearly fell over. She went through the door with her coat in her hand, put it on outside, walked into the night with long strides.

There was a small clump of pines within the compound. She headed blindly toward them. He caught her arm just as she reached them. He turned her around gently.

"Look. I didn't want to say the wrong thing. If this is just one of those days when you—remember too much, please forgive me, Francie. I'd never do anything to hurt you."

She held onto his wrist with both hands. "Clint, I'm so—terribly mixed up I don't know what to do."

"Let me help you if I can."

"Clint, what is the most important thing in the world to any individual? It's their own happiness isn't it? Tell me it is?"

"Of course it is, but you don't need a definition of terms. Isn't happiness sort of a compound?"

"How do you mean?"

"Don't too many people confuse happiness with self-gratification? You can be happy if you have self-respect and also what an old-fashioned uncle of mine used to call the love of God."

She was crying soundlessly. "Honor, maybe?"

"That's a word, too. Little dog-eared through misuse, but still respectable.

"Suppose, Clint, that somebody saved your life and the only way they could do it was by violating all the things you believe in. Would you be grateful?"

"If someone saved me that way I think I'd begin to hate them, and hate myself too, Francie. But don't think I'm a typical case. I'm a little top-heavy in the ethics department, they tell me."

"I married that sort of man, Clint. I understand."

"You still haven't told me how I can help you."

She turned half away from him, knowing that unless she did it quickly, she would be unable to do it at all. She unbuttoned the red coat, the jacket under it, the blouse under that. She found the folded packet of onionskin sheets and held it out where he could see it.

"You can help me by taking that, Clint. Before I change my mind."

He took it. "What is it?" he asked.

"A copy of what Tom dictated today," she said tonelessly.

"Why on earth are you carrying it around?" he demanded sharply.

"To give it to someone on the outside."

After a long silence he said, "Holy jumping Nellie!" His tone was husky.

"I was doing it to save Bob's life," she said.

"Your husband? But he's dead!"

"I found out yesterday that he's alive, Clint. Alive and in prison." She laughed, dangerously close to hysteria. "Not that it makes any difference. Now he *will* die."

He shook her hard but she could not stop laughing. He slapped her sharply, and she was able to stop. He walked her across the compound, unlocked a door, thrust her inside, turned on a light. The small room contained a chair, table, double bed, and bookshelf.

"Please wait here," he said gently. "I'll be back in a few minutes with Dr. Cudahy. Handkerchiefs in that top drawer."

Cudahy and Clint Reese were with her for over an hour. Clint sat beside her on the bed, holding her hand, urging her on with the story when she stumbled. Cudahy paced endlessly back and forth, white lipped, grim. When he interrupted her now and then to ask a question his voice was harsh.

At last they knew all there was to know. Cudahy stopped in front of her. "And you, Mrs. Aintrell, were planning to give them the—"

"Please shut up, Doctor," Clint said tiredly.

Cudahy glared at him. "I'll require some explanation for that comment, Mr. Reese."

Clint lit two cigarettes and gave Francie one, while Cudahy waited for the explanation. Clint said, "I don't see how a tongue-lashing is going to help anything, Doctor. Forget your own motivations for a moment and think of hers. As far as this girl knows, she has just killed her husband—just as surely as if she had a gun to his head. I doubt, Dr. Cudahy, whether either you or I, under the same circumstances, would have that same quality of moral courage. I respect her for it. I respect her far too much to listen to you rant at her."

Cudahy let out a long breath. He turned a chair around and sat down. He gave Clint a sheepish glance and then said, "I'm sorry, Mrs. Aintrell. I got carried away with a sense of my own importance."

Francie said, tonelessly, "Bob told me once that they put him in a brown suit and made him expendable. I married him knowing that. And I guess my life can be as expendable as his. He said we had to be tough. I know they made him write that. He isn't the kind of man who begs. I almost—did what they wanted me to do. It isn't courage, I guess. I'm just—all mixed up."

"Francie," Clint said, "Dr. Cudahy and I are amateurs in the spy department. This is a job for the experts. But I'm in on this, and I'm going to stay in. I'm going to make it certain that the experts don't foul up your chances of getting your husband back. We're going to make the Jacksons believe that you are cooperating. The experts can't get here until tomorrow. Do you think you can handle it all right when they contact you tonight?"

He looked at her steadily.

"I—I think so. I can tell them that I didn't do any transcriptions today."

"Don't give them any reason to be suspicious."

"I'll try not to."

Clint Reese walked her to her car, stood with the door open after she had slid under the wheel. "Want me to come along?" he asked.

"I'm all right now."

"The best of luck, Francie."

He shut the door. The guard opened the gates. She drove down the gravel road toward Lake Arthur.

Betty Jackson, in ski pants and white cashmere sweater, was sitting on the bunk reading a magazine. The fire was burning. Her jacket was on a nearby chair.

Betty tossed the magazine aside and smiled up at her. "Hope you don't mind, hon. I nearly froze on the porch and I only had to make a tiny hole in the screen, just where the catch is."

Francie took off her coat, held her hands toward the flames. "It's all right."

"Got a little present for us, dear?"

"I couldn't manage it today. I took a lot of dictation and then I was put to work filing routine correspondence."

Betty leaned back, her blond head against the pine wall, fingers laced across her stomach. "Stew was pretty anxious. This might alarm him a little, hon. He might worry about whether you're cooperating or double-crossing. You know, he told me last night that lots of war widows got so depressed they killed themselves. I'm not threatening you. That's just the way his mind works sometimes."

"I dropped J. Edgar Hoover a personal note," Francie said bitterly. "It's so much simpler than getting a divorce."

"You don't have to be nasty, you know. This isn't personal with us, dear. We take orders just as you do."

"Tell your husband, if he is your husband, that I'll have something tomorrow."

After the woman left, Francie stood and bit at the inside of her lip until she tasted blood. "Forgive me, Bob," she said silently. "Forgive me."

It had been done. Now nothing could save him.

She found the lure on the shelf over the sink, at eye level. The body carved to resemble a frog. After she stopped trembling she forced herself to pick it up and throw it on the fire.

The men arrived in mid-afternoon the very next day. Three of them. A slow-moving, dry-skinned sandy one with a farmer's cross-hatched neck. He was called Luke Osborne and he was in charge. The names of the other two were not given. They were dark, well-scrubbed young men in gleaming white shirts, dark-toned suits. Cudahy and Clint Reese were present for the conference.

Osborne looked to be half asleep as Francie told her story. He spoke only to bring out a more detailed description of the Jacksons.

"New blood," he said, "or some of the reserves. Go on."

She finished, produced the letter. Luke Osborne fingered it, and held it up to the light before reading it. He handed it to the nearest young man, who read it slowly and passed it on to the other young man.

Osborne said, "You're convinced your husband wrote that?"

"Of course!" Francie said wonderingly. "I know his writing. I know the way he says things. And then there are those references— the housecoat, Willy."

"Who is Willy?"

"We bought him in Kansas. He's in storage now. A little porcelain figure of an elf. We had him on the mantel. Bob used to say he was our good—"

Suddenly she couldn't go on. Osborne waited patiently until she had regained control.

"—our good luck charm," she said, her voice calm.

"It stinks," Osborne said.

They all looked at him.

"What do you mean?" Reese demanded.

"Oh, this girl is all right. I don't mean that. I mean, the whole thing implies an extent of organization that I personally don't believe they have. I just don't believe that in a little over thirty days they could fix it so Mrs. Aintrell, here, is balanced on the razor's edge. Three months, maybe. Not one."

"But Bob wrote that letter!" Francie said.

"And believing that he wrote it, you opened up for Reese here?" Osborne asked.

"I almost didn't," Francie told him.

"But you did. That's the point. You won't get any medals. There are a lot of people not getting any medals these days." Osborne's smile was an inverted U.

"What are your plans?" Dr. Cudahy demanded.

The office was very still. At last Luke Osborne looked over at Francie. "I'm going to go on the assumption that your husband is alive, Mrs. Aintrell, and that he wrote this letter. At least, until we can prove differently.

"Dr. Cudahy, have you got a file on some line of research that proved to be valueless? A nice, fat file?"

Cudahy frowned. "Things are so interrelated here that even data on unsuccessful experimentation might give us a line on the other stuff."

"Pardon me, sir," Clint Reese said. "How about that work Sherra was doing? And you couldn't make him stop. Wasn't that—"

Cudahy thumped his palm with a chubby fist. "That should do it! I had to have progress files made to keep him happy. That work bore no relation to our other avenues of approach, Mr. Osborne."

"And if Mrs. Aintrell gives them Sherra's work, a bit at a time, as though it were brand-new stuff, it won't help them, eh?" He thought an instant, then asked: "But will it make them suspicious?"

"Only," said Cudahy, "if they know as much about what is going on here as I do."

"Reese, you turn that file over to Mrs. Aintrell. Mrs. Aintrell copy enough each day to turn over to Jackson, so he won't get suspicious. Better make six copies or so and give him the last one. Fold it up as though you smuggled it out of here. Can do?"

"Yes," Francie said quickly.

"That should keep your husband alive, if he is alive. We have channels of communication into the likely areas where he'd be. It will take nearly two months to get any kind of a check on him, even if we started yesterday. The better way is to check through the Jacksons." Luke Osborne was regarding her steadily.

"What do you mean by that?" Francie demanded. "You can't go to him and—"

Osborne held up his hand and gave a rare smile. "Settle down, Mrs. Aintrell. Even if your husband weren't involved, we'd hardly go plunging through the shrubbery waving our credentials. They use their expendables on this sort of contact work, just the same as we do. We want the jokers who are buried three or four layers of communication back. I want Jackson to be given the dope, because I am anxious to see what he does with it, and who gets it."

"But—"

"Just trust us, Mrs. Aintrell."

Francie forced a smile. There was something about Luke Osborne that inspired trust. Yet she had no real confidence that he could match his cleverness with the Jacksons. Both Stewart and Betty seemed so supremely confident.

"I'll need your letters from your husband, Mrs. Aintrell. Every one of them. "

Francie flushed. The overseas letters, since they had been subject to censorship, were written in a doubletalk understandable only to the two of them. But the letters he had sent her that had been mailed inside the country had been full of bold passages that had been meant for her eyes alone.

"Do you have to have them?"

"Please, Mrs. Aintrell. We will have them for a very short time. Just long enough to make photostats for study. When this case is over our photostats will be burned."

"But I can't imagine why—"

He smiled again. "Just call it a hunch. You have them at your cabin, I judge."

"Yes I do."

Clint Reese followed her home in his car at five-thirty that evening. They walked down the trail together. A fine, misty rain was failing and the rustic guard rail felt sodden under her hand.

Francie unlocked the door and went in. She looked on the porch and turned to Clint. "Nobody here," she said, relief in her voice.

She took the candy box full of letters out of the bureau drawer and handed it to him. "You'll be back at nine?"

"Thereabout," he said. He slipped the box into his jacket pocket. Then he put both hands on her shoulders. "Take care," he whispered.

"I will," she said. She knew he wanted to kiss her, and also knew that he would not, that his sense of rightness would not permit him. He touched his lips lightly to her forehead, turned, and left.

She turned on the gas under the hot water heater, and when the water was ready she took a shower. While she was under the water she heard someone call her.

"In a minute," she called back. She dressed in tailored wool slacks, a plaid shirt cut like a man's. She walked out unsmiling. Betty sat on the bunk, one heel up, hands laced around her knee.

Francie said, "I brought something this time."

Betty smiled. "We knew you would. Stew is on his way over now.

Francie sat down across the room from her. "Did you get Stewart into this sort of thing, or did he get you in?"

"Clinical curiosity? We met while I was in college. We found out that we thought about things the same way. He had contacts and introduced me. After they started to trust me I kept needling Stew until he demanded a chance to do something active. They told us to stay under cover. No meetings. No cells. We did a little during the war, and a little bit last year in Canada. Satisfied?"

Stewart came in the door, shivering. "Going to be a long winter," he said.

"Here's what you want," Francie said, taking the folded sheets from the pocket of her slacks.

"Thank you, my dear," Stew said blandly. He sat down on the bunk beside Betty and they both read through the sheets skimming them.

"Dr. Sherra's work, eh?" Stewart said. "Good man, Sherra. I think he was contacted once upon a time. Got stuffy about it though, and refused to play. He could have lived in Russia like a little tin king."

Jackson refolded the sheets, put them carefully in his wallet. "Did you have any trouble getting these out, Francie?"

"Not a bit."

"Good! " Stewart said. He still held the billfold in his hand. He dipped into it, took out some money, walked over, and dropped it into her lap.

Francie looked uncomprehendingly at the three twenty-dollar bills. "I'm not doing this for money."

He shrugged. "Keep it. It isn't important. Buy something pretty with it."

Francie fingered the bills. She folded them once, put them in the top left pocket of her plaid shirt.

"That's better," Stewart said. "Everybody gets paid for services rendered. Canada and London, Tennessee and Texas."

Francie remembered her instructions from Osborne. She leaned forward. "Please let them know right away that I'm cooperating. Bob's letter said he was sick. I want to know that he's being cared for."

Osborne had said to cry if she could. She found that it was no effort.

Stewart patted her shoulder. "Now don't fret, Francie. I was so certain of your cooperation that I already sent word that you're playing ball with us in every way that you can. I'd say that by the end of this week, no later, Bob ought to be getting all the attention he can use."

"Thank you," she said, meaning it completely. "Thank you so much."

Betty stood up, stretched like a plump kitten. "We'll see you tomorrow night, huh? Come on, Stew."

"I'll have more for you."

Francie stood up, too. She made herself stand quite still as Jackson patted her shoulder again. There was something about being touched by him that made her stomach turn over.

She stood at the side window and watched their flashlights bob down the trail through the trees. She made herself a light meal. Clint Reese arrived a little after nine. She took the box from him and put it back in the bureau drawer.

Clint gave an exaggerated sigh. "Osborne's orders. We got to go to the movies together. That gives me an excuse for coming down here, if they happen to be watching you. Ready to follow orders?"

She shivered. "I—I know they're watching me. I can feel it," she whispered. "I do want to be out of here for a little while."

As they went out the door she stumbled on the wet boards. He caught her arm, held it tightly. They stood quite still for a few moments. It was a strange moment of tension between them, and she knew that he was as conscious of it as she was. The strain of the past few days, strain they had shared, had heightened an awareness of each other.

"Francie!" he said, his voice deeper than usual.

Shame was a rising red tide. Certainly her loyalty to Bob was sinking to a new low. To take the step that must lead to his death, and then take a silly pleasure in a strong male hand clasping her arm.

She pulled away, almost too violently, and said with false gaiety, "But I buy my own ticket, Mister."

"Sure," he said with no lift in his voice.

When they were in the car Clint said, "I'm always grabbing hold of females. Sort of a reflex. Hope you don't mind."

The car lights cut a bright tunnel through the wet night. "I didn't mind that. It was the sultry tone of voice that got me."

"Look. Slap me down when I get out of line. After the movies, to change the subject, we meet Osborne."

"It frightens me, having those people around. Suppose the Jacksons catch on."

"To everybody except you and me and Cudahy, they're new personnel on the project. And they're careful."

The movie was a dull musical. The crowd was very slim and no one sat within twenty feet of them.

I can't help it, Francie," he said suddenly blurting it out like a small boy. "I—"

"Clint, please listen to me. You told me once that you would never do anything to hurt me. This whole thing has torn me completely in half. I don't know who I am or where I am. I'm attracted to you, Clint, and I don't like that. I must ignore it, get over it. I have no other choice."

For a long time he did not answer. When he spoke again, the familiar light note had come back into his voice: "If you will permit me, madame, I shall finish my statement. Quote: I can't help it, Francie. I've got to have some popcorn. End quote."

She touched his arm. "Much better."

"What's better than popcorn?"

The movie ended and they filed out with the others. As they walked toward the car a match flared startingly close, and the flame-light touched the high, hard cheekbones of the face of Stewart Jackson. Betty was a shadow beside him. Francie caught hard at Clint's arm, stumbling a little, her breathing suddenly shallow.

"Evening, Francie," Stewart said, a mild, sly triumph in his tone.

"Hello, Stewart. Hello, Betty," she forced herself to say, proud that her voice did not shake, knowing that the presence of Clint Reese had given her strength.

Once they were in the car and had turned out of the small parking lot, she said, "Oh, Clint they were—"

"They just went to a movie. That's all. And found a chance to rattle you."

Clint turned off the main road onto a narrower one and turned off lights and motor and waited for a time. No car followed them. He drove slowly up the hill and parked in a graveled space near some picnic tables. He gave Francie a cigarette, and she rolled her window down a few inches to let the smoke out.

When Osborne spoke, directly outside her window, he startled both of them: "Let me in before I freeze, kids."

She opened the door and slid over close to Clint. Osborne piled in and shut the door. "Let's have it, Mrs. Aintrell."

"They seemed pleased. Mr. Jackson told me that he'd already sent word to have Bob looked after, knowing in advance that I'd cooperate. And he gave me sixty dollars. He made me take it. Here it is."

"Keep it all together. He'll give you more. They love to pay off. They take some poor, idealistic fool who wants to help the Commies because he was nuts about *Das Kapital* when he was a college sophomore. When the fool finds out what kind of dictatorship he's dealing with and wants out, they sweetly remind him that he had accepted the money and he thereby established his own motive, and it is going to make him look very bad in court. So bad he'd better keep right on helping. By the way, thanks for the loan of the letters. The boys are tabulating them tonight."

"What do I—?"

"Just keep doing what you're doing. Feed them dope from the Sherra file."

"Oh, I forgot. Jackson mentioned that Sherra was contacted once. Is that important?"

"We know about it. Sherra reported it."

"Can I have that last letter back? The one from the prison camp?"

"You'll find it in the box with the others. I'll get a report from the handwriting experts soon."

"That's a waste of time. I know Bob wrote it. It sounds like him."

"Take her home, Clint, before she convinces me," Osborne said, getting out of the car. "Night, people." The blackness of the night swallowed him at once.

On Wednesday and Thursday Francie turned more copies of the Sherra file over to the Jacksons, receiving each time, an additional twenty-dollar bill, given her with utmost casualness and good cheer by Stewart Jackson. On Friday afternoon Francie was called into Dr. Cudahy's office by Clint. Cudahy was not there. Just Luke Osborne. He looked weary.

As Clint paused uncertainly in the doorway, Osborne said, "Sit in on this, Reese."

Clint pulled the door shut and sat down. Osborne was in Cudahy's chair.

"What have you found out?" Francie demanded.

"How long can you keep playing this little game of ours, Mrs. Aintrell?"

"Forever, if it will help Bob."

Osborne picked up a report sheet and looked at it, his expression remote. "There's this report of the handwriting. They say it could be his handwriting, or it could be a clever forgery. There are certain changes, but they might be the result of fatigue or illness."

"I told you he wrote it."

Osborne studied her in silence. He looked more than ever like a prosperous Midwestern farmer worried about the Chicago grain market.

"Now can you take it on the chin?"

Francie looked down at her licked hands. "I—I guess so."

He picked up another sheet. "Tabulation report. It has a cross reference of the words in previous letters. We have numbered all his letters chronologically. Letter Four uses the term 'crumb-bum.' In Letter Sixteen there is a sentence as follows: 'Put old Satchmo on the turntable, baby, and when he sings "Blueberry Hill," make like I'm with you in front of a fireplace. Letter Eighteen has a reference to Willy in it. And Letter Three mentions—uh—the green housecoat."

Osborne colored a bit, and Francie flushed violently as she remembered the passage to which he referred.

"What are you trying to tell me?" she asked, in a low voice.

"There are no new words or phrases or references in that letter Stewart Jackson gave you. They can all be isolated in previous letters. We can assume that Jackson had access to those letters during the first few weeks you worked here."

"I don't see how that means anything," Francie said. "Of course, Bob would write as he always writes, and talk about the same things in letters that he always talked about. Wouldn't that be so?"

"Could be. But please let us consider it sufficient grounds—that and the handwriting report—to at least question the authenticity of the letter Jackson gave you. Remember, the handwriting report said that it could be a forgery."

Francie jumped up. "Why are you saying all this to me? I go though every day thinking every minute that if you slip up, just a little, Bob is going to die, and die in a horrible way. I'm doing the very best I can to keep him alive. If you keep trying to prove to me that he's been dead all the time, it takes away my reasons to go through all this—and I just can't see it like—"

She covered her eyes and sat down, not trying to fight against the harsh sobs.

Osborne said, "I'm telling you this, Mrs. Aintrell, because I want you to do something that may end all this, before you crack up under the strain. I never like to have anybody follow orders without knowing the reason behind the orders."

Francie uncovered her eyes, but she could not answer.

Osborne leaned forward and pointed a pencil at her. "I want you to reestablish friendly relations with these Jacksons. Talk about your husband, talk about him all the time. Bore them to death with talk about your husband. Memorize the three items on this little slip of paper and give the slip back to me. I want those three items dropped into the conversation every chance you get."

Francie reached out and took the slip. There were three short statements on the paper: "Willy wears a green hat." . . . "Bob broke the Goodman recording of the 'Russian Lullaby' accidentally." . . . "You met in Boston."

It gave Francie a twisty, Alice-in-Wonderland feeling to read the nonsense phrases. She read them again and then stared wildly at Osborne, half-expecting that it would be some monstrous joke. "Are you quite crazy?" she asked.

"Not exactly. And not all those words appear in the letters. We know you are clever, Mrs. Aintrell. We want you to tell the complete truth to the Jacksons, except for those three statements on that slip of paper. We assume they have a photostat of those letters, too. Nothing in the letters contradicts those three statements. You are not to repeat them so often that the Jacksons will become suspicious. Just often enough to implant them firmly in memory. Then we shall wait for one of those false statements to reappear, either directly or by inference, in the next letter you get from your husband."

"And if they do, it will mean that—"

"That the army's report of your husband's death was correct. And that the Jacksons have been working one of the nastiest little deals I have ever heard of. Very clever, very brutal, and, except for your courage, Mrs. Aintrell, very effective."

With forced calmness Francie said, "You make it sound logical, and it might be easier for me if I could believe it. But I know Bob is alive."

"I merely ask you to keep in mind the possibility that he may not be alive. Otherwise, should that second letter prove to be faked, you may break down in front of them."

"She won't break down," Clint said.

Francie gave him a quick smile. "Thank you."

"Just be patient," Osborne said. "Keep turning data over to them. Skip a day now and then to make it look better. We're trying to find their communication channel. When we find it we'll want you to demand the next letter from your husband. Maybe we can have you risk threatening to cut off the flow of data unless you get a letter. But get friendly with them now, and work in that information."

That night Francie walked down the shore path to the Jackson camp. She saw Stewart through the window in the living room. He let her in. Betty sat at the other end of the room, knitting.

"A little eager to deliver, this time, aren't you?" Stewart asked. He shut the door behind her and she gave him the folded packet. He glanced at it casually.

"Is something on your mind, Francie?"

"May I sit down?"

"Please do," Betty said.

Francie sat down, sensing their wariness at this deviation from routine. "This is something I have to talk to you about," she said. "I—I know I'd never have the nerve to consciously try to report you. But I am afraid of giving Dr. Cudahy or Mr. Reese a clue involuntarily."

"What do you mean?" Stewart demanded, leaning forward.

"It's just this: I think about Bob all the time. I think about how he is going to come home to me. It is the sort of thing a woman has to talk about, and there is no one to talk to. Sooner or later I may slip and mention Bob to either Dr. Cudahy or Mr. Reese. On my record it says that Bob is dead. They both know that. You see, I just don't like this chance I have to take every day, of my tongue slipping."

"You haven't made a slip, have you?" Stewart asked.

"No. But today I—I almost—"

Betty came to her quickly, sat on the arm of the chair. "Stew, she's right. I know how it would be. Hon, could you talk to us, get it off your chest?"

"It might help, but—"

"But you don't particularly care for our company," Stewart said.

"It isn't that exactly. I don't like what you stand for. I hate it. But you are the only people I *can* talk to about Bob."

"And perhaps get into the habit of talking about him? So that you'd be more likely to make a slip?" Stewart asked.

"Oh no! Just to have *someone* listen."

Stewart stood up. "I want to impress on your mind just what a slip might mean, Francie. Not only would it mean you'd never see Bob again, but you wouldn't be around long enough to—"

"Leave her alone!" Betty said hotly. "A woman can understand this better than you, Stew. We'll be substitute friends for a while, Francie. You go ahead and talk your head off. Stew, it will be safer this way."

Stewart shrugged. Francie said, uncertainly, "I may bore you."

"You won't bore me," Betty said.

"I'm bursting with talk. Saving it up. I've been wondering what to do when he gets back. He'll be weak and sick, I suppose. I won't want to be here. I'll try to get a transfer back to Washington. I could rent a little apartment and get our things out of storage. I keep thinking of how I'm going to surprise him. Little ways, you know. He used to love our recording of 'Russian Lullaby.' The Benny Goodman one. And then he stepped on it. I could buy another one and have it all ready to play.

"And after I got the—the telegram, when I packed our things I was sort of shaky. I dropped Willy and chipped his green hat. I saved the piece, though, and I can have it glued on. You know, I can't even remember if I ever told him about saving the flowers. I pressed them—the ones I just happened to be wearing the day we first met in Boston. White flowers on a dark-blue dress. I can get some flowers just like them. When he comes into the apartment, I'll have the record of 'Russian Lullaby' playing and Willy with his green hat fixed on the mantel and a blue dress and those flowers. Do you think he'd like that, Betty?"

"I'm sure he will, Francie."

"He isn't the sort of man who notices little things. I mean, I could get something new for the apartment and I'd always have to point it out to him. He used to—"

She seemed to be two people. One girl was talking on and on, talking in a soft, monotonous, lonely voice, and the other girl, the objective one, stood behind her, listening carefully. But the ice had been broken. Now she could talk about Bob and they would understand just why she had to. The words came in a soft torrent, unbroken.

After that, the days went by, and the constant strain was something she lived with, slept with, woke up with. The Sherra file was exhausted, and after careful consideration of the three team leaders, Cudahy brought Tom Blajoviak into the picture. Tom was enormously shocked at learning what was transpiring, and he was able to go into his personal files to find the basis for a new report on work that would in no way prejudice the current operations.

Stewart Jackson, although disappointed at the way the Sherra reports had reached negative conclusions, was pleased to begin to receive the Blajoviak reports.

Francie knew that she was becoming increasingly dependent on Clint Reese. No one else could make her smile, make her forget her precious moments. It was a quality of tenderness in him, of compassion, yet jaunty in its clownface.

And since that one night he never again put any part of his heart into his voice when he spoke to her. She thought that she could not bear it if he did.

During a frigid mid-November week Betty Jackson went away on an unexplained trip. Stewart collected the daily portions of the Blajoviak report. He smiled at Francie too much, and made clumsy, obvious passes which she pretended not to notice.

Betty left on a Tuesday night. She was back Friday night. Saturday morning Luke Osborne talked to Francie alone in Tom Blajoviak's tiny plywood office. Osborne was having difficulty concealing his jubilation behind a poker face.

"What have you found out?" Francie demanded, her voice rising.

"Nothing about Bob," he said quickly.

She sagged back into the chair and closed her eyes for a moment.

Osborne went on, "But we've gone places in another direction. Can't tell you too much, of course. But I thought you'd like to know. Evidently, they've been under orders to keep contacts at a minimum. I believe that Mrs. Jackson acted as a courier for everything accumulated up to date. She has good technical training for the job, but I don't think she has the feet for it. We put enough people on her so that even if she could push a button and make herself invisible, we'd still stay with her.

"Her contact is from one of the control groups we've been watching. She met him on a subway platform and went through a tired old transfer routine. He gave the stuff to a deluded young lady who works in Washington, taking a one-day vacation in New York. She took an inspirational walk when she got back to Washington. Visited national shrines by night and was picked up by the traditional black diplomatic sedan. By now those no-good reports have cleared Gander, chained to the wrist of a courier from one of the cold war countries. "

"Why are you telling me all this, Mr. Osborne?"

"It's time to get impatient. We know all we have to know. It has been a month since the first letter. How has it been going?"

"All right, I think. I don't think I've overworked those three things you told me to say. But it seems so pointless. I've been friendly. I help her with those lures they make, enameling them. And we talk a lot."

"Start tonight. No letter, no more reports. My guess is that they'll tell you one is on the way."

"One probably is."

"Please, Mrs. Aintrell, keep planning on the worst. Then if I'm wrong, it will be a pleasant surprise." Osborne smiled. "Young lady, you are doing fine, but, remember, give them a bad time tonight."

That evening fat, wet flakes of the first November snow were coming down as she walked down the trail toward the Jackson camp. She walked slowly, rehearsing her lines.

She went up on their porch, knocked, and opened the door.

Betty put her knitting aside. "Well, hi!" she said. "Off early today."

Stewart was near the fire, reading. He put his book aside and said, "An afternoon nip to cut the ice?"

Francie stripped off her mittens, shoved them in her pocket. She unbuttoned the red coat, looking at them somberly. She saw the quick look Betty and Stew exchanged.

"I came over to tell you that I didn't bring you anything today. And I'm not going to bring you anything from now on."

Stewart Jackson took his time lighting a cigarette. "That's a pretty flat statement, Francie. What's behind it?"

"We made a bargain. I kept my end of it. A month is more than up. As far as I know, Bob may have died in that military prison. When I get the letter you promised me, the letter saying that he's better, then you get more data."

"Hon, we can understand your being impatient," Betty said, in an older sister tone. "But don't go off half-cocked."

"This isn't just an impulse," Francie said. "I've thought it over. Now I'm doing the bargaining. You must be reporting to somebody. They're probably pleased with what you've done. Well, until I get my letter they can stop being pleased, because you're going have to explain to them why there aren't any more reports."

"Sit down, Francie," Stew said. "Let's be civilized about this."

Francie shook her head. "I have been civilized long enough. No letter, no reports. I can't make it any clearer."

Stewart smiled warmly. "OK; there's no need of hiding this from you, Francie. We just didn't want to get you too excited. A letter is already on the way. I'm surprised we haven't gotten it already. Now, do you see how foolish your attitude is?"

It startled Francie to learn how accurate Luke Osborne's guess had been. And the rightness of his guess strengthened her determination. She turned from them, took a few steps toward the fire.

"No letter, no reports."

Stewart's smile grew a bit stiff. "You are being paid for those reports."

"I thought you'd bring that up. But it doesn't matter. I don't care what might happen to me. Here is step two in my ultimatum: Either I get my letter within a week or I consider it proof that Bob is dead. Then I'm going to go to Dr. Cudahy and tell him about you and what I've been doing."

She took pleasure in Stewart's look of concern, in Betty's muffled gasp.

"You wouldn't dare," Betty said.

"You're bluffing," Stewart said. "Sit down and we can talk it out."

Francie pulled her mittens on and turned toward the door.

Stewart barked, "I insist that you act more reasonably, Francie!"

"Look me up when you've got mail for me," Francie said crisply.

She slammed the door behind her and walked along the lakeside trail. She felt neither strength nor weakness—just a gray, calm emptiness. When she got home the fire she had lit was blazing nicely. She sat on the floor in front of it, looking for Bob's face in the flames.

On Monday after listening to her report, Osborne said, "Now, understand this: You'll get a letter. If the letter proves by content to be a fake, it will be up to my superiors to make a policy decision. Either we take them into custody or we flush them and see which way they run. If the letter doesn't prove anything one way or another, then we go on as we are and wait for the report through Formosa. That may take until Christmas.

"If—and I am recognizing this possibility—the letter shows beyond any doubt that your husband is still alive, we'll continue to play along and use every resource to try to get him back for you. Just remember one thing: No matter what the letter shows you are to act as though you have no doubt. Can you do that?"

"I can try."

"We've asked a great deal of you, Francie. Just this little bit more."

THE JACKSONS CAME OVER to the cabin on Wednesday, minutes after Francie's arrival from the lab. They stamped the snow off their feet, and came in smiling.

"So you doubted me, eh?" Stew said cheerfully. "It came this morning."

As he fumbled for his pocket, Francie realized that Osborne's doubts had shaken her more than she knew. She was afraid of the letter—afraid to read it.

It seemed to take Stewart an impossibly long time to undo myriad buttons to get at the pocket which held the letter. Francie stood, looking beyond him, hand half outstretched, and through the windows she saw the shale of new ice that reached tentatively out from the shoreline into the lake. She heard Betty prodding the fire.

"Here you go!" Stewart said, holding out another folded sheet of the familiar cheap-fibered paper.

Francie took it, her finger tips alive to the texture of it. Betty knelt in front of the fire, bulky in her ski suit, head turned, smiling. Stew stood in his shaggy winter clothes, beaming at her.

"Well go on!" Betty said. "You going to stand and hold it?"

Francie licked her lips, "Could I—read it alone please? It means so much."

"Read it now, honey," Stewart said. "We want to share your pleasure with you. It means a lot to us, too, you know."

She unfolded the letter. At first the pencil scrawl was blurred. She closed her eyes hard, turned her back to them, opened her eyes again.

> *Baby, now I know they weren't kidding when they said you'd get that other letter. I guess you're doing all you can for me. Anyway, I seem to be a guest of honor now. Sheets, even. Baby, don't feel bad about helping them. Maybe it's for the best. They've got something I've never understood before. For the first time I'm beginning to see the world as it really is. And now, darling, that fireplace seems closer than ever. And so do you. You still got those two freckles on the bridge of your nose? When I get my hands on you, baby, we'd better turn Willy's face to the wall.*

Francie stopped reading for a moment and took a deep breath. A breath of joy and thanksgiving. He had to be alive. Nobody else could sound like that.

> *Remember that I love you and keep thinking that we'll be together again. That's what really counts, isn't it? Figure on me being back in the spring when all the world is turning as green as Willy's hat.*

She stared at the last words. How could Bob have made such a grotesque and incredible mistake? The figurine wore no hat! How could he possibly—? And she read it again and saw the whole letter begin to go subtly false. This new letter and the one before it. False, contrived, artificial. It was all so clear to her now.

Bob, under the circumstances he described, would never have written in such a pseudo-gay way. His other letter had been like that because he had been trying to keep her from worrying about combat wounds or combat death. Now these letters, these fake letters, sounded absurdly light-hearted.

Still looking at the letter, her back turned toward them, Francie saw how they had taken the most precious part of her life and twisted it to their own ends. Bob was dead. He had died during the retreat. Had any doubt existed they would have labeled it *Missing in*

Action. She had been the gullible fool. The stupid sentimental fool who clung to any hope, closing her eyes to its improbability.

Involuntarily she closed her hands on the letter, crumpling it, as though it were something evil.

Stewart Jackson had walked over to where he could see her face. "Why are you doing that?" he asked, his voice oddly thin.

She fought for control, masking her anger. "I—I don't know. Excitement, I guess. To think that he'll be back in the spring and— we can—" But that was a spring that would never come.

In i's own way this letter was far more ruthless than the original telegram. She couldn't pretend any longer, not with the two of them watching her so carefully.

She looked at them, hating them. Such a charming civilized couple. Stewart's face, which had seemed so bland and jolly, was now merely porcine and vicious. Betty, with features sharpening in the moment of strain, looked menacingly cruel.

"Filth!" Francie whispered, careless now of her own safety. "Filth! Both of you."

Stewart gave a grunt of surprise. "Now, now, after all we've done for—"

"Grab her, you fool!" Betty shouted. "It went wrong somewhere. Just look at her face!" Betty jumped to her feet.

Stewart hesitated a moment before lunging toward Francie, his arms outspread. In that moment of hesitation Francie started to move toward the door. His fingers brushed her shoulder, slid down her arm, clamped tightly on her wrist. The meaty touch of his hand on her bare wrist brought back all her fear.

His lunge had put him a bit off balance, and Francie's body contracted in a spasm of fright that threw her back. Stewart was pulled against the raised hearth of the fireplace. As he tripped, his hand slipped from her wrist and before she turned she saw him stumble forward, heard the thud his head made striking the edge of the fieldstone fireplace, saw both his hands slide toward the log fire.

As Betty cried out and ran toward Stewart, Francie found the knob and pulled the door open and ran in panic toward the trail. She went up the first slope, reached the handrail, caught it, used it to pull herself along faster.

She glanced back, gasping for breath, and saw Betty, her face set, her strong legs driving her rapidly up the hill.

Fear gave Francie renewed strength and for a few moments the distance between them remained the same. But soon she was fighting for air, mouth wide, while a sharp pain began to knot her left side.

Betty's feet were so close that she dared not look back. Her shoulder brushed a tree and then Betty's arms locked her thighs and they went down together, rolling across the sticky trail into the base of a small spruce.

Betty slapped her hard, using each hand alternately, slapping until Francie's ears were full of a hard ringing and she could taste blood inside her mouth. But she could hear the ugly words with which Betty emphasized each blow.

"Stop!" Francie cried. "Oh stop!"

The hard slaps ceased and Francie knew that she had learned a great deal about Betty's motivations during those brutal moments.

"On your feet," Betty said.

Francie rolled painfully to her hands and knees. She reached up and grasped a limb of the small spruce to help herself to her feet. The limb she grasped was only a stub, two feet long. It broke off close to the trunk as she pulled herself up. She did not realize that, in effect, she held a club, until she saw Betty's eyes narrow, saw the woman take a step backward.

"Drop it, Francie," Betty said shrilly.

Francie felt her lips stretch in a meaningless smile. She stepped forward and swung the club with all her strength. It would have missed the blond woman entirely, but Betty, attempting to duck, moved directly into the path of the club. It shattered against the pale-gold head.

Betty stood for a moment bent forward from the waist, arms hanging, and then she went down with a boneless limpness. She hit on the slope, and momentum rolled her over onto her back.

Francie, laughing and crying, dropped to her knees beside the woman. She took what remained of the club in both hands and raised it high over her head, willing herself to smash it down against the unprotected face, her temples pounding.

For a long moment she held the club high, and then, just as she let it slip out of her hands to fall behind her, Clint Reese came down the wet path. He was half running, slipping on the wet snow, his overcoat fanning out behind him. When he saw Francie the tautness went out of his face. He took her arm and pulled her to her feet.

"Get off the path," he said roughly.

"They—"

He pulled her with him, forced her down, and crouched beside her. She heard the shots then. Two that were thin and bitter. Whipcracks across the snow. Then one heavy-throated shot, and after an interval, a second one.

She moved and Clint said, "Stay down! I came along to see if you were getting all the protection Osborne promised."

"Oh, Clint, they—"

"I know, darling. Hold it. Somebody's coming."

It was Luke Osborne, walking alone, coming up from the house. He walked slowly and the lines in his face were deeper. They came out to meet him. Osborne looked down at Betty Jackson. The woman moaned and stirred a little.

One of the young men, a stranger, came down the road.

Betty sat up. She looked vaguely at Osborne and the young man. Then she scrambled to her feet, her eyes wild. "Stewart," she screamed. "Stewart!"

Osborne blocked her as she started forward. "Your partner is dead, lady," he said. "Quite thoroughly dead."

Betty pressed the knuckles of both hands against her bared teeth. Instinctively Francie turned to Clint, and pressed her face against the rough top-coat texture. She heard Osborne saying, "Get her up to the car, Clint."

AFTER GIVING FRANCIE A shot the doctor sent her to bed in the Cudahy guestroom. As the drug took hold she let herself slip down and down, through endless layers of black velvet that folded over her, one after the other.

On the fourth day, Clint Reese took her from the Cudahy house back to her cabin. He helped her down the trail and pointed out where Osborne's men had been trying to protect her as much as possible without alarming the Jacksons.

He lit a fire, and tucked a blanket around her in the chair. And then he made coffee for them. He lounged on the bunk with coffee and cigarette. "Take tomorrow off," he said expansively.

"Yes, boss."

"Remember when I was going to say something in bad taste and you stopped me?"

"I remember."

"Oh, I'm not going to try to say it again, so don't look so worried. I'm going to say something else. Lines I memorized last night, in front of my mirror, trying to wear in appealing expression. The trouble is, they still happen to be sort of—well, previous. So I won't say them, either.

"But I'll keep practicing. You see, I've got to wait until you give me the go-ahead. Then I'll say them some day. Old Reese, they always said, a very patient guy. Got a master's degree in waiting, that one has."

"It is too soon, Clint. Especially after all that's just happened."

"Well, I'll stick around and wait. The way we work it, you show up some morning one of these years with a lobster trap in your left hand and a hollyhock in your teeth, humming 'Hail to the Chief.' That will be our little signal—just yours and mine. I'll catch on. Then I'll spout deathless lines you can scribble in your diary."

He stood up for a moment. His eyes were very grave.

"Is it a date?"

"It's a date, Clint."

"Thanks, Francie."

He left with an exaggerated casualness that touched her heart. She pushed the blanket aside and went to the window to watch Clinton Reese go up the trail.

Now the Adirondack winter was coming, and during the long months she would watch the frozen lake and let the snow fall gently on her heart. A time of whiteness and peace, a time of healing. By spring Bob's death would be a year old, and spring is a time of growth and change and renewal.

Francie recalled the look of gravity and warmth and wanting in Clint's eyes, the look that denied the casual smile.

Possibly with strength and luck and sanity, it might come sooner than either of the them realized. For this might be the winter in which she could learn to say good-bye.

Authors' Biographies

Sir Arthur Conan Doyle

Doyle (1859–1930) was the creator of the most successful detective of all time, Sherlock Holmes, whose exploits took on a life of their own to thousands of mystery readers around the world and still resonate with a large audience today. His creator studied medicine at the University of Edinburgh, served as a senior physician at a South African field hospital during the Boer War, and was knighted in 1902. Doyle's writing career had been well established by then, with the tales of Holmes and his chronicler and companion John Watson passing from literature into legend.

Edward D. Hoch

Hoch makes his living as a writer in a way that very few other people can attest to—he works almost entirely in short fiction. With hundreds of stories, primarily in the mystery and suspense genres, he has created such notable characters as Simon Ark, the two-thousand-year-old detective; Nick Velvet, the professional thief who steals only worthless objects; to the calculating Inspector Leopold, whose appearance in the short story "The Oblong Room" won his creator the Edgar Award for best short story.

Michael Collins

Michael Collins is the most famous pseudonym of author Dennis Lynds, who is the creator of Dan Fortune, the one-armed private investigator who has sleuthed his way through more than fifteen novels. Lynds served in World War II, earning the Bronze Star, Purple Heart, Combat Infantry Badge, and three battle stars. After the war he used his bachelor's degree in chemistry for various careers, including editing several chemistry magazines. In the 1960s he turned to mystery writing, and he has been at it ever since. A former president of the Private Eye Writers of America, Lynds received the Mystery Writers of America's Edgar Award in 1968.

José Latour

Latour has been an avid reader of crime fiction since he was a teenage; and, for reasons that would take too long to explain, American authors are the most important influence on his present profession. He began writing at night and on weekends in 1987, while working as a financial analyst at the Cuban Ministry of France. In 1990 he gave up his government position to become a full-time writer. Latour is also the AIEP/IACW vice president for Latin America and head of the organization's Cuban branch. His works include, under the pen name of Javier Moran, *Choque de leyendas*, *Fauna Nocturna*, and *Medianoche enemiga*.

Arnaldo Correa

Correa got his start in fiction at age sixteen, when a short story of his was bought by Cuba's most popular magazine. Deciding to be a writer, he tried to follow Jack London's example and traveled the world trying out various pursuits, such as mucker in the mines of Nevada, sailor on the Mississippi, waiter, and engineer. While biding his time to write about his experiences, he has published five collections of short fiction and one novel. Correa's latest book is about the exploits of Sherlock Holmes's Cuban grandson.

Jürgen Ehlers

Jürgen Ehlers is a member of the International Association of Crime Writers. He lives and works in Germany.

Stuart M. Kaminsky

Kaminsky's two mystery series characters are as different as night and day. Inspector Porfiry Rostnikov is an intelligent Moscow policeman forever distrusted by his superiors and always being assigned "impossible" cases, which he solves with aplomb. Private detective Toby Peters lives and works in and around the Hollywood of the 1940s, taking on cases for stars such as Judy Garland and the Marx Brothers. A former president of the Mystery Writers of America, Kaminsky has also written plays, screenplays, and biographies on such noted celebrities as Clint Eastwood and director John Huston. His short fiction has appeared in anthologies such as *Guilty as Charged* and *The Mysterious West*.

Bob Mendes

In 1997 Mendes was awarded his second Golden Noose Award, the top mystery fiction prize in the Netherlands, for his novel *The Power of Fire*. Born in 1928, he became an accountant at age twenty-four and eventually rose to become senior partner and manager of an association of accountants. He began writing in 1984, producing a collection of poetry, and in 1988 he published his breakthrough novel *A Day of Shame*. Since then Mendes has published ten novels, several short stories, and two plays. He also was president of the Antwerp Basketball Club and won several national championships with his team. Currently, he plays tennis and golf.

John Jakes

Americans love success stories, and few success stories match that of John Jakes's. Following a long career in advertising, during which he wrote innumerable novels and short stories, he found his literary fortunes waning. Then, in the 1970s, he was commissioned to write the American Bicentennial series and very quickly became one of the world's bestselling authors. Jakes has written virtually every kind of fiction and excels at all of them. Recently, he edited a collection of the best western stories of the twentieth century.

Mark Twain

Mark Twain was the pseudonym of Samuel Langhorn Clemens (1835–1910), and he is widely regarded as one of America's greatest authors. His biting satire of then-contemporary times brought to light social injustices such as racism and slavery. Twain's best-known works include *The Adventures of Tom Sawyer*, *The Adventures of Huckleberry Finn*, and *A Connecticut Yankee in King Arthur's Court*.

John Lutz

John Lutz is one of the most skilled mystery writers today, with his most recent novels being *The Ex* and *Final Seconds*, which he coauthored with David August. His settings and descriptions always have a ring of authenticity, whether he's writing about the blues scene in New Orleans or the relationships between men and women. Lutz's series characters are also in a class by themselves, whether it be the hapless Alo Nudger or the more traditional detective Fred Carver. Neither appear in "Winds of Change," a flawless short-short stand-alone with a stunning conclusion.

Guy de Maupassant

Although de Maupassant's (1850–1893) horror fiction numbers only thirty stories, a tenth of his total writing output, they have left an indelible mark upon the genre. His stories of unnatural creatures, madmen, and ghosts caused quite a reaction when they were first published in the 1880s. Unfortunately, de Maupassant contracted syphilis and, after an unsuccessful suicide attempt, entered an insane asylum, where he died at the age of forty-two.

Jack Ritchie

Ritchie (1922–1983) was another writer who excelled in short fiction. A master of the short, sharp detective or suspense story, his work was reprinted in the Best Detective Anthology Series seventeen times, and it has appeared in virtually all of the hardcover Alfred Hitchcock collections. Adept at both humorous and serious fiction, Ritchie developed characters that ranged from the vampire detective Cardula to a ten-year-old detective. The story included in this anthology is a classic example of writing by a classic mystery author.

Ambrose Bierce

Bierce (1842–1914) was second only to Edgar Allan Poe in terms of literary achievement, and he is often considered Poe's successor when it comes to writing tales of supernatural terror. But Bierce was far more accomplished in life than Poe, serving on the Union side during the Civil War and advancing to the rank of major. He also was a famous columnist for several major city newspapers, including the *San Francisco Examiner* and the *New York Journal*.

Jean-Hugues Oppel

Jean-Hugues Oppel is a member of the International Association of Crime Writers. He lives and works in France.

Carmen Iarrera

Iarrera is the only female Italian author currently writing spy novels. Although she earned a degree in political science, she writes full-time, producing short fiction, cartoons, and teleplays. She is the author of the novel *Never with Paintings*, which was cowritten with Italian art expert Federico Zeri, published in 1997, and translated into German and Japanese. Her short stories have been published around the world, including in *Ellery Queen's Mystery Magazine* and publications in Germany, Spain, and Japan. Iarrera is also the president of the Italian chapter of the International Association of Crime Writers (IACW).

Howard Engel

His Benny Cooperman series is Engel's best-known work, featuring a hapless yet persistent Yiddish detective who lives and works in Canada. Before turning to writing full-time, he was a freelance radio broadcaster, executive producer, and literary editor. He was a cofounder of the Crime Writers of Canada organization and a member of the Mystery Writers of America as well as the IACW. Engel also has written nonfiction, most notably a book about executioners. He also edited an anthology of short mystery fiction by Canadian authors.

Janwillem Van de Wetering

Born in Rotterdam, the Netherlands, Van de Wetering, a former policeman and businessman, now lives in rural Maine. In 1971, at the age of forty-one, he launched his writing career by publishing *The Empty Mirror*, an autobiographical account of his experiences in a Buddhist monastery. Inspired by the mystery fiction of George Simenon, he tapped into his experience in the Amsterdam Special Constabulary, which he joined in lieu of being drafted into the military. He has written more than a dozen novels featuring Adjutant Grijpstra and Sergeant de Gier, as well as nonfiction and children's books.

Brian Garfield

Garfield has been writing novels and short fiction for more than thirty-five years. He is best known for the novel *Death Wish*, later made into the successful movie of the same name starring Charles Bronson. During his youth Garfield traveled all over the world, writing about a particular place or event as he encountered it. He has written western novels and screenplays and has edited several anthologies.

John D. MacDonald

MacDonald (1916–1986) wrote sixty-nine novels during his more than thirty-five years as a writer, but it is his Travis McGee books that have earned him a permanent place in the mystery canon.

Described as "a tattered knight on a spavined steed" by his creator, McGee was the epitome of the private detective in the 1960s and 70s. MacDonald received the Mystery Writers of America Grand Master Award in 1972, the American Book Award in 1980, and he was the guest of honor at America's premier mystery convention, Bouchercon, in 1983.

Copyrights and Permissions